A SILENT SONG IN WINTER

DRAGONS OF ROKAHN • BOOK TWO

M. H. WOODSCOURT

Edited by Sarah B.

Map by CartographyBird Maps

Cover design by MiblArt

Published by True North Press

www.mhwoodscourt.com

Paperback ISBN: 978-1-959619-16-1

Hardback ISBN: 978-1-959619-18-5

To my beautiful friend,
Cheryl Benner.

I'm sorry you didn't get to read this series before you crossed over to the Other Side. May you soar through the clouds with dragons.

Fly high, Lady of Light!

PAE'TAL
LIRSHON
THE FLAME FOREST
ELENTH
ANDYAN MOUNTAI
DRAGON KING'S WAR CAMP
SIMYNSHIN
CIT HYA
ROKAHN
VORSAH
TO DISTANT SOUTHERN SEAS

TO UNCHARTED NORTHERN WATERS
THE FAE LANDS
TESHRELLE
SERIELIAS
THE ISLES OF KWILAJ
BLIGHTED LANDS
DRAJIN
THE SPIRE
THE PILLAR
CIMIN
CRESTFEL
OCEANA
RELVIN PROVINCE
BONE COVE
NAUTTIA
LINTHA
HOLORE
THE ISLES OF TEN GOLD
THE MANY LANDS OF
SIRINHIGHA
MAPPED
IN THE PRESENT AGE

Pronunciation Guide

People

Akonn – uh-KAHN
Athonen d'Ereth – uh-THAWN-en d-AIR-eth
Atlanse Chenta – AT-lanss CHEN-tuh
Brentin – bren-tin
Crim – krim
Dalter – DOLL-ter
Donivan Kriv – DON-uh-vinn Kriv
Drayve – dray-v
Eddan – ed-DON
Elayorah – el-lay-OR-uh
Feresse Chehta – Fur-EES CHEN-tuh
Fontinn – FAWN-tin
Gredd – gr-edd
Hilker – HILL-ker
Jensirin – jen-SEER-inn
Jonatten – JAHN-uh-ten
Jossen – JOSS-in
Kalet – KAL-ett
Karrad – KARR-odd
Katanni – ka-TAN-aye
Kevva – KEV-uh
Larkynven – LARR-kin-ven
Latta Chenta – LOT-uh CHEN-tuh
Maya – MAY-uh
Milannetirin – mee-LAN-eh-TEER-in
Mikoneh – mee-KO-nay
Minno – MIN-no
Namirsha – nuh-MEER-shuh
Nilo – n-AYE-low
Owenekiras – oh-WEN-uh-KEE-*ras* (roll the R)
Penn Lendir – pen len-DEER
Prettem Chenta – PRET-em CHEN-tuh
Rathana – ruh-THON-uh
Rokahn – RO-kawn

Sariolin – SAW-ree-OH-lin
Sathe – SAY-th
Seranni – SARE-un-NYE
Suld – SOO-ld
Tayvin – TAY-vinn
Teev – teeg
Ter N'Avea – tare NAH-vay
Thyfinn - th-EYE-finn
Tikar – tee-KAHR
Tryss – tris
Vomm – vom
Zevier – ZEV-eer

PLACES

Andyan Mountains – ANN-dee-ehn
Cimin – KIM-inn
Crestfel – crest-fell
Elemeer Plains – Ell-eh-MEER
Elenth – ELL-en-th
Hyanython — HYE-uh-NYE-thon
Holore – hol-ORE
Kagon – KAG-on
Kenooshin – ken-OO-shin
Kwilaj – kwee-LAJJ
Lintha – LIN-th-uh
Mithrinn – MITH-rinn
Nauttia – NAW-tee-uh
Oceana – oh-shee-ON-uh
Pae'Tal – pay-TAL
Relvin Province – REL-vin
Rokahn – RO-kawn
Serielias – seer-ee-EL-lass
Simynshin – SIM-in-shin
Sirinhigha – seer-in-HYE-uh
TeshRelle – tesh-rell
Vorsah – VOR-suh

TERMS

Complété – kom-play-TAY
Firia Leaves – FEE-ree-uh

Jarsui – jahr-SWEE
Korta – KOR-tuh
Renemm – REN-em
Tiassana – TEE-uh-SAWN-uh

RACES

Celes – sell-ESS
Ephe'ahn – eh-FAY-on
Nijaal – nee-TSAWL
Undrik – un-drik

A SILENT
SONG
IN
WINTER

CHAPTER 1

WEARING A TARGET

"No one truly understands the Spirits Elemental."

- *A Treatise on the Magic of the Hidden Realm* by Sariolin the Solitary

Under a sliver of waning moonlight, fog flanked the icy streets like faceless spirits—watchful, restless.

Equally watchful, Mikoneh strode behind Owenekiras Rokahn, careful to avoid stepping on the Dragon King's cloak hem where it slithered across the snow-dusted cobblestones. At Mikoneh's back walked his twin sister Maya, and their friend and comrade, Penn. Also in the company was Akonn, leader of the legendary League of the Sword, and Hilker, a Master Wind Elementalist. They all wore heavy winter wear, though only Penn needed it to fend off the night's chill. The rest wielded elemental magic that subdued the cold.

Despite the darkness of the night and the shadows cast by the looming Simynshinian-style buildings to either side of the company, Mikoneh had no difficulty seeing the details around him. He'd always had keen hearing and vision, far above average. Only recently had he learned why.

He was a dragon—and the son and heir of the Dragon King. In one hellish month, Mikoneh had gone from a rebel sentenced to death, to the captive of a monstrous Mage, then to Dragon Prince and an heir to the throne of Rokahn.

It had only been a week since his rescue. Mikoneh's mind and soul were still reeling—but he'd come now to the kingdom of Simynshin to prevent war, or at least to contain it. His feelings—his recent trauma—would simply have to wait. He preferred that anyway. He didn't relish the idea of examining the hollowness inside too closely. He was afraid he might discover he was more broken than he felt beneath the numbness.

They'd flown from Owenekiras's war camp on his mount—the black and red dragon Larkynven—and been dropped off at the northern gates of Elenth, Royal Capital of Simynshin on the western coast. Quaking, the sentries had let them pass without incident. Judging by their pale faces and stammering tongues, the armored men knew Owenekiras at a glance—that or they'd never seen a dragon in flight before.

Elenth was quiet in the middle turns of night, especially with the early winter snows. Beneath her heavy hood and cloak, Maya was whispering to Penn about her excitement over meeting the Songbird Princess of Simynshin.

The small company had come to Elenth to sniff out a traitor selling vital information to Dark Mage forces. Owenekiras had been warned of the treachery by a peculiar boy called Minno. Ironic, really, considering that Minno had also betrayed the Dragon King not so long ago.

Adjusting his fur-lined hood, Mikoneh studied the looming castle in the dark ahead. He'd always hated royalty and nobility. He'd resented them with every thread of his soul. Now, he was one of them.

Fa taught you better than that. People are as good as their actions, not their stations.

Often, the two seemed to align, with those in power using that influence for their own selfish ends, but hadn't Mikoneh seen exceptions? Penn was nobleborn and nothing like his vile father, Drayve Lendir, Earl of Relvin Province.

Then there was Owenekiras Rokahn.

Walking at the man's back, Mikoneh found his attention wandering to his father repeatedly. Their goals were similar. Despite Owenekiras's power and influence, he was dead set on stopping the Dark Mages from enslaving all magic beneath their leader, the Mage Queen, a figure of legends whose identity was shrouded in mystery.

The street gave way to a courtyard where a tall fountain gurgled. A statue stood at the center amid an ice formation crafted by the cold. Despite the ice, water still gushed from the figure's palms, as though the sculpted man had conjured it. A Water Elementalist of importance, perhaps? Magic was real, after all—which Mikoneh hadn't believed until recent weeks.

He'd known so little.

He didn't blame the man and woman who'd raised him. Fa and Mama had been protecting him and his sister from what hunted them. Mikoneh now understood what that meant. His mind veered away from fresh memories. He couldn't think about his captivity below ground. Not now. Not yet.

A tingle shot up Mikoneh's spine. He paused, even as Owenekiras gracefully halted upon the slick cobblestones. Something was wrong. Maya's faint chatter faltered, and the whisper of cloth and chink of metal suggested Penn had reached for his sword. Probably Captain Akonn, too. Hilker might have his poleaxe at the ready.

Owenekiras turned, his silver eyes slicing into Mikoneh. He said nothing, but his message was clear. Ambush.

Mikoneh drew his sword while fire licked at his fingertips, willing him to summon flame. He resisted, uncertain what enemy they were about to face, or how much control he had over his element. The battered sword would do to begin with. He slid his feet wide apart, the familiar weight of Fa's weapon comforting.

Shadows stretched across the courtyard. The fountain still flowed, yet the air felt cold, even with Mikoneh's fiery blood. His bones ached in the chill. *Hollow. Dark Mages.*

He searched the buildings looming around the company. *Any moment now…*

Quick steps approached from beyond the half-frozen fountain—a single set. The tension broke. The shadows fell away as though they'd been severed.

A cloaked figure split from the darkness, then halted beside the trickling water. The figure pulled a hood back to reveal a man in his late thirties. His eyes were a hazel color, and his hair was deep auburn flecked with premature white. He wore an open smile and bowed his head toward Owenekiras.

"Welcome back to Elenth, my lord. It's been too long."

"Thank you, Lord Crim," said the Dragon King like nothing had been amiss mere breaths before. Penn inhaled sharply while Owenekiras spoke on. "Is Prince Atlanse awake?"

"Yes," answered Crim, "and waiting for you in his private parlor."

"Lead on."

As Mikoneh followed the two men, he sheathed his blade and glanced to his right. Penn stood close, eyeing the newcomer with wonder. He'd drawn back his fur-lined cloak to get a better look, revealing his long blond hair and thoughtful brown eyes. Penn was two years older than the twins' twenty years and had several inches on Mikoneh in height. According to Maya, he was an attractive fellow. Mikoneh took her word for it.

"What is it?" Mikoneh asked his friend in a low voice.

"Lord Crim is a well-known nobleman even in Oceana. He's perhaps the wealthiest noble merchant on the continent, entirely independent of King Prettem or his court. My father always said Crim can weave wheat into gold."

"Good head for agriculture, then?"

"Quite," said Penn. "His landholdings are the most expansive outside the Royal House of Chenta. He also married the daughter of the head of the merchant guild of Lintha, so he dabbles in textiles as well. What sets him apart is his mind. He's a wizard about finance."

A nobleman who didn't thrive on his family heritage alone was a breath of fresh air to Mikoneh, but he remained skeptical. Ties to the greedy kingdom of Lintha to the southeast were hardly comforting. And while accumulating wealth might be impressive to some, far more important was what Lord Crim did with his money. Hoarding it certainly wouldn't serve the world.

That's rich coming from a dragon.

Not that Mikoneh had any wealth. He didn't know if he would hoard it or not. He couldn't deny being drawn to gold and gems, but what he prized most was his twin and keeping her safe. He glanced over his shoulder to find Maya. She was still following close, eyeing the buildings, the shadows, the cobblestones with a wariness he could well appreciate. His nerves remained on edge, and he double-checked more than one shadow in his path. Why had the Mages fled at Crim's arrival? Had they really been Dark Mages, or had he imagined the bitter cold of their Hollow magic?

Beyond the ice-encrusted city stretched an expanse of open

road separating the castle from its capital. Before the castle walls, a moat cut across the frozen earth. A bridge spanned the gaping darkness. The gray stone walls rose high and thick, lit by hundreds of torches whose flames sparked higher as Mikoneh drew near. Lord Crim led them across the moat, beneath the portcullis, and into the bailey proper. Mikoneh relaxed a little but kept his hand on his sword pommel.

A handful of guards watched them. Their backs straightened fast upon seeing Owenekiras Rokahn. Even if they somehow didn't recognize him in his trademark black armor and dragon scale cloak, his presence could halt a stampede.

Across the bailey, thick scrollwork doors pulled aside, admitting the company into the warm castle. Half a dozen servants ushered them into a dimly lit vestibule. Two more ornate doors flanked the entryway. Another exquisite door stood at the center of the vestibule, barring entry into the main partition of the ancient castle. Boldly, Lord Crim took them through that door. The servants streamed ahead of them, carrying lanterns to chase off the gloom.

Crim led them down a stone passageway, hung with tapestries that whispered of the ancient history of Simynshin. Despite their long walk, the company kept quiet. No one wished to disturb the other residents of the castle. A secretive hush lay across the whole affair, and Mikoneh wondered what politics were at play. He knew something of King Prettem Chenta, but he couldn't rely on hearth stories for information.

The fact that Owenekiras had come to see Prince Atlanse rather than his father, the king, was certainly telling.

Mikoneh reached behind his back. Maya's gloved hand caught his bare fingers, and his nerves settled a bit more. Whatever they were walking into, they were together.

The castle was grand and large—much larger than King Nilo's austere domain in Oceana on the east coast. Mikoneh's sense of direction had always been acute, but he questioned himself as he traveled along the myriad passageways, up two flights of stairs, and eventually down a tapestried hallway. Glancing out a window, he found the ebony sky and familiar Unicorn constellation that told him he was walking along the western side of the castle, toward the ocean.

Near the end of the passage, a servant, holding her flickering lantern high, moved ahead of the company. She nudged a door open then swept aside to let Owenekiras and Lord Crim enter. Mikoneh pulled Maya with him, and they stepped inside. Penn stayed on their heels, Akonn and Hilker following close.

The chamber was wide and warm, with a cheery fire in the hearth. A great stone mantle hung over the bright flames where fire spirits glutted on wood and cackled at each other. Mikoneh started toward them before he caught himself. The smell of woodsmoke tickled his senses. He turned his back on the flames to take in the rest of the chamber. A man stood before a wingback chair, a tome clutched in his hands, a quiet smile on his face. He cut a trim figure, well dressed in a silver doublet, with charcoal pants, and high-top black boots. Wavy brunet hair hung loose down his back, and his eyes flashed like sapphires in the fire's glow.

"Welcome back, my friend." The man—presumably Crown Prince Atlanse Chenta—extended one arm toward Owenekiras. In his other hand, he kept his hold on his book.

The Dragon King maintained his stoic expression. "I wish it were under better circumstances."

"Please shed your cloaks and sit." Atlanse motioned to the circle of chairs surrounding his preferred wingback, then he sank into the plush, crushed velvet cushions. His eyes strayed to Mikoneh, widened only a margin, then danced toward Maya. His smile deepened, drawing faint lines around his eyes. He couldn't be far into his fourth decade, but the telltale signs of laughter had etched into his face.

Lord Crim claimed a chair near his prince, and Owenekiras took the opposite chair.

Mikoneh led Maya to the silk settee. After draping their cloaks on a spare chair, Penn joined them. Akonn stood behind Owenekiras's seat and clasped his hands behind his back. Hilker moved to the fire to warm his fingers. His unusual maroon eyes turned red in the ember light.

The atmosphere wasn't tense like Mikoneh had expected it to be. Atlanse slipped a bit of yarn between the pages of his tome to mark his place, then sat back, eyeing Owenekiras with that quiet, knowing smile. It might have been an after-dinner party among close friends. Mikoneh wouldn't be surprised if Atlanse broke out a bottle of brandy.

If not for the somber air shared between Owenekiras Rokahn and his fae captain, Mikoneh might let his own guard slip. But then, perhaps not. This was still a foreign place with strange customs and unknown factions. Not to mention, Simynshin was wearing a target the Mages had set their sights upon. And likely, Mages were lurking outside.

"Your children, I presume?" asked Atlanse.

Owenekiras's silver eyes flicked toward the twins, then away. "Yes."

Atlanse's eyes brightened. "They both look very handsome." He leaned forward. "I'm Prince Atlanse, King Prettem's son and heir. Welcome to Simynshin. I'm honored to meet my friend's children." He hesitated. "We did meet once before, but I highly doubt you remember it."

"Nice to meet you—again," Maya answered, her voice like warm honey. "I'm Mayanaleh, though I prefer Maya. This is Mikoneh. And with us is our friend, Viscount Penn Lendir of Oceana."

"Your Highness." Mikoneh offered a curt nod.

Atlanse searched their faces, one at a time, then flashed a grin at Owenekiras. "They *look* like you, but neither has your disposition, I think."

"That's probably for the best," Lord Crim piped up. "I mean no offense, Prince Owenekiras, but by the Celes, there can only be one of *you* at any given time."

Hilker grunted in agreement while Akonn tried to school his face.

"He's much kinder than he looks," Maya chimed in.

Mikoneh squeezed her hand, frowning. "We came here to discuss matters in Simynshin, right?"

The atmosphere shifted. Atlanse's smile faded, and Crim studied his hands where several rings sparkled. The gems were finely cut, and each was worth more than the whole of Relvin Province back home. Mikoneh pried his eyes from them, fixing his attention on the crown prince.

"True enough, Prince Mikoneh," Atlanse said. "Matters are grave. Sympathies are veering toward dark paths."

"There's been vocal support for the Mage cause," Crim said. "Not loud yet, but even a whisper unsettles me. It's largely because of the new queen."

Mikoneh's brows pinched together. He'd heard the old king of Simynshin had taken a new wife, but he'd been preoccupied with leading a ragtag rebellion, and matters so far removed from Oceana had felt like another world.

Not anymore.

"Who is the new queen?" asked Maya.

"A merchant's daughter from Lintha," Crim answered. "Like my own wife. But they each have vastly different views on whether to bring their country's politics here to Simynshin."

"Most Linthians want to swallow the world," Penn muttered.

"True." Atlanse sighed. "My new stepmother favors that way of thinking. And she's a pretty, young, vivacious woman. My father is quite enamored, which makes him easy to sway."

"Is there any sign of her desiring to produce an heir to threaten your position, Your Highness?" asked Captain Akonn. His green eyes and white hair, framing his pointed ears, were painted orange in the firelight. The metal clasps of his crisscrossed chest belts glinted.

"None yet," Atlanse said. "Give it time." He shifted, and the ease of his body vanished. His jaw set. "The lady queen is targeting my daughter instead."

Akonn frowned. "Trying to change her worldview?"

"Trying—and succeeding—with much of the court," Atlanse said. "But not with Latta. She's not easily persuaded. With Latta, she's trying to isolate her." His gaze settled on Mikoneh. "Luckily, you're here now."

Disquiet slithered up Mikoneh's spine. "We'll do what we can to help—"

"You haven't told him." Atlanse shot Owenekiras a sharp look.

"No," Owenekiras said. "I haven't."

"Told me what?" Mikoneh's insides squirmed.

Atlanse leaned back, frowning. "Well, it's simple enough."

Hilker snorted. "Sure."

The crown prince of Simynshin cleared his throat. "You and Latta were betrothed at birth. A matter of tradition and security."

Flames erupted across the hearth. Mikoneh shot to his feet. "Over my *dead* and *rotting* corpse."

Chapter 2

Play at Peace

"Even the rare Elementalist gifted enough to control all five aspects will admit that the nature of these ethereal spirits is enigmatic at best."

- *A Treatise on the Magic of the Hidden Realm* by Sariolin the Solitary

In the ringing echoes of Mikoneh's refusal, every spirit in the hearth perked up. The fire roared.

"It's not what it seems, Prince Mikoneh," Atlanse said, batting at the air with one hand. "It's merely a formality. A security measure, as I said."

Mikoneh's heart pounded against his ribs. "I'm not betrothed to *anybody*."

"Technically, you are," Crim said gently. "But as His Royal Highness mentioned, it's merely a formality—and a helpful tool. It gives Rokahn more influence in Simynshin, allowing Owenekiras to keep his army hidden within this kingdom."

Mikoneh swung around to stare at his father—a man he respected by reputation but hardly knew personally. "I don't want to marry a princess. Or anyone else." He'd meant to argue against being a political device, but the panic was mounting. His ears hummed. His lungs pinched. Eloquence had abandoned him.

"You won't if that's your wish," Owenekiras said. "Both Atlanse and I understood that in the beginning. The betrothal will ultimately be dissolved, but it may be useful to keep for the present if you're willing to aid us." He folded his hands over his lap. "The choice, Mikoneh, is yours alone."

"Please hear them out, Your Highness," Crim said.

Since his elemental magic had awakened, Mikoneh's body temperature had remained consistent—except during the ordeal with Dark Mages and the unwanted bond Sathe had forced on him. Yet now, the chamber was stuffy, and Mikoneh's collar clung too tight to his throat. He tugged against the fabric, desperate to bolt, but Maya caught his wrist and pulled him back down to the settee. He folded himself onto the cushions, rigid-backed, fighting his adrenaline rush. Her eyes were fixed on him, but what she was thinking or how Penn had responded to the news, he didn't bother to guess. His head was ringing with fear.

Atlanse spoke. "My daughter Latta has known of this betrothal all her life. So has the court. There have been several loud factions who demanded it be broken off due to..." he glanced at Owenekiras "...unrest within Rokahn."

Mikoneh knew about that. The succession was a tangled mess. Owenekiras Rokahn was the rightful heir, but he'd been accused of regicide after his parents were found murdered in some occult sacrifice. The accuser and sole witness? Owenekiras's younger sister, Elayorah, who now sat on the throne of Rokahn and allied herself with the Mage Queen by all reports. Mikoneh didn't know where Owenekiras's younger twin brother was, or why he hadn't ascended the throne—nor why Owenekiras had never stood trial for his alleged crimes.

I don't know anything about my blood kin.

Though Owenekiras had never been crowned king of Rokahn, most folk called him the Dragon King regardless. Likely because, though the Rokahnians had forgotten their draconic heritage, the dragons whose blood had awakened bowed to the rightful king just the same and the title had caught on.

Dragons were real. Yet no one seemed to know that except for the Mages, a handful of humans, and the hidden fae of the world.

Crim spoke, carving through Mikoneh's thoughts. "We must consider that if Owen's heir acknowledges the betrothal, it will feel more valid, and certain factions may become volatile."

Hearing the Dragon King's name shortened startled Mikoneh. He eyed Crim with renewed interest. The lordling must be a close friend indeed.

"I'm fine with the risks," Atlanse said. "Latta will be as well. Already my father's court extends itself too far. Too many are willing to forget the true threat the Mages pose in order to play pretend."

"Pretend, Your Highness?" asked Penn.

Atlanse nodded. "Play at peace long enough and you can easily forget what freedoms you've given up in attaining the illusion of it."

"Are that many courtiers tempted by the Dark Mages?" asked Akonn.

"They're an alluring trap these days," Crim answered. "Things have been difficult here for a long time while Lintha appears to be thriving since they declared open trade with Mages."

Mikoneh frowned. "I hadn't realized the Mages were out in the open. In Oceana they were skulking in shadows until very recently."

"Oceana's made up of suspicious farmers and sailors who don't want to believe in magic," Hilker growled. "Mages had to be careful there while they wooed the nobility. But Lintha is a merchant country—incidentally well versed in killing fae. They deal in selling wares—and now causes." He shrugged. "They can make a battered pot sound like a golden scepter at bargain price."

Atlanse set his tome aside. The gilded title, *Warfare of the Coasts, 1298-1342 AB*, glinted in the guttering light. "My stepmother brought that same showman's spirit to her new marriage, and it's causing a ripple effect within her realm of influence. The ladies at court are more interested in fine wares than they've ever been before, and in their turn, they're influencing their husbands. Always, we Simynshinians have prided ourselves on our grounded practicality. Agriculture is our life and trade—not silks, lacey fans, and shiny buckles. But the new queen is changing all that, making it sound like the Mages can alter our very livelihoods. Producing pearls from thin air." He scoffed. "As if that wouldn't affect the economy badly."

Mikoneh blinked. He'd misread Atlanse. Beneath the crown prince's mild exterior, embers burned. Shifting, Mikoneh caught the man's gaze. "How does my...betrothal play into your game of politics?"

"No one outside of this room—and the few household servants I trust—knows you've arrived," Atlanse said. "Tomorrow, we will announce you, when it's too late for anyone at court to counter the move. You will be introduced to Latta and spend a great deal of time with her, in the name of custom and good sense. After all, you're to be wed"—he lifted a hand—"only insofar as the court is concerned. But it gives you a great deal of freedom to move about. More than any normal outsider. You'll be treated as part of the Royal House. Where Latta goes, you go. Where you go, she goes. You'll be of great interest to all factions, especially given that the kingdom of Rokahn has remained politically neutral. Where *you* stand will be a matter of curiosity to all. Some will attempt to bribe, blackmail, threaten, befriend, or otherwise persuade you to the side of whatever cause they laud."

Mikoneh grimaced. "Sounds like fun."

Penn snorted.

"Oh, it can be," Crim said. "You just have to be ready with a counter move in these matters. That's what I'm here for. To guide you—if you agree to let me, Your Highness."

Mikoneh stiffened. "Please don't call me that. 'Mikoneh' is fine."

"I'm afraid that's impossible, Your Highness," Crim said. "You're a prince, and this is a matter of royalty and succession. Your title is why we need your help."

Dragging a hand down his face, Mikoneh exhaled a low breath. "I've only known about my *title* for a few days. Maybe a week. This is going to take a lot of getting used to." He could feel every eye on him. Maya's concern bled in deepest. He caught her wrist and squeezed. How she could be so calm about finding herself a princess, he'd never know. But then, she *loved* princesses.

"I realize this is a great weight, Prince Mikoneh," Atlanse said. "I appreciate your willingness to help in a matter that must be foreign to you."

Mikoneh fell utterly still. No, it wasn't foreign. Not anymore. Not after Sathe. Perhaps before that, he'd have scoffed and stalked off at the idea of aiding royalty for *any* reason. But not now. He understood—perhaps better than most—what the Mages were really like. The horrors they dealt out. The monstrosities they crafted. The damage they intended to wreak.

Maya's arm pressed against his. She must be trying hard to send every reassurance into him, to combat the trauma he wasn't ready to face. He'd been free of Sathe's hold for such a brief time. Mere days. He hadn't processed it—hadn't dared.

Do it later.

Rubbing his hands across his thighs, he dragged in a bracing breath. "I don't know much about politics, or castles, or anything that goes on in them. But I'll do what I must to thwart the Mage Queen's spy. Just so long as the betrothal is dissolved afterward, in writing at least."

"If that's your price, I accept it," Atlanse said. "Thank you, Prince Mikoneh."

"You're a bold one, Your Highness," Crim said, grinning. "I respect that."

"It's late." Atlanse sat forward. "Crim will lead you to your shared suite—all of you—and we'll begin in the morning by introducing my daughter."

As Mikoneh climbed to his feet, his lungs pinched. Meeting a princess...one he was engaged to... How had his life gone from mounting a rebellion and an impending execution to court intrigue and a betrothal to a princess he'd never met?

I'd almost rather burn at the stake again.

After all, that wasn't really a threat anymore. His eyes coasted over the fireplace where several flaming spirits waved at him.

"This way," Crim said, already aiming for the door.

Mikoneh, Maya, and Penn started after the lord, but the others didn't follow. Mikoneh glanced back.

"We will come shortly," Owenekiras said, remaining in his seat. "I have a private matter to discuss with His Highness." His silver eyes settled on Atlanse.

Mikoneh wasn't sure whether to feel relieved or annoyed that he was left out. Twenty years ago, these two same men had tied his fate to another, simply for the convenience of the thing.

He grimaced but nodded, then left the chamber to follow their guide down the corridor. A long walk and several junctions brought them to another suite where Crim ushered them into a circular common room with a blazing hearth, several fine pieces of furniture, and a tray set with mulled wine, sweet cakes, and an assortment of fruits. Despite the lateness of the night, Mikoneh's stomach rumbled, and he rummaged through the bowl of fruit to find the least sweet variety. Maya plucked up a frosted cake. Penn poured himself some wine.

"If you'll excuse me," Crim said near the open door, "I'll be on my way. Pleasant dreams. See you in the morning." He bowed his head, then retreated. The door shut with a soft snick.

Penn lowered his goblet and licked his lips. "Will you really go along with their scheme?"

Dread coiled in Mikoneh's stomach. "Don't have a lot of choice. It's a solid plan—even if I hate it."

"Latta might be a lovely person," Maya said.

"Lovely or otherwise," Mikoneh growled, "I'm not marrying a perfect stranger. Or anybody. Not for a long, long time."

She shrugged. "At least meet her before you dismiss the possibility. I want to meet her, too."

He did want to meet his *intended*, but not for a potential life partnership. He'd been mulling over Sathe's final words— words that had to do with Prince Atlanse and his daughter. Sathe had claimed the Mages were targeting the prince directly, and that Latta was his weakness. What did that mean? Was Latta as loyal to her father, as unswayed by the changing tides at court, as Atlanse believed, or had her loyalties shifted along with the other courtiers Crim had mentioned—taken with pearls, silk, and other petty frippery?

"I'm going to bed." Mikoneh tossed the core of his green apple into a bin near the refreshment table, then headed for the nearest door set in the circle of adjoining rooms around the broad chamber. Peeking inside, he was pleased to find a bedroom—and a fine one at that. A four-post bed loomed before him, draped in pale blue curtains, a matching coverlet, and stuffed feather pillows. It looked cozy enough to swallow him. Every muscle ached from his ordeal of mere days ago, yet the idea of entering the room twisted his stomach.

"Goodnight," Maya called.

Shaking off the feeling of dread, he waved acknowledgment and shut the bedroom door, cutting off the light from the attached chamber. The moon pooled across the floor, turning the blue bedding silver. Mikoneh stood in perfect stillness, absorbing the shadows. Chills crawled up his limbs. He was alone. For the first time since escaping Sathe's clutches, he was entirely alone.

It's fine. Maya and Penn are in the other room. Sathe is dead. I'm in a castle surrounded by thick walls and patrolled by capable guards.

I'm safe.

That last was a lie. No matter where he went, no matter who stood with him, he was far from safe. Dark Mages sought him and his twin. They might already be in Elenth judging by the brush of Hollow he'd felt in the city. The world was on the brink of war. His father was the most notorious and hated man in all Sirinhigha—and Mikoneh was his heir.

And he'd just agreed to play court politics in a country he knew nothing about beyond what any Oceanean farmer might know.

I'm in over my head.

He curled his hands into fists. He was no stranger to fear—but he was its superior. He never gave in for long. He wouldn't start now.

Unbuckling his sword, Mikoneh marched to the bed, ignoring the needles across his spine. Sitting on the edge of the mattress, he took a moment to appreciate its plushness before he pried off his boots, stripped down to his smalls, and curled under the coverlet with Fa's sword close at hand. Warmth. Comfort.

No hint of Sathe.

He shut his eyes.

NIGHTMARES ASSAULTED HIM, full of violet flames, cold earthen tunnels, and whispering voices frigid as deep winter. He tossed, turned, called out—but nothing saved him from his dreams until dawn spread its golden rays across the wide room. A knock fell on the door, then someone flew inside the chamber. He shot upright, groping for his sword.

Just Maya. She raced to the bedside, gowned in pale pink, her blue-black hair loose and flowing down her back. Her gold eyes caught fire in the morning glow.

"Good morning, sleepyhead." She searched his face, frowning. "Bad dreams?"

He scrubbed at his eyes. "Yeah. Thanks for waking me up."

Her footsteps padded nearer. Fingers brushed his hair. "I'm sorry, Mikoneh."

"It's fine." He lowered his hands and pushed a smile to his lips. "Nightmares I can handle. It's real-life Mages that might be a problem." He drew a breath. "And then I'll just focus on toasting them." His fingers prickled, nearly conjuring flame before he stopped them.

She sat on the bed's edge. "You don't need to be brave for me, you know."

"Nah, I know. I need to be brave for me." He held her eyes. "Really, Maya, I'll get through the nightmares. I'm more worried about what I have to do when I'm awake." He tugged on her satin sleeve. "That's fancy. Where'd you steal it from?"

"From the same tailor who's waiting just outside your door to give you a fitting. Lord Crim arrived a while ago, with heaps of food and a handful of servants. There's a tub, too, so you can get as clean as you please."

"Sounds thrilling."

"Come on, up with you." Maya rose and twirled around, showcasing the sleek flowing ripples of her dress. She gracefully halted facing him, and the smile on her face warmed him through. Less than a year ago, she'd been little different than a corpse. Now, her golden eyes were ringed with pearlescent light from her wind element and her cheeks were rosy.

"All right," he said in the grumpiest tones he could muster, "but get out. I'm not exactly dressed, you know."

She laughed and darted to the door, cast him a last radiant smile, then slipped out.

The tailor poked his head inside. A quill pen was tucked behind his ear. His clothes were fine but wrinkled and askew. He was a lanky man in his third decade, with a sharp nose and lively dark blue eyes. His sandy hair was shoulder-length and caught back in a ribbon. "If I might intrude, Your Highness, I've come to collect a few measurements before you don your clothes."

The idea of standing in his smalls before a stranger set Mikoneh's teeth on edge. Sathe had humiliated him by denying him clothes, forcing him to stand naked in nearly all their dealings.

This is different.

In defiance of the dead Dark Mage, Mikoneh tossed aside his coverlet, then positioned himself on a plush rug. The tailor looked him up and down, then set to work, his movements fluid and practiced. Though the ordeal made Mikoneh's flesh crawl, and every brush of fingertips made painful memories flash across his mind, he held still and waited for the tailor to finish. At last, the man stepped back and jotted a series of numbers down on a heavy slip of parchment.

"Thank you, Your Highness. Your proportions are excellent, which will make my task an easy one. I brought a few articles of clothing that should suffice while my staff crafts your wardrobe. Is that acceptable?"

"Sure," Mikoneh said. "Thanks."

"Of course." The man tucked the quill behind his ear and smoothed his rumpled shirt. "And please don't fret. You'll look finer than me by far." A smile darted across his face, then vanished. The tailor offered up a bow that looked like a dancer's moves, then he glided from the room as though he walked upon the air above the flagstones.

Mikoneh stared after him. *That's an odd one.*

But then, this was a different world from what he'd always known.

And now we're stuck in it.

He shook that off and climbed into his worn clothing gifted by the Ephe'ahns of Kagon Village in the North. It was plain garb, especially for a castle. He barely cared. Food and a bath did sound good, even if servants attended them.

Sucking in a breath, he stepped out into the posh common room—and into a completely new life.

CHAPTER 3

FROST ROSES

"Only the surface nature of each spirit type has been studied. We know, for instance, that wind is mischievous while earth is more gentle and arguably the most loyal of these strange creatures."

- *A Treatise on the Magic of the Hidden Realm* by Sariolin the Solitary

After a warm bath that smelled of sandalwood and cinnamon, Mikoneh slipped into the fresh apparel the tailor had left for him. Then he sat down to a breakfast large enough to feed an entire village in Relvin Province. Penn and Maya joined him, along with Akonn and Lord Crim. Where Owenekiras and Hilker had gone, no one said, and Mikoneh spent his energy on eating rather than asking questions. Maya passed him some *tiassana* tea, steeped from red leaves meant to soothe broken bonds. As he sipped the steaming red drink, the ache in his soul lessened.

Crim filled the silence with idle conversation about the winter onset and how the harvest had been. Simynshin had experienced a much milder transition from autumn than Oceana had, though it had still come early.

After breakfast, Mikoneh returned to his bedroom and slipped on his leather boots. The Simynshinian wardrobe wasn't much different from what he'd seen Penn wear. It consisted of a loose blouse, a brocaded vest, and tight-fitting trousers. The tailor had a good eye. Mikoneh's borrowed apparel—muted tans with accents of burgundy—fit him like it had been tucked and pinned already. Strapping on Fa's battered sword, he checked himself in the gold-framed looking glass standing in one corner of the ornate chamber. Good enough, royalty or no royalty.

He usually kept his long, black hair back in a tail, but it was still wet.

He started for the exit, then hesitated. Could he dry his hair with his element?

Mikoneh held out his palm and summoned a fire spirit. The wispy little creature, formless and flickering like a flame, appeared over his hand and crackled an inquiry.

"Could you dry my hair without setting it ablaze?"

The spirit slipped into his palm. Warmth traveled up his arm, his neck, into his head. A soothing energy accompanied it. The warmth bled into his hair, and steam rose from his tresses until his hair hung dry and straight.

The warmth traveled back to his palm, and the little fire spirit reappeared. It resembled a hand-sized dragon made of flame and looked very pleased with itself.

"Thanks." Mikoneh set the fire spirit on the nearby wash-stand, tied his hair back with a black cord, then scooped up the spirit to place it on his shoulder. Together they entered the common room.

Maya stood up from the couch where she and Penn had

been sitting. Looking her twin up and down, she chuckled. "You certainly make a statement."

"That *is* the point," Mikoneh said.

Crim approached for a closer examination. "You cut the figure of a true Rokahn. Few will mistake you." He nodded, rubbing his smooth chin. "Yes, you'll do well. Despite our efforts to keep things hushed up, the castle is abuzz with the news of your abrupt late-night arrival. Princess Latta is waiting in her garden for a formal introduction."

Mikoneh arched his brow. "Isn't it cold for a garden stroll?"

"Not if you want to see the first frost roses."

"That sounds lovely." Maya looped her arm around Mikoneh's. "Shall I come along to make certain he doesn't offend the princess straight away?"

Mikoneh shot her a glower. "I know how to be polite."

"Yes, but you're out of practice."

Penn snorted.

Mikoneh switched his glare to his friend. "Traitor."

The viscount grinned and shrugged. "Your tongue is the one who betrays you most, my friend."

A retort welled up, but Mikoneh bit it off. No sense proving Penn's point further. "Well," he glanced at Crim, "I think we're as ready as we're gonna be."

"Then please follow me, Your Highnesses." Crim motioned toward the door.

Akonn took up a position behind the twins, and Penn joined the leader of the Sword. Mikoneh arched one eyebrow at his friend.

Penn's grin widened. "I wouldn't miss this for all the dragon gold in the world."

Shoving down an urge to slug Penn on the jaw, Mikoneh

followed Crim from their suite and into a corridor brightly lit by the east-facing windows. Their walk was a long one, slowed further by both twins taking turns staring out the windows to the world beyond. Despite a crust of snow covering the fields and forests around Elenth, and the snowcapped mountains to the northeast, the Royal City itself was bustling with activity. Only a faint powdering of fresh snow had stuck to the roofs or streets.

The aromas of baking bread, roasting fish, and manure mingled with the more distant fragrance of the forest, and the briny smell of the western coastline. Mikoneh let the whiffs of the outside world curl over and through him, grounding him in the present, away from his nightmares.

Perhaps he could convince Princess Latta to give him a tour of Elenth later. To be among people—honest, hardworking people—might help him accept this as reality.

Latta. His stomach clenched. She was the Songbird Princess. She could carry a tune exceptionally well. That was all he knew. Prince Atlanse had dropped a few other hints the previous night, but those could have meant anything. Was she haughty, timid, fierce? Women his age tended to make him nervous—particularly after Kevva's betrayal—and he rarely got along well with his peers. Could he manage this farce? Would she be in the know, or had Atlanse conveniently forgotten to tell her the betrothal wouldn't last?

I should've asked more questions.

Too late now. He'd simply have to muddle his way through. Typical.

Maya tugged him to a halt, and he found himself staring up at a portrait. It showcased Prince Atlanse, a decade younger and draped in his finest royal raiment, with fewer worries burdening his shoulders—or the artist had left them out.

Beside the crown prince, a woman with dark brunette hair and deep brown eyes stood looking serene and lovely in a gown of deep green. Between them, shorter than both, stood a girl of ten years, with large sapphire blue eyes and rich brown hair. She wore a white dress, and a bird perched on her small fingers.

Princess Latta Chenta. The young woman he must pretend he was going to marry. Mikoneh shivered. Crim cleared his throat, and the company moved along the passage.

"Even back then, she was lovely," Maya whispered. "You might truly fall in love."

"Not happening," Mikoneh grumbled.

Penn's snickering earned him another glare. Mikoneh made a mental note to kick him later.

Light flooded the passage ahead. Crim's step quickened, leading them through two wide-open doors. Mikoneh flinched until his eyes adjusted to the outdoor sunlight. The princess's garden was a blanket of white in a labyrinth of evergreen hedges. Crim took it at a confident pace, obviously familiar with the paths. He led them to a pavilion swathed in pale green curtains guarding the warm interior.

Taking the three steps up, Crim aimed a smile at Mikoneh. "The princess is within." He drew the curtains aside. The fire spirit still perching on Mikoneh's shoulder perked up and chirped a note. Torches within the pavilion flared higher in answer.

Mikoneh, Maya, Penn, and Akonn entered. Crim came last.

Seated at a table set with tea service, the little girl was all grown up. Latta was lovelier than her mother's portrait. Her blue eyes were stunning just like her father's. She wore a delicate slender gown of blue and silver, and her dark curls ringed her face and spilled down her shoulders, softening a smile that was slightly tight.

An urge to run nearly overcame Mikoneh, but Maya gripped his arm harder and pulled him further into the pavilion. He'd kill her later.

Princess Latta stood and dipped into a fluid curtsey, all grace and propriety. "Welcome, Prince Mikoneh, Princess Maya." Her eyes skimmed Penn. "Lord Penn." Her smile eased a tad. "Welcome back, Captain Akonn."

"Your Highness," Akonn said, sweeping into a bow. "I hope you've been well."

"I haven't," Latta answered. "But I'm improving."

'His daughter is his weakness,' Sathe had said.

Tugging free of Maya's grasp, Mikoneh offered a bow of his own, more rigid than Akonn's, but it would have to suffice. "Your Highness, it's a pleasure to meet you. I'm glad your health is improving."

The shocked silence behind him was strangely satisfying. He might not *like* it, but he would play his part to the best of his ability. He straightened. "I hope you and Maya will be good friends."

That shook his twin from her shock, and she took several steps forward before she remembered to curtsey. "That would be lovely, Your Highness."

Latta eyed them with the same neutral smile. "Please, 'Latta' will suffice. If we all say 'Your Highness' all the time, we'll never know which of us we're talking about."

Maya laughed. "True. I did wonder how that worked in a castle."

"Ah, yes. I understand you were sent into hiding as children. Have you never visited your home in Rokahn?"

"Never," Mikoneh said. "Not even the harbors."

The princess's brows shot up. "That's very sad. Rokahn is a magnificent country. I hope you're able to remedy that soon."

Her tones were so well controlled, Mikoneh couldn't read

whether she was horrified by their ignorance or by their circumstance. Maybe it was both.

"How is your father?" Latta asked, and her smile warmed again. "I've missed him."

"He's here," Maya said, then looked toward Akonn in a sudden panic. Mikoneh read her question clearly: Had she given away a secret?

The Captain of the Sword stepped forward. "He is indeed here, Princess Latta, and sends his greetings. He'll be observing the welcome feast this evening, where your betrothal will be officially announced."

Strain touched Latta's jaw. "Thank you, Captain. I look forward to seeing Uncle Owen again." She motioned to her table. "Please, sit. My father thought it best to meet ahead of the feast, and I quite agree." Her eyes swept over Maya and Penn again. "I'm glad you're in company. A first meeting is always so awkward."

The knots in Mikoneh's stomach relaxed. She was as uncomfortable as him. That was something. He helped Maya into her seat while Crim offered the same to Latta. Penn waited, then took his seat once both ladies had folded into their chairs. Mikoneh mirrored him. Crim seated himself last.

Latta poured the tea, offering up honey, cream, and pink-frosted dainties to all. Mikoneh declined all but tea—straight—and sipped the fragrant mixture with more relish than usual. Anything to occupy his hands.

The princess *was* lovely, and a perfect stranger. The desire to run struck him again, but he set his feet and ignored the impulse.

"Lord Crim mentioned frost roses," Maya said. "I've never heard of those. May we see them after tea?"

Latta's smile was more genuine this time. "I'd love to show

you. They're a rare breed anywhere south of the high mountains. My father brought them from the Nijaalin forest for my birthday years ago. They only bloom in winter."

Maya leaned forward, sprinkling crumbs from her dainty. "We've seen the Nijaalin forest. It's enchanting."

Latta's eyes lit up like gems. "Have you, truly? I'm envious. Father promised to take me, but with the state of things..." She took a sip of tea, then set her cup down with a faint *clink*. "Perhaps someday I'll go."

"You must," Maya said. "Lady Katanni is the loveliest creature I've ever seen."

"I have met her," Latta said, "and I agree with you wholeheartedly." Her attention danced toward Mikoneh. "I did expect to find Ter in company with you."

Akonn answered. "He had business off-world. He'll return soon."

Off-world. Mikoneh's skin tingled. Another allusion to places beyond Sirinhigha. He let his mind drift away from the vastness of that, afraid it might choke him. To keep himself busy, he selected a dainty, but he didn't eat it.

"You must be twenty by now," Latta said. "If I recall, your birthday is in the autumn, right?"

"Yes," Maya said. "Funnily enough, it was almost our deathday, too."

Latta nearly dropped her dainty. "What do you mean?"

Maya happily launched into the tale about their near-execution and subsequent escape. Latta's eyes grew wider with each turn in the story, and she glanced at Mikoneh several times. Maya wisely avoided any mention of Dark Mages, but she touched on their visit to the fairy lands, the old ruins of Hyanython, and the Ephe'ahn villages.

Latta sipped her tea and nibbled while she listened, then

shook her head once Maya wound down to the present. The holes where Sathe should be were glaring, but the princess either hadn't noticed or didn't want to press.

"It sounds so terrifying and exciting." Her gaze flicked to Mikoneh again. "You look remarkably well for all that."

He blinked. "We've had a few days to recover."

Latta took another sip. "You'll find few adventures in Elenth, I'm afraid."

Mikoneh's mind flashed to the previous night's lurking shadows, but he wasn't certain if he'd only dreamed them up.

"We don't mind," Penn said. "Frankly, a few quiet weeks sound wonderful after everything."

The princess eyed their cups and plates. "Would you like more refreshment, or would you prefer to visit the frost roses now?"

"Roses," Maya exclaimed. "Please."

Latta stared at Mikoneh's plate. "Did you not like the cake?"

He hesitated, torn between stuffing the dainty into his mouth and being honest. The latter won out. If he played at pretend too much, he'd eventually reveal himself and risk ruining any goodwill he'd built. "I don't really like sweet things. At all."

Maya chuckled. "He's always been that way. I don't understand it. Can you imagine hating dessert?"

A genuine smile broke through Latta's polite mask. "No, I can't. Do you like fruit?"

"Not really," he said.

"Leaves more for the rest of us," Penn said.

The group murmured assent.

Mikoneh rolled his eyes. "Should we be on our way?"

Latta pushed her chair back and rose. Her skirts straightened around her with a whispering hiss. She led the way outside the pavilion, and the rest of them followed. Lord Crim moved to Mikoneh's side and cleared his throat.

"You might want to walk with her," he whispered.

Mikoneh set his jaw and nodded. He quickened his pace, then fell into step beside Latta. She nodded at him, then looked away.

"You grew up in Oceana, right?" she asked.

"Yeah. In Relvin Province, southwest, near the inner bay."

Latta twisted a plain gold ring on her finger. "I've been to Oceana several times, but we traveled from Cimin to visit King Nilo in Nauttia. Never farther inland."

"Not even to see Lintha?"

She shook her head. "We took a ship from Nauttia to Holore."

Mikoneh had never visited Lintha across the wide bay to the south of his childhood home. Fa had few kind words to say about their southern neighbors, and Mama even fewer. Both soldiers had disdained materialism.

"Nauttia is beautiful in its austere way," Mikoneh said, pushing memories of Sathe from his head. "The ocean was dazzling."

"I do love open waters."

He nodded, unsure what to say to continue the conversation. The soft chatter behind him set his skin itching. He'd never been great at small talk. He preferred useful discussion.

Small talk is useful if it helps you get to know her.

He scratched his wrist. "Your mother. She's from Cimin, right?" He recalled hearing that somewhere.

"She was, yes."

He winced. "I'm sorry. I didn't realize she was..."

"She's not dead," Latta said stiffly. "Not strictly, at least. It's...rather complicated. According to the laws of Cimin, she's dead. And by the same law, her marriage to my father is dissolved. So, she's not really Ciminian, nor is she technically my mother."

"Laws can't erase blood."

"No, but they can make blood ties foolhardy to keep. At least, that's my mother's philosophy." Latta sighed. "It's for the best. She didn't like living in Simynshin. She says the women here are repressed and dull. I suppose from her point of view that's true."

Mama had often said something similar about Oceanean women. Compared to a warrior's dangerous life, running a household was dull indeed. "Does your mother live in Cimin even though they disavowed her?"

"I haven't any idea where she is." Latta twisted her ring again. They turned a corner, and the princess quickened her pace. "The frost roses are just up ahead."

Despite her level tones, Mikoneh read the underlying emotion threading through her voice. Loneliness. He knew it too well to miss it, no matter how composed Latta was. He also knew it well enough to let the matter drop.

Keeping up with her, he turned his attention ahead. There, before a green hedge dusted with fresh snow, strange crystalline roses grew. They were translucent blooms with glass-like stems that caught the sunlight and sparkled like rainbows. Behind him, Maya gasped.

Drawing closer, Mikoneh caught the fragrance. Crisp, cool, like snow, but sweet like honey and berries and spring meadows. He brushed his fingers against the nearest bloom, expecting the smooth coolness of glass. The petals were velvety like other roses and bent at his touch.

Latta drifted toward Maya, who had stooped over to breathe the fragrance in more deeply. "You may cut a few for your room if you wish."

"May I?" Maya straightened up. "Oh, but I don't want to rob from your garden."

Latta drew a small knife from a hidden pocket in her gown. "It's no trouble. Observe." She cut one stem about twelve inches below the bloom and handed it to Maya. Where the stem had been cut, another bud curled up. "Tomorrow, it will reach the same height as its fellows and unfurl into full bloom. The roses flourish all winter."

"That's marvelous!" Maya accepted the knife from Latta and began building herself a bouquet of frost roses.

Mikoneh caught Latta's eye. "You made her whole day. Thanks."

"She's a sweet girl. I'm glad that hasn't changed."

He looked at her, puzzled. "Who told you about us?" He couldn't imagine Owenekiras chatting about his infants, nor had he been in their lives since he gave them to his two trusted generals.

"Oh. I remember meeting you."

He stared at her. "We've met?"

Latta nodded. "We were very small, and I'm a little older, so my memory might be better than yours. Your father brought you here, and we played near a suit of armor. Maya knocked it over, then blamed you."

Mikoneh's brows flew up. "And you call her sweet? She was always pulling stunts like that."

"She confessed and apologized later."

"Sounds exactly right." He tossed his twin a fond scowl, but she was busy handing off roses to Penn who patiently added them to a growing pile in his arms. The viscount had broken his forearm a while back, but it seemed to have mended well.

Mikoneh fingered a crystal rose petal. Swirls of frost decorated the edge. "You'd think I'd remember that incident."

"You were only three."

Three. Had he and Maya lived with Owenekiras and their birth mother as long as that?

"How old are you?" he asked.

"Twenty-two."

He grunted, distracted by the fire spirit sashaying down his arm. The little creature had taken on a humanoid form with long hair that flowed and sparked across the air. Reaching the frost rose, the spirit curled its wispy hands around the petals and breathed in deeply. Then it lit upon the bloom and set it on fire.

"Hey, don't do that." Mikoneh plucked the fire spirit from the rose—and started. The flower wasn't injured, though a flame engulfed the delicate petals. Latta inched closer to him.

"It's lovely. You've gotten very good at fire."

He narrowed his gaze on her. "Was I wielding fire at three years old, too?"

She nodded. "You caught your bed curtains on fire one night during your visit, but your father put the flames out before any damage occurred. Your mother was so proud."

Mikoneh's fingers tightened around the fire spirit. It crackled a protest and vanished with a huff. He hardly noticed. "You met my mother?" His voice cracked.

Latta nodded gravely. "She was Ciminian, just like mine. They were friends. My mother and I both cried when we learned about..." She frowned. "I'm sorry, this must be painful for you. We can talk about something else."

"No." His voice was faint. "I know nothing about her. I'd like to learn more."

Latta fell still. "You don't remember anything?"

"No."

"That's so sad." She twisted her ring faster. "She's the loveliest woman I've ever known—apart from Lady Katanni, of course. And I don't mean outward beauty alone. There was something...so bright about your mother. She was..." her eyes fell on the fiery rose "...like that."

Mikoneh studied the flames curling around the crystal petals with renewed interest. "Do you know her name?" His voice was still low, soft, as though he was afraid to hear his own question. He'd never known her—or at least, his memories had faded past recall. Instead, he'd been raised by two rambunctious but kind and honorable warriors, and he wouldn't trade them for anything.

Yet, she'd been his mother once. She'd birthed him. Named him. Nursed him. And Maya, too. Didn't they owe her something? It wasn't a betrayal toward the people who had raised the twins as their own, was it? Ter had said as much, hadn't he?

So, why am I terrified?

"Her name was Rathana," Latta said. "She had dark auburn hair and amber eyes if I'm remembering right. I always thought that's where you and Maya got your gold eyes—from the mixing of silver and amber."

Maya's lilting voice had grown silent. Mikoneh twisted around and found her eyeing Latta with a sad smile.

"Rathana is a beautiful name," Maya whispered. "I can almost picture her face. Gentle, but with a fierceness in her eyes."

"That's her." Latta nodded.

As Mikoneh glanced between them, his chest tightened. He couldn't picture anything—couldn't remember *anything*. Not a scent, not a sound.

"She was a swordswoman," Latta went on. "One of the best. Ciminian swords are light and fast—and she used her blade most eloquently."

"Do you mean elegantly?" asked Penn, shifting his armload of frost roses.

Latta shook her head. "The swordplay of Cimin is a language all its own, and she wielded that language with the eloquence of a master. Women in Cimin are fierce, and she was among their fiercest ranks."

The idea of his mother being a warrior loosened the knot in Mikoneh's chest. The parents who'd raised him had both been fighters as well. It was familiar. Mikoneh fingered the burning rose again, trying to imagine his mother, sword gleaming, hair lashing, eyes blazing.

Maya spoke up. "If Mikoneh could use his element back then, what changed? Ter said it woke up when we were about to be burned alive."

The princess shook her head. "I'm not sure. After your long-ago visit to Elenth, I heard nothing for months. Then I saw my mother crying and my father trying to comfort her. She wouldn't tell me why, but my father told me Rathana had been killed, and you were going far away. After that, matters in Rokahn worsened, and for years I assumed you would grow up fighting your aunt."

"No." Mikoneh scowled, cupping his hands around the rose until the flame snuffed out. "We were hiding in Relvin, tucked away from everything."

"Yes, my father told me that eventually," Latta said gently.

He couldn't blame Owenekiras for making that choice. They'd been small children, and he'd just lost his wife. What protective parent wouldn't do the same?

Even so, all the secrets grated. Why was everyone tiptoeing around the twins' past, their heritage, and their future? He wanted someone to spell it all out, to help them understand what exactly was on the line and how to prepare properly for their roles in the war against the Mage Queen. He and Maya weren't children anymore.

Latta turned from the frost roses. "You'll need a large vase for those," she told Maya. "Come, let's head inside. It's getting chilly." She linked Maya's arm through hers, then caught Mikoneh's arm with the other. The three royals set the pace from the garden, with Penn, Crim, Akonn, and a fleet of servants at their backs. The whisper of old secrets seemed to flutter through the air, chasing Mikoneh inside.

CHAPTER 4

LOSS HAD SHARPENED HIS EDGES

"Scholars surmise that the Spirits Elemental are guardians born to defend and revitalize the world. They purify magic, especially where taint has bled into the ground. The process is slow, but the spirits never tire of their work."

- A Treatise on the Magic of the Hidden Realm by Sariolin the Solitary

Latta offered to give them a tour of the castle, and Mikoneh accepted at once. He needed a good look at his surroundings and the chance to memorize the hallways.

He'd always viewed castles as ostentatious and bloated—but while Elenth Castle had scrollwork and intricate trappings, it was tasteful, rather than gaudy. In many ways, the decor and architecture reminded Mikoneh of the ruinous Citadel of Hyanython. Latta knew a great deal about her home's history, and she relished the chance to share the fascinating points about past sieges. The foundations of Elenth Castle had existed as far back as the Age of Dragons, though the structure had been badly damaged and restored several times over twenty-thousand years.

"Your knowledge is impressive, Princess Latta," Penn said. "Do you aspire to become a scholar?"

She laughed. Throughout the tour, Latta had grown more relaxed, and her smile came easily now. "No, Lord Penn. But I suppose I can't escape my blood. Ciminians are proud of their history. Which must come from dwelling so near the Spire."

Mikoneh missed a step but caught himself. He'd heard whispers about the Spire of Northern Cimin. A place where witches dwelt, the village hearthwives had always insisted. Mama had said that was nonsense and that the Spire was a place of learning and record-keeping.

"Is it true," asked Maya, "that witches learn their magic there?"

Latta's laugh was brighter still. "Is that what they say in Oceana?"

"Yes," Maya said, "and with the next breath, they insist there's no such thing as magic. But they seem awfully afraid of witches despite their skepticism. I always found that odd."

"Superstition is a magic all its own," Akonn said.

Crim grunted. "Too right, Captain." He paused as the company came to a crossroads. "I regret that this is where I must leave you all. I've avoided my duties for too long. Luncheon will be ready within half a sandglass turn in your parlor, Princess Latta." He offered up a bow, kissed the air above Latta's knuckles, then swept down the hall with a flourish.

Latta shook her head, but mirth edged her lips. Mikoneh looked at her curiously, and she shrugged in reply. "Crim's a bit eccentric, but he's a good man. My father relies on him."

Penn inched closer. "The Spire, my lady. Can you tell us about it? Have you ever been there?"

Mikoneh choked back a snort at his friend's eagerness. The Viscount of Relvin was a bit of a scholar in his own right, and never stopped asking questions. Small wonder he'd want to know the truth about the strange ways of the Spire Folk.

"I have," Latta said, "once. My father took me when I turned five." She cast a glance at Mikoneh, her eyes twinkling. "It was arranged by Lady Rathana."

Mikoneh tensed. Maya inhaled a breath.

"She was one of them?" asked Penn.

Latta nodded. "Rathana's father is an important scholar at the Spire. Or...well, he was. I'm not sure whether he's still alive, I'm sorry to say."

Maya shifted. "I hope he is. I've always wished we had a grandfather."

"Seems like we don't on the Rokahn side," Mikoneh said.

"True." Maya frowned, then shook herself. "What does the Spire look like?"

"Rather like a spire," Latta said, her smile turning crooked. "It's a great, tall, towering red rock ending in a point. The interior is carved from the stone, mostly made for their archives. The whole history of Sirinhigha resides there, carefully preserved by its protectors and by magic."

"It's something you'll never forget once you see it," Akonn said.

"You've seen it, too?" Penn's voice dripped with envy. "I asked my father if I could travel there, but he laughed and said that was a waste of time and effort. 'Who cares about the old ways?' he always said. 'They're gone for a reason.'" Penn shook his head. "He's always been a fool."

Latta clicked her tongue. "Fools like that are the reason the old ways are forgotten and wars brew again." She blinked, her cheeks reddening. "Oh, but I apologize for insulting your father, Lord Penn."

The viscount shrugged. "Truth is truth."

"Even so, it's not polite." She twisted around. "Shall we continue?"

As they made their way to the princess's private parlor, Latta described rows and rows of tomes and scrolls within the Spire. She also described ceilings that looked like the sky and rooms filled with silver orbs. Eventually the company reached the parlor to find food laid out along a cozy table set for four. Akonn moved off to sup at a separate placement while the three royals and young lord took their seats.

Mikoneh was grateful to dine on cold cuts, steamed vegetables, and fluffy bread, rather than dessert. The meal was light but flavorful, and the water was cool and fresh. He sat quietly while Maya chatted about her new wardrobe to Latta, delighted by the fashions of Simynshin. Penn eyed Latta with subtle admiration, and Mikoneh nearly leaned over to tease his friend—but thought better of it. This wasn't a holiday. It was subterfuge, a deadly game no matter whether it was played in the backwoods of Relvin or beneath the high beams of Elenth Castle.

No wrong steps. Not one.

His mind drifted along the hallways they'd trod, committing the route to memory. Fire spirits had greeted him from every torch. Servants had avoided eye contact. Maya had been drawn to several windows where the wind whistled. She'd gotten stronger in her element under Hilker's tutelage, and she conversed with the breeze like it was a friend.

Still, they both had a lot left to learn. Maya had a tutor. Mikoneh didn't. He'd learned from Sathe—a fact that galled him—but it wasn't enough to call himself a Master Elementalist, not for years yet. That was fine. He doubted whether Sathe had taught him the proper boundaries of wielding fire. Dark Mages bent rules to their wills, even if it meant tainting nature.

Mikoneh must find someone new to teach him. He'd hoped Ter could help, but the Ephe'ahn was absent—and besides, he wasn't a Master of Fire. Surely, someone in Elenth could train Mikoneh.

He stirred in his chair. "Princess Latta?"

She lowered her goblet. "Yes, Prince Mikoneh?"

The formal title tightened his gut. He winced, then caught the sparkle in her eye. "Right. Sorry. *Latta.* I just wondered if you know of any Master Elementalists nearby, besides Hilker."

She hesitated. "Yes, I suppose so. But they're not fond of court. Do you have need of one immediately?"

He shook his head. "I'd just like to continue my training."

She nodded thoughtfully. "A Fire Master. Those are more common than some, but that's not saying a great deal. They're reclusive these days, being targets of Mages. Several were murdered during the Summertide Tourney last year."

"Murdered? Openly?" asked Maya.

Latta nodded. "Sadly. The Mage ambassador assured us that a *rogue* Mage was responsible, not anyone from his own cabinet, but my father and I don't believe him."

"Simynshin has a Mage ambassador?" Mikoneh's lungs pinched. Panic tolled in his head.

Latta's grimace was telling. "Unfortunately, we've had one for two years now. Unpleasant fellow. He puts me in mind of a weasel, with those shifty eyes and his scampering ways."

Mikoneh stared at the table, trying not to reflect on Sathe and the undead Mages that had accompanied him. They were all shifty, all scampering. All unpleasant. He'd killed Sathe himself, but he still had difficulty believing the monstrous being was dead.

"Could a Master Fire Elementalist be summoned?" Penn asked.

"I'll inquire of my father," Latta said. "He'll respect the

desire to train one's element, being an Elementalist himself. He's a wind user. Hilker trained him."

"Really?" Maya leaned over the table. "Hilker's an absolute tyrant as a trainer, but I've learned so much from him."

Latta chuckled. "That's what Father always says, too. I think they're fond of each other, but some days it's difficult to tell." She turned back to Mikoneh. "I'll mention it at the feast tonight."

He tensed. He'd forgotten about that ordeal. He yearned to avoid further social engagements after such a full morning and the long, exhausting night before, but he knew better than to skip out on the formal announcement of the twins' arrival and his betrothal. He needed to be seen, known, and sought after.

That means being nice, he told himself. Once, such a thing had been easy. His manners were smooth and his smile quick, but loss had sharpened his edges and dulled his humor. And after everything with the Mages, he wasn't sure how much worse he was behaving.

You're just gonna have to pretend.

He expected that to be difficult, but what choice did he have? No matter what he must do, he wouldn't let the Mages win. Besides, he wanted to return to his truest self, bit by bit.

"Are you an Elementalist, Latta?" asked Maya.

"No." Latta pushed food across her plate. "I'm sure I could be—most can if they try—though few become masters. My talents lie in a different realm."

"Politics?" quipped Mikoneh.

"Ha! That doesn't take talent, just money and rank." Her answer brought the edges of his mouth up. She went on. "I'm —well, I was a singer."

Penn leaned forward, his eyes bright. "Yes, we know. The Songbird Princess, some call you. Your voice is said to hold magic."

Latta's cheeks grew pink. "Of a sort, I suppose."

Akonn snorted from his spot across the parlor. "She can charm the birds from the trees. I've seen it."

"But you say *was*," Penn said.

"Yes." The color in the princess's face drained. "A few months ago, I fell ill. Since then, my voice hasn't been the same. The physicians told me it would likely come back. I can sing now, but it's not as it was." She shrugged. "No more charming the birds from the trees."

"I'm very sorry to hear that, Your Highness," Akonn said gently.

She shook her head. "No need for that, Captain. I can make do. I'm most sorry for my father. I could always cheer him up after a hard day with my music, but now hearing me sing only makes him sad."

Mikoneh frowned, weighing her words. *Atlanse's weakness.* "What did your music do? Aside from bird charming."

"My voice healed things," Latta said. "Not physical wounds, mind you. Those require a level of magic no human I know possesses. It's more of a soul-cleansing. Like a healing balm."

"That's an impressive gift," Mikoneh said.

"Thank you." Latta sighed. "I miss it."

"Could it be used in other ways?"

"I'm not sure what you mean."

"If it can soothe and heal, might it be used to hurt or taint?" He pushed his plate away and laced his fingers together on the table. "In the wrong hands, could your song be used for evil?"

Latta's eyes widened. "I don't know. I've never tried."

"But theoretically, do you think it could?"

"Maybe. I really don't know."

"What illness did you have?"

She searched his face. "A bad fever, accompanied by a terrible cough."

"At the time, was that a common illness in Simynshin?"

"No."

"Did anyone else in the castle have it?"

She tipped her head to one side. "I don't think so."

"Anyone since then?"

"No. What are you thinking?"

Mikoneh shook his head. "I'm just narrowing down possibilities." He could feel Maya's gaze on him, but she didn't interrupt.

"What sort?" asked Latta.

"I think your talent might've been robbed."

The parlor fell silent. Everyone stared at Mikoneh, and he could sense their tension like a taut rope. Still, he held Latta's eyes, ignoring the rest. He wasn't an expert in magic. He knew little about the world outside of Oceana. But his time spent with Sathe had given him enough insight to recognize magical manipulation and control.

"What were you doing in the days leading up to your illness?" he asked. "Can you remember if you went anywhere different, or spoke to someone unfamiliar? Did the Mage ambassador return from a trip around that time or visit you privately or anything unusual?"

"I..." She dropped her eyes to her lap, probably twisting her ring around and around. "No. I always avoid speaking with him. I did ride with my protector into the foothills a few days prior, but that's routine for me."

"You trust your protector?"

"Implicitly." Latta raised her head to meet his steady gaze. "I can't think of anything... Wait. There *was* a strange storm. I was in my garden when it struck. Snow fell out of season, and my frost roses bloomed for a full day before the snow melted.

That was perhaps two days before I fell ill. The physicians assumed the cold had shocked my body."

"Did the snow fall across all of Simynshin? Or only in Elenth?" asked Mikoneh.

"Only Elenth, I believe." Her brows pinched together. "Do you think it was a Mage storm?"

"Yes. And I think it was directed at you."

"To steal my voice and use my music for evil?" She shook her head. "That's like a hearth story."

"Hearth stories come from truth," Akonn piped up. "Mikoneh, you should tell your father your theory. He'll wish to know."

Mikoneh nodded. "I planned on it." He stood. "I've enjoyed my morning. Thank you, Latta."

She rose along with the others. Though a shadow still touched her face, she offered a bright smile. "Thank you for accompanying me. I look forward to knowing all of you better."

"Likewise." He bowed, then caught Maya's arm, and they withdrew from the room. Penn and Akonn followed.

"Owenekiras is probably back by now," Akonn said.

"Where did he go?" asked Mikoneh softly.

"To his war camp on the plains. He needed to make sure everything there was still in good order."

Mikoneh nodded. They'd left Kagon Village in the north and came straight here, not daring to detour to Owenekiras's camp. It made sense the Dragon King would need to head there and see to matters under his care.

Meanwhile, Mikoneh must see to things here. He turned his theory about Latta's voice over and over in his head. "Do you think her song could be used for evil, Captain?"

"All talents and tools can be used for evil as much as for

good," Akonn answered. "The choice always lies with the wielder."

"Any chance we can use magic to find the thief?"

Akonn's eyes glinted. "There's one possibility, but the timing needs to be right. I'll discuss my idea with Hilker."

They moved toward their suite at a quick pace. Mikoneh was glad for a respite from socializing, even though Latta was a more sensible woman than he'd suspected any princess to be.

Maya's technically a princess, too, you know. He smiled wryly.

Still, he'd assumed that there would be a big difference between a princess who grew up in a castle and one who grew up in a cottage with no idea of her lineage. Latta proved that his assumption wasn't fair. Even so, he was glad the betrothal was only a front.

They reached their borrowed suite. Entering the common room, he found it had been cleared from breakfast, tidied from the tailor's visit, and stocked with snacks to tide them over until the feast. For the first time, he absorbed the plush nature of the room, with its rugs and tapestries and the swath of curtains framing an enormous glass-paned bay window over-looking an outside courtyard shadowed by the castle walls. Owenekiras Rokahn was standing at the window, eyeing Mikoneh with his usual closed expression.

Extracting himself from Maya's arm, Mikoneh strode toward his father. "Would the Mages want Latta's musical talent?"

"Possibly," Owenekiras said. "What did you learn?"

Mikoneh explained his interview with Latta, then shrugged. "Could her talent be used to manipulate or hurt anybody?"

"Yes, given enough practice," Owenekiras said, "and if the Mages have learned how to tap it, that's a very dangerous weapon. It might explain their ability to influence the court at Elenth.”

“Could it influence you?”

Owenekiras paused to weigh that. “To some degree, yes. The issue lies in the fact that Latta’s gift requires the presence of the wielder. If someone is tapping her gift, they would need to rely on their own voice, and they would need to sing.”

Mikoneh frowned. “That’s a bit obvious. Would they risk it?”

“I doubt highly that the Mage ambassador would be so bold. If they are tapping into Latta’s magic, it must be to some purpose elsewhere or the wielder is not a Mage.”

“So,” Mikoneh rubbed a finger against his jaw, “it comes back to the leak rather than direct Mage interference.”

Just like Minno had said. Memories of the gray boy put Mikoneh’s teeth on edge.

“Possibly so,” Owenekiras said. “Time will tell us. We must remain vigilant.”

“Guess that’s all we can do,” Mikoneh sighed. “And wait for someone to start singing.”

Silence fell between them, neither knowing what else to say.

Maya swept across the room. “Father, Latta remembers our mother.”

A faint line appeared between the Dragon King’s brows, then he nodded. “She has a good memory. I’m not surprised.”

“Her name was Rathana, then?” asked Maya.

“Yes,” Owenekiras said without emotion.

Mikoneh looked away from Owenekiras’s face. He was unwilling to intrude on his father’s private pain, but he was equally unwilling to shut his twin down. She had the right to ask questions. They’d been robbed of knowing the woman.

“And she was from Cimin, right?” Maya went on.

"She was."

"Is our grandfather dead? Rathana's father, I mean."

Mikoneh twisted around in time to catch a faint smile on his father's lips.

"He's alive," Owenekiras said. "Few things could kill that man."

"Really?" Maya caught her father's arm. "Could we meet him?"

"Someday. Perhaps soon."

Maya's face lit up like an Ephe'ahn village tree. "Does he live in the Spire of Cimin?"

"Yes. He's a scholar there."

Mikoneh couldn't resist a question of his own. "Could our mother fight? Latta seemed to think so."

Owenekiras nodded. "All scholars of the Spire can fight, and well. They must protect history. There is no clan within Cimin more skilled than that of your grandfather's people."

"He leads them?" asked Maya.

"Certainly." Owenekiras's smile deepened, warming his glacial eyes. "By her own right, Rathana was a princess."

The man's short answers lodged in Mikoneh's chest, touching a hollow place he'd never noticed before. It was strange not to know the woman who'd given the twins life. Stranger still to think she'd loved them yet Mikoneh had no memory of her—only a deep pain that distance hadn't healed.

He wondered if such pain ever faded away, or if like his trauma, he would wear the scar forever.

Chapter 5

The Hope of Spring

"There is proof that the taint of TeshRelle has lessened since the Age of Dragons, but without the Complété it may take another 20,000 years before it is habitable, even with the ceaseless aid of the Spirits Elemental."

- *A Treatise on the Magic of the Hidden Realm* by Sariolin the Solitary

Long before Mikoneh reached the wide-open double doors to the enormous chamber where the feast was in progress, the fragrance of roasting meat and unfamiliar spices made his mouth water. The twins walked side by side, with Captain Akonn at their back. Penn had asked to stay behind, claiming a bad headache—the lucky man.

Both twins had changed for the evening. In the afternoon, the tailor had appeared with a dozen articles apiece and recommended that both wore what he called "Rokahnian colors" for the feast. They donned charcoal gray and deep burgundy, with blue and silver accents. The style was different from both Oceana and Simynshin.

Maya's dress was beautiful, with buckles, a laced bodice, a pocketed skirt that went to her calves, supple boots, and a belt for a ruby-studded dagger, which she proudly wore. Mikoneh was similarly dressed—with loose pants, a finely embroidered vest, and plenty of pockets—and wearing Fa's sword as proudly as Maya wore her dagger.

Above the lull of stringed instruments, the din of voices rose and fell in merriment, ringing through Mikoneh's sensitive ears. The noise warned him back despite the tantalizing scents. Too many people, too many staring eyes. Only Maya's firm grip on his arm brought him through the doors and into full view.

He stared at the dining courtiers, gentry, knights, guards, servants, and foreigners seated along the crammed tables. Countless candles and braziers edged the room, brightening the gold-threaded tapestries along the stone walls. At the head of the chamber stood a high table running across a dais. There sat King Prettem, along with his son Atlanse, Princess Latta, and another young woman who couldn't be much older than the princess. Probably the new queen. She was draped in velvet finery sewn with tiny gems that glittered and winked in the flickering light.

"It's so grand," Maya whispered.

Mikoneh scowled. It was certainly grand and foppish enough to belong in Drayve's court back home. Seemed like royalty and nobility the world over knew precisely how to waste time and coin on frivolity while people starved and died in the byways of Sirinhigha.

Maya dragged him forward. He allowed himself to be led while he scanned the high table again. A chill raced across his bones, and he jerked to a halt. His eyes met the cold green gaze of a man robed in purple and black. A Dark Mage, seated near the young queen. Probably the ambassador.

Mikoneh lifted his chin and held the man's gaze. Defiance charged through him, banishing the chill.

The braziers and candles brightened as if in answer.

The young queen leaned toward the Mage to murmur in his ear, forcing the man to break off eye contact to answer her. Mikoneh moved toward them.

Prince Atlanse noticed the twins coming along the aisle, and he perked up. The crown prince stood, and the music drifted into silence, warning the crowds to still. They did, one table at a time, and countless eyes searched for the cause of the interruption.

Maya reached the high table, then subtly guided Mikoneh onto the dais and around the table itself, toward the empty chairs waiting for them.

"Welcome," Prince Atlanse said, grinning at them. "My lords and ladies, I have the great privilege of presenting two very important personages: Prince Mikoneh Rokahn, and the lovely princess Mayanaleh Rokahn. I'm certain many of you remember them well."

The gaping silence was deep enough to swallow the Isles of Molten Gold.

Mikoneh faced the massive chamber, held his head high, then gave a tiny bow as Akonn had instructed. Maya curtsied at his side. At the closest table near the head, Mikoneh's gaze snagged on Lord Crim. The merchant nobleman stood up, holding a goblet, his smile radiant.

"Your Majesty," Crim said, "Lady Queen, Crown Prince, and the rest of the High Table, on behalf of the nobility of Simynshin, may I give a hearty welcome to the heirs of Rokahn. Too long has it been since they honored our lands with their presence. They've grown strong and comely, and with them comes the hope of spring after a long, dark winter." He lifted his goblet. "Long live the Dragon Throne!"

Everyone stood. Shouts of "hear, hear!" resounded across the room, though Mikoneh marked more than one sour face among those below the dais.

Cold eyes settled on him, hungry, probing.

Mikoneh set his teeth and bowed to Lord Crim, ignoring the sensation.

When the toast finished, the room settled back down, but Atlanse remained standing. So did the twins, since neither knew whether it was appropriate to sit yet. The prince smiled at them in a reassuring manner, then addressed the room again.

"Many of you will also recall a long-ago promise between Simynshin and Rokahn." Murmurs drifted from the tables, but Atlanse pressed on. "I am pleased to announce that the betrothal between Princess Latta and Prince Mikoneh Rokahn remains an honorable and worthy tie between our two lands. May it unite us under any conflict now and in the future."

A man in his later years pushed to his feet. "But, Your Highness, he's the son of the traitor!"

Mikoneh stiffened.

Murmurs of assent sparked over the air.

Hostile eyes flashed over him, then away.

Atlanse's gaze turned cold. "Owenekiras Rokahn is my friend and ally, Lord Verett. Not a traitor."

Several faces twisted into scowls, but someone threw a dismissive hand toward the protesting lord. "Sit down, you old fool, before you crack your head again."

A smattering of laughter followed that statement, and Atlanse managed a smile.

"Simynshin honors its promises, Lord Verett. As it always has." The Crown Prince of Simynshin lifted his goblet. "To our continued alliance with Rokahn, and the coming union between two good young people."

Chairs scooted back. Goblets lifted. Cheers rang out.

Silence followed as everyone drained their goblets.

Mikoneh had to lock his joints so he wouldn't run. Maya held on for good measure. When goblets lowered, Atlanse motioned, and everyone sat back down. Jewels winked and sparkled, eyes darted between Mikoneh and the Simynshinian princess, and chatter started back up. Stringed music began anew.

"I think we can sit now," Maya whispered.

Mikoneh remembered how to bend his knees and followed his twin's example. The chair was plush—that was something. Unwillingly, he found himself glancing toward Latta. Their gazes collided. He looked away at once, unable to maintain eye contact.

Her eyes had been bright, her smile warm. Did she know this was a ruse? Had her father already talked to her?

I don't want to hurt her feelings later.

He resolved to ask Atlanse at the next opportunity.

Maya shifted closer. "Why do you think Owenekiras didn't come to the feast?"

"Can't you *feel* that disquiet? He'd only make it worse."

"Yes but...if they *are* allies, and if there *is* unrest—which is clearly the case—shouldn't he work to alleviate that by appearing less remote, more human?"

Mikoneh offered her a crooked smile. "There's just one problem with that, Maya. He's not human. Neither are we."

Her smile faltered. "True. I...I suppose I just haven't fully accepted that yet."

"Understandable." If Sathe hadn't drilled into him exactly what he was, he'd likely still be struggling with the idea, his mind caught between the truth and old mental habits.

Once you turned into a dragon—even a cat-sized one—you could never go back to thinking you were human.

THE FEAST DRAGGED ON ENDLESSLY. As the wine was poured and the music became livelier, the hostile glances diminished. Outlandish toasts were raised. Even Verett seemed more at his ease after the first turn or two. At last, toward the middle turns of the night, Prince Atlanse signaled that the twins could depart. The feast could go on without them. After bowing to the royal family, Mikoneh led the way toward the side door where Captain Akonn stood waiting. Numerous eyes watched them until they stepped out into a torchlit corridor.

Maya exhaled a heavy breath. "That was terrifying."

Mikoneh grunted his agreement.

"Royal functions like that take a lot of getting used to," Akonn said.

Mikoneh choked back a comment about not wanting to get used to any of this. Like it or not, he was stuck in this new world, caught by the threads of a heritage he knew almost nothing about. He ran his thumb along his sword pommel, contemplating the foreign clothes he wore. Their cut, their color, their symbolism.

"Does Owenekiras intend to take back the throne of Rokahn?" he asked.

Akonn glanced at him. "If he does, the Sword will have his back."

"You don't know?" asked Maya.

Akonn shook his head. "Your father is fighting a war far bigger than one lone island. He would probably prefer his brother to take the throne. Or you." He nodded toward Mikoneh.

"Not likely," Mikoneh muttered.

"He'll never force the point." Akonn motioned them down the hallway, and the three headed for their suite.

Maya snapped her fingers. "That's right. He does have a younger brother."

"A twin," Akonn said. "His name is Milannetirin, though most folk call him Milann."

"I heard he went missing," Mikoneh said.

"He did, yes, but Owenekiras rediscovered him a few years ago. That's not common knowledge."

"Is he all right?" Maya asked.

"He's got a wife and child, and lives a nomadic life." Akonn turned down a new corridor, heading toward their suite. "The child is a daughter, I believe. Your cousin."

Mikoneh's step faltered. He'd gone from an orphaned peasant and defeated rebel leader to a royal prince with a large family tree in a mere month.

"That's wonderful," Maya breathed out. "How old is she?"

"Eighteen, I think." Akonn smiled at her. "She's a fierce young woman. Very independent."

Maya glanced toward Mikoneh. "Sounds familiar."

He ignored that. "Does Milann have any plans to take the Rokahnian throne from his sister?"

Akonn shook his head. "He's...caught up in other affairs."

"Will we meet them?" asked Maya.

"Not soon, I'm afraid." Akonn started up a stairwell. "Owenekiras doesn't dare bring attention to them. And Milann's wife prefers that he stay far away."

"Seems like a lot of people don't like the Dragon King."

"I don't think it's a matter of dislike in this case," Akonn said. "More a matter of protecting her family. But yes, many people despise your father. It comes from being powerful and just."

Mikoneh rubbed his sword pommel faster. He had yet to

form a personal opinion about the man. What he knew and respected was largely secondhand knowledge, and though he trusted Fa and Mama's stories of their time serving under the Dragon King, respecting a leader was a different prospect from judging an estranged father.

Yes, Owenekiras had rescued him from the Dark Mages—and yes, their objectives were the same. But beyond that, they were strangers. Mikoneh couldn't begin to guess who Owenekiras Rokahn truly was under his icy façade or what he wanted once the war concluded.

Maya trusted him, but she was prone to trust everyone.

Do I want to trust him?

Eyeing Akonn's back, he wondered if the captain could give an objective view. The captain seemed to border on hero worship, and really, who could blame him? Like the man or hate him, no one could help but respect the rightful heir of Rokahn.

I'm better off watching and waiting before I make any hasty judgment calls.

They soon reached the suite, where Penn sat reading in a chair near the blazing hearth fire. He looked up from the tome cradled in his arms and smiled, his chocolate brown eyes almost amber in the glow. "How did it go?"

"Step one complete," Mikoneh said. "How's the headache?"

"Quite a bit better. I just needed some silence to shake it off."

"Good book?" Mikoneh nodded toward it.

"Fascinating." Penn lifted it to reveal the title: *Agricultural Wars: Simynshin's Shift to a World Power.*

"Looks riveting," Mikoneh said dryly.

"It is." Penn flashed him a grin. "So, you're officially a betrothed man."

"I don't want to talk about it." He plucked up a throw pillow and tossed it.

Penn batted it aside. "She's lovely, you must confess."

"Sure. So is the sea—but I don't have to marry *that*."

Maya chuckled. "If you weren't so shy, I bet you'd win her heart. It could be very romantic."

"It's more than shyness," Penn said. "It's terror."

Mikoneh rolled his eyes and tramped toward his room. "I'm not scared of women. I'm scared of *eligible* women."

"No need for all that now," Penn said. "You're promised. You only need to be scared of *one*."

Mikoneh paused at his bedroom door and glanced over his shoulder. "You're such great friends. Thanks so much. And goodnight." He slipped inside his room, shut the door, and leaned against it. Why he was shaking, he couldn't say. It wasn't fear of a fake betrothal—that only made him nervous now that he'd come to terms with it.

He pressed his palms against his face to shut out the moonlight, the shadows, the nameless shapes across the chamber. Outside, the wind whistled, and the scent of imminent snow filled his nostrils.

"You're safe," he whispered to himself. "You're alone. Safe and alone."

He didn't believe his words.

INTERLUDE I
WATER

"In what other realm is found a soul more gentle than yours?"

- From the Corpse Poet's 3rd Sonnet

The blue world was clearer than usual. He walked the familiar watery path, looking for a glimpse of his white-cloaked companion. Everything was eerily silent. Only the faintest breeze stirred the ancient trees and rustled the hem of his long, shadowy cloak.

There were no birds. No insects.

His insides tightened. His steps quickened. At last, the pathway rolled into a clearing made of water. Tall, wide trees circled the pool. He scanned the vicinity. Its familiarity nibbled at his mind. Those weren't just trees; they were homes. The Nijaal lived here.

Ripples cascaded out in all directions as he stepped onto the surface of the pool, his feet staying above the water.

There, at the center of the depthless pool, she knelt and

wept, folded forward into her hands. Her cloak was spread around her. Her cowl had fallen across her back, revealing her long, wheat-blonde tresses.

He stooped beside her, resting one hand on her trembling shoulder. "What's wrong?"

She tensed, then straightened and twisted to meet his gaze. Her emerald eyes were wide and glistening with tears. Her cheeks shone. "They've taken him, too. Minno is gone."

Chapter 6

In the Memory of Light

"A widely accepted theory regarding the innate nature of each Spirit Elemental type is drawn from studying the human and fae wielders of each aspect, but this is a flawed premise. While Fire Elementalists have been known to be temperamental, I've met too many level-headed wielders to think it a rule of nature. There are simply too many exceptions."

- *A Treatise on the Magic of the Hidden Realm* by Sariolin the Solitary

Eyes watched him. So many of them. Whispering voices followed at his back.

A clawed hand reached for his arm, raking his flesh.

'You can't escape forever, Firebrand.'

He jerked upright, gasping. Sweat dripped down his chin.

"Good morning." The bland monotones came from the window.

Mikoneh turned toward that voice, his heart slamming into his throat. There, on the cushioned seat below the open window, knelt Minno. The boy wore his customary gray outfit, which exactly matched the cloudy shade of his hair and eye color. In his arms, he held the mallard he'd named Duck.

"What are *you* doing here?" Mikoneh growled. "Trying to hand me back over to the Mages?"

"Not today," Minno said. "I came for information."

Mikoneh's scowl deepened. "I'm not going to tell you where Lady Katanni is if that's what you're after." The ageless gray boy, who looked no older than ten, was trying to meet the Nijaalin woman—though why Minno was so fixated on that remained a mystery. It was clear no one trusted him anywhere near her.

Minno shrugged. "Perhaps your sister will."

"Not gonna happen." Mikoneh threw his coverlets aside and grabbed his pants to slip on over his smalls. "You can leave now, preferably by the same way you entered."

Minno glanced at the open window. "It's snowing."

"Even better. Goodbye."

Minno unfolded himself and slipped off the window seat. "You're an unpleasant person."

"Who's nice to their enemies?"

"I'm not your enemy."

Mikoneh fumbled with his loose white shirt, then slipped it over his head. He pinned a glower on Minno. "What do you call that stunt you pulled with the Mages back in that forest?"

"A scheme," Minno said.

"Yet you don't see me as your enemy?"

"I kill my enemies," Minno said. "I don't sell them."

Mikoneh fell still. "And what do you call people you sell?"

"Pests," Minno said in the same blasé tone. "You've stepped in where you're not wanted."

"In what way?"

Minno's grip around his duck tightened. "That isn't your business."

Mikoneh blinked. "Come again?"

"You heard me."

"Yeah, except if I'm involved, doesn't that make it my business?"

"Just stay out of affairs between Owen and me."

"Who said I wanted—"

Owenekiras's voice came from the door. "Minno. What are you doing in here?"

Mikoneh's heart jumped into his throat. He spun toward the Dragon King while his hand reached for his sword and closed over nothing but air. "Wha—"

Owenekiras's cold eyes were pinned on Minno. "You shouldn't enter people's rooms unannounced."

"That goes for both of you," Mikoneh growled again.

"That's true," Minno said. "You didn't knock, Owen."

Owenekiras turned to Mikoneh. "My apologies."

Mikoneh shrugged into the vest folded on the chair beside his boots. "As long as it's understood." He reached for his sword belt. "Is breakfast ready?"

"Would you care for a sword bout before your morning meal?" Owenekiras asked.

"Against you?"

"If you like. Akonn is organizing matches in the south training room."

"Another chance to put me on display?" The words came out gruffer than Mikoneh had meant them to be. He understood the stakes. He knew his purpose. It was no more dangerous than any soldier's part in a war. If anything, what he struggled against was his isolation in a complex political game. He much preferred the blunt honesty of steel against steel.

While the Dragon King's face remained as unreadable as

ever, Mikoneh recognized that it wasn't cold—not strictly. There was a wall, yes, but perhaps...just maybe...there was also a gate.

"If you cannot handle this affair on the heels of your captivity," the Dragon King said, "we can adjust course. You're not a captive here." He spoke with the same levelness he always wielded. Did Mikoneh imagine the gentle undertone?

This man is my father.

Cloying emotions swirled within Mikoneh, making his chest tight. He'd been raised by a good man—one of the best—but Jonatten was dead. In his place, unasked for, unwanted, stood a stranger—but one who'd given up his family to protect them. Didn't he deserve a chance, too? Hadn't Mikoneh decided to allow that back in Kagon?

Everything from the past few days was fuzzy at the edges.

What am I supposed to do? Throw myself in his arms like a child because I'm afraid?

Mikoneh's hands curled into fists. They could only hope to forge a relationship as two adults. Training seemed like a good starting point. "I'm fine. I'd rather move around than sit still and think for too long."

"Doubtless, you would struggle with the latter," Minno said.

Mikoneh ignored him. To do anything else might provoke a fist fight, and if anyone walked in on him beating up a child, he couldn't justify himself. Even if the child in question was millennia old and deserved it.

"Lead the way," he told Owenekiras.

The Dragon King motioned to the common room, then set his cold eyes on Minno. "You should remain in the castle. I must discuss something with you later."

"Very well." Minno stroked Duck's head. "We'll stay close."

Mikoneh slipped from the bedroom and glanced around for his twin. She wasn't in the common area. Had she slept in? Penn wasn't there either.

Owenekiras came up behind him. "Your sister was invited to an early breakfast with Princess Latta. Penn requested access to the library. Both left a sandglass turn ago."

Mikoneh wasn't used to sleeping longer than his companions, especially by a full turn, but he chose not to dwell on what that might imply. Owenekiras moved ahead of him, and entered the corridor beyond. Together, they walked toward the training room. Mikoneh kept himself one step behind his father. His thoughts dripped like tree sap, and he was unable to conjure up any conversation he dared to speak in public halls.

"How is the pain?" asked Owenekiras.

"Pain?"

"Sathe's rooting about in your soul will have left a mark. The pain cannot have subsided yet, even with the Lady's touch and the *tiassana* leaves."

True. There was certainly pain. A deep, aching, nebulous kind. But Mikoneh had set it on one of the shelves of his mind, not eager to examine it, or even acknowledge it... "It's not too bad."

"It should be treated again." Owenekiras glanced at him. "Minno is one of the most adept Spirit Elementalists I know. I realize you harbor no trust toward him, and no one would blame you for saying no, but I recommend you let him treat your soul."

"He's not *touching* me."

"It isn't invasive."

"Not happening." Mikoneh flinched at the vehemence of his tone. Growling again, he ran a hand through his hair. His fingers caught on a tangle. He hadn't brushed it. Pulling his fingers loose, he exhaled. "If you know any other adept Spirit

Elementalists, I'll consider the idea. But Minno doesn't get to come within five feet of me. Not after what he did."

The Dragon King nodded. "I do understand. Minno's story is a...complicated one. But his actions were unconscionable."

"Too right," Mikoneh muttered.

"If you could overcome that, however, it might be best for your sake."

Mikoneh's eyes narrowed. "You don't seem the type to push a point." He didn't understand how his father could overlook Minno's betrayal so quickly after everything, but something within Mikoneh couldn't balk against the man's reasoning tones. Was it possible some part of Mikoneh was beginning to trust Owenekiras after all?

"I'm usually not," Owenekiras agreed, "but Minno is the *best* in terms of spirit of spirit. Few equal him. Fewer still surpass him. And you wield spirit, as well as fire. Minno would be my first pick to train you."

"No thanks." Mikoneh rubbed at his sword pommel. "I'll stick with fire for now if you have any good mentor candidates that way."

Owenekiras halted, then turned. "Minno wields all five elements. He's a master. You could not do better if you wish to excel at your own."

Chills spidered down Mikoneh's spine. He set his feet. "I don't care if he's the foremost authority on dragons, Mage killing, or harnessing the sun. I won't deal with him."

Owenekiras dipped his head. "Very well. Lord Crim is also quite skilled at fire. He's volunteered to train you. I understand you spoke with Latta about the matter, and she brought it to Atlanse's attention while we were conversing early this morning."

Mikoneh breathed out through his nose. "That will work fine. I like Crim, as far as nobles go."

"He's a fair and reasonable man, and he will teach you how to harness your element as much as his limits allow."

Was that disapproval? Mikoneh dismissed it. He could start with Crim and perhaps find a master once he understood the basic etiquette and proper techniques of his newfound power.

A frown edged his lips. "What about the other thing?"

"What other thing?" asked Owenekiras.

"My...my dragon...thing."

They entered an outer hall flooded with sunlight. Passing through the light staining the flagstones, Mikoneh gazed outside. The pristine cloak of snow covering the great lake ports of Elenth glittered under the dawn's ephemeral light. He halted, dazzled. A deep ache to draw out his wings and soar above that lake nearly overwhelmed his senses.

Owenekiras's voice sounded beside him, disembodied in the enveloping morning glow. "I've arranged for someone to mentor you in dragon matters. Your education on that subject will not begin for a week or two, when he arrives."

Thank the Nijaal, the man wasn't proclaiming Minno as the foremost expert on dragon kind after all.

"Shall we continue?"

Mikoneh almost shook his head. Swimming in sunshine, lost in the memory of light, he didn't want to return to the castle halls and dim chambers, with all their politics and subterfuge. He didn't want to deal with the war against the Mage Queen and her undead armies in the north. He didn't want to face the conflict in Rokahn or his usurping aunt on the throne to the south.

Grimacing, he wrenched around and followed after Owenekiras, blinking away the afterimage of the glittering lake.

Perhaps later he could sneak away and fly. Maybe Maya would want to come with him. After all, she was a dragon, too.

CHAPTER 7

BRED FOR WAR

"Also of note is that any one elemental aspect is not hereditary. Even twins rarely share the same spirit type. That is not to say breeding a specific type into one's family line hasn't occurred, for records offer proof that such a thing has happened."

- *A Treatise on the Magic of the Hidden Realm* by Sariolin the Solitary

Maya entered the training hall, arm in arm with Latta. They'd spent a lovely breakfast together, discussing trivial things. It had been divine. Because she'd been raised differently than the other village girls back in Relvin, Maya had little experience with young women her own age. Most had eyed her askance every time she drew a sword or handled a quarterstaff. The fact that her parents were warriors only added to the divide between the twins and their peers.

Certainly, she'd tried to be friendly with everyone, and she'd thought she had a dear friend in Kevva, but that had proved false when the auburn-haired girl betrayed Mikoneh's army because he'd jilted her—unwittingly.

Since the village girls saw Maya as an outsider, they'd tended to act haughty and unfriendly when she was around. Latta wasn't like that. She was troubled, that much was easy to read. And it seemed a deeper trouble than even her stolen song. Latta looked like she was being hunted. It was so much like Mikoneh, plagued by night terrors and nervous of his own shadow.

The clash and clatter of wooden weapons pounded across the wide chamber, jerking Maya from her reverie. Mats were strewn across the floor, and racks along the walls held every kind of weapon Maya could imagine. Wide windows lined the southern end of the room, letting in ample light.

Mikoneh stood across the chamber, wooden sword in hand, hair tied back in a sloppy tail. Sweat glistened on his brow. He'd shed his vest. His blouse was half unlaced and stuck to his sweaty back.

His opponent, draped in full chainmail, cut a looming and impressive figure. Owenekiras Rokahn. Father. Maya found herself smiling. She'd been afraid Mikoneh would reject the man outright, deny their shared blood, and drag Maya back home to fight a losing battle in the backwoods of Oceana.

Fortunately, Mikoneh had more sense than that.

"They're both impressive," Latta said.

Maya nodded. "Bred for war." Whether that was true of all dragons or only those of the royal Rokahn line, she didn't know, but the statement rang true for these men.

All other training in the room had ceased. Every eye was fixed on father and son. Despite the difference in their height and experience, Mikoneh's motions were graceful, swift, and purposeful. Jonatten and Seranni had taught their adopted children to waste no energy on fancy twirls and flourishes.

Showing off got a man killed. Mikoneh was skilled and careful.

But he'd lost weight in his captivity, and as a result, he got tired more quickly. Maya winced when he stumbled backward, retreating from a block he should've been able to take. Yet his jaw was set. His eyes were bright.

He was angry.

Maya's heart throbbed. He was behaving just like Kevva said he had after their house burned down: unnaturally calm at first, then throwing himself into his work, growing angrier and more brooding. Maya had fallen apart, leaving him to pick up all the pieces—and he'd changed.

She couldn't blame him. Not then, and not now. Not after being held captive by Dark Mages for a month. She didn't know all that Sathe had done but guesses and fears swirled in her head like a storm. She ached for Mikoneh to talk to her, to lance the wound and not let it fester and rot.

What can I do to help him?

Owenekiras backed him against the edge of the mats. Mikoneh's slitted gold eyes took on a feral sheen. Maya started forward, her stomach flipping—but a new emotion flickered over his face, then a grin cracked his lips.

He did step forward—but it was a purposeful motion. Steady. Controlled.

Owenekiras responded by retreating. Their wooden blades crashed into each other. Held. Mikoneh pressed, then stumbled back after Owenekiras's swing. The younger man sank to his knees and held up one hand.

"I yield." Mikoneh's voice was strong, despite his panting breaths.

The room broke into applause. Maya raced forward, Latta right on her heels.

"That was magnificent," the Simynshinian princess said.

Maya nodded. While she'd seen few men who could equal Mikoneh with a sword, it didn't surprise her that the Dragon King was better. Still, her twin had held his own.

Mikoneh staggered to his feet and wiped a trickle of sweat from his chin. "It was definitely educational." A faint line appeared on his brow. He was frustrated, but not angry. He'd come to manage his emotions better, even when he lost.

Several men and women moved closer to the mat. Admiring eyes followed Owenekiras—and many darted toward Mikoneh with equal respect.

"This is your son, my lord, isn't he?" asked a young man, clutching a wooden sword close to his chest. By his grip, Maya could tell he wasn't a seasoned swordsman.

"So he is," Owenekiras said. "Mikoneh Rokahn."

Mikoneh slipped into a fluid bow, then straightened. His eyes darted to Maya, and his smile warmed. "This is my twin sister Mayanaleh."

"An honor, Your Highnesses," the young man said with a deep bow. His sword clattered against the floor. Behind him, an older man sighed.

"Remember it's a weapon, Seval."

"Yes, Master Donivan." Seval straightened up, his face bright red.

Donivan strode forward, carrying himself like a proper warrior. He was a man in his forties, with dark brown hair streaked with faint silver threads, and eyes like rich chocolate. For a man double Maya's age, he was beautiful. Lean, well-toned, with powerful hands. The sword master—for what else could he be?—inclined his head to Owenekiras.

"Thank you for a wonderful demonstration on what *real* swordplay is." He turned an appraising eye on Mikoneh. "Your skills are well beyond your years, Your Highness, though that comes as no surprise. I've never met a Rokahn who didn't excel at every craft of war. My name is Donivan Kriv, by the way."

Mikoneh's grin twitched toward a grimace. "It's the art of peace I'd prefer to master, Master Donivan. But maybe that'll come with a new season."

"Celes willing." Donivan's dark gaze settled on Maya. "Do you also excel at fighting, Daughter of Rokahn?"

Maya's cheeks warmed. "I'm fair with a sword, but I'm better still with a quarterstaff."

Mikoneh laughed. "True. She bests me all the time when we duel with polearms."

"Well, then," Donivan said, "I'd love a demonstration for my afternoon class. Would you be opposed, Princess?"

"Not at all," Maya said cheerfully, "so long as I'm not pitted against Ter."

"Is he here?" asked Donivan.

"No," Owenekiras said. "Not for another week, I suspect."

Donivan nodded. "I'll arrange a bout against Zevier. He's my swiftest student with any polearm. I look forward to seeing your footwork, Your Highness."

The title sent a thrill through Maya. She dipped into a hasty curtsey, then whirled on Latta. "Will you come and watch?"

Latta laughed. "I wouldn't miss it." The princess's sapphire eyes fell on Mikoneh. "Just as I'm glad I didn't miss this bout. When we were young, you said your father was the strongest man alive, and one day you'd be just like him. It seems you're well on your way, Prince Mikoneh."

A dry smile brushed his lips. "I doubt I was that articulate —and I don't know if I'll ever walk around in full armor in an ally's castle to find out how similar we are."

Several sword students laughed.

"That's our favorite Rokahnian royal for you," Crim said

from the back of the crowd. "Always prepared for a possible knife in the back." The students parted to let him through. The merchant lord walked closer, then halted to bow at the assembled royalty. "Brunch is ready in the adjacent hall, my royal lords and ladies."

Maya was still full from her hearty breakfast, but she followed her twin, her father, and the rest of those invited to join in the midmorning meal. She scanned the sea of faces, frowning.

"What is it?" asked Mikoneh, inching closer.

"I haven't seen Hilker since we arrived. I hope he's all right."

"He's visiting his family," Owenekiras answered. "He'll return in two days."

"Oh." She grinned. "I didn't know he had a family. Somehow, he struck me as a loner, especially since he left Elenth to train me."

Akonn moved up from the back of their train. "Actually, he has eight children."

Maya froze, and Mikoneh had to tug her into the adjacent chamber. The room was bright with sunlight. Food spread across the long table. The fragrance of meats, fruits, cheeses, and fresh bread wafted over the air. Covered tureens promised unique dishes Maya couldn't identify by scent.

At Crim's gesture, Owenekiras sat at the head of the table. Mikoneh took the seat near him, and Latta positioned herself across from her betrothed. Maya placed herself beside her twin, and Crim claimed the next chair. A few others filed in, but most of the students stood at the door, watching, until Master Donivan shooed them off and shut the door to give the group some privacy.

Akonn stood behind Owenekiras's chair, his hands clasped behind his back.

"Does Hilker really have eight children?" asked Maya.

Mikoneh snorted into the goblet he held.

Akonn's mouth quivered. "Yes, Your Highness. And a very lovely wife."

"I'm happy for him." Maya selected some fruit from a dish to occupy herself while Mikoneh filled his stomach. His appetite was fair, though she wished he looked less distracted. Mostly, he ate meat. Was that because his dragon blood was fully awake?

Movement caught her attention. Owenekiras withdrew the pale, shelled fruit called *korta*—dragonfang fruit—from some hidden place beneath his cape. He unsheathed long black claws, sliced the fruit in half, and peeled it apart to reveal the iridescent fruit within. Maya's mouth watered.

Owenekiras passed the fruit to Mikoneh, who accepted it without blinking and sank his teeth into the soft flesh. Maya tensed. Were those *fangs* in his mouth? She ran her tongue across her teeth, half afraid, half fascinated. The Dragon King had been giving her *korta* every morning, after explaining that eating it each day would awaken her dragon blood gently. That last word tightened her chest. Doubtless, Sathe hadn't been gentle with Mikoneh. He'd come into his blood through torture.

Dark circles marked Mikoneh's eyes, and his distance was something almost tangible—especially since he was throwing himself into a role he hated. But if it kept him going, Maya wouldn't argue.

Latta spun her ring around her finger. "Since Maya's demonstration for Master Donivan won't be until this afternoon, would you both care to join me for a tour of Elenth's market squares once Mikoneh is finished eating?" She glanced at Owenekiras. "You would be welcome to come as well, my lord."

Owenekiras shook his head. "I'm afraid I would cause a riot. Best I play least in sight among the common folk of your fair city."

Latta frowned. "The common folk have more good sense than my grandfather's courtiers. They'd be more likely to throw flowers than stones if you rode the streets with us."

"Perhaps. But I have a meeting with your father in half a turn and it could go on a long time. Better not wait for me."

The princess's frown deepened, but she didn't press the point.

Mikoneh ate another slab of roast beef, then sat back. "I'm ready for that tour any time. You mentioned riding. Horseback or carriage?"

"Which do you prefer?" asked Latta.

"Horseback."

"Then that's what it will be."

Maya rose with them, then hesitated. "You know, I think I'll stay behind if that's all right. I'd like to get some practice in ahead of my demonstration. You both go on without me."

Mikoneh's narrowed glance was brief, but she caught it— and certainly it was deserved. She couldn't help herself. Maybe Mikoneh would remain stubborn, but Latta was obviously a kind person, as well as lovely, and he could do far worse. And if all the princess did was help him to overcome his shyness around women, that was just as good.

Maya started to leave, then paused and glanced over her shoulder. "You owe me a bout, too, Father."

Owenekiras fell still, then nodded. "If you wish."

"I do." She skipped across the chamber, pleased with herself all around. Her life would never be the same as it was before Fa and Mama died, but that didn't mean it had to be bad.

Chapter 8

The Cost of My Country

"I've studied the Spirits Elemental these past forty years, and will state with confidence that while personality traits can, and often do, determine which Elementalist type a person may become, it is also common for the spirits to choose the wielder later in life and for any number of reasons. There are cases across history to support this."

- *A Treatise on the Magic of the Hidden Realm* by Sariolin the Solitary

Draped in an ermine fur-lined blue cloak, Princess Latta led the way to the royal stables across the snow-dusted grounds. Mikoneh followed behind her, careful not to reveal his reluctance. He was relieved that Akonn and the princess's protector—a large man built like a bear—came along.

Snow drifted down like lazy feathers, and the sky glowed with silvery light in its battle to hide the sun. Latta entered the stable and moved to a stall near the entrance, drawing back her voluminous hood. Dust motes swirled in the air, and the musty odor of hay and horsehair filled Mikoneh's nose.

"Here's your riding mate," Latta said, stroking a black nose.

Mikoneh drew near to peek inside the stall. He blinked. "Rook?"

The black warhorse tossed his head and offered up a cheerful greeting. Mikoneh reached out, still not believing his eyes. He'd left his stolen mount—along with Maya's and Penn's, and even Ter's pony—in the Ephe'ahn village before he was captured. By Maya's report, they'd flown straight to the Dragon King's war camp from there, leaving the horses behind.

Yet hadn't Ter once brought the horses across space using gateways made of Void? Magic appeared to make the impossible possible, for good or ill.

He stroked Rook's nose, murmuring a soft greeting. Though he'd stolen the horse from Lord Drayve, Rook seemed to hold nothing against Mikoneh. Considering how badly the earl rode, Mikoneh wouldn't have been surprised if Rook was grateful to escape his master.

With scuffing steps, an adolescent stablehand, around sixteen years old, approached and bowed. His straw-colored hair was tousled, and he looked—and smelled—like he'd been mucking out the stable. His light brown eyes were fixed on Latta adoringly. When he glanced at Mikoneh, ice flooded those eyes. And something else. Hatred?

Akonn noticed, too, and inched closer.

The stablehand backed up a step. "Would you like me to saddle Firechaser, Princess?"

"Yes, please," Latta said, "and this fellow." She stroked Rook's neck. "Thank you, Brentin."

"Very good, Princess." The young man moved to a nearby stall and guided a dappled gelding into the walkway. After shooting Mikoneh one last daggered glare, he guided Firechaser to a rack where a polished saddle sat ready.

Mikoneh glanced at Akonn, who frowned back. The captain held his sword in a deceptively casual stance.

If Latta had noticed the hostility she gave no indication. She whispered to Rook, then motioned to the stall across the walkway. "Maya's horse is in there, and Lord Penn's, just there. We even have Ter's pony. They arrived yesterday."

"That's a relief. Thank you." Mikoneh rested his forehead against Rook's muzzle and breathed in the stallion's scent. Magic was a wondrous thing. "We've gone through a lot together. They deserve to be treated like royalty."

"They will be." Latta glided past him, approaching the stablehand. She hummed a few sweet notes, then caught up a brush from the tools laid out on the table. "You enjoy riding, Mikoneh?"

"I do when I get the chance—unless I'm running for my life."

She glanced at him. "Perhaps tomorrow we can ride to the foothills. The forests are dense and old, and sometimes they sing." Her eyes sparkled. Dust motes swirled around her like minuscule fairies.

"I'd like that," he said. "Perhaps Maya could join us, now that she has Fairy."

Latta laughed. "Is that her horse's name? It's delightful. *She's* delightful. Such a sweet soul. I relish the chance to become true friends."

Mikoneh fingered the hem of his tailored Rokahnian vest —this one black with blue embroidered trim. "She's certainly special. And she's been through a lot."

"You both have." Latta watched him steadily. "I can read it in your countenance. Your burdens have been beyond description."

His breath caught. He shifted his feet and blew out air, trying to silence the fears screaming in his head. "It's war. We all suffer."

"Some more than most," Latta whispered. "Your part...it's a heavy one."

He shrugged. "I'm not complaining."

"No." She stepped closer, until the sweet fragrance of roses permeated the air around them. "That's what impresses me most, Mikoneh Rokahn."

He nearly moved back but resisted the urge. Instead, he hefted his head and met her gaze. Her expression was earnest, bright, but not intimate.

"I want to be your friend," she said. "And Maya's. And even Penn's. Whatever the future holds for us, let's begin that way." She reached out and caught his hand. He tensed. Every nerve screamed at him, but he held still. He was surprised by the softness of her fingers.

"I'd like that," he whispered.

She tipped her head to one side. "Then why do you look completely terrified?"

"It's nothing." He pulled his hand loose. "Just...don't like to be touched these days."

Latta retreated in a few graceful steps. "I'm sorry." She didn't look sheepish—just compassionate. "My father told me you'd suffered torture recently. I didn't think of that. Forgive me."

"It's fine." He turned to Rook, trying to ease his tense muscles. "I think—" His voice cracked. He swallowed and tried again. "I think I'll saddle Rook myself. He's a bit temperamental, and we can head out faster."

"His saddle is here," said Akonn, hefting the ornate black saddle off a hook.

"Thanks." Mikoneh accepted it and deftly saddled the

warhorse, trying to keep his thoughts focused on his task, away from the whispering shadows of his mind and the twinge of pain in his chest where Sathe had once been connected.

A few moments later, the two royals and their protectors left the stable and the glowering stablehand behind. Mikoneh relished the motion of the horse beneath him. It wasn't the same as flying—but it was as close as any human might get. He'd take it in the interim.

Latta was an excellent rider. With a laugh, she nudged Firechaser into a gallop across the snowy grounds, targeting the castle gates standing between them and Elenth proper. Mikoneh urged Rook after her, and the warhorse caught up in a few easy bounds. The protectors fell behind, but that might've been intentional to let the royals chat.

Nearing the gates, Mikoneh slowed, and Latta matched his pace. The sentries signaled, and the rumble of the lifting portcullis filled Mikoneh's ears. The guards bowed, letting their princess and her guest through the gate and across the moat. Mikoneh glanced below the bridge. The water hadn't frozen yet, but thin patches of frost framed the banks of the murky depths.

A cool breeze tugged on his hair. His body warmed to combat the chill, keeping him comfortable without a cloak.

Across the bridge and along the road, no one spoke. But as they neared the town proper, Latta drew her mount closer to his. "I'm sorry about Brentin. He's not usually so hostile."

So, she had noticed. Mikoneh scanned the large cobbled square spread before them. Snow frosted the roofs. Carts clattered past with wares and foodstuffs. A contingent of the city guard came around the northside corner and halted, giving their princess passage along the main city street. Several of the guards glared at Mikoneh, then dropped their eyes before Latta glanced toward them.

"Seems Brentin isn't the only hostile Simynshinian," Mikoneh said.

Latta fingered her ring while clutching the reins. "I'm afraid the people are split between Owenekiras's supporters and his...naysayers. We trade a great deal with Rokahn, and Queen Elayorah has denounced your father as a traitor and a dread lord. She all but threatened war against any kingdom harboring him. Many fear him more than the Mages."

Mikoneh mulled over that, rubbing his thumb along the leather reins. "That my aunt would denounce him without a public trial baffles the mind. At least Drayve had the decency to put Maya, Penn, and me through the motions, rigged or not."

"Elayorah is a hard woman. Strong and cold as a mountain." Latta shook her head. "I've only met her once, and she frightened me enough that I had nightmares. I used to think *she* was the Mage Queen. She certainly fits the image."

Memories of Sathe, cold and strong, swelled in Mikoneh's mind, threatening to choke him. He inhaled. "So... Simynshin is afraid to upset the balance and ruin trade. But, surely, Elayorah can't follow through on her threat when you're the agricultural trade center of Sirinhigha. No one dares mess with Simynshin, or they'd starve."

"That's true for all countries save Rokahn. That island is self-sustaining. It doesn't need any trade agreements. Besides, even on the mainland, that sentiment has been shifting. Where before Simynshin maintained its autonomy, now it's... teetering."

"Because of your new queen."

"Exactly." Latta sighed. "On her own, she's nothing but the fluff of dandelion down, but her presence holds sway."

"I'd heard the ladies at court are enamored with silks and lace from Lintha."

"Not all of them, but many practically *drool* over frippery these days." Latta's disdain dripped from every word. "And while I do appreciate a beautiful gown as much as the next woman, I would *never* favor it at the cost of my country."

"I can respect that," he said. "If the new queen is addled-brained, who's guiding her actions? The Mage Ambassador?"

"That's one influence," said Latta. "Queen Feresse also has her personal attendants, and I wouldn't trust *any* Linthian with a firestick. No matter who they're married to."

"Arsonists, hm?" Mikoneh chuckled. "Oddly enough, I don't think that'll be a problem."

"True. Not for a Dragon Prince with your skillset." Latta pointed up the road. "My favorite bakery stands there, and often a flower vendor parks beside it. She keeps trying to convince me to sell her a few frost rose cuts. I won't, though. Lady Katanni asked me not to share them far and wide."

"Why is that?" asked Mikoneh, studying the solid structure of the bakery as they passed. The aroma of fresh bread wafted out, making his mouth water though he wasn't hungry.

"She said the roses needed her blessing wherever they were planted, or they'd not survive. I don't think that's her only reason, but it's enough for me. I won't subject my roses to death."

There was no stall bursting with blooms today, but Mikoneh hadn't expected any different in the wintertime. What did a flower vendor do for money out of season? Could Earth Elementalists keep flowers alive in the cold months?

"Up ahead is the main market square," Latta said, "and adjacent to it, the theatre district. There's a playhouse there where a troupe is currently performing *The Minstrel and the Dragon,* which is a delightful story taking place shortly after the Age of Dragons. I doubt it's historically sound, but you may enjoy it."

Mikoneh shifted in his saddle. "You know a lot more about me than I do."

"I doubt that. I know a lot of facts, but not your soul. Not anymore. I can tell you about who you once were, when you were small—but you've changed, which is to be expected."

He frowned. "It's odd that I remember nothing about visiting you. I thought my memory was better than that."

"Children remember different things. You're more likely to recall the first caterpillar you found in a tree than you are a political visit to a far-off kingdom. The former is much more interesting to a boy of three years."

"Maybe." He studied the close-set stone buildings, then spotted the fountain of the man spouting water from his palm —except the water was frozen now. "I remember playing in a puddle with Maya, but I'm confident that was outside our cottage in Oceana. I remember wrestling with Jonatten and cooking with Seranni. I recall a hundred-thousand things...but nothing that wasn't centered around that cottage. No long trips, no setting fire to any bed curtains—we never had bed curtains. No suits of armor in castles. No you."

Latta frowned. "Does your twin remember more?"

"I haven't asked her. I didn't know it was bothering me 'til now."

"If it eases your mind—though I'm not sure it will—I've heard that trauma can make a person lock up certain memories. I don't know the particulars of your mother's death, but I think you were with her in hiding when it happened. Perhaps you needed to block everything out to avoid recalling a terrible moment."

Her words were like claws raking his chest. Breath exploded from his lungs. He darted a look around the square, feeling eyes watching him. Staring. Hungry. Blackness bled in from the edges of his vision, circling, swallowing the world.

"What's wrong?" asked Latta.

"N-nothing." He shuddered. "I'm...fine."

"He's lying," said Akonn, bringing his horse to Mikoneh's side. "Maybe it's too soon for you to be out and about, Your Highness."

"Captain, is he ill, or does this have to do with...?"

"The latter, I think." Akonn pried the reins from Mikoneh's fingers. "Let's head back."

"Sorry," Mikoneh mumbled.

"None of that," whispered Akonn. "Come along, Prince Mikoneh."

Hearing his name eased the darkness a little. It was grounding, remembering who he was. *My name. Mine.*

They turned the horses around and headed for the castle. Mikoneh clutched the saddle horn and focused on breathing.

Chapter 9

Dreamsnare

"Likewise, in the past Spirits Elemental have been held captive and forced to offer their core magic to their captor. This, I fear, is how a single aspect can be bred into a family line."

- *A Treatise on the Magic of the Hidden Realm* by Sariolin the Solitary

Breathing heavily, Maya slammed her quarterstaff against her opponent's. Bones rattled. Zevier's eyes widened, and he rocked back to disengage, then swung from the left. Wind whistled a warning, but she was already moving.

Maya caught the young man's staff with hers. Ducking, she feigned a right leap, and the young man moved to defend against it. Tossing her polearm into her left hand, she brought her quarterstaff in from that angle, ramming the wooden pole into his side.

Air exploded from his lungs. His staff fell with a clatter, and he sank to his knees. She lowered her quarterstaff, heart pounding in her ears.

"I yield," he gasped, rubbing his ribs.

Donivan Kriv applauded along with the rest of the training class. "An excellent bout!" the master called above the din. "Very impressive, Your Highness."

Maya knelt before Zevier. "Are you all right?"

He blinked his gray eyes, then grinned. "Apart from my numb hands, I'm brilliant, Your Highness. You're marvelous with that staff."

Heat bloomed across her cheeks. "As are you. It was a close duel. I'd love a rematch."

He chuckled. "Let me feel my hands again, and we can go right now if you like."

"Maybe tomorrow," Maya said, laughing. "I'm a bit winded myself."

The door across the chamber burst open. Penn flew inside, his long blond hair a net around his face. Maya straightened up, insides tight.

"Is it Mikoneh?"

Penn nodded. "He's...sick."

Maya shoved her borrowed quarterstaff at Zevier. "Thank you, Master Donivan. Zevier. I must go." She rushed to Penn's side. Together they left the training room and raced for the suite. It had never felt so far away.

"What happened?" she asked above the noise of her feet slapping along the stone corridor. Luckily, for the quarterstaff bout she'd traded a dress for a long, loose top and tights provided by the proficient tailor. Running was easier in pants and boots.

"While he was in Elenth, he started to panic," Penn explained. "Latta said it came on suddenly, but she feels responsible. They were discussing your mother. Your blood mother, I mean."

She nodded. "That's been weighing on me, too."

"What has?"

"All of it. She was killed. It's a sad thing to know she loved us, raised us, and even died for us—but we don't remember her."

"I understand that very well."

Maya glanced at him, her heart clenching. Of course, he understood. His mother had died shortly after giving birth to him. Drayve had always blamed and hated him for that.

They raced on in silence until they reached the suite. Throwing herself into the common room, her gaze fell on Mikoneh spread out on a settee, a thin blanket tucked around him. Akonn stood close, along with Lord Crim, Princess Latta, and Owenekiras Rokahn. Maya slipped up next to Latta and stared down at her twin's pale face.

She expected him to be asleep. Instead, he scowled right at her.

"Will you tell these hovering hens to leave me alone? I'm fine. It was nothing."

Latta twisted to face Maya. "He nearly fell off his horse on the way back."

"It was just a dizzy spell," Mikoneh muttered.

"Respectfully, it was considerably more than that," Akonn said.

Maya squeezed between the princess and Crim to kneel beside the settee. She rested a hand on Mikoneh's cheek. It was warm, but that was normal these days. "Dizzy spell or something worse, you've definitely pushed yourself too hard. Like always. And don't argue with me, Mikoneh Rokahn." She was surprised at the ease with which she used his full name. They hadn't grown up with a surname in Oceana. Peasants rarely had one.

His mouth snapped shut, and his scowl deepened. He slumped his head back and stared at the ornately carved ceiling. Maya studied the gauntness of his cheeks, the dark circles under his eyes, and the haunted light shimmering in them.

"You need rest."

"Can't."

She tapped her finger to the tip of his nose. "*Must.*"

His scowl deepened more.

"No tantrums." She twisted to search for her herb kit, which she'd left on a nearby table, but Penn had anticipated her and held it out. She smiled her thanks, then took it and rummaged around for valerian root. "I need hot water for tea."

Footsteps moved off to obey—probably Penn.

"And the curtain should be drawn."

"I'm not sleeping right here and right now," Mikoneh growled, trying to rise.

"If someone could please keep him still?" she said, ignoring him.

Akonn leaned over the settee and pushed Mikoneh against the throw pillows. "Please lay quietly, Your Highness."

"Don't call me that."

"Yes, Prince Mikoneh."

Latta chuckled, and Mikoneh's scowl shifted into a grimace.

The window curtains pulled shut, darkening the room. Maya moved off to brew a tea mixture with valerian, chamomile, and passionflower while Penn assisted. Latta drifted over to their side.

"It's my fault," the Songbird Princess said.

"Nonsense." Maya crushed the dried herbs together using her pestle. "Mikoneh is solely responsible for overexerting himself and not telling anyone. After what he's been through, sword-training and horseback riding on the same day were foolish decisions." She frowned. "Which I should've recognized. So, it's my fault as much as his. Maybe more so."

Penn shook his head but kept his peace. He wrapped Maya's spare herbs back up and packed them in her herb kit.

Latta watched Maya strain the herbs in hot water.

"You're a genuine healer." Latta's voice was warm with admiration. "That's amazing, Maya."

Flushing, Maya poured the tea into a cup. "It seemed a practical thing to learn with two battle-hungry parents and a brother following suit."

The princess snorted. "Yes, I'm confident your skill with a quarterstaff doesn't signify a similar disposition."

Maya shrugged and moved back to Mikoneh's side. "Who can really say?" She knelt, and Mikoneh meekly sipped the tea, not even having the decency to cringe at the bitter taste or the heat. When she pulled the cup back, he licked his lips.

"That's good," he said.

Maya rolled her eyes. "You're a menace."

He cracked a smile, took a few more sips, then settled back. Whether because the herbs were potent, or he was simply tired enough, he drifted off almost at once. His dark lashes fluttered, then stilled.

Maya breathed a sigh. "I know he's been having nightmares. Hopefully the herbs will help."

"Use this, Mayanaleh." Owenekiras's voice startled Maya. She'd half-forgotten he was there, he was so quiet. The Dragon King drew a large blue stone from beneath his cloak and held it out. It wasn't a sapphire. It was too pale and cloudy. Still, it was lovely, and it hummed sweet notes as her father set it on the arm of the settee near Mikoneh's head. "This is a Dreamsnare gemstone. It will capture every dream, good and bad alike, until it's full. That should allow him uninterrupted rest for a few turns."

Maya's throat tightened. She set the half-drunk cup of tea

down, rose to her feet, and flung her arms around her father. "Thank you!" Tears of relief and gratitude pricked at her eyes.

Owenekiras stood rigid. After several breaths, his whisper drifted into her ears. "You're welcome, Mayanaleh."

She pulled back and caught his gaze. She wouldn't let him escape. "This is new for all of us, but it's not bad. We want you in our lives—and I know you want us, too." She pinched his dragon scale cloak with her fingers. "You wouldn't have sacrificed *everything* for us otherwise."

He searched her face. Then he offered a slow nod. "It's as you say. I'm here."

She reached up, stroked his cheek, then slowly pulled back. "Good. Because I want to know you."

Another nod was his only answer.

A crooked smile played on her lips. Maybe she was reading him wrong, but it appeared he wasn't cold—though his exterior remained icy. Instead, he seemed...uncertain. Taking a chance, she leaned close and whispered, "I promise we don't bite."

His blink was telling. And she didn't think she imagined the upward twitch of his mouth.

"Perhaps you should," he said. "After all, you are dragons."

She laughed. "That reminds me, when do I get to learn how to fly?"

"Once your teacher arrives."

"Oh." She tipped her head to one side. "You're not going to teach us?"

"I've found you someone far better at it—and Hilker will continue to oversee your mastery of wind while Lord Crim trains your brother."

Maya glanced at the ginger-haired merchant lord, who bowed his head.

"I'll do what I can," Crim said, "though your brother appears to be a quick study. He'll likely surpass me swiftly."

Maya grinned. "That he will, my lord. Mikoneh is smarter than he looks."

The lord folded his arms. "That's alarming, considering how clever he *does* appear."

"Best watch yourself."

"I appreciate the warning."

Maya knelt beside the settee again and brushed back strands of Mikoneh's dark hair. "I'm going to bathe and change. Can someone stay and watch over him?"

"I will," Crim said.

"Thank you, Crim," Owenekiras said. "I'll be off at once and return as soon as is possible."

Maya twisted toward him. "You're leaving?"

"It can't be helped." Owenekiras frowned. "Matters in Oceana have escalated since the attack on King Nilo's castle and Sathe's death. I must answer."

Her stomach clenched. "Is it open war?"

"We're on the cusp of it, but that was inevitable. Right now, it's skirmishes and power plays."

"Where is Drayve in all this?"

Owenekiras hesitated. "Mages have taken up position in his fortress. Relvin Province belongs to them. Sathe made sure of that long ago."

Maya nodded, mulling over the ramifications. She and her twin hadn't known just how deep and twisted the corruption at Drayve's court had been—or what they had really been fighting. Sathe had only been a court magician as far as they knew, but he was responsible for their parents' deaths. Had Fa and Mama even known what they were pitting their rebel force against?

She clenched her fists. "I won't ask you to stay here, but come back safely and soon."

The ice flecks in his silver eyes softened into something liquid. "I promise." He moved off toward the door, his cloak billowing behind him.

When he left the room, Crim let out a sigh. "That man terrifies me, friend or not."

Penn grunted his agreement.

Akonn chuckled. "If he didn't, he'd cease to be Owenekiras Rokahn, and we don't want that."

"No, indeed." Latta rested a hand on Maya's shoulder. "Your bath is ready in your room. Go clean up. Your brother is safe here."

"It's the Mage incident, isn't it?" asked Crim. "That's what's giving him nightmares."

Latta sucked in air. "*Mage* incident?"

Crim nodded. "He was captured. Tortured. By Mages. That's what Prince Atlanse said."

Akonn cleared his throat in warning, but Maya stood up.

"It's true," she whispered. "They had him for a month."

Latta's eyes widened. "I've never heard of survivors after so long."

"They didn't want to kill him," Akonn said. "He's too valuable."

"That makes sense." Latta dropped her eyes to Mikoneh. "Even so, he must be incredibly strong to resist their control."

"He's a Rokahn," Crim said, "and the rightful heir. Of course he's strong."

Maya smiled weakly, then drifted toward her bedchamber. The appeal of the bath had lessened after Crim's mention of the Mages, but she was determined to care for herself. Otherwise, she couldn't be there for Mikoneh, and she refused to fail him.

Not ever again.

Chapter 10

The Fiend Folk

"Core magic is the center of magic planted within a chosen Elementalist. Many are born with it. Others are chosen by the spirit guardian later in life. Many humans are chosen as adults while the fae and fantastic almost always come into the world with their element already manifesting."

- A Treatise on the Magic of the Hidden Realm by Sariolin the Solitary

The faint chatter of fire spirits drew Mikoneh from a deep dreamless sleep. He cracked his eyes open. Luckily, the chamber was dark, and his vision adjusted straight away. He stared at the ornate pattern embossed on the ceiling. Shadows played across them in the guttering hearth light.

"I knew your parents well," a soft voice said.

Mikoneh jerked his head to his left. He was startled to find Lord Crim sitting in a chair he'd drawn close to the settee. Glancing around the common room, Mikoneh found no one else present.

"I'm keeping watch," Crim said, anticipating his question. "A servant will bring food around soon, I'm certain."

Mikoneh's stomach was hollow, so he didn't protest. His mind ran back over Crim's first statement. "My parents, my lord?"

"The ones who raised you. I was very sorry to hear of their passing."

A lump lodged in Mikoneh's throat. He looked away, blinking back a sudden mist. All the times people had mentioned their deaths, he'd never cried. Why now? "You were friends?" he asked in a muffled voice.

"Yes. Seranni was a Simynshinian. Jonatten, a Rokahnian."

"I didn't know that."

"I doubt they dared to speak much about it. After your blood father was unjustly disgraced in Rokahn, they gave up their past lives to follow him. People are fiercely loyal to Owenekiras once they see who he really is."

Mikoneh chewed on that. He could see it a little, in the way the Dragon King conducted himself. Perfect calm. Perfect control. And a rigid determination to do the right thing. If Mikoneh was honest with himself, he knew that he'd inherited that last trait from his father—but he'd honed it from watching Jonatten.

The ache of their loss thrummed through him, but warmth followed. Crim had known Fa and Mama. He'd been their friend.

"How did you meet them?" Mikoneh whispered.

"I knew Seranni when we were children. We're of a similar age. She was the first woman I ever loved." Crim's laugh was sheepish. "Of course, she never felt the same. She could only love someone as fierce and alive as herself. When she introduced me to Jonatten, I knew they would wed. I told her as much, but she denied it emphatically. They despised each other." The merchant lord shook his head. "Sometimes animosity becomes the seed of love, though I'll never understand it."

Mikoneh's mind flitted to Kevva, who'd betrayed him for rejecting her. "Me neither, my lord." It was strange to imagine his surrogate parents ever hating each other. They'd been inseparable. Utterly in love. Revoltingly so, at times.

"Well." Crim slapped a hand against his thigh. "Enough reminiscing. I've been asked by Lord Rokahn to train you to wield fire. I'm proficient, but not a master, so I don't know how much help I'll really be. But I'm willing if you are."

"Thank you." Mikoneh sat up. "I accept your help, and I promise to be an attentive student."

"That I don't doubt." Crim snorted. "You have the Rokahn look."

"Meaning?"

"You take life very seriously. You'll go far in whatever you pursue—but don't let it keep you from appreciating the simple moments, Your Highness. Those count the most."

Mikoneh studied his hands resting on his lap. He allowed himself a smile. "I agree with you, my lord. My twin's always been good at reminding me."

"She's a lively one," Crim said. "Very observant, too. And beautiful. She'll have no end of suitors."

"Is she also betrothed to a perfect stranger, or isn't she that lucky?"

"She has none that I know of, though that's possibly because the Crown Prince of Cimin was killed in his youth— or hidden away if you believe the hearth stories. Otherwise, who could say? I've heard of greater age gaps." Crim glanced toward Maya's bedroom. "It seemed to me that she and Lord Penn are rather close."

"They are," Mikoneh said, "but they're too much alike. She needs...someone different."

"Overprotective brother, are you?"

"No. If I thought Penn was right for Maya, I'd encourage it. But..." He scrubbed the side of his scalp. "I dunno what I'm saying."

"You're tired and overwrought." Crim rested a hand on the edge of the settee cushion. "There's no sense pushing yourself. Instead, spend today resting. Tomorrow—if you're much improved—we can begin training right after breakfast. Make sure to eat well, then come to the northwest tower. I think that's a good spot to begin."

Something in Mikoneh's chest eased. "Very well, Lord Crim."

"Good man." Crim stood and straightened his silk surcoat. His jeweled rings flashed, drawing Mikoneh's focus. Crim chuckled. "Dragons..." He bowed. "Until tomorrow, Your Highness."

The man started for the common room's exit before Mikoneh remembered something: "Is Minno still here?"

Crim glanced over his shoulder, his eyes wide. "Was *that* creature lurking nearby?"

"He sneaked into my room early this morning."

"That one unsettles me..."

"Me, too," Mikoneh said.

"Your father left to handle a situation on his front lines. It's likely Minno went with him. The boy is fixated on the Dragon King like a dog on a bone."

"I'd noticed," Mikoneh said.

Crim frowned. "Minno is an odd one. I don't know much about him—only that he's terribly dangerous and unhinged. I'd avoid him if I were you."

"Thanks for the warning," Mikoneh muttered, "but I did learn that much."

The lord's hand hovered at the doorknob. "Captain Akonn is just outside, but do you want me to stay?"

"No, you're fine." He shifted his blanket. "I think I'll just sleep a while longer. Maya's nearby if I need anything, right?"

"Yes, she's napping in her room. Penn went back to the library."

"I'll be fine." Mikoneh worked up a reassuring smile. "Thank you, Lord Crim."

The man inclined his head, then slipped from the room and shut the door. The fire spirits crackled a farewell chorus, then returned to gnawing on the logs in the hearth. Mikoneh slid his legs from the settee and angled himself toward the fireplace to observe the tiny creatures. Woodsmoke teased his nostrils.

On impulse, he lifted one hand. A stray ember drifted toward him, then shifted into a fire spirit in the shape of a tiny dragon. He chuckled and let the winged creature settle on his palm.

"Tomorrow, we'll get to know each other a little better," he whispered. "You'll play nice, right? No mischief just to show off to my mentor, you hear me?"

The fire spirit tossed its mane and flicked its long, spined tail.

Mikoneh rolled his head. "You're a menace—"

Glass shattered behind him. Mikoneh whirled. Daylight flooded the room, and a silhouette stood against the glow from the broken window.

The figure charged toward him. A sword flashed in a gloved hand.

Mikoneh flung the fire spirit at the imposing shape. Brentin—the adolescent stablehand—stumbled backward to avoid the flame. Then he adjusted his grip and darted toward Mikoneh, swinging his blade.

Leaping from the settee, Mikoneh groped for his sword—but his belt had been removed when he'd been brought to the room. He staggered back and slammed into Crim's empty chair.

Brentin vaulted over the settee, landed on the cushions, and stumbled sideways. His sword tip sank into the blanket.

Mikoneh leapt at the stablehand, throwing his full weight into the young man. The settee fell backward, and both men rolled across the floor. Mikoneh's foot caught on a table leg. A vase teetered off and shattered.

He wrestled with Brentin for the sword.

The stablehand rammed his knee into Mikoneh's thigh, then swung a fist at his face. Mikoneh took the hit on the jaw, unwilling to relinquish his grip on Brentin's sword arm.

He could call on fire, but he hesitated. Killing a Simynshinian, even one trying to murder him, could prove to be a fatal political move. And he wasn't confident he could control the flames enough to merely incapacitate.

A door burst open. Maya's gasp prickled down Mikoneh's spine.

"Stay back!" he cried.

Her indignant scoff was followed by the howling of wind. Brentin's charging fist met hard air rather than Mikoneh's jaw, then his hand slammed to the rug under the power of invisible fingers. The stablehand grunted, squirming against the air holding him flat.

"You can get up," Maya said, drawing close with a rustle of skirts. "He's not going anywhere."

Mikoneh scrambled backward, then stood, panting. He shoved hair from his face. "That's a handy trick."

"Isn't it?" Maya narrowed a look on Brentin, then flicked

her hand. Wind pried the sword loose from the would-be assassin's fingers. Brentin let out a cry, but he didn't so much as twitch a limb. "Who sent you?" she demanded.

The stablehand clamped his mouth shut.

"His name's Brentin," Mikoneh said. "He works in the royal stables." Mikoneh set his bruised jaw and stooped beside the young man. Lifting one palm, he let a fire spirit light upon it. The creature took the shape of a visible flame—at least, he presumed it was visible. "We can make you talk one way or another. Answer her question: Who sent you?"

Brentin's eyes widened. "No one," he growled. "I wanted to rescue Princess Latta."

Maya snorted. "From what exactly?"

"Me, I think," Mikoneh said.

Brentin's eyes hardened. His body quivered—though with wrath or fear, Mikoneh couldn't guess. "Rokahn won't take her away from me!"

"From you?" asked Maya. "What, you're her secret lover or something?" The scorn in her voice was surprisingly strong. "Somehow, I doubt it."

"She doesn't love me," Brentin said, "but I would die for her."

"Better to live for her," Mikoneh said. "More sensible, less messy all around." He shook his head. "All this because you disapprove of our betrothal? You realize you could be executed for attacking me, right? Royalty doesn't take kindly to attempted assassinations."

"I doubt he thought that far ahead." Maya sighed. "Move away, Mikoneh."

He started to ask why, but when he glanced at his twin he recognized that determined look on her face. He knew better than to battle with her when she was in that mood. He rose and stepped back.

Maya flicked her hands, and Brentin was lifted into the air. The stablehand yelped, his eyes bulging with fear. She gestured again, and his legs lowered to hover just above the rug. "I could dangle you out that window, drop you, or make you soar. Do you understand?"

Brentin nodded vigorously.

"You tried to kill my brother without understanding him. You climbed into this room"—Maya's eyes swept over the glass shards littering the floor—"*somehow,* and attacked a perfect stranger over a betrothal he has no more control over than *you* do. Why, Brentin?"

"Better answer her," Mikoneh said, keeping his palm up with the fire spirit. "She's even moodier than I am."

Maya shot him a glower, then marched to the window while turning Brentin to keep him facing her—and his potential doom. "Answer me."

When Brentin swallowed, his throat bobbed. "He's one of the fiend folk."

Maya's brow arched. "What are they?"

"R-Rokahnians. Some say they take on the shape of terrible beasts."

Maya folded her arms. "Are you suggesting *I'm* one of the fiend folk?"

The stablehand paled. "N-no."

"Really?"

"No, my lady. You're too beautiful to be one of them."

She gave her captive a slow blink. "You do realize I'm *his* twin, don't you?" She jabbed a finger at Mikoneh.

Brentin's face screwed up. "But they said—"

"Who said?" Mikoneh asked.

Maya stepped toward Brentin. "Yes, who's talking about fiend folk?"

The young man swallowed again and flexed his fingers in

their invisible chains. "Lots of people. They talk about orders coming from Dreadlord Rokahn's camp—that he'll soon march on Elenth."

"That's false," Maya said. "He and Prince Atlanse are friends."

"Bewitched, he is."

"Atlanse?" asked Maya.

Brentin nodded.

"That's stupid," muttered Mikoneh. He strode to Maya's side and faced the stablehand. "We're fighting a war, but it's not against Simynshin. We're allies."

"The queen hates you."

Mikoneh stilled. "Who says that, Brentin?"

"Soldiers." Brentin's eyes slid sideways like he was trying to see behind him. Fear lit his irises. "Other folk, too."

"Queen Feresse doesn't know us yet," Maya said, her voice gentling. "Brentin, look at me."

He obeyed, admiration warring with terror.

Maya smiled. "If I'm not one of the fiend folk, neither is Mikoneh. And neither is our father. We only want to stop Dark Mages from controlling everything. We find Simynshin beautiful, and we both like Princess Latta. She's our friend. We would never harm her."

Brentin licked his lips, staring between them. His attention settled on Mikoneh, and something hardened in his eyes. "You're going to wed her."

"That's not my fault," Mikoneh growled.

"She deserves to be happy."

"We agree with you," Maya said. "We'll do nothing to make her sad."

"She cries," Brentin said sharply. "In her garden, she cries all the time."

Mikoneh quirked an eyebrow, cold frosting his insides. "What were you doing in her garden?"

Brentin fell still, the last of his blood draining from his face. "It—it's close to the stable."

"Hardly," Mikoneh said.

"I—I—I just go to watch. Just to watch."

"You realize that's a crime—and incredibly creepy, right?" Mikoneh stepped closer. "I begin to think this one's not right in the head."

Maya's frown hardened into a glare. "You spy on Latta, Brentin?"

He shook his head quickly. "I just like to watch her. She's so beautiful. I—I love her. I'd never, ever harm her."

"Stalking someone is harmful," Mikoneh snapped, "no matter how you justify it." He reached up and caught the stablehand's collar. "You tried to kill me, but your other offense is far worse." He jerked his hand free and marched across the room. "Akonn!"

No one answered.

Mikoneh reached the door and hesitated. Hadn't Crim said the captain was just outside? If not, where was Akonn?

Think, Mikoneh.

Surely, the captain would've heard the vase breaking and come running.

Mikoneh lifted his flame and wrenched the door open. The fire spirit crackled and pointed a flaming finger to the floor. Mikoneh's gaze dropped.

Six men lay upon the flagstones, blood oozing around them. Five were strangers dressed in unobtrusive clothing like messengers or servants. Captain Akonn lay among them, his sword near one hand. A knife jutted from his back. Dark blood pooled around him.

"Maya!" Mikoneh twisted to face the common room. "Herb kit, now! Akonn's hurt."

She snatched up her satchel, raced to the door, and stared down at Akonn with a stricken expression. "Don't move him," she said, then crouched beside the captain, her skirts spreading around her. "What happened?"

"Ambush, I suspect. Maybe Brentin knows these men." Mikoneh scanned the corridor. No sign of Crim. Had the man left before the attack—or had he been the one to stab Akonn?

"If the boy does know," Maya said, "wring it out of him."

Mikoneh nodded and darted back across the chamber to face the captured young man still hovering in the air. "You said you came alone, but you couldn't climb the castle walls unnoticed or without equipment. How'd you get up here? Are those your friends out in the corridor? Akonn killed all of them—in case you thought they'd be of any help."

Brentin lifted his lips in a snarl. His eyes flashed black, then back to brown. **"Your time grows short, Prince of Fiends. We will claim you soon."** Froth welled up at the corners of the stablehand's mouth.

"No!" Mikoneh caught Brentin's shirt. "You don't get to escape like this."

Brentin's body convulsed. The froth rolled down his chin, and his eyes rolled up into his head. His convulsions grew more violent, but the air held him fast.

"Maya!" Mikoneh shouted, but he knew it was too late.

She appeared in the doorway, eyes wide, a hand pressed to her mouth.

Brentin gurgled, then gave one last spasm—and fell limp. Suspended in the air, he looked like a Ciminian marionette abandoned halfway through a show, dangling from strings.

Trembling, Mikoneh tried to look away from the hanging corpse, but he couldn't get his body to move.

Maya vanished from view to focus on Akonn again.

Mikoneh's knees shook. He let his body buckle and buried his hands in his face, but he couldn't block out the young man's last words: *We will claim you soon.*

CHAPTER 11

THIS I VOW

"At first, Mages were not born with an element. Some were chosen later. Others had to steal the power, and sadly, many of the little guardians were destroyed in an effort to extract their essence. I am convinced it was this action that led to the Mages falling into darkness."

- A Treatise on the Magic of the Hidden Realm by Sariolin the Solitary

Shouts sounded along the corridor.

How much time had passed between Brentin's last breath and the pounding of boots up the passage, Mikoneh couldn't guess. The clatter of armor approached. Something told Mikoneh to run, before Simynshinians arrived to arrest him and Maya, but he couldn't get his legs to work. The world hummed around him.

Voices congregated outside the common room. Was that Lord Crim?

A breath later, the red-headed merchant lord entered, his expression grave. His arm was bandaged and wrapped in a sling. Blood smeared his cheek. Nearing Brentin, he hesitated, then moved around the corpse.

"Forgive me, Your Highness," Crim said. "Akonn and I were attacked by those men. The captain told me to run for help. I barely got away, but this entire floor was cleared of any guards. I had to go searching for them."

Mikoneh found the strength to stand, and his eyes fell to the sling. "You took the time to get treated."

Crim grimaced. "It's a hasty job. I was losing too much blood. The healer insisted." His eyes darted to the doorway. "I only hope we weren't too late to save Captain Akonn." He turned back to Mikoneh. "Are you injured?"

"No." The word was a hoarse whisper. "Maya isn't either."

"Thank the Celes for that."

"Do you know who did this, Crim?" he asked.

"We'll find out."

"I already know." Mikoneh turned to the broken window. "Mages."

Silence answered. Crim's sigh followed, low and resigned. "That much I could already guess. But they had to have someone on the inside."

"The ambassador."

"No." Crim shook his head. "He's watched too closely. He knows better than to make a move himself. He must have help."

"Is it you, Crim?" Mikoneh met the man's hazel eyes. "Do you work for the Mages? Did you stab Akonn and then injure yourself to evade suspicion?"

Crim clapped a fist to his heart. "I swear to you, I would never harm Seranni's children. Not for anything."

"We're not her children." Mikoneh's voice was low and thin.

Crim frowned. "You don't believe that."

"Do you?"

The lord sank to one knee, caught Mikoneh's hand, and kissed the air above his knuckles. "My life belongs to you, Prince Mikoneh Rokahn. I will protect you at all costs. This I vow."

Mikoneh studied him through a haze of weariness that had settled deep in his bones. "And Maya?"

"I pledge the same to her."

"Then I accept your oath, Lord Crim. Rise."

The lord obeyed, releasing Mikoneh's hand. He smoothed his surcoat and straightened his sling. "We'll clear the room." He glanced at Brentin. "If your sister will be good enough to release...this thing."

"I think he was being controlled by Mage magic," Mikoneh said. "But he was stalking Princess Latta even before that. He was more than a little besotted with her."

Crim grimaced. "An unpleasant fact to take to the crown prince, but I thank you for telling me." He motioned two guards into the room. "Haul this unsightly figure out of here."

The guards obeyed, grabbing Brentin's elevated corpse by his tunic and towing him across the room. The sight was unnerving, especially with the stablehand's head wagging back and forth. Bile rose in Mikoneh's throat, but he choked it down and turned away.

"I think we'll move you to a new suite," Crim said. "Too many people know where you're staying."

"That won't change anything if you don't know where the leak is," Mikoneh said.

"True." Crim clicked his tongue. "What a mess."

A grunt was Mikoneh's only answer.

"I'll request Hilker to return immediately. That much I can manage right away. And I'll offer up several of my own men to guard the window and the door, inside and out. Of course, we'll also repair the glass."

"Do what you need to do." Mikoneh drifted toward the door.

His insides were tied in knots too tangled to unravel. The only thing he knew could ground him was Maya's nearness. Stepping into the hallway, something in him did ease. Maya looked up from a wad of bandages, her smile strained but not hopeless.

Mikoneh set his focus on Akonn. "Will he make it?"

She nodded. "If he doesn't push himself."

Crim poked his head around the doorframe. "Knowing him, that's a tall order."

Maya finished wrapping the captain's exposed waist. "Not with what I'm going to dose him."

Mikoneh flashed a grin at the merchant lord. "Maya doesn't play fair in matters of healing. It's her way."

"Good. And unsurprising." Crim chuckled. "You really could be her children."

"Whose?" asked Maya.

"Seranni's." The name scraped over Mikoneh's tongue, painful. "He knew her. They grew up together."

She blinked up at the lord, then turned back to Akonn. "I'd love to hear some of those stories later, my lord."

"Gladly." Crim's voice was thick with emotion. "I'd love to hear about her from both of you as well. I miss her."

Maya leaned back. "He's stable enough to move to a bed now." A frown flickered across her mouth, then a breeze stirred her hair. The slightest gesture of her hand lifted Akonn off the floor, and Maya directed him into the common room under the power of wind.

Mikoneh darted past the unconscious captain, opened the man's bedroom door, and stepped aside to let Maya bring her patient in. The room was draped in rich green curtains, bedding, rugs, and tapestries, highlighted with copper accents. Wind flipped the coverlet over, and Maya laid Akonn gently across the mattress. The coverlet fell over him.

She reached the bed and checked his bandages, then nodded. "Still stable."

Crim coughed out a laugh behind Mikoneh. "With powers like that, you're both indisputably Rokahns."

Mikoneh leaned against the door jamb, folding his arms. "For good and ill. Ready or not."

CHAPTER 12

EVERY DEEP FEAR

*"Dragons have a special affinity with the Spirits Elemental.
While fire is the most common for these great beasts, the other
elements—and sub-elements—manifest in many of the clans."*

- *A Treatise on the Magic of the Hidden Realm* by Sariolin the Solitary

Evening descended on the world, bringing a pall of gray clouds that promised more snow. Latta arrived in the gloom with the Wind Master, Hilker, in tow. Both went immediately to Akonn's room where Maya had remained since the late afternoon.

Mikoneh sat brooding near the fire. The common room had been put back together, and servants had stretched thick cloth across the broken window, with assurances that the glass would be replaced within the week. If the covering let in more cold, Mikoneh couldn't feel it.

The fire spirits had taken to entertaining him like an acrobatic troupe, balancing on the log in the hearth, flipping, twirling, dancing, and presenting various other death-defying feats that were arguably less deadly or defiant when wisps of flame performed them. Still, he smiled a little, grateful for their efforts.

His mind kept tugging at the memory of Brentin, mouth foaming, body convulsing, eyes black.

'*We will claim you soon.*'

He hunched forward, resting his arms on his legs, staring into the embers. He tried to drink in the warmth to banish a chill deeper than bone.

Voices sounded from Akonn's room. The door swung open. Out stepped Latta, her brow furrowed, eyes glittering with unshed tears.

Mikoneh stood up, his heart stammering. "Is he—?"

She ran to him, flung her arms around his chest, and clung tight. Mikoneh tensed up, ready to bolt—but he caught the impulse and shoved it down fast. Wrapping his arms around the princess, he let her weep.

Maya stepped out of the bedroom a moment later. Hilker was right behind her. Mikoneh met his twin's eyes. She frowned but didn't look heartbroken. Maya walked to his side, and rested a hand on Latta's trembling shoulder.

"I really do think he'll pull through, Latta," Maya whispered. "He lost a lot of blood, but he's fighting hard. The wound itself isn't terrible. I just need to keep infection from setting in."

Mikoneh stared down at Latta's head. If Akonn had a fair chance, why was she so upset?

The answer clicked.

Maya drew closer and rested her head against Latta's. "You're in love with the captain, aren't you?"

Latta started to shake her head, but her sobs deepened.

Mikoneh tightened his hold as something in his chest eased. She was in love with someone else. She didn't want this betrothal any more than he did. The relief trickled over him like gentle rain, loosening every deep fear.

"He'll be fine," Mikoneh whispered. "Trust me, Maya's the best. Under her watch, patients don't die."

Maya shot him a warning glance.

He shrugged. "It's true. The only men in my army back in Oceana who died were under the care of other healers. Maya doesn't fail."

His twin looked ready to argue, then snapped her mouth shut. She ran fingers through Latta's dark hair. "I'll do everything I can to save him—everything."

Latta bobbed a nod, her sobs slowing. A moment later, she grew quiet and pulled back. Her eyes were red-rimmed, and threads of hair stuck to her wet cheeks, but she wore a faint smile. "You're both wonderful. Thank you."

Maya caught her arm and pulled her free of Mikoneh's grasp. The women moved together to the fire and sat down on the settee. Mikoneh studied them for a moment, then strode to Akonn's bedroom. Hilker hovered at the open door, and they peeked into the shadows of the chamber.

"How bad is he?"

Hilker shrugged. "Maya's more worried than she's letting on. The weapon didn't strike any vital organs, but he did lose a lot of blood. Had you found him any later, he'd be a dead man, sure as I'm standing here." The Wind Master glanced at the settee. "Is it true, wha'cha said? Does Maya heal everyone under her care?"

"She's never lost anyone yet."

Hilker rubbed the stubble on his chin. "That's a rare gift, if gift it be."

"I think it's skill and pure stubbornness combined," Mikoneh said. "No magic required."

"Whether it's magic or not doesn't diminish a gift." Hilker

swung the door shut, closing Akonn off from the faint noises of the common room. "I need to report this attack to Owenekiras. He won't like it."

"Who does? Even the instigators didn't get what they wanted."

Hilker grunted. "Crim's men are at the door, and he stationed a few trusted guards in the courtyard below that there window." He nodded toward the blanket covering the view. "Further attempts'll be hard-pressed."

"Good to know. Thanks."

The man shrugged. "Not my doing. All I can manage is continuing your sister's training, make her more of a force to be reckoned with."

"You've done a good job so far," Mikoneh said. "She incapacitated that stablehand all on her own."

Hilker grinned. "She's a quick study. And feisty besides. Can't help but like her."

"Few can."

Hilker snorted, then offered a nod before he moved off to a corner of the common room where a writing desk stood with parchment and quills.

Standing alone, Mikoneh hesitated. Should he join the women at the fire, or should he retreat into his bedroom? He recognized his inclination to isolate himself. He'd experienced it after their cottage fire. He knew better than to indulge it, but he also longed for quiet.

You won't get that with all the demons in your head.

Squaring his shoulders, he moved toward the settee, but footsteps outside the chamber door slowed him. Voices exchanged words, then the door opened, and Penn stepped inside. Concern lined his brow, and he clutched several heavy tomes in his arms. His eyes darted from Maya and Latta, to Mikoneh, to the covered bay window.

"What happened? Where's Akonn? Why are there new guards?"

Mikoneh adjusted course and steered Penn toward a separate set of chairs. They sat, and he explained about Brentin's attack after assuring his friend that he and Maya were both fine. Penn's eyes were wide throughout the story, and his gaze darted toward Akonn's room as Mikoneh described the captain's wound. Last, Mikoneh touched on Brentin's death and the eerie warning.

Penn lowered his head, absorbing the information. He traced the embossed lettering on a Simynshinian history book propped on the stack in his lap. "Confirmation that we're not safe here. Not surprising, really."

"No," Mikoneh agreed. "We're still being stalked, but this time, there's nowhere to run."

Penn blew out a breath. "At least we have allies."

"Yes, and spies pretending to be allies."

Penn shrugged. "Welcome to politics."

"Thanks, I hate it."

The viscount chuckled. His dark gaze flicked to Latta, then away. "Is she all right?"

Mikoneh hesitated. "Seems she has feelings for Akonn."

Surprise flickered over Penn's face. "Oh. That makes sense. She did seem very happy to see him during our first meeting in her garden."

Looking back, Mikoneh supposed she had. "Is it a doomed match?"

Penn offered him a slanted smile. "Asks the man who's betrothed to her?"

"That's temporary."

Penn dropped his gaze. "For both your sakes, I hope so. But I've never heard of a betrothal getting annulled. Politics aren't based on whims and feelings—at least, they're not meant to be." He drummed his fingers against the leather book cover. "Just brace yourself for your father's maneuvers. We don't know how reliable his promises are."

"I know. But don't think for one instant I'll stick around if he changes his mind about Latta and me. I'm not getting married."

His friend shrugged. "I don't doubt your desire to flee. I just doubt how far you'll get. This isn't as big a world as we thought back in Oceana. No matter how far from home, some things don't change. Politics are one of those. I've been reading up on Simynshin."

"I noticed."

"It's a fascinating kingdom, but a lot of its grievances and upheavals stem from the same issues we have in our neck of the woods." Penn grimaced. "Or rather, mine. You're Rokahnian."

"Oceana is still home," Mikoneh said. "I'm still going back to end Drayve's plots if I have to nibble his legs off as a mini-dragon."

Penn's brows lifted. "Mini-dragon?"

Mikoneh shifted, his collar feeling suddenly too tight. "Never mind."

The nobleman leaned toward him. "Can you become—wholly dragon? Can you shrink down? How small do you get?"

"Drop it, Penn." Mikoneh couldn't meet his gaze.

"Wow. So, you can."

"I said to drop it."

Penn shook his head. "Sorry, no. You need to show me."

"Not gonna happen."

"Please."

"Never."

"Please?"

"Absolutely not." Mikoneh jumped to his feet and

marched across the room, cheeks blazing with embarrassment —and terror. Sathe had made him take on his true dragon shape. He'd become vulnerable, and his mind had shifted into a strange worldview. One he couldn't accept. Not after... everything.

He slipped into his room and shoved the door closed. Leaning against the barrier, he shut his eyes and breathed.

Get control of yourself. You can't keep running.

But he didn't know how to gain control of his fear. Not yet...

Not while he still felt hunted.

CHAPTER 13

FROM A SINGLE EMBER

"Many scholars are certain that the Dragon King can wield all five main elemental types, as well as the sub-elements. I've been unable to confirm this."

- *A Treatise on the Magic of the Hidden Realm* by Sariolin the Solitary

At dawn, Mikoneh dressed to train at the northwest tower as Crim had instructed. A night of troubled dreams had dragged him from bed early, eager to face a day of intense training—to keep his thoughts on the present.

He peeked in on Akonn before heading out. Maya had fallen asleep in a chair at the captain's bedside. Akonn looked pale, deathly so, but his breathing wasn't as shallow. Surely, he would recover. Maya's skills would be enough.

Mikoneh didn't know Akonn well, but from all he'd observed, the fae captain was good-hearted and deeply loyal. To lose such a man would be a tragedy, even beyond Latta's tender feelings for him.

Tiptoeing from the suite, Mikoneh saluted the two guards stationed at the door, and started down the hall. Crim had told him to eat, so he stopped a maid along the way to ask for directions to the kitchen—or at least the nearest place he could find sustenance.

She directed him south, and he took a wide corridor populated with staff hard at work dusting, sweeping, and otherwise tidying up ahead of the day's activities. The scuff of footsteps and the faint rattle of armor behind him suggested he was being tailed, probably by one of the guards he'd greeted.

He found a dining hall at the end of the southern corridor. Sitting at the head of the table, Crown Prince Atlanse looked up from several scrolls whose seals had been broken. Mouth full of buttered bread, the crown prince only nodded to Mikoneh and gestured toward the nearest seat.

The table was laid with an assortment of complicated dishes. The aroma of succulent meat made Mikoneh's mouth water. He dropped into the proffered chair and, though he'd not had an appetite in days, he piled his plate with anything that looked or smelled tempting.

Atlanse released the scroll under his fingers, and the parchment sprang back into a coil. "Good morning, Your Highness. I'm profusely sorry about what occurred yesterday. That it happened under this roof is unacceptable."

"Thank you, but it's not your fault," Mikoneh said.

"Agree to disagree." Atlanse skewered a berry with his fork. While he chewed it, he studied Mikoneh with an earnestness that he didn't bother to hide. "You're very much like Rathana."

Mikoneh tensed. His birth mother. What should he say to that? Thank you?

Atlanse's probing gaze dropped, and the crown prince ate more food. "Lord Crim told me what you learned about the stablehand's...habits."

"You mean him stalking your daughter."

Atlanse cringed. "That, yes. Thank you."

"I didn't do anything."

"You and your sister dispatched a threat."

"We didn't kill Brentin."

"You incapacitated him."

Mikoneh speared steamed vegetables and shoved them in his mouth to avoid answering. When he swallowed, he glanced at Atlanse. "Mages were controlling him."

"So I understand."

"Though he was stalking your daughter, I'm not sure he would have acted on any vile impulses on his own."

"That we'll never know," Atlanse said in cool tones. "What's done is done."

"True." Mikoneh pushed more vegetables across his plate, then cut into his slab of cold ham instead. "But his family lost someone precious to them."

"He has no mother, only a drunken father. I doubt the man will notice his absence in any meaningful way—only in the ending of his tavern coin."

Mikoneh stared at his plate. "That makes it all the sadder."

"I agree with you." Atlanse sighed. "As for the men Captain Akonn killed, we don't yet know how they entered the castle undetected, and no one can identify them. My guess would be mercenaries. In any case, security has been tightened. You'll be kept away from lesser nobility except during major events, and when showcasing your relationship with my daughter is required."

"That's reasonable." Mikoneh hesitated. "May I ask a question, Your Highness?"

"You may," Atlanse said.

"Does Latta know about the *particulars* of our betrothal?"

Atlanse paused in heaping jam onto a thick slab of fluffy bread. "She knows as much as you do, Prince Mikoneh."

"Good." Mikoneh stood, his appetite gone. "Good day, Your Highness."

"And to you, Your Highness. Give Lord Crim my regards. Best of luck with your training."

Stifling a grimace, Mikoneh bowed his head, then strode from the room, keeping his back erect. He had no reason to dislike Atlanse—the man was sensible, even pragmatic, which were two traits Mikoneh respected. But Atlanse was still royalty, with the cold efficiency that shielded them from feeling regret at the sacrifice of human lives.

If I ever become like that, may lightning strike me down.

He moved along the passages at a quick pace, determined to lose himself in Crim's lesson and not think about anything but fire. He ignored the sound of armor keeping up with him.

At last, he reached the northwest tower steps. He moved up the spiraling flight, taking the stairs two at a time. Armor clanked close behind him. At the end of the tower steps, a trapdoor lay open, revealing a brilliant blue winter sky. Mikoneh caught the edges of the opening and lifted himself through.

Crim stood at the parapet, leaning his arms across the stones behind him. He wore a crooked smile. A mild breeze stirred his auburn hair. "Ready?"

Mikoneh glanced down at the passage below and met the eyes of the guard. Definitely one of those stationed at the suite door. An urge to kick the trapdoor shut and lock the man out swelled up, but he suppressed it, turning his attention on Crim.

"Ready."

"Good." Crim shoved off the parapet. "Call on fire."

Mikoneh let heat build in his blood, then held out his palm. A fire spirit burst into life above it.

"Good. Now multiply that. Give me ten."

Mikoneh hesitated but focused on producing more heat. Another spirit popped into life. Then another. Another. The intensity of the heat made the air around him grow stifling.

Four was his limit. Any hotter and he'd scald his insides, dragon or not.

"Keep going."

"Can't," Mikoneh said.

Crim bobbed a nod, like he'd expected as much. "Your instinct is common in the beginning, but false. Producing more heat isn't the way to conjure more spirits. You're tapping into an inferno when all you really need is a spark. Think of it this way: Every fire spirit is born from a single ember."

"That's a lot of spirits."

"It is." Crim held out his gloved hand. With a pop and crackle, a dozen little wisping fire spirits danced across the air above his hand. He grinned. "The trouble isn't in having enough spirits. Too many and you can't control them. They're mischievous, passionate, and whimsical. They won't stay on task. And you don't need that many. Fire spirits aren't fire itself. They guard it. Strengthen it. And one is usually enough to muster a fire hot enough to melt stone—if you can train yourself to handle that heat. *That* is what the inferno is for, and it takes a *long* time to develop a resistance to soul burn when you deal with heat of a tremendous temperature." Crim grinned. "You have an advantage I don't, being Rokahnian."

"Such as?" asked Mikoneh.

"You're a fire dragon."

Mikoneh flinched, glancing toward the trapdoor where the guard waited on the landing below. "Does everyone in Simyn-shin know about that?"

"No. Sadly, few outside of Rokahn believe dragons are more than feral beasts—or even real—anymore." Crim lowered his hands, letting the fire spirits ride the stirring wind. They shaped into humans, clasped fiery little fingers, and danced in a circle across the air. The merchant lord continued. "The heritage of Rokahn has been forgotten in Simynshin for centuries, but I don't think that will remain the case much longer. With Dark Mages on the battlefield, we'll have no choice but to return to our roots. Magic is something we humans fear, and anything magical is shunned. But it's our only hope against the wave swelling yonder." His eyes flicked northward to the Andyan Mountains. Somewhere in that range of peaks, the Mage Queen lay hidden. "Best come into your own quickly, Dragon Prince. We'll need you in the sky."

Mikoneh snorted. "Oh, yes. All ten pounds of me."

"Probably closer to twelve. Dragon scales aren't light."

"Oh? Then how, by all the ocean sands, do full-sized dragons leave the ground?"

Crim waggled his fingers. "Hollow bones and ancient magic."

"Cop out answer," Mikoneh shot back. "Give me scientific explanations for magic."

The merchant lord laughed. "Fair enough—but I can't. I'm no dragon. You'll have to wait for your *other* instructor for that. And he'll likely give you a whole slew of historical facts as well. Best you learn them, Your Highness. The Royal House of Rokahn will take center stage in this next act in the play for Sirinhigha."

Scrubbing his hand against his thigh, Mikoneh stared out at the nearest mountain roots blanketed with snow-dusted forests. The view tickled at something within him. A yearning. The wings hidden under his shoulder blades burned.

He needed to fly.

Crim cleared his throat. "Let's work with one fire spirit today. Don't be surprised when more answer. As I said, each ember sparks a spirit. But only focus on *one*. Use it like you would a captain in your army. They can muster more soldiers if they need, but you command the leader, who commands the forces."

"Got it."

Crim lowered himself to the stone floor, crossed his legs, and waited for Mikoneh to follow suit. Once he did, they worked with their two spirits, bringing the heat up, then cooling it off. Mikoneh caught on to the purpose swiftly. Control was everything. Without it, he could burn up his bed curtains. With it, he could dry off without crisping his hair.

"You and I can handle far greater heat than your twin," Crim said, "so it's important to adjust temperatures instinctively, without hesitation. Practice with Princess Mayanaleh. Carefully learn her thresholds. But also bear in mind that she's wind. She can fan your flames and make you lose control. The two of you can also work in beautiful harmony, and down the line, we'll bring her into our lessons to hone that. But not yet. First— Ah, you're getting too hot. Cool it down."

Mikoneh concentrated. His head throbbed and his vision faded as he turned the fire spirit white-hot, but he managed to stay conscious. Bringing the flame to an almost blue-violet glow, he swiped at perspiration on his brow and kept the high heat as long as he could. Crim nodded his approval. After that, Crim had Mikoneh cool the flame to an almost burgundy color. The flame snuffed out twice before he kept it steady.

"Good!" Crim clapped his hands, snapping Mikoneh out of an almost meditative state. He blinked under a broad sun. "That's enough for today," the merchant lord announced. "I'm famished. It must be past lunch time. Let's find something to eat."

Mikoneh stood up and closed his fist over the flame,

dousing it. He and Crim climbed down onto the stair landing, where they found the sentry sound asleep.

Mikoneh nudged the man with one boot, feeling less annoyed after burning away some of his tension. "Hey, wake up, sleepyhead. Time for food."

The guard jerked awake and clambered to his feet, rubbing at one eye. "Yes, Your Highness. Forgive me."

The three men moved down the steps in single file, then came out into a corridor bustling with servants. Mikoneh tried not to notice the curious eyes tracking him. The sentry moved closer, hand tight on his sword. Crim also stayed near, plowing his way through the crowd.

"Seems busier than normal," Mikoneh said.

"And so it will remain," said Crim. "They're preparing for the Winter Tourney next month. Every lord and knight across Simynshin will attend—especially with rumors of your presence here. You'd be welcome to join in the festivities if you wish."

Mikoneh blinked. "A tourney? That's...reckless." But he supposed it couldn't be helped. Tradition offered a sense of normalcy even in wartime, helping to keep chaos at bay—something Fa had explained to the twins years ago. To give up life's simple pleasures was to snuff out hope, and without hope, people lost their sense of purpose.

Still, the influx of nobility, gentry, and courtiers would make finding the traitor harder.

"Will the affair include jousting and swordplay?" Mikoneh asked.

"Certainly," Crim answered. "Each day features a main event, and acting troupes from across the kingdom—and even beyond our borders—will present their skills each evening during the five feasts."

"It goes on for five days?" asked Mikoneh, an alarm tolling in his head.

"Yes. It's our second largest event of the year. The first takes place at Summertide, naturally."

"Naturally." Back in Oceana, they had similar events at the summer and winter solstices, but nothing so grand—at least not in Relvin Province. Dread coiled in his stomach, but Mikoneh resigned himself to a week of pomp and politics. Yet again, he had no choice. At least it wasn't for another month. Maybe he could find the spy and escape before then.

"Is it an outdoor event?" Mikoneh asked to maintain the conversation.

"Mixed. Most fighting events take place outside on the tourney field, but not the feast and stage plays. And in the case of inclement weather, we can move everything inside."

"What constitutes inclement weather?"

"A blizzard."

"Right."

They turned down a less congested corridor, and Crim led them to a chamber where spices wafted over the air. Platters of meat and tureens of soup crowded the table. Mikoneh blinked, recognizing it as the same room where he'd eaten only a few turns before. Crown Prince Atlanse wasn't there now, but a few other familiar faces sat at the table, finishing up their meal.

Maya caught sight of them and jumped to her feet. "There you are!"

Mikoneh flinched. "Sorry, I should've left a note."

"Yes, that might've been nice." She shook her head but smiled patiently.

Penn climbed to his feet, followed by two tousle-headed, long-robed strangers. One was male, the other female. "Mikoneh, these are scholars of Elenth. They gave me a tour of the lower catacombs this morning. There are some fascinating old records down there." The viscount's eyes were bright.

"I'm really happy for you, Penn."

"It's a great honor to meet you, Your Highness," the female scholar said.

"Um. Likewise." Mikoneh glanced at his twin. "How's Akonn?"

Penn sat back down and murmured to one of the scholars. She nodded, then flashed a grin at her companion. Beside Penn sat a stack of scrolls—probably his allotment of reading for the day.

"He's a bit fevered, but sleeping deeply," Maya answered. "Latta has an indoor herb garden where she keeps a lot of useful plants, including several that help with blood loss."

"That's very good news," Crim said. "I'll come visit him this evening if that's fine with you."

Maya's smile warmed. "Certainly, Lord Crim. Oh, Mikoneh, you remember Ter, of course."

Mikoneh blinked and turned to follow his twin's gesture. Sitting near the foot of the table, his eyes bright blue and shining, sat Ter N'Avea, the child-sized Ephe'ahn. His short wavy blond hair framed his eight-year-old face. He wore his traditional green woodland garb, though his quiver of arrows was missing.

"Warm greetings from the stars," Ter said. "You look better than before, my lad." One of his long, pointed ears twitched.

"We weren't expecting you for a week," Mikoneh said. "Did you accomplish what you needed to?"

"Ah, yes. I was able to slip away a bit sooner than expected, and I'm here to stay for a bit. And I did not come alone—but that is a matter for another turn." He tapped the table. "Sit, sit. Eat up. You look famished. But then, training your element does take a great deal out of you in the beginning."

Maya grunted. "At least *your* mentor isn't a tyrant." She rubbed her elbow. "Hilker put me through my paces this morning."

Chuckling, Mikoneh fell into the nearest chair and ladled himself a creamy soup that smelled of chicken and fresh herbs. He ate with more relish than he'd felt in days, filling every corner in his stomach with warm buttered bread, rich soup, and tart berries that stained his fingers a deep purple. He also found a pot of the red-tinted *tiassana* tea. Mikoneh poured himself a cup and sipped it between mouthfuls of food. The hollow place in his chest shrank a little.

Beside him, Crim consumed food at almost the same rate. The others looked on, but Mikoneh ignored them until he'd crammed a last bite of fresh bread into his mouth, then sat back in his chair with a satisfied smack of his lips.

"Well, Lord Crim," said Penn. "You're a miracle worker."

Maya nodded. "I think fire training should be mandatory every day."

Mikoneh rolled his eyes and dabbed at his mouth with a cloth napkin. "Only if wind training is for you."

Maya's grimace was gratifying.

Crim finished chewing the mouthful of bread he'd used to mop up the remnants of his soup, then he folded his napkin and set it aside. "Speaking of training, there *is* another lesson I've arranged for both of you—jointly."

"Is it archery?" asked Maya. "We're both fair at it, but I'd love to get better."

Crim shook his head. "You're welcome to use the archery range, but that's not it. In fact, it's nothing to do with warfare of the traditional variety and everything to do with politics."

A haze of dread wafted over Mikoneh. "Tell me it's not table etiquette."

Crim snorted, but he pressed a hand over his mouth to

muffle the sound. "No, no. You both seem adept enough at that when you're not half-starved." He glanced at Mikoneh's neglected utensils. "This is something far more important and practical. Can the two of you dance?"

Mikoneh's heart fell into his stomach. "No!" He hadn't meant to shout.

Maya's eyes widened until the gold of her irises sparkled. She inhaled. "Oh. Oh, I'd *love* to learn. We never did. Fa and Mama never danced."

Crim was nodding sagely. "Yes, I recall my one dance with Seranni all too well. Nothing short of a fiasco. Couldn't feel my toes for a week."

Maya giggled. "She *loathed* dancing. Fa told her that was only because she was so bad at it."

"Jonatten was always a clever fellow." Crim shook his head. "But no better a dancer than his wife. So, I thought it safe to assume neither of you had ever learned."

"I've done some village dancing," Maya said. "There's a maiden circle dance every girl participates in from her sixteenth year until she's wed, and I didn't do too badly."

"She didn't," Mikoneh agreed. "Except for stepping on poor Herett's skirt and ripping it off."

Penn cupped a hand over his mouth to hide a smile. Mikoneh flashed him a grin.

Maya winced. "That was only my second time participating. I got better."

"Right," said Mikoneh. "The third and last time you participated." After that, the twins had been too caught up in the rebellion to risk showing their faces in Relvin openly.

Crim chuckled. "Well, this time should go much better. Your dance instructor is the best, and it's critical you learn swiftly. I've already mentioned to Mikoneh that the Winter Tourney is soon upon us, and it always opens with a ball."

Mikoneh buried his face in his hands and groaned.

"A ball!" Maya's delight was almost palpable. "I've always dreamed of wearing a beautiful gown and dancing through the night."

"Now's your chance, Your Highness," Crim said. "And what's more, your brother won't be the only one suffering through the long festive sandglass turns. Your father is planning to attend—though he detests the idea."

Mikoneh lifted his head. "He said as much?"

"It was the look in his eyes, actually," Crim said. "Nevertheless, Prince Atlanse insists he attends to *humanize* him—if you'll allow the expression. With matters so tense right now, and so much hostile sentiment toward House Rokahn, it's vital that we showcase your family in a positive light. A ball and a tourney are just the things—and *you*, Mikoneh, must take center stage, alongside your betrothed."

Mikoneh scowled at his empty soup bowl. "Or I could disappear."

"True." Crim's voice was gentle. "You *can* still bow out."

That same longing to fly away—far away—maybe as far as the Nijaalin Woods—filled Mikoneh up until he couldn't breathe. But he clenched his hands into fists, drawing his heart back from the fae lands, into the reality of war. "No," he whispered. "I can't. I've agreed to help, and my word is my bond."

Crim's approving nod was strangely fortifying. "I admire your zeal, Your Highness." He turned back to Maya. "You'll have several gowns made up. The tailor will likely visit your suite for several fittings leading up to the ball. Same for you, Prince Mikoneh. Meanwhile, dance lessons every afternoon."

"What if we simply can't dance," Mikoneh said.

"Yes, what if Mikoneh's hopeless?" asked Maya.

He tossed her a glare.

"Nonsense," said Crim. "You're both from the House of Rokahn. Royal Rokahns can always dance."

As Crim sketched out their daily schedule for the next several weeks, Mikoneh tried to imagine Owenekiras Rokahn dancing. He found it as impossible as imagining himself leading Latta over the floor, surrounded by ostentation and subterfuge.

His stomach flipped.

Even so, he'd made a vow, and he would keep it—dance or no dance.

CHAPTER 14

CONCERNING DRAGONS

"There is evidence to support the idea that the Spirits Elemental worked in harmony with the Complété, and that once they were more fae-like, not so whimsical. If that is the case, is it any wonder that when the fabric of the Universe collapsed, the spirits became more childlike and—some scholars will insist—even mad?"

- *A Treatise on the Magic of the Hidden Realm* by Sariolin the Solitary

After Crim excused himself, the twins led Ter and Penn back to their suite. The Ephe'ahn would be staying in one of the spare bedrooms. Once there, Mikoneh and Maya would have one full sandglass turn to mentally prepare themselves before a servant came to guide them to their first dance lesson.

Along the corridors, Maya was treading clouds, humming to herself and spinning in circles now and then.

"A ball, Mikoneh," she sighed.

"Yeah. So exciting."

She only laughed at his flat tones. "You wouldn't understand. You're a man."

"Not all women like dresses and dancing," Mikoneh muttered.

"And that's their prerogative—just as enjoying those things is mine." Maya twirled outside the suite door. "I won't be robbed of my joy."

"I'd never dream of washing it away," Mikoneh said. "Just stop dripping it so close to me."

She laughed and flicked her fingers at him, as though she were indeed drenched in joy. Then she pranced into the common room, twirled again, and raced to Akonn's room. Halfway there, she froze.

Mikoneh felt the strange presence at the same moment. He spun toward the fire—and let out a cry, half of fear, half of wonder.

"Rev—" He cut off. Reven wasn't the man's name. Mikoneh stepped toward the hearth. "Jensirin, it's so good to see you."

The dragon lord, once confined to a specter's existence and chained to Sathe's will, looked whole now. He was tall, lean, with long snowy white hair hanging in waves down his back, and skin almost as pale. His eyes were a silvery lavender framed by long white lashes. He wore black armor and a long cape of crimson.

Jensirin moved from the fire, his gaze trained on Mikoneh. The haunted look was still there, more raw than before, perhaps because he wore flesh again. Reaching Mikoneh, Jensirin rested a gauntleted hand on his shoulder. It was solid, weighty, yet strangely brittle.

"My prince," the dragon lord whispered, then sank to one knee. "My dear prince." He caught Mikoneh's hand and kissed his knuckles.

Dumbfounded, Mikoneh remained still, staring at the man. Swallowing, he tried to find words. "Don't." It was something, but it meant nothing. He dropped to his knees before Jensirin. "None of that. You're my friend, not my liegeman. We saved each other. Remember?"

Jensirin lifted his head as though it weighed a thousand tons, then locked eyes with Mikoneh. Probing. Searching. The faintest smile touched his pale lips. "Your friend, my prince?"

"*Yes*, definitely. Now, please drop the title, or I'll call you Lord Scaly Britches for the rest of our lives."

Maya laughed nearby, and Mikoneh turned to find her only inches away, her gaze riveted on Jensirin.

Mikoneh twisted toward her. "Maya, meet Jensirin, formerly the Revenant."

She dipped into a graceful curtsey. "It's an honor to meet you formally."

"Jensirin, this is my twin sister, Mayanaleh—Rokahn, I suppose."

The dragon lord rose, caught her hand, and stooped to kiss her knuckles. "The privilege is mine, my princess."

She sucked in a breath, her cheeks blazing pink. Wrenching her hand from his, she backed up. "Well, I—I need to...it's important... Akonn needs me." She spun and raced into the captain's chamber. The door slammed behind her.

Mikoneh laughed. "Well, my lord. You flustered her beyond words. That's something few have ever managed, and none so dramatically."

Jensirin stood stock still. His hand remained outstretched. He blinked, then turned to Mikoneh. "Did I offend her?"

"Nah. You're just far too beautiful for your own good." Mikoneh clapped him on the back. "Pay it no mind. She'll recover." His lips twitched up. "Though, not quickly, I hope."

He glanced over and found Penn, still clutching his scrolls, looking a bit torn. Sympathy welled up, but Mikoneh shoved it aside. He turned back to the former Revenant. "This is my friend, Viscount Penn Lendir of Oceana. Penn, meet Jensirin."

"Hello, Lord Jensirin," Penn said, inclining his head.

"Viscount," Jensirin replied, mimicking Penn's motion. "It's an honor to know any friend of Prince Mikoneh."

"I'm honestly surprised you've come so quickly," Mikoneh said. "Lady Katanni led me to believe your recovery would take several weeks or longer."

Jensirin drifted toward the hearth, then turned back to face him. "I insisted on returning with Ter as soon as he arrived in *Serielias*. I do not wish to sit idly when I may be of some help to you, my—friend."

Mikoneh nodded. "I won't lie and say I'm not happy to see you, but it's dangerous here. Mages are closing in."

Something flashed across Jensirin's face. "All the more reason to stay near."

Ter spoke from where he'd perched himself on one arm of the settee. "Jensirin is not here passively. Owenekiras has asked him to be your mentor. He will teach you all things concerning dragons."

Mikoneh blinked. "Oh. That's what he meant." He searched Jensirin's face. "Will that cause you any pain?"

The dragon lord shook his head. "I am glad to help."

"More than that," Ter said, "he's quite eager. And an apt teacher, I might add. Few are as knowledgeable in dragon history, culture, and etiquette. He is quite old, after all."

"I won't argue," Mikoneh said. "Honestly, I'm relieved. Now the only lesson I'm dreading is dance."

Penn's snicker earned him a scowl.

"Still," Ter said, "it is best to keep Jensirin from overexerting himself. Do keep an eye on him."

"Don't worry," Mikoneh said. "I won't have the chance.

Maya will insist on keeping track of his health, and he'll feel marvelous in no time." His lips twitched up again. "As soon as she recovers from his looks." He moved toward the settee, sat, then motioned to the nearby wingback chair. "Please join me, Jensirin. You look ready to shatter."

The dragon lord drifted from the hearth like a lost feather and settled into the cushions of the plush chair. He set his gaze on Mikoneh. The haunted look was still present, but in the fire's glow it felt less...broken.

Shifting, Mikoneh folded his hands together and leaned his elbows against his legs. "We can begin our lessons tomorrow if you like. After elemental training and dance." He grimaced. "It'll be something to look forward to."

"A reward for good behavior," Penn added.

Jensirin nodded at Mikoneh. "I will be ready."

"Be sure to attend his class with an alert mind," Ter said, still seated on the settee's arm. He swung his short legs back and forth above the floor. "If that means rearranging Crim's time frame, I recommend doing so."

"I'll talk to Lord Crim this evening," Mikoneh said. "I don't know what his schedule's like, but I imagine he's a busy man."

"No doubt of it." Ter's ears fluttered. "Speaking of busy, it seems you've settled in nicely. One assassination attempt down already."

Jensirin stirred. "Someone tried to kill you?"

Mikoneh shrugged. "It was a poor attempt. Hardly an assassin either. He was just a boy. And now he's dead."

"You killed him?" Jensirin's voice was neutral.

"No. Dark Mages were controlling him, and when Maya imprisoned him with her wind spirits, they found him... expendable."

Jensirin lowered his head. "That does not surprise me." His

words were slow, deliberate, like he was trying to remember how to use his voice.

"Still." Mikoneh flopped against the settee's straight back. "It's been safe enough otherwise for the moment. Everyone's on high alert. I can't imagine it'll stay secure though. Rokahns aren't popular here."

"Hm, so I've heard," said Ter. "It was to be expected. Atlanse himself is out of favor these days. Queen Ferrese has already all but accused him of making advances on her."

Mikoneh blinked. "That's rubbish."

"No doubt of it," the Ephe'ahn agreed. "Atlanse is generally a composed man, and no kind of cad. Owenekiras wouldn't be his friend if he were."

"They do seem like an odd friendship though."

"'Tis an old one, from their childhood. They have both changed much, but the roots of their friendship only deepen."

Mikoneh turned that over in his head. Owenekiras's life was still shrouded in mystery. Most hearth stories agreed he'd grown up not so long ago in Rokahn—and Fa and Mama's tales aligned with them—yet more recent stories hinted that he'd also lived during the Age of Dragons twenty thousand years ago. Had the man somehow traveled across time to that ancient battlefield? Was such a thing possible like Ter had once implied?

I doubt he would lie to me.

Penn spoke, drawing Mikoneh from his thoughts. "What do you know about Latta, Ter?"

"She's a sweet lass, though prone to melancholy."

"Has she always been prone?" Penn gently pressed.

Ter shook his head. "No. She was a girl of sunshine in her youth. Alas, hard times change us."

Mikoneh sat silently. That was an understatement. "But it doesn't have to be a bad change."

"Change in itself isn't bad, my lad," Ter agreed. "It is necessary, like a butterfly in chrysalis. But we choose the colors of our wings upon emerging."

Mikoneh shifted. "So, it's too late for people like Latta?" *And me?* he finished silently.

"No, no, dear boy." Ter's ears fluttered. "You are changing. The change isn't ended. Each hard incident and how you cope adds a new stripe, dot, or splash to your wingspan. It is a long, slow process across a lifetime."

"Sounds horrible."

"It is life," Ter said with a chuckle.

Mikoneh nodded toward Jensirin. "His is a long life, but one of suffering. How much longer before he leaves his chrysalis?"

"That," Ter said, "is up to him."

"I thought it took a lifetime."

"We can live many lifetimes in a single year," Ter said. "Do not take my analogy so literally as that."

Flopping back again, Mikoneh let out a breath. "It still sounds exhausting. But if you're right, it seems like I have the chance at more than one set of wings."

"Indeed," Ter said. "That is the great gift. We have more than one chance to paint our wings with broad, bright colors." One ear twitched, then Ter sprang up and moved toward the shuttered window. "I think I shall wander Elenth today. Get a feel for things. I will return later."

"'Kay." Mikoneh didn't move. "Have fun."

Silence answered, and he twisted around on the settee to find the space empty where Ter had stood. Mikoneh shifted back toward Jensirin, catching a glance of Penn reading in a corner. "That Ephe'ahn's an odd one."

The solemn dragon lord nodded. "He is very old."

"Remind me not to live *that* long."

Jensirin rested his hands on his chair arms. "We must discuss my debt to you."

"There's no debt," Mikoneh said. "None."

"You freed me from a place worse than death."

"I freed you because we were both prisoners, and you gave me hope. Without you, I might've given up."

Jensirin shook his head. "Not you."

"You don't know that."

"But I do. The fire in your eyes never dimmed. You were far from broken."

Mikoneh dragged a hand down his face. "I feel broken." He dropped his hand and met Jensirin's gentle gaze. "I don't know how you're able to stand. Or breathe. Or...anything."

"What is fresh for you is something I accepted long ago as my new reality. And then you reminded me what it is to feel. It did not cause pain so much as relief. You were a soothing balm. I am restored because of you."

"You can't tell me you're all healed now."

"No. I may never be fully healed. But I *am* healing, and that is only possible because of you." Jensirin scooted forward on his chair. "Whether you accept it or not, I am indebted to you forever. You have given me new life, my prince."

Mikoneh flinched. "I'm not your prince, Jensirin. I'm your friend."

"You are both." The words were firm. Jensirin leaned back and sank into the plush cushion behind him. Surprise flitted over his face, then he settled in, and his eyes closed.

Mikoneh studied the former Revenant for a long time, smiling faintly. "I'm glad you're here, Rev."

Though Jensirin's eyes remained shut, his lips tugged up. "As am I, Mikoneh Rokahn."

CHAPTER 15

LIKE A SWAN TO WATER

"It's unfortunate that so few scholars have studied the Spirits Elemental beyond the generalities of their kind. It is by studying each type in its differences that we learn more about them as a whole."

- *A Treatise on the Magic of the Hidden Realm* by Sariolin the Solitary

The twins' first dance lesson was torture. The second and third lessons were likewise dreadful. After a full week, Mikoneh detested dancing like he detested dessert. The torture was made worse by their dragon lessons being delayed, as Jensirin looked so fragile, Maya had insisted they defer anything formal until the dragon lord had settled in.

Maya obviously enjoyed the dance lessons, despite tripping over her own skirts and tromping on Mikoneh's feet half a dozen times. He tromped back, not bothering to stifle his pettiness while the instructor clapped his hands and chanted out rhythms like a bleating sheep. The man was longsuffering, clearly well paid to dole out compliments aplenty, even as he flung veiled insults.

Maya's feet were hooves—from a prancing unicorn, of course. Mikoneh's step was as rigid as the sturdy stones of the Andyan Mountains—which must be wonderful for marching orders.

Still, it wasn't a complete loss. Certainly, Lord Crim seemed to find amusement in their torment when he came to observe at the week's end. Mikoneh shot him daggered looks more than once, then proceeded to collide with Maya in time for another slew of poetic invectives.

"Very close—if you were aiming for a battle dance," the instructor said after the fourth collision. "Try again and imagine yourself a thundercloud. It will give you better movement than mimicking a battering ram."

Mikoneh did picture a thundercloud, with lightning striking the insufferable man. He whirled Maya around, narrowly dodging her toes. She glanced up at him, determination bright in her eyes, even as she tried, again, to lead him. He stumbled but corrected himself—but not before the instructor let out a little groan he tried to disguise with another clap of his hands, slightly off rhythm.

Crim cleared his throat and shoved off the distant wall he'd been leaning on. "May I try something, Master Vomm?"

The instructor dipped his head, likely to hide his displeasure at the interruption. "If it pleases you, my lord."

Crim crossed to the twins and held out one hand. "If I may, Princess Mayanaleh?"

She tossed a questioning glance at Mikoneh, then accepted Crim's hand. "I'll butcher your feet, my lord."

Crim chuckled. "They can survive a little bruising." He caught Mikoneh's eye. "Observe, Your Highness. You can learn just as much from standing there, watching us, as your sister will learn in my arms."

The instructor sighed but didn't argue.

Crim led Maya across the dance floor, murmuring instructions. "No need to tug. That's right. Turn. Turn again." They stumbled. Maya trod on the lordling's toes, but Crim merely offered soft instruction. Halfway through a turn, Crim stopped, frowning. "You've the grace for this, but no vision." He tapped a finger against Maya's hand, then nodded. "Imagine wind, Princess. Imagine flight. Don't pull. Don't tug. *Flow.*"

They started again. Maya's steps changed slightly. The rhythm fell into place. Mikoneh blinked, startled by the newfound grace of his twin. Maya did start to flow, her skirts sweeping out, then twirling in. Crim led her through several motions, and each one grew softer, gentler. Maya's stiffness faded. Her smile bloomed.

Mikoneh inched closer, studying Crim's feet. The steps were consistent, just as the instructor had shown them in the beginning, but this somehow looked...right. Not rigid like a mountain. The rhythm matched the steps.

Crim drew nearer to Maya, turn by turn, then he spun her outward—she gasped, laughing—then he brought her back in. He stepped back, offered a low bow, then rose and grinned at Mikoneh.

"Your turn."

"I'm not dancing with you."

Crim laughed. "No, no. With your sister." He motioned to Maya. "She's a natural."

With less reluctance, Mikoneh strode to his twin's side, caught her hand, and pulled her in for another bout. The first step was awkward, but Maya pulled in rather than out, letting him guide her. The next step came easier, and each one after that grew into a fluid series of steps not unlike sword movements. Mikoneh let himself fall into the rhythm. Let himself pretend there was no ground, no ceiling, no walls. Only air between them and everything else.

Flight. Flow. Dance.

He caught her toes once, but she offered an encouraging smile, and he found his rhythm again.

"Good! Excellent." The instructor shattered the illusion of blue skies and snow-capped mountains. Mikoneh blinked in the dingy ballroom. Maya blinked with him, and they froze in place.

Crim strolled over alongside the instructor.

"That was well done, Lord Crim," Vomm said.

"Thank you." Crim inclined his head. "It dawned on me that these two have never witnessed a true ball, so dancing—apart from folk festivals—was outside their experience." He winked at Maya. "I did tell you you'd both be quick studies. You just needed experience to lend a helping hand."

"Thank you, kind sir," Maya said with a curtsey.

"My pleasure," Crim said, bowing.

"It really was impressive," said a new, feminine voice across the chamber.

Mikoneh tensed, hand falling to his sword belt—but the weapon was gone, at Vomm's insistence. That was for the best if he could startle easily enough to draw it on an unarmed woman.

The woman in question crossed the chamber, her silvery-blue skirts flowing behind her, a netted headdress fluttering down her back, half-hiding her curly golden-brown hair. Eyes like azure sparkled in the light from the high windows.

"Ah, Namirsha." Crim held out his hand, and the woman took it when she came close enough. Her sparkling eyes flitted between the twins, and she slipped into a graceful curtsey. Rising, she offered a smile that was quiet but keen.

"Introduce me, Crim," she said.

"Of course." He used his free hand to motion. "Prince Mikoneh Rokahn and Princess Mayanaleh Rokahn. She prefers Maya, however." He shifted his gaze to the woman. "This is my wife, Lady Namirsha, formerly of Lintha."

Namirsha curtseyed again, then rose. "It's a pleasure, Your Highnesses. You're as lovely as the rumors say, though far less dreadful."

"Dreadful?" Mikoneh quirked an eyebrow.

Crim chuckled. "It's traditional in Simynshin to paint all Rokahnians as frightful specters. The fact that you both sparkle with life is *not* in keeping with said tradition. You're not nearly grim or fierce enough. Thus, the rumors are trying to repair that."

Maya laughed. "We could try to be grim, but I think we'd fail. Certainly, I would." She glanced at Mikoneh. "He's more sullen than grim. But he *can* be fierce."

Mikoneh fastened his attention on the Linthian woman. "Who started these rumors, my lady?"

She shook her head. "They spread too fast to be certain, though many come from the highest peak, I'm certain."

"You mean Queen Feresse."

She offered a shrug. "Simynshin will never hold a candle to Lintha's gossip vine."

"Another tradition," Crim said.

"Do you gossip?" asked Maya.

Namirsha's smile crooked. "My dear sweet girl, it's practically a requirement for any respectable woman to gossip, else she knows nothing and believes anything."

Maya fell silent, no doubt trying to chew on that peculiar life philosophy.

"Are you in the Lady Queen's circle, by chance?" asked Mikoneh, thinking of Latta's earlier inference about Linthian influence at court. It was clear the Songbird Princess didn't trust Crim's wife. Best to keep an eye on her.

Namirsha's smile sharpened. "As the only other Linthian woman at court, where else would I be?"

"Makes sense." Mikoneh caught Maya's arm in his. "I wonder if you would be kind enough to formally introduce my sister to Her Majesty if the chance presents itself?"

Namirsha inclined her head. "Your Highness, the only chances that present themselves are marriage proposals and illnesses. All other things are *made* to happen. I will certainly do as you request, and I hope in return you might introduce me to the young lord from Oceana who traveled here with you."

"You mean Penn?" asked Maya. "Certainly. He'd be honored."

"I thank you." Namirsha dipped her head again. "It's my understanding that he's quite the catch, and several young ladies are eager to make his acquaintance."

"But he's Oceanean," Mikoneh said flatly.

The lady laughed. "That might have been a deterrent in the narrow minds of my own compatriots, but here in Simynshin, Oceana is something of a novelty, especially since half the court knows you grew up there, Your Highness. Backwoods are only backwoods until the sun shines on them, and we discover—lo! the world isn't as small as we thought." Her smile grew more sly. "Imagine so many other interesting places existing outside our own countries."

Mikoneh snorted. "Shocking."

"Quite." Namirsha drew a fan from a hidden pocket in her skirts and snapped it open. "I've stayed just long enough, I think, to remain fascinating without risking fatigue. I shall take my leave for now, and hope to see you both for dinner at my husband's home before the new week is out. Agreed?"

"We'd love to," Maya said ahead of Mikoneh's murmured acceptance.

"Perfect," Crim said. "We'll look forward to it. If you'll allow, I'll escort my wife, and see you tomorrow for our next elemental lesson."

"Of course," Mikoneh said. "I'm eager to learn more."

"Good." Crim bowed, then tucked his wife's arm in his, and led her from the room.

Vomm cleared his throat. "One more movement, Your Highnesses, then you're free to depart."

Mikoneh pulled his eyes from the winsome couple and took Maya back in his arms. He fell into the steps, with only a few hesitations before the rhythm returned to his feet. Maya followed well, taking to the motions like a swan to water.

"They seem happy," she said.

"Crim and his wife?"

"Yes."

"They do." He smiled. "I'm glad he got over his feelings for...for Seranni."

"Me, too. Though it is rather romantic."

"Unrequited love isn't romantic."

"It is a little," she said.

"Only in your fuzzy head. Not in real life."

Maya rolled her eyes. "I'm not fuzzy-headed."

"Sometimes you are."

She tramped on his foot. "You're a petty, petty man."

"Likewise."

"I'm not a man."

He snorted. "No, I suppose not."

"Now be quiet, and let's dance."

He led her through the last steps, as far as they knew them, and Vomm acknowledged enough improvement to release them until the next day. As they left the dance hall, Maya sighed. "Do you think Penn will find the women here very pretty?"

"Some of them, yes," Mikoneh answered. "Just like you find several of the men so."

"I do not."

"Not even Akonn or Jensirin?"

Maya missed a step, then caught up with him. "That's different. They're—well, different."

"I hate to tell you this, Maya, but there are lots of interesting and different women in Simynshin, too. And Penn isn't going to miss seeing that."

They walked in silence, then Maya sighed again. "True. The world *is* awfully big, isn't it?"

Mikoneh eyed a shadow as he passed an adjoining corridor. He relaxed. Not a person. "Not big enough to hide in," he whispered.

Chapter 16

Connection with the Spirits

"Since so few scholars have the time or interest to directly interact with the Spirits Elemental, I've chosen to undertake it myself. If we don't understand the how of the world, we'll never understand the why."

- A Treatise on the Magic of the Hidden Realm by Sariolin the Solitary

While Mikoneh trained in the northwest tower, each morning Maya made her way to the northside courtyard to meet Hilker. Stepping outside, the bite of winter penetrated her simple gray training dress, but it didn't chill her blood like it used to. Instead, it invigorated her.

Hilker stood at the dead center of the courtyard, surrounded by heaps of sculpted snow he'd doubtless ordered the wind spirits to scoop up and pile into symmetrical patterns. Maya could guess what she'd be doing this fine, brisk morning, judging by the remaining snow left in the corners of the walled space. She crunched her way across the fresh powder, smiling at the drifting flakes being swept up from the castle eaves by bored spirits.

"You're late," Hilker growled.

Maya only beamed at him. He always said that, even when she arrived first. After the first few lessons, she'd decided to make him not look like a liar by allowing his statement to be true. Every morning, she arrived a quarter turn late, no more and no less.

"What's on today's agenda?" she asked, bending down to scoop up a fistful of snow. It was too dry to stick, so she tossed it into the air and watched the glittering flakes flutter around a cluster of wind spirits who twirled and danced with it.

"Training, what else?" Hilker sounded more grumpy than usual.

"Is something bothering you?"

He scowled, then sighed. "Nothing that would interest you. Just a family issue. Leave it be."

She eyed him for a moment, assessing his expression. He really didn't want her to ask judging by the tightness around his mouth. Hilker had once told her he was part fae but that the human side was winning out. Did his mixed blood affect his home life in some way? Were his children bullied? Was his wife insecure?

It's not my place to ask.

"Very well. But if you change your mind, I'm here to listen." She motioned to the nearest corner and willed the wind spirits to reshape the crystals into the shape of a dragon. Delighted, they complied, following the imagery she fed them with her mind. The translation wasn't exact. Her mental connection with the spirits was tenuous at best—something she was working on.

Hilker watched the dragon take shape, then grunted. "How close is the likeness?"

"My unicorn was better," Maya admitted.

"Sad, considering what you are." Hilker reached up to rub the back of his neck, the flash of a gold ring glinting in the sunlight. He muttered something that sounded distinctly like a curse word, then toed the nearest snow pile with his worn boot. "Try again."

Maya shrugged, dredging up her memory of Larkynven, Father's dragon mount. She still couldn't quite accept the oddity of the Dragon King riding a dragon of his own, but what did she know of magic or royal traditions? Concentrating on the dragon's majestic form, she fed the imagery more slowly to the wind spirits, who knocked over the first dragon sculpture with a relish to begin again.

"How is Jensirin settling in?" Hilker asked, reforging his own pile of snow into a castle not unlike the one looming over them in the growing sunlight.

"Slowly," Maya admitted. "He meant to start training us at once, but he's so listless and pale that I demanded he wait a few days. I don't think he's ready for any commitments yet. Mikoneh agrees with me—for once. Wintertide miracles *do* happen, it seems."

The Wind Master snorted. "Let's hope so. I could do with a few myself."

Maya eyed him in her periphery but didn't press for details. Perhaps his wife was annoyed with his long absence—but it was none of Maya's business. She had no romantic relationship of her own, so how could she hope to offer up counsel or proper sympathy?

The second dragon sculpture was much better than the first. Even Hilker grunted approval before he had the wind spirits collapse it and ordered her to start again. Maya worked for over a turn, until her nose was numb despite her element.

"That's enough," Hilker said, tugging his cloak around his neck. "I've got a meeting to get to. Head back in and check on your brother. He's still not himself."

Heat flamed against Maya's cheeks. "Would you be, after everything?" Her voice was terser than she'd expected.

Hilker paused, then shook his head. "I suppose not. I didn't mean to sound insensitive."

Shuffling her feet, Maya smiled faintly. "And I didn't mean to lose my temper. Sorry."

Hilker waved that off. "Go on, take a hot bath. Get that nice viscount to give you a shoulder rub."

She scoffed at that. "If only he'd stick around long enough to ask! Penn's more the scholar than the noble these days. I think he's consuming more books than food."

They moved toward the doors leading into the castle proper.

"What's the lad reading about?" asked Hilker.

"Sands if I know. Wheat, maybe. And he's making friends with all the scholars. I think he was reading out in yesterday's storm. He came in sopping wet."

"That's dedication." Hilker chuckled. "I'm not a great reader myself."

"Neither am I, though that's not because I wouldn't like to be. There just doesn't seem to be much time for books—either because of rebellions, executions, Mage hunters, dance lessons, or learning how to be a Dragon Princess."

"Tough life," Hilker said dryly.

Maya rolled her eyes, nudging him with her elbow.

Within the castle, warmth enveloped her, and she drank in the fragrance of cinnamon and beeswax. "You know, I'm getting excited for Wintertide."

"It's a special time here in Elenth." Hilker took a deep breath. "It was even more so when the previous queen was alive."

"King Prettem's wife?" Maya frowned. "I never heard much about her."

"She was...a good woman." Hilker looked away. "A good woman."

Maya opened her mouth to pry, but footsteps thundered up the passage.

"HILKER!" The bearded man who approached was tall, stately—and royal. A handful of guards trailed after him.

Maya's eyes widened. She swept into a hasty curtsey before King Prettem.

"I've been looking for you every which way," the king said with venom. "I expected you half a turn ago."

"Apologies," Hilker said, not sounding the least bit sorry. "I was escorting Princess Mayanaleh." He gestured toward her.

The king glanced her way, not hiding a scowl. "Is she lost?"

"Good morning, Majesty," Maya said, applying her most cheerful smile. "I'm not a bit lost. Hilker's simply being a gentleman."

The king snorted. "That would be a first."

Hilker wore a longsuffering look while one hand flexed at his side. "This is where I leave you, Princess Mayanaleh." He turned toward her, bowed, then twisted back toward the king. "Shall we, sire?"

Prettem looked off balance, then nodded and spun away to march down the hall, stroking his beard. Hilker followed him, and soon they turned down a new corridor and out of sight. The handful of guards followed, armor clanking. Their footsteps faded into a silence stirred only by the faint crackle of the nearby torches.

Maya stared into the gloom for a moment, then shrugged

to herself. Turning, she made her way toward her shared suite. She'd not been sure what to think of King Prettem at the feast their second night in Elenth Castle. Now she was positive he was a pompous, condescending jerk—exactly the sort of royalty Mikoneh despised most. He'd be delighted.

Interlude II
The Sea's Wrath

"Whence comes the storm which has brought you back to me?"

- From the Corpse Poet's 38th Sonnet

Ocean waves crashed against the breakers, singing an ancient, eerie song. He stood at the edge of the cliff, ignoring his long hair lashing in the windstorm. The taste of salt prickled his tongue and gnawed at his nostrils.

A ship far out among the monstrous waves struggled in vain to fight the sea's wrath.

He reached a hand out, as though he could grasp the tiny vessel, but his fist closed over damp air. A wave rolled above the ship, folding over it, swallowing the crew.

"They will not give them back."

He turned toward the voice. She stood beside him, cloaked in black, mourning.

"Make them," he growled.

"I've tried. So did the Dragon King."

He turned back to the sea, empty now of any vessels. "We'll find them. I won't rest until I do."

"You cannot interfere," she whispered.

"I'll do what I must. No matter what."

Chapter 17

Playing Court Games

"Fire Spirits are the most straightforward. They are temperamental, quick-witted, and honest. The same can be said of Fire Elementalists as a rule, though I stand by the idea that this is a narrow view of the wielders."

- *A Treatise on the Magic of the Hidden Realm* by Sariolin the Solitary

Dawn crept in through the window, overcast and snow laden.

Mikoneh sat up, dragged hair from his face, then climbed out of bed. He threw a silk robe on and tied it at the waist. Wind wailed, rattling the glass panes. If it was colder than yesterday, he couldn't feel it. Padding to the window seat, he touched the frosted glass. Under the heat of his palm, it cracked.

He flinched back.

He hadn't dreamed of *her* in two weeks. Maybe longer. What did it signify? He couldn't recall enough details to guess.

They always seemed to slip away the harder he tried to grasp onto them.

A knock fell on the bedroom door.

He turned, wary, nerves raw. "Who is it?"

"Me," said Maya.

He exhaled, crossed the room, and cracked the door open. "You're up early."

"The storm woke me," she said. "Why do castles feel so eerie when the wind rages?"

He cracked a smile. "This coming from a Wind Elementalist."

She squeezed into the room. She wore a delicate silver robe over a pale seafoam green nightgown. Her long hair was braided and disheveled from sleep. "I think it's worse, knowing what the wind is saying. It's angry. Unrest in the east, near Oceana. Death and heartache." She shivered.

Mikoneh wrapped an arm around her shoulders and drew her to the edge of his bed. They sat on the mattress, sinking deep into the plushness.

"I know what we're doing is important," she said. "But it feels so wrong to be here, playing court games, while good folk suffer out there."

"We can't save them all," he whispered.

"I *wish* we could."

"Me, too."

She snuggled up against him, resting her head against his shoulder. "I'm frightened."

"Of what? Not King Prettem. You were fearless with him."

"Of meeting Queen Feresse. Of spying for information. It's so far beyond what we know. I only handled the king well because he caught me off guard."

"Do you know how unique that is? You'll be fine, Maya. Everyone likes you."

"That's not true."

"Fair. Not everyone knows you yet." He turned his gaze to the window and found the fine crack across the lower pane. "Out there, we're more trouble than help. Here we can do something to make a difference. Saving Latta and her father. Keeping Simynshin from joining the Dark Mages' followers. That's worth a lot in this war."

"I know." She blew out a breath. "But I'm homesick."

His stomach twisted. "Yeah. But there is no home. Not anymore."

"I know." She fingered the ties of her robe. "Do you think...once this war is over...do you think Owenekiras will let us live with him?"

"I don't think he has a home either, Maya."

She paused. "That's so sad."

Mikoneh tracked the faint dawn light growing across the floor. "I need to get ready for my lesson with Crim."

"In that storm?"

Mikoneh shrugged. "Might be good to pit my fire against snow."

"Don't catch cold."

He shrugged loose and stood. "I'm not sure I can."

"May I come with you?" She stood.

"If you want." After all, Crim had said to involve her in training once he got better control, and over the past week he'd been improving steadily.

Maya beamed. "I'll go get changed." She raced out of the room, leaving the door ajar.

Mikoneh trudged over, shaking his head, and kicked the door shut. Then he crawled into the new clothes the tailor had left neatly folded near the wardrobe. Another Rokahnian set, with the same grays, burgundies, and blues, in a different cut. Checking himself in the looking glass, Mikoneh found he was coming to like the practical but ornate designs. After brushing his hair and tying it back, he entered the common room to find Maya already waiting.

"That was fast," he said.

She ran her hands over the simple gray gown she'd chosen. It was decidedly Simynshinian. She'd also left her hair loose, like Latta often did. "I wear this when I train with Hilker. Shall we?"

He motioned toward the door, but his attention snared on Jensirin standing at the hearth with his back to the room.

"Good morning," said Mikoneh. "Did you sleep?"

The dragon lord turned. He was draped in the same crimson cloak he'd worn since his arrival. "The night was restless. Sleep betrayed me." He looked more pale than usual.

"I could've given you some tea," Maya said. "Wake me next time. I'm happy to help."

Jensirin nodded. "Thank you, Your Highness."

Her cheeks reddened. "It's my pleasure." She caught Mikoneh's arm and tugged. "Shouldn't we be on our way?"

He found himself dragged from the common room, ready or not. Chuckling, he let his twin guide him halfway up the corridor before she halted.

"Where are we going?" she asked.

"That's what I was wondering." He took the lead, ignoring the clink of metal indicating his usual protective shadow was with them. "How's Akonn today?"

"Improved, but still weak from blood loss. There's no infection, which is a very good sign."

"Good."

"He should recover in time for the ball. I hope so. I might be able to finagle a way for him to dance with Latta."

Mikoneh frowned, pulling Maya down a new corridor.

"That might not be wise. She has feelings for him, but *he* may know nothing about them."

"I wonder," Maya said in a dreamy tone that signaled danger.

Mikoneh stopped and whirled toward her. "Leave it alone, Maya. Feelings are complicated enough without external meddling."

She sighed. "I know you're right, but..."

"I thought *you* liked Akonn."

"I do. But nothing like her."

"You don't find him attractive?"

Maya rolled her eyes. "I do. But I barely know him."

"And Jensirin is more your type?"

Maya scowled. "You're an idiot, Mikoneh." She marched past him, heading up the corridor alone. Mikoneh followed, content to let her get herself lost for a few moments while she brooded. He knew he shouldn't poke fun, but it felt good to act normally. To pretend his soul wasn't cracked and bleeding.

He needed that.

And he suspected Maya needed that from him, too.

He caught up a few breaths later and led her toward the breakfast room. They grabbed a few crab-stuffed rolls to munch on, then carried on toward the northwest tower in comfortable silence.

Crim was waiting at the bottom of the tower steps. "Good morrow," he said cheerily. "With the storm, I thought we'd—" He glanced at Maya. "Welcome, Princess. Ready to be a little cold?"

She nodded. "The wind shields me from the worst of the chill."

"Very good." Crim started up the stairs. "I thought we could have fun battling nature."

Mikoneh grinned. "I was hoping you'd say that."

Theyspent a productive morning melting snow. Crim started with handfuls of icy white clumps pressed against Mikoneh's palms, which were easy enough to melt. The lone fire spirit enjoyed itself immensely, cackling as the snow shrank into a puddle. Then Mikoneh was instructed to concentrate on emanating enough heat from his body to melt the falling snow at different radiuses.

The challenge came when Crim met Mikoneh's eyes with a grin and said, "Now, try melting only one snowflake before it hits the ground. *Without* touching it. Just use fire."

"Can the fire spirit touch it?" asked Mikoneh.

"Sure," Crim said. "If you can get it to melt the right snowflake."

In theory that was easy, but the fire spirit couldn't see through Mikoneh's eyes, and kept going after the wrong snowflake. Balls of fire proved too big and unwieldy to target a single tiny flake without melting any of the others swirling close by.

Mikoneh kept at it, having no success, until Crim slapped his palms together and rubbed them.

"Enough for today. Time for lunch, and then you have more lessons this afternoon, right?"

Mikoneh sighed and jumped down from the parapet where he'd taken up residence to practice. The fire spirit settled on his shoulder, taking the form of a flaming bird. Maya stood up from the stone floor where she'd been watching. Her hair fluttered around her, almost like a living force, and her eyes were bright despite the overcast day.

"You weren't making that more difficult for me, were you?" he asked.

"No," she said, grinning, "but it was fun to watch the wind spirits tease you."

"Oh, yes. So much fun." He stomped over to the trapdoor, dislodging the snow that had caught on his clothes, and jumped down into the stairwell, hungry and tired enough not to care that he was sulking. Up until Crim's last exercise, he'd taken to fire like—well, like he'd been born to it. But targeting a single snowflake was impossible.

The scuff of boots behind him turned him around halfway down the tower. "Can you do it, Crim?"

The merchant lord grinned at him. "I only ever managed it once."

Mikoneh's gaze narrowed. "You're trying to make me do something you haven't even mastered?"

"Certainly. You're a Rokahn. You're meant to excel."

Mikoneh rolled his eyes. "I'm beginning to think that's an excuse more than a compliment."

"It's both," Crim offered. "We mere mortals look up to your family, we envy you, and we also fear you. It's best for all concerned if you master your gifts early on."

"Afraid I'll burn down the castle?"

"Among other things, yes." Crim moved up to his side and slapped his shoulder. "Ease up, Dragon Prince. I didn't expect you to get it during your second week of lessons. But I'm confident you'll catch on fast."

"You did it only once. It's really hard, right?"

Crim frowned. "My single victory was a fluke. Yours won't be—of that I'm certain."

"Because I'm a Rokahn?"

"Because you're stubborn. More stubborn even than most Rokahns."

Mikoneh sighed and started down the stairs again. The guard stood in the corridor below, armor glinting in a pool of murky sunshine. The man positioned himself at the back of the procession leading to the nearby dining hall.

"By the way," Crim said, "my wife has made arrangements for you to come to dinner tomorrow night if that's acceptable? She's anxious to host you, and she forgot she had another commitment at week's end."

"Wonderful!" said Maya. "She's a lovely woman."

"She is that," Crim said, chuckling. "Warm and vivacious. I'm lucky that she married me for my money."

"Surely not," Maya said.

He laughed. "You're right. She tells me frequently it's purely for that, but we're very much in love."

"Do you have children?" she asked.

"Not yet. But I married late, you see. We only exchanged our vows last summer."

"Then you're newlyweds! That's very sweet."

Grimacing, Mikoneh let his thoughts drift away from the chatter, flicking one finger out to light his fingernail, then curling it in to extinguish the flame. He repeated the action until they reached the food-filled chamber, trying to imagine aiming a single tiny flame at a snowflake with any kind of accuracy.

Flopping into a chair, he reached blindly for food. He couldn't use a fire spirit for precision. How then to target one small object among millions?

Conversation surrounded him. He didn't care—not until a familiar voice spoke.

"You seem *very* distracted."

He jerked his head up from his plate and met Latta's sapphire eyes. She was seated next to him, her dark hair caught up in a complicated coif, her deep green dress glittering with tiny diamonds. As she reached for a goblet, the ring on her finger flashed.

He grabbed a drumstick from a platter. "Sorry. I didn't mean to be rude."

"You're not," she said. "Lord Crim tells me you're coming into your element swiftly. That isn't surprising, though, considering—"

"Considering I'm a Rokahn," Mikoneh grumbled. Then winced. "That *was* rude, sorry."

She studied him. "You're frustrated."

"Often," he said. "Right now, specifically, I'm frustrated by a heritage everyone understands better than me. I'm a Rokahn so I *must* excel, but why and how, I have no idea."

"No one understands Rokahns except Rokahns—and even then." Latta sipped her wine, then set her goblet aside. "It's really not that Rokahns are all a certain way. They're just inclined to be true to themselves—which is more than I can say for most people. Don't feel pressured to live up to a legacy you don't know. It's far more important to carve out your own path and create your own legacy. *That's* the Rokahn way."

He chewed a bite of chicken, finally tasting the herbs smothering the tender meat. Swallowing, he set the drumstick down. "Thank you, Latta. I'll try not to overcomplicate things."

She softly laughed. "Ah, but that, *too*, is the Rokahn way."

CHAPTER 18

BORN TO FLY

"What too many so-called scholars miss is that mastering each spirit type requires different behaviors, especially for combat. Fire prefers mental fortitude and internal command while wind wants imagery and hand gestures to direct them."

- *A Treatise on the Magic of the Hidden Realm* by Sariolin the Solitary

The next dance lesson went better than the previous one, though Mikoneh was distracted by a growing anticipation. Once he and Maya were dismissed by Master Vomm, they would return to their suite, where Jensirin waited to teach them about dragons. At last.

Vomm had brought in a musician to play a stringed instrument, which helped with the rhythm, and his passive insults were less frequent. Mikoneh threw himself into learning the new steps in the dance's second movement, treating it like he would a sword lesson. That helped, along with Crim's tip to treat the dance like flight.

After they'd danced through a dozen songs, Vomm clapped his hands together, cutting off the music. "Better, but there's still room for improvement. Tomorrow we will focus on combining movements one and two of the Frost Trot. Dismissed for today, Your Highnesses."

Mikoneh caught Maya's arm, and dragged her toward the door.

"Thank you, Master Vomm," Maya called out.

They entered the corridor, and their guard followed after them.

"Why such a hurry?" asked Maya.

"Jensirin's next. Dragon lessons." He shook his head. How could she forget?

With so much going on, the twins had done little more than train their elements, learn new dances, and sneak in occasional weapon bouts with Master Donivan. Movement around the castle had been discouraged since Brentin's attack, making their job of sniffing out potential spies tricky. Mikoneh was growing stir-crazy. At least Jensirin's instruction would offer something productive to do.

They arrived at the common room a little breathless. Slipping inside, they found Jensirin standing at the window, hands clasped behind his back. The blanket covering had been removed, and new glass sparkled under strands of sunlight. The storm had passed, leaving the world outside white and glittering.

The dragon lord turned toward them. He'd removed his crimson cloak and armor, and wore a style of clothing different from any Mikoneh knew. They were layers of charcoal robes, though tailored to fit his form, unlike what the Mages wore. A belt tied the ensemble together, and an embroidered green dragon twined up the sleeves, the hems, and along the chest of the outermost robe. He looked like a foreign king from distant lands.

Maya stood dumbfounded.

Mikoneh tugged his twin forward. "We're ready for our lesson."

Jensirin nodded. "We will go out." He turned and unlatched the wide window, then pushed it open. Cold wind wafted into the room. Maya's hair lashed in a swift breeze more enthusiastically than the two men's long tresses.

She hesitated. "I don't know how to fly. The wind spirits can hold me up, but they're...flighty and easily distracted."

Jensirin considered her. "Your father has been giving you *korta*, yes?"

"He has."

"Then your blood will be awake by now. Draw out your wings."

"How?"

"Close your eyes. Think of flight. Answer the question."

The man's words stirred up Mikoneh's desire to fly, and his midnight-blue wings slid out from his back, quivering with anticipation. The tailor had cleverly sewn slits into Mikoneh's shirt back, keeping him from tearing his clothing every time he wanted to fly. In human form, his wings adjusted for his height and build, appearing much larger than when he was in his tiny dragon form.

He glanced at Maya. Her brow was pinched in concentration, and after a moment, wings slid out from her back in a graceful, fluid motion. Her clothing had sewn slits as well. He expected the same wing coloring he had, but rather than the deep blue scales on the outer wings and fiery webbing underneath, Maya's wings were pure white, with black underside membrane streaked with lightning blue veins.

Her eyes flew open, and her gasp of delight brought a smile

to his face. She spun in a circle, nearly knocking over the replacement vase on the decorative side table.

"This is amazing," she breathed, spinning the other way.

Jensirin stood in silence, though a faint smile touched his lips.

Mikoneh caught the edge of her wing before she could make another full turn. "It's even better when you're in the sky."

Maya twisted toward Jensirin. "Am I ready to fly now?"

"You were born to fly, Princess." Jensirin stepped aside to give passage to the window. "Go and claim the clouds."

Maya raced to the large bay window, leapt onto the ledge, then sprang out into the broad blue expanse. Mikoneh followed, laughing. His wings thrummed, then he was bounding out the window and soaring, higher, higher—into the endless heavens.

Maya swooped low, then spun, more confident than Mikoneh had been at first, but that made sense. She could see wind spirits and knew they wouldn't let her fall. Her black hair streamed behind her like a banner, declaring for all the world that she was a free and noble creature.

A Dragon Princess.

Mikoneh glanced back and found Jensirin—still in human shape, like them—flying behind the twins, the glistening blue-green scales of his wings flashing in the sun. Slowing, Mikoneh positioned himself near the dragon lord.

"As far as first lessons go, this one's excellent," Mikoneh said.

Jensirin's quiet smile returned. "It seemed fitting. This is my first flight in centuries."

Pain flashed through Mikoneh, tightening his throat. He swallowed hard. "Definitely overdue."

Jensirin nodded. His long white mane of hair streamed

behind him, and his robes billowed in the wind. "You have not known flight outside of your captivity, have you?"

"Only briefly at TeshRelle," Mikoneh said. "Though I suppose Sathe still had my blood, so I wasn't entirely free." He tracked Maya's backward loop across the sky. "Thank you for this, Jensirin."

"Tomorrow, we will touch more on dragon history and heritage. Your sister needed to catch up with you first."

Mikoneh chuckled. "I'm not sure that's fair. But then, you don't know Maya yet. Just wait, she'll surpass me in no time."

"I think not," Jensirin said. "Wind is her advantage in the air, but it does not help her on solid ground. Fire is grounded, deep, and abiding. You will catch on to other aspects of your dragon blood at a faster rate than she. And where each of you is weak, the other will bridge the gap. Dragon twins are rare and wonderful. You will complement each other as few dragons do."

"Why are her wings white? I expected the same color scales I have."

"Dragons in their true form do not always align with their human forms. Nor do families always bear the same coloring. Twins you may be, but your elements define your dragon appearance."

Mikoneh nodded, beating the air with his glistening wings. He tipped his head up. "I think I'll go higher."

"Do what your instinct demands. It will aid in your healing."

Mikoneh started upward, then paused. "Coming?"

Jensirin shook his head. "I am not quite ready."

Mikoneh frowned but chose not to push the point. He aimed for the nearest stand of clouds, shoving against the wind, fighting at snatches of current. A grin spread over his face, and his troubles melted away, until all that remained was the joy of flight.

Maya joined him, and together the twins flew toward the sun, wing to wing.

CHAPTER 19

VIOLET WATER

*"If one views the five main types of the Spirits Elemental as
siblings, all in the same family but with their own quirks and
traits, it becomes easier to accept the differences."*

- *A Treatise on the Magic of the Hidden Realm* by Sariolin the Solitary

Crim promised to send his private carriage to collect
Mikoneh and Maya the next evening. After their
dance session, Jensirin had intended to give them a
lesson on dragon history, but he'd backed out, claiming he
wasn't up to it. He'd looked so pale and lost, the twins hadn't
argued.

Mikoneh hated to leave his strange new friend behind for a
dinner party outside the castle, but Penn promised to keep an
eye on Jensirin after assuring the twins he was taking a break
from his stacks of books on theology, agriculture, and whatever
else the viscount had grabbed from the library shelves. Maya
was disappointed Penn wasn't coming with them to Crim's

estate, but the viscount consoled her by asking for a dance at the upcoming ball.

Standing in the bailey outside the castle, bundled in stylish fur cloaks neither twin needed, Mikoneh and Maya stood on the slushy cobblestones and watched the sentries on the outer wall prowl along the parapets. Armor and spearheads glinted in the waning daylight. The crisp air brought the fragrance of snow and pine from the eastern woods.

Feet scraped stone behind them. Mikoneh glanced back, instincts prickling, though he expected to find his assigned guard inching closer.

It wasn't his guard.

Princess Latta stood against the backdrop of her own, rather large protector, both wrapped in matching green cloaks lined with white fur. Latta smiled at the twins, brushing back a lock of dark hair.

"Good evening to you," she said. "Lord Crim kindly invited me to attend his dinner party tonight and suggested I ride with you."

Mikoneh froze. It made sense, considering he and Latta were supposed to be seen together often, but the entire prospect of the dinner left him feeling uncomfortable, and his writhing worsened at the idea of conversing with the princess throughout the ordeal. They'd already covered the few topics they had in common over the past two weeks. What could he possibly talk to her about now?

The rattle and clatter of the approaching carriage saved him from an immediate response. The party turned to watch the driver steer two fine gray horses before a scarlet carriage trimmed in gilded swirls along the frame and doors. The conveyance came to a halt before them. A footman sprang from the back, folded into a practiced bow, then swung the door aside to admit them into a plush interior of crushed velvet.

They settled inside, and the footman produced blankets for their laps. Mikoneh took one to be polite and caught Latta's fleeting smile. Her protector remained outside the carriage and swung onto a horse someone brought over. The twins' guard mounted another horse, and the two men flanked the carriage. A dozen more armored men on horseback took up the rear before the footman closed the door.

The driver clicked his tongue, and the carriage lurched into motion. Hooves clattered over cobblestones. The curtains covering the carriage windows swayed, tassels bobbing. Latta's perfume hung in the air, floral and sweet.

"How are your dance lessons?" she asked.

"Wonderful," Maya answered, sparing Mikoneh from lying. She leaned forward in the seat she shared with her twin. "At first we were both terrible, but Lord Crim showed us how the dance was meant to look—and feel—and we caught on after that. I love dancing!"

Latta's smile warmed at the edges. "That does my heart good to hear."

Maya reached for Latta's hand and squeezed her fingers. "You look unwell."

"I'm all right," Latta said. "Just tired."

"Why?" asked Mikoneh.

Maya shot him a glare, but he ignored her and leaned forward. The rumble of the rolling wheels changed as they drove across the moat bridge, then struck the gravel road.

"Why are you tired, Princess?" he pressed.

Latta hesitated, then shook her head. "No reason I can think of. I've been careful not to push myself since my illness. Perhaps it's worry for my father, and not sleeping much. Not since..." Her lips pulled sideways in a sort of apologetic expression. "I was told about Brentin. About him watching me. It was unsettling."

"I wouldn't be able to sleep either…" Maya said gently.

Tears welled in the princess's eyes, and she ducked her head.

"Don't be ashamed," Maya whispered. "You've done absolutely nothing wrong. *Nothing.*"

Latta shook her head again, but kept her chin tucked. "I'm not. It's not shame. It's…gratitude."

Maya stood, hunching over, in the rocking carriage. She moved to sit beside Latta on the opposing seat and wrapped an arm around the other woman to pull her close.

"You're very lonely, aren't you?" Maya said softly.

Latta fell still.

An old Oceanean song fell into Mikoneh's mind: *A lonely soul sings a silent song in the barren fields of winter.* The irony of Latta's predicament wasn't lost on him.

"It's all right," Maya whispered. "In Oceana, our family was so peculiar, we never fit in. We can understand why now, but it doesn't change the fact that the villagers were unkind. A lot of the boys I knew growing up called me ugly and spindly. They called Mikoneh a lot of cruel things, too. But we always had each other and our parents." Her voice cracked.

Mikoneh studied the calluses on his hands, swallowing down a lump in his throat. *A lonely soul sings…*

"When we lost them," Maya went on, "it was like the sun had been snuffed out. But we still had each other. I can't imagine feeling all alone without my twin."

Latta rested her head on Maya's shoulder. "But you did lose your twin." Her gaze flicked to Mikoneh, then away. "He was captured."

Maya's eyes shut. "That's true. I did wonder if I would become completely alone."

"But she's not." Mikoneh leaned back against the velvet

cushions. "Neither are you, Latta. And we're not going to let that change."

A carriage wheel struck a rock, throwing Mikoneh forward. He caught himself, narrowly avoiding ramming his head against Latta's. They blinked at each other, then she slumped backward, laughing.

"It's true, I don't feel nearly as lonely anymore," she said, glancing between the twins. "Not with my friends returned to me."

Maya caught the princess's hand again. "Good. Please know it goes both ways."

Latta started to nod. Shouts outside wrenched the royals' attention to the slowing carriage.

"Stand down," boomed a voice that could only belong to Latta's behemoth protector.

The crack and whistle of a releasing crossbow kicked Mikoneh into action. He flung himself over the princesses, dragging them to the carriage floor. The crash and tinkle of glass was followed with a heavy *thunk*, then Mikoneh jerked upright to glance out the shattered window. As he shifted, shards of glass crunched beneath his boot.

Hooded figures surrounded the carriage along the tree-lined road. Latta's protector fought off several with his glaive. The bladed tip flashed in a strand of sunlight. The sound of drawing swords and rattling armor filled the gloom.

Mikoneh caught his sword hilt, but Maya snatched his arm.

"They're after *you* as well as us," she whispered.

He shrugged her off. "If we stay in here, it'll be easier for them to steal the carriage and drive off with us."

"That crossbow wasn't a hostage tool," she hissed.

"Maybe they only need one of us." He unlatched the door, sprang out onto the snow-crusted road, and drew his blade.

Two hooded figures detached from their fight against Mikoneh's nameless protector to charge him. He brought up his sword and caught the first swing. Gritting his teeth, he summoned fire. Flames raced up his arms, forcing the second attacker off kilter. Mikoneh pressed his advantage, willing the flames to roll along the steel of Fa's sword—not too hot, but intense enough to stave off his enemies.

A quick glance told him two dozen men had ambushed the carriage just inside the eastern wood. The armored knights on horseback were fending off half. That left another dozen.

Not terrible odds.

He swung his flaming sword, and the two attackers backed off—but a third lunged from behind him. At the same moment, another man flung the driver off the carriage's front seat. Before the driver hit the ground, he halted in the air, hovering slightly above the snowy road. Maya emerged from the carriage, a dagger in hand, black hair whipping around her fur-lined cloak. Her golden eyes raged like a storm. She jumped down and stabbed a finger toward the hooded man standing on the driver's bench. Eyes wide, he flew backward, hands scratching at the air for purchase. A shout escaped his lips, then he slammed into a fir tree with a grunt.

Maya winced, then whipped around, seeking her next victim. The nearby fighting had ceased, every head turned toward her. Perhaps they hadn't expected a second burgeoning Elementalist to be inside the carriage, but that seemed odd, unless...

They're not after us. They want Latta.

Mikoneh backed toward the carriage, keeping his blade lifted against any comers. The hooded figures recovered slowly, like a ripple ran through them. Then Mikoneh's two assailants charged him again, both of their swords raised. A quick glance told him half the castle guard was dead, horses scattered.

Contain them fast. No accidents. No mistakes.

He squeezed his sword hilt, willing the ever-present flame within him—fueled by anger and regret—to brighten and grow hotter. The flames licked up his arms, down his sword, and across his shoulders. His vision sharpened, and he could *see* the natural heat blazing in his enemies. He saw other inner fires, fourteen of them—other men, hidden among the bare trees.

He launched forward, throwing his opponents off balance. Flames whipped out from his sword as he swung it, and the two hooded men dodged rather than parried. Wind roared behind him, and one of the hooded men rose into the air with a yelp.

Maya darted around her twin, her hands lifted, guiding the airborne man higher into the trees. Mikoneh focused on the second attacker, but the hooded man backed away, then raced off into the woods.

Others were retreating.

Only three of the castle knights remained upright, but they'd dispatched the remaining attackers. Whoever the enemies were, they weren't common toughs.

Mikoneh spun toward Latta's protector to find two cloaked men down, and one pinned beneath the glaive, alive and quivering. His hood had fallen back, revealing a blessedly human face. Something in Mikoneh's chest loosened. Had he been expecting an undead Mage?

Latta stepped down from the carriage, her breath misting before her face. She strode toward her protector. At the same moment, Mikoneh's armored protector moved from the other side of the carriage. There was a nick on his cheek, oozing blood. Otherwise, he was hale. The man looked Mikoneh and Maya up and down, then lifted his gaze to the figure still suspended in Maya's private wind torrent.

"Handy trick, that." He nodded toward the floating prisoner. "Wish I'd been any good at my element."

Mikoneh doused his fire, studying the man's face closer. "You trained?"

"Yes, but..." The man grimaced. "Can't do more than sense water for digging wells. No spouts. No cleansing."

Maya glanced at the two of them, then turned back to her prisoner. "As fascinated as I am by the topic, I can't hold this fellow much longer. Where do I put him?"

"Down," said the guard, motioning with his sword. "I'll take custody of him."

Latta and her protector approached. Mikoneh managed to return the Songbird Princess's tight smile with what probably looked like a grimace, then he glanced past her to find the quivering prisoner trussed up like a calf bound for market day.

With a creased brow, Maya lowered her prisoner on threads of wind. Sweat beaded her face.

Mikoneh moved up next to her. "Don't tax yourself."

"It's surprisingly difficult to harness wind, especially outside."

He snorted. "Something I don't think you'd have said six months ago."

"No, indeed," she laughed.

The guard and the massive protector bound the second prisoner with thick ropes while Latta and Maya moved to the driver's side to see if he was injured. Mikoneh glanced around for the footman, but the little fellow had vanished.

Adjusting his hold on his blade, Mikoneh rounded the carriage. He came up short, breath catching. The footman was dead. Blood puddled around his chest, and he stared glassy eyed at the winter sky.

"Guards!" He strode toward the corpse, skin crawling. It looked like a stab wound, but something was off. It felt *cold*.

Instinct clawed at him. He summoned flame. A fire spirit sprang into being above his free palm.

The two protectors came around the carriage at a run. The smaller man came up short, swearing. The behemoth moved to Mikoneh's side and stooped.

"It's—" The large man cut off, gagging. He slumped forward, clutching his throat. Foam appeared at the corners of his mouth. The whites of his eyes turned red, like they were filling with blood. Mikoneh found a deep gash in the man's back, as if he'd been stabbed, but no blood poured from the wound.

Mikoneh wrenched back, his flames dancing higher. But he couldn't abandon the man. "Tell me how to help you."

The man waved him off. "Get—back—"

Maya and Latta rounded the carriage from the front. The driver caught up the reins from the ground. The harnessed horses shied, nickering.

"Mikoneh!" Maya shrieked.

He spun, and his flames roared higher. Through the tongues of fire, he caught sight of his guard. The man had changed. Violet water poured from his hands, and his eyes danced with the same eerie light.

"Stand down, Rokahns." The guard's voice sounded as if a chorus of a hundred souls spoke through him at once. "We only need the Songbird Princess today."

Mikoneh narrowed his eyes. "Not on my watch."

"Or mine." Maya slipped in front of Latta. Her hair stirred in a quickening breeze.

The guard snarled. "Two burgeoning Elementalists are nothing to us."

"Stop, Jossen!" Latta screamed.

Mikoneh caught motion in his periphery. He barely lifted his blazing sword in time to block the behemoth's glaive. Bones rattling, Mikoneh stumbled sideways. Violet water shot toward him, and he crashed to his knees to avoid his flames taking the hit.

Maya threw her hands forward, and wind roared across the frozen ground. Snow swirled toward the guard, but he only grinned wider.

The behemoth—Jossen—charged Mikoneh like a bull.

"Jossen, I order you to stop!" Latta shouted, but the giant man looked dead already, head swinging from side to side, eyes bloodied and vacant. He was a mere puppet, just like Brentin. He swung his glaive. Mikoneh narrowly dodged again.

Latta stood back, twisting her ring, her eyes wide and violet-hued in the flashing light. Maya and the nameless guard were caught in a dance of water and wind, cutting and splashing at each other. But Maya was flagging.

Mikoneh felt his own strength bleeding away. The flames were lower, and his knees shook. He had yet to recover his full strength after his captivity.

Can't give up now!

Should he draw out his wings and claws, or had he weakened too much for that to do any good?

The driver scrambled on top of the carriage and brandished a whip. He lashed it, and it fell against Jossen's back with a resounding crack. The behemoth didn't flinch. He merely swung at Mikoneh again, his glaive whooshing through the air.

Latta tackled Jossen from behind.

"Stay back," Mikoneh growled.

Too late. Jossen lifted his glaive over his head to skewer her.

"No!" he screamed.

Latta released the guard, fell from Jossen's back, and landed on the ground, stunned. The glaive missed her.

Mikoneh dropped his sword and summoned more fire, willing it to burn hot enough to melt steel. It blazed blue.

Jossen swung at him again. The vicious-looking curve of the glaive's tip came out of Mikoneh's flames glowing. It rushed past his face, missing him by less than a finger's width.

His back struck a tree.

Maya shrieked.

Tearing his eyes from Jossen's glaive, Mikoneh found his twin wrapped in a coil of water. She was trapped within the liquid, unable to breathe, but she stared at him more in wonder than fear.

The nameless guard circled the watery prison. "Don't kill him, Jossen! We need them alive." Beyond them, Mikoneh found the three castle knights trapped in water just like Maya, all of them writhing and struggling for air.

The giant faltered.

The sound of a crossbow cracked across the air. Its bolt caught the smaller guard in the throat, and the man lurched back, gurgling, clutching at his throat.

The watery prisons exploded, sending droplets across the frozen air.

Horses thundered into sight up the road from deeper in the forest. At their head, riding like a windstorm, rode Lord Crim. His eyes burned with fury. He loaded another bolt into his crossbow. He aimed at Jossen, but the giant guard had fallen to the ground, his strings seemingly cut.

The horses slowed, and Crim brought his stallion to a stop before Latta. "Are you wounded, Princess?"

Latta was still seated on the ground. She shook her head, her tear-stained cheeks glistening in the light of Mikoneh's fire. She couldn't seem to speak.

Mikoneh shook himself free of shock and raced toward Maya. She was strangely calm, kneeling before the body of the nameless guard. Slowing, Mikoneh inched toward the body.

"Not too close," Crim said from right behind him.

Startled, fire sprang into Mikoneh's palm. The lord eyed it, then flashed an approving grin at him. Crim lifted his crossbow and aimed it at the guard.

"Jossen is dead," Crim said.

"I know," Mikoneh said. "He was controlled. By the other guard, maybe."

Crim grunted, then set his finger against the trigger, and released it. The bolt plunged into the guard's skull. Maya looked away with a sob. The body jerked, then fell still. Crim moved closer, then knelt near the head and checked for a pulse.

"Dead." Crim stood up, and turned to Maya. "All right, Princess Mayanaleh?"

She shook her head, swiping at her eyes. "How is Latta?"

"Shaken, like all of you." Crim turned to Mikoneh. "Good thing your flames lit up the sky. My wife was worried when you didn't arrive on time, but I figured you were merely delayed, until my watch reported a fire." He clapped a hand on Mikoneh's shoulder. "Are you wounded?"

"No." Mikoneh found himself staring at the smaller guard's corpse. "Just tired."

Crim squeezed his shoulder. "All of you must remain at my estate tonight. I'll send word to Prince Atlanse of the attack and of your staying over. We won't risk any of you traveling back in the dark." He glanced at the darkening sky. "Come. There's hot food and baths half a league up the road. I'll send my servants to tend to the fallen."

Mikoneh helped Maya to stand, then moved with her toward the carriage. He climbed inside after Latta and Maya while avoiding looking at the bodies littering the forest road, surrounded by crimson-stained snow.

CHAPTER 20

BELOVED CELES

"Yes, fire and wind are both mischievous, but wind loses interest quickly while fire can fixate for days on a single action. This is why mountains weather over ages while forests burn down overnight."

- A Treatise on the Magic of the Hidden Realm by Sariolin the Solitary

When the carriage slowed, Mikoneh stuck his head out the broken window.

Lord Crim's estate boasted a large fortress lit under the power of hundreds of torches. The walls were sturdy and gray, and the parapets were solid, square, and festooned with dormant ivy. The structure was much like Elenth Castle, though the watch was double, judging by the shadows passing along the outer walls.

Glancing toward Crim riding alongside the carriage, Mikoneh found the lord watching him.

"We can't be too careful," Crim said. "The eastern woods are dangerous these days."

"Mages?" asked Mikoneh.

"Not yet. But dark creatures."

An image of the giant toad-like Undrik, creatures who ate magic and conjured nightmares, swelled up in Mikoneh's mind. He shuddered. His two encounters with those creatures had been brief, but...

Don't think about it.

In the bailey, the carriage rolled to a stop outside two wide-open doors flanked by blazing torches. Fire spirits danced and chirped within the flames, then paused and turned toward Mikoneh. He stepped from the carriage, then offered his hand to Latta and Maya in turn. Crim swung from his saddle and escorted the royals to his front door with a smile.

"Come inside and get warm." His hazel eyes flicked to Mikoneh. "Except for you, my good sir. No need for the latter, eh?"

Mikoneh couldn't help but grin. His nerves were easing now that stone walls stood between him and the forest. As he passed the torches, several fire spirits leapt from the flames and settled on his shoulders.

Maya leaned close. "Show off."

"Can you see them?"

"I see twin flames perched on you."

"But not as spirits?"

"No. Just flames."

Mikoneh studied one fire spirit from the corner of his eye. Could they reveal themselves at will even to a non-Fire Elementalist? He really needed to ask more questions.

The interior was a sweeping reception hall lit by chandeliers and sconces. The massive, rectangle-cut stones that made up the thick walls were softened by the forest tapestries covering them. A long carpet cut a line across the center of the room, aiming for a well-lit chamber beyond. Standing before that chamber, Lady Namirsha waited.

She was gowned in gold. Her hair was loose, curling down her back. Her eyes sparkled in the candlelight. She curtsied to the royals, then offered her hand to Crim.

"Welcome back, beloved," she murmured.

Crim kissed her ring-bedecked fingers, then stepped to one side to allow the three royals admittance. As Latta and the twins passed, Namirsha inclined her head to each of them in turn, her expression guarded as she greeted the Songbird Princess. Her diamond earrings sparkled with each movement. Mikoneh dodged her eyes. He had little experience with women, and even less with married ladies. He didn't want to give a false impression that he was a cad, especially with Crim's wife. She was too beautiful to avoid admiring.

The inner chamber was a dining hall, and the table was laden with the usual assortment of Simynshinian fare from roasted meats to creamy soups, steamed vegetables, fresh bread, plump berries, and roasted nuts. The succulent aromas tugged at Mikoneh's senses, and he eagerly took a cushioned seat near the head of the table, across from Latta. Maya took her place beside Mikoneh, and Crim claimed the head. His wife sat two chairs down from her husband, giving way to Latta's rank.

Crim placed a hand to his brow, lifted his head to the vaulted ceiling, and offered a prayer. "Beloved Celes, we offer gratitude for this bounteous meal, for those who have worked to provide it, and for the safety of our guests. Bless Sirinhigha and all who fight for right. Nevertheless, to thee I do yield."

Murmurs of assent rolled down the table.

Mikoneh had expected other nobility to be present, but only servants took up the spaces of the chamber, bustling over to fill goblets, set a last tureen down among the soups, or straighten the edge of the silk tablecloth.

"Regretfully," Maya told Namirsha, "Penn couldn't come tonight. He's otherwise occupied. He asked me to present his apologies."

"I understand. Perhaps next time," Namirsha said.

"If I may ask, who or what are the Celes?" asked Maya. "I've been meaning to inquire. People reference them like Oceaneans do the Nijaal."

Crim glanced up while he filled his bowl with a hearty clam soup. "It seems Seranni didn't give you a well-rounded education, but that shouldn't surprise me. I think she forsook her Simynshinian heritage when she wed Jonatten. Rokahnian tradition was always more of a fascination for her, especially since they embrace female warriors. Her sword instructor was Rokahnian, I believe, but I digress."

"Celes are guardians," said Namirsha. "Saints, you might say. They watch over us, each within their sphere."

"Like gods?" asked Mikoneh. He recalled Ter mentioning the Celes before, but he'd just been rescued from Sathe and hardly recalled that conversation.

"No, not quite gods." Crim set the ladle in the tureen, and plucked up his spoon. "There is only one God in Simynshin."

"Oceana used to believe that," Maya said, "but Fa said they adopted all kinds of gods to help with all their superstitions. Such as the Nijaal."

Crim chuckled. "That sounds exactly right. Oceana has always had something of an identity crisis. Lintha plucked their deities from fae legends for their gods, so Oceana had to do the same."

Mikoneh shifted and glanced at Namirsha. "As a Linthian, which theology do you prefer?"

She smiled. "I like the weight and consistency of Simynshin

far better than my homeland's tendency to pounce on the next popular faith. But personally, I subscribe to no religion."

"My wife is a skeptic," Crim said. "That makes sense, considering how much of a goddess she nearly is."

"Flatterer." Namirsha shook her head, but she looked pleased with the compliment.

Crim laughed, then sipped his soup.

Mikoneh heaped four types of meat onto his plate, then added a few vegetables for good measure. He didn't know what a dragon's diet was meant to be, so all he could do was follow his instinct. It was definitely more carnivorous these days.

"Are there Celes over each element?" asked Maya.

"There's one over all of them combined, I think," Crim said, then shrugged. "If you want to know the details, I'm not the man to ask. Devout as I am, I'm no theologist. I have chosen one Celes to whom I pray, and I let the rest have their province."

Mikoneh swallowed a bite of tender red meat. "About the Spirits Elemental. Maya can see the two fire spirits"—he shrugged one spirit-laden shoulder—"but not as themselves. Only as a flame. Is that because she's my twin, or because they allow her to see them on some level?"

"An excellent question." Crim glanced at his wife and winced. "But perhaps better left for our regular lesson time. I promised my dear wife we'd not bore her guests." His gaze darted to Princess Latta, then away.

"I don't mind," Latta said, not looking at Namirsha even once. "I have a fascination with the Spirits Elemental as well—and I can see the two flames on your shoulders, Mikoneh, so it isn't only your twin."

"Very well," Crim said. "I'll indulge this one question, but then we should discuss other subjects."

"Such as the attack on the road," Latta said. "I think we

shouldn't bury that just to be polite." Her gaze flicked to the hostess of the feast, her mouth tight, then she looked away.

The atmosphere dimmed, despite the dancing flames in the chandelier overhead. Mikoneh pushed a cabbage-like sprout across his plate, mixing the buttery liquid with the juices from a porkchop. "There's that, too."

Crim cleared his throat. "Very well. First, the matter of fire spirits. Yes, they can be seen by *all* as a flame—but it's one of the rare exceptions, since we can see fire naturally. Each element manifests itself in some way, like Princess Maya and her rather lively hair."

Mikoneh glanced at his twin. Her long tresses *were* still rippling in a private breeze.

"But I thought our eyes manifested it," he said.

"That's only one manifestation—internally. The spirits like to show off. They want to be *seen* in some way, too. So, they often present themselves. Fire spirits are the most...theatrical. They will themselves into visible fire in order to be acknowledged, when they wish to be."

"What does earth do?" asked Mikoneh. "And water?"

"It varies," Crim said. "Sometimes, plants perk up around an Earth Elementalist. Or grass grows under their feet. Or they smell like verdure. With water, it's more subtle, which tends to be the way of Water Elementalists. Perhaps it rains more around them, or you may not *notice* them standing nearby. Water goes hand in hand with mirrors, storms, and stealth." He glanced at his wife. "Right?"

"Right," she said.

Mikoneh's mind flashed to the nameless guard wielding Hollow-tainted water. "Do any particular Elementalist types lean more toward darkness than others?"

"No," Crim said. "I've seen good and bad come from the use of any Spirit Elemental. Each can be used for tremendous destruction, or for great good. Few are born with the strength to do either. But you're both—"

"Rokahns, yeah. We know." Mikoneh glanced at Maya. She'd dried off before they'd reached Crim's estate, thanks to her wind magic—but she could've drowned. Powerful bloodline or not, they were both still novices.

She looked up from her plate and smiled at him. "Stop fretting."

"It's my right to fret as much as it is yours," he said. "That Mage could've killed you."

"But he didn't." Maya glanced down the table toward the servants, then met her twin's eyes again. "Actually...it was odd."

"What was?"

She leaned forward, her eyes twinkling. "I could *breathe* in the water."

"You could wha... How? Is that—is water your second element?"

Maya shrugged. "I don't know. But I could."

"It's your blood," Latta said. "Uncle Owen once told me —" She cut off at Mikoneh's expression, then laughed. "I'm sorry. That must've surprised you. He's not really my uncle, but I've always called him that."

"You've said it before. I'd just forgotten. Go on." He set his fork down.

"Well, he said that dragons can breathe underwater. You can open gills"—she tapped the skin beneath her right ear—"and swim for several turns. Perhaps even days."

"I didn't know that," Crim said. "Extraordinary. You'll need to test its limits, Your Highnesses."

Mikoneh nodded, his thoughts flitting through the possibilities. Gills suggested no underwater limits—and Maya had done it in human form, not even as a small dragon. He needed to speak with Jensirin when they returned to Elenth Castle.

Mikoneh rubbed his forehead with his hand. The weight of his sleepless nights, his malnourishment, and this most recent attack pressed against his frame. Would he ever feel rested again?

THEY SPENT the rest of dinner discussing the details of the attack without shedding any new light on the experience. Afterward, Crim led the twins to a suite all their own while Namirsha deposited Latta in a private suite in the same wing. At their door, the lord of the keep assured the twins he would station guards outside their door and on the grounds below their windows.

"Nothing unwelcome will come into my keep while I draw breath," Crim said, "but it never hurts to be cautious."

"Thank you, my lord," Mikoneh said.

"We're very grateful," added Maya.

Crim's eyes twinkled. "You'll thank me more profusely for the baths, I think. They should be in each of your bedrooms, ready and waiting, with soap, oils, and the softest towels in Simynshin."

"Sounds lovely," Maya sighed. "Goodnight, Lord Crim."

The merchant lord bowed. "A pleasure, Princess." He caught Mikoneh's eye, offered up a friendly grin, then retreated with a snip of the door.

Maya drifted over to a set of furniture clustered around the center of the common room. She flopped down into a wing-back armchair crammed with pillows.

Frowning, Mikoneh strode to the chair and crouched down before it. "You're sure you're not hurt anywhere?"

She nodded, keeping her eyes shut. "I'm shaken, but the food helped."

He caught her wrist and squeezed. "You'd tell me if it was anything more, right?"

"Promise."

"Good." He stood up. "Then I'm going to take that hot bath. You should, too."

"I *am* looking forward to those soft towels." She shoved off the chair and rose, smoothing her skirts. A tear in the fabric caught her fingers, but she didn't seem to care.

"Well, then." Mikoneh started for the nearest bedroom door and peeked inside. Steam rose from a wide tub set over a plush rug. A soft pink robe and matching nightgown were laid out beside it on a stand, along with an assortment of colored bottles. "I think this is your room." He moved to the next door and found the same situation within, but the robe and night-shirt were light gray. "Yeah, this one's definitely mine."

Maya pranced to the first door, peeked inside, and sighed like she could already feel the hot water on her skin. "It looks heavenly. Goodnight, Mikoneh." She drifted inside and shut the door.

"'Night." He stepped into his borrowed chamber, letting the steam curl around his face. The heat was welcome, though it didn't change his body temperature. It only promised cleanliness, which was more than enough.

Stripping down, he brushed away the two clinging fire spirits, then entered the tub. He sank into the water with a long exhalation, settled back, and drifted toward sleep.

"Awfully rude not to say hello first."

Mikoneh yelped and shot forward, splashing water across the rug.

Standing before him, draped in his usual gray, stood Minno.

CHAPTER 21

AT YOUR DOORSTEP

*"Meanwhile, water is more solitary—a trait I well relate to—
and stand-offish. It doesn't socialize. Scholars have lumped earth
in with water as a result of both being quiet, but where water is
indifferent, earth is merely observant. Its shyness is often
mistaken for aloofness."*

- A Treatise on the *Magic of the Hidden Realm* by Sariolin the Solitary

"**G**et out."

"I was here first," Minno said in level tones.

"Doesn't matter. Out. This is my room, my suite." Heat rolled down Mikoneh's arm, and he allowed flame to bloom above his palm.

Minno eyed the fire spirit with his usual blasé expression. "Do you really think you can fight me with fire?"

"I'm willing to try."

"Stubborn. And foolish. I would reconsider."

"Then reconsider," Mikoneh growled.

Minno moved from the relative shadows near the four-post

bed, his gray eyes burning in the light from the nearby brazier. His steps were slow and deliberate, sending Mikoneh's senses skittering toward self-defense.

"You're letting your titles go to your head," Minno said.

"I am not." Mikoneh flushed at his childish retort. Why did this *creature* rankle him so much? "Why are you here? Weren't you with Owenekiras?"

"He sent me away—"

"I don't blame him."

"—to protect you."

The crackle of the logs in the hearth filled the silence.

"Liar," Mikoneh snarled.

"It's true."

"After the stunt you pulled? You're behind the attack tonight, too, I'd wager anything. Well, sorry to have to inform you, but your pet Mage is dead."

"I have no pet Mages." Minno neared the edge of the tub.

Skin crawling, Mikoneh reached for a towel, flung himself from the water, and wrapped the soft cloth around his waist. "You'll understand if I don't believe you."

"Believe what you want, but I rarely use the same trick twice." Minno hesitated. "Except for one."

Mikoneh stared at the boy, trying to comprehend the oddity that was Minno. "Whether you really believe Owenekiras sent you here to protect Maya and me or not, we don't want your help. We don't want you anywhere near us."

"You think I desire this arrangement?" The gray boy rounded the tub, coming closer. His tones remained flat, yet something deadly curled beneath his level voice. "You think I enjoy watching you steal what is mine?"

"Then take it—whatever it is!" Mikoneh's voice rose, then cracked. "None of this is what I wanted either!"

They stared at each other, Minno the portrait of indifference tinged with something lethal. Mikoneh breathing heavily, blood roaring in his ears. Then Mikoneh scrubbed at his face with one hand. Weariness pressed down on him.

"Please go away."

"I can't. Owen asked me to stay."

A growl was the only answer Mikoneh could muster. Frustration clawed at his chest. He lifted his head and glowered at Minno. Drawing a breath, he tried to collect himself. "Why bother doing what he asks? You betrayed him once already."

"Which is why I need to atone." Minno shuffled his feet, the only indication he might be feeling anything at all. "Turning you over to the Mages was a mistake. One I would repeat if it served me, but it...didn't."

"How penitent of you."

Minno offered him a slow blink. "Not really."

"It was— I was being sarcastic. You're really strange, you know that?"

Minno shrugged. "You think I care?"

"Evidently not." Mikoneh inched around the far side of the tub and snatched up the gray robe. He wrapped it around his body and tied off the waist, relieved to feel less exposed before this oddity. "Listen. I'm perfectly safe in Lord Crim's estate. So, go away. Tell Owenekiras we're fine." He eyed Fa's sword leaning against the nearby wall.

"You mentioned an attack," Minno said.

"Which we *handled*. We're fine."

"This is the second attack in a matter of days." Minno frowned. "It bodes ill."

"So do you. Go away."

"Were they after you, or your twin, or both of you—or Princess Latta?"

"I—I don't know. I thought Latta, at first. They said as much. But they were Mages—and they tried to drown Maya."

"That would be foolish of them. Mages ought to know dragons can breathe underwater."

"So we found out," Mikoneh muttered. "Why do you care?"

"Because..." Minno drifted toward the bed, then he pulled himself onto the mattress and hung his legs off the edge. "Why do you think the Mages want you?"

"Because I'm a dragon?" Mikoneh let heat lick at his tones.

Minno gave him another slow blink. "Do you think they snatch up dragons left and right?" He paused. "They used to, of course, but that was another age. Literally."

"I can't imagine dragons are that easily captured."

"True. Only young ones, on their own—but they are usually well protected."

"Well, then. There you have it. We haven't been protected until recently. So now we're fine. Go away."

"You *were* protected, until Sathe destroyed those protections."

Mikoneh fell still. Memories of the burning cottage lanced through his mind, then Sathe's claim that someone was out to ruin Mikoneh, but he shoved everything back. "What's your point? Trying to emphasize my royal standing? Thank you, but I already know."

Minno exhaled through his nose. "You mean you've never considered why *you*?"

"Of course I have!" Mikoneh raked a hand through his hair. "Because I'm a prince. And Maya's a princess."

"Maya isn't as useful to them."

"I—Why?" He scowled. "Stop asking questions and explain yourself."

"One last question: Why you and not your father?"

Mikoneh threw out his hands. "Like I *know*? Maybe because he's huge and powerful and terrifying!"

"There's one more reason." Minno's calm was infuriating.

"Care to elaborate?"

The boy shrugged. "You're bondless."

The simple words trickled in slowly. Mikoneh caught and weighed them. "You mean…a bonded dragon can't be forced to connect to a Mage."

"Precisely. And female bonds are different."

"How?"

"The fundamentals are distinctive. They cannot be controlled. The bond is only formed through friendship. It cannot be tainted, cannot be coerced. Otherwise, the Mage Queen wouldn't use her generals to capture and control dragons. She would do it herself. Female dragons are different."

Something loosened in Mikoneh's chest. Maya was safe—at least from that fate.

"That is," Minno said, "until the Mages manage to properly corrupt bonding magic to make it serve them better. It's been done before, though never perfected."

Knots formed beneath Mikoneh's ribcage. "You're so reassuring."

"I don't mean to be."

"Again, sarcasm."

"Ah." Minno scooted himself further onto the bed. "Princess Latta is a different matter. She's no dragon nor an Elementalist. It must be her voice they want."

Mikoneh scowled. "I think they already have it."

"Do you? Why?"

He explained about Latta's recent illness and subsequent inability to sing as she had before.

Minno rubbed his chin while he listened, then nodded. "It stands to reason. Mages favor stealing and corrupting pure magic. It feeds their war and their sadism simultaneously."

Mikoneh shuddered, recalling Sathe's icy touch. He shoved

that back, too. "If you have to stick around, can you focus on protecting Latta instead of me? That would be some peace of mind. Assuming we can trust you."

"You act as though I can't handle both." Minno slid from the mattress and landed lightly on the floor. "Don't worry so much. I'm not doing this for you, but I won't fail when Owenekiras is counting on me."

"He was before, you know."

Lines appeared between Minno's brows. "Yes. He was." He tugged on his gray tunic, straightening it. "Get some rest, Mikoneh Rokahn. The storm is at your doorstep. It will break soon."

Chapter 22

At the Edge of a Battlefield

"As for the elusive fifth spirit, that of spirit itself, there is not much we can state definitively. Most is guesswork."

- *A Treatise on the Magic of the Hidden Realm* by Sariolin the Solitary

Despite Minno's counsel, Mikoneh spent the night tossing under his covers, trying to stave off dreams of his recent captivity. Worst was a dream about the village he'd been forced to massacre. He woke up sobbing and wiping his hands against his nightshirt, though there was no blood.

At last, dawn broke, stormless but gray. Snow had dusted the world outside, covering the dense trees surrounding Lord Crim's keep.

Dressed and groomed, Mikoneh stood for a long time at the wide window in his borrowed bedroom. He knew he needed to return to Elenth Castle, but that would require a second carriage ride through the forest...

No. It didn't. Couldn't he fly back?

Maya could, too. But that left Latta behind. She wasn't a dragon. He frowned, trying to work around that difficulty. Could he carry her? Surely, his body heat could keep them both warm.

Something to discuss, at least.

A knock sounded at the door.

"Come in."

Maya swept inside, gowned in crimson. Her dark hair lay long and silken against the fabric. "Isn't it stunning? Lady Namirsha lent it to me."

He smiled. "It suits you."

Maya twirled. Wind tossed her hair rather elegantly, and the skirt flared out as though a breeze was showing it off. Which it no doubt was. She halted, facing him, and studied his torn tunic. "You don't have a change of clothes."

"I'll survive until we get back to the castle. Promise."

She nodded to the open door. Her voice dropped. "Hilker arrived this morning, bringing Prince Atlanse."

Mikoneh tensed. "Were they that..." He trailed off. Of course, they were worried. Atlanse's daughter might've been captured or killed, and the foreign royalty in his charge had also been threatened. "Well, let's go assure them we're fine."

"Oh." Maya hesitated. "Minno is here, too." A flash of anger brightened her golden eyes.

"Yeah. I know." Mikoneh caught her arm and tugged her after him. "Play nice for now." They moved into the common room to find the Crown Prince of Simynshin standing with his face to the marble mantle above the fireplace. Hilker was at his side, and Lord Crim was present, looking a bit out of sorts, his auburn hair tousled. He was still wearing his sleeping robe.

Despite that, Crim turned a bright smile on the twins. "Good morrow, my dragonish friends. Sleep well?"

"Could anyone, after last night?" Prince Atlanse asked the

flames. He turned around, revealing his own dark circles. Yesterday, he'd been caught in important meetings all day long, and according to Latta, he'd asked Hilker to attend him, presumably to carry more weight against his political foes. What Hilker's actual position and influence was, Mikoneh hadn't yet identified—but it had to be more than Master Wind Elementalist.

The crown prince lingered on Mikoneh's face for a moment, then he nodded as if to himself.

"Princess Latta is fine," Mikoneh said, "all things considered. She wasn't injured."

"I understand I have you to thank for that," Atlanse said in strained tones.

"Mikoneh threw himself over us to protect us from the initial attack," Maya said, her eyes glittering with a quiet challenge. "He then fended off the ambushers outside."

Atlanse blinked, then batted the air. "I don't mean to sound ungrateful. I am. Truly." He rubbed his temple with two fingers. "It's been a long night."

Mikoneh grunted agreement. Motion caught his attention, and he turned to find Minno sitting cross-legged on the floor near a crushed velvet chaise lounge. The gray boy was helping his mallard duck preen its feathers. Minno looked up at him and offered a solemn nod.

Hilker waggled his fingers at the boy. "He claims you agreed to let him stay."

Caught between a glower and a grimace, Mikoneh shrugged. "I don't know how to get rid of him. I'm open to suggestions."

No one spoke.

"That's what I thought." Mikoneh shoved his thumbs into his belt. "Presumably, you've brought a full contingent to escort us back to the castle, and we're not to leave said castle grounds again under any circumstances. I won't fight you on that point—except when it comes to flying lessons."

Maya bobbed a hasty nod. "Right."

Atlanse blew out a breath. "I appreciate your good sense… but…"

"There's something else?" asked Mikoneh.

"It's just Hilker here assures me that locking you up in my father's castle will keep you from doing what you've come to do, and likewise, I need to keep Latta visible. Like bait." His lips curled down.

Mikoneh slid a glance toward the Wind Master. "Hilker's not wrong. My freedom will make things easier."

"Besides, Your Royal Highness," Crim spoke up, "the Winter Tourney begins in mere weeks. He can't miss that. Neither can the princesses."

"No." Atlanse tapped his finger against the sword hilt hanging at his hip. "No, they can't."

"I *won't* let anyone hurt your daughter, Your Royal Highness," Mikoneh said.

Atlanse grimaced. "I appreciate the sentiment—and your valor—but you're out of your depth, as we all are, where Dark Mages are concerned."

"He and Princess Maya handled themselves beautifully last night," Crim said. "Especially Maya. You should've seen the way she went at those Mages. If they'd been any less skilled, they would all be captives by now."

Maya's face lit up like a Nijaalin shrine at festival time. "It's all thanks to Hilker."

Atlanse glanced at the Wind Master. "Yes, he knows what he's about."

Hilker shrugged. "The aptitude of the student is important."

Crim coughed. "Yes. About that." He glanced at Mikoneh.

"While I'd love to continue your instruction, I've had a chat with Master Minno and—"

"No." Mikoneh folded his arms. "Absolutely not."

"Hear me out." Crim raised his hands in a placating motion. "I'll be present for the lessons going forward, and I'll offer my insights as may be helpful, but Minno is a better teacher and a Master Elementalist. He can instruct you better than I can—in both of your elements."

Flames licked at Mikoneh's insides. "I already told Owenekiras no." He shot a glare at Minno. "I don't trust him."

Minno's slow blink was his only statement.

"That's why I'll be supervising," Crim said. "I swear you'll never be left alone with him."

Frustration bubbled up in Mikoneh's chest. Frustration and fear. But he needed to learn his elements. Both of them. And if Owenekiras was this insistent...

"Fine. But I want my protest to go on record."

"Noted," Crim said. "And now, breakfast awaits. I think it might help with the general mood, don't you?" He cast his question toward Maya.

"Oh, yes," she said. "Mikoneh is at his worst before a meal."

He bit down a petulant reply, aware it would only prove her case. Instead, he fell back, allowing Crim to lead Maya from the room, with Atlanse and Hilker next. He hung back until Minno set his duck on the floor and climbed to his feet, his movements unhurried.

"Don't forget about protecting Latta," Mikoneh growled.

Minno blinked at him, then stooped to scoop up the mallard. Duck let out a patient quack, and Minno started for the door. "As I said before, I can handle both. Besides, aren't the two of you going to be wedded? The more time you spend together, the easier for all who seek to protect you."

"And capture us," Mikoneh muttered.

"That, too." Minno nudged the door open a little more, then motioned for Mikoneh to exit first. Spine prickling, Mikoneh adhered, putting several feet between himself and the ancient child.

"I never wanted any of this," Mikoneh said.

"Then walk away," Minno said flatly.

"I can't. Not now. The Mages will still find me—thanks to you in particular." He glanced back to find Minno stopped in the corridor. The boy was frowning at the floor, ignoring the duck nibbling at his sleeve.

"Yes, that's true," Minno whispered, his shoulders drooping. "There is no going backward." He looked lost and broken, like a small child at the edge of a battlefield.

Pity squirmed through Mikoneh. He stepped toward Minno. What had caused the boy to become so warped? So cruel? Mikoneh lifted his hand to rest it on Minno's shoulder, but the boy blinked and lifted his head. Their eyes met.

"If you want a hug, try your sister," Minno said. "I don't care for them."

Mikoneh jerked back and snapped his arm to his side. "You're mental, you know that?" He spun away and marched up the hall, ignoring the boy behind him.

"Yes," came a soft, monotone voice. "I know that."

Atlanse had brought none of his entourage, but all of his personal guard. After a quiet breakfast—where only Crim, Namirsha, and Maya made polite conversation—Atlanse announced he was ready to return to Elenth Castle. Latta stood at once, and Mikoneh was right on her heels.

"I'm sorry your visit was ruined, Your Highnesses," Crim

said, standing at the front doors of his keep, one arm tucked around his wife's waist. "I hope we can settle matters enough to allow for a more leisurely dinner next time."

"I look forward to it," Mikoneh said. "As it is, your efforts weren't lacking at all. Thank you for your hospitality." He bowed, then bowed again to Namirsha without meeting her eyes. "And to you, my lady."

As he rose, she brushed her fingers against his arm. "Come again soon, Prince of Rokahn. We look forward to your company, and that of your delightful sister." She smiled warmly at Maya, never glancing at Latta.

"Except for the incident on the road, I've had a lovely time," Maya assured her. "And since that wasn't technically in your home, I don't think either of you should feel ashamed for what happened."

Crim shrugged. "Even so, we feel responsible." He turned back to Mikoneh. "If those flying lessons go well, do consider dropping by unannounced sometime. We're always open to entertaining."

"Indeed," Namirsha said.

"Thank you. I'll consider that." Mikoneh inclined his head again, then gently pulled Maya with him down the front steps and into one of two royal carriages. Atlanse and Latta sat in the other. Two dozen men-at-arms flanked the carriages. Minno perched on the driver's seat of the twins' conveyance, acting as their personal protector.

Moments later, the carriages rolled with a crunch across the bailey, over the bridge with a clatter, and out onto the forest road. Sitting across from Mikoneh, Maya peeled back the curtain to stare out into the trees.

"If it weren't for the Mages, we'd be having a lovely time," she said.

Mikoneh settled back against his seat. "You would, maybe. I'm exhausted just thinking about another dance lesson."

"You like dancing, admit it."

"I love flying—dancing is merely a counterfeit."

She snorted. "For most people, it's as close as they come."

"Like I said, counterfeit."

She rolled her eyes. "I hope Penn is well. He's barely come up for air since he discovered the Royal Library."

"Leave him to it," Mikoneh said. "He's helping in his way."

"By burying his nose in a book?"

"By studying Simynshinian history, tradition, economics, and who-knows-what-else. Leave the book wizard to his research, and we'll thank him sooner or later for supplying us with some worthy tidbit."

"I just hope he's taking care of himself. He keeps getting wet."

"He'll be fine."

A wheel struck a rock, jostling the twins. They righted themselves, then Maya smoothed her dress out.

"Do you think Jensirin is better today?" she asked.

"I hope so. I don't want him to push himself too hard."

"He seems very kind."

"He is."

They didn't speak again until they rolled into Elenth Castle's bailey. The knights dismounted and flanked the path to the front doors. Prince Atlanse led the way, his daughter on his arm. The twins followed, and Minno and Hilker took up the rear.

Inside, warmth embraced the company. Mikoneh shed his cloak and passed it off to a servant, but his eye fell on the figure standing ahead of them. The Mage ambassador, draped in dark robes.

"What do you want, Karrad?" asked Atlanse, not disguising his annoyance.

"I've not had a chance to be formally introduced to the royal twins from Rokahn, Your Highness," the Mage said in a low, simpering voice. "I came to rectify that."

"Introductions were made at table," Atlanse said.

"Yes. Generally." Karrad slithered forward, his smile stretched taut, his skin deathly pale. "I had hoped for an audience with—my lord and lady."

Every muscle in Mikoneh's body tensed. His stomach flipped. "Sorry," he said, willing his voice to stay level. "Our schedule is packed today."

"Ah, then perhaps tomorrow." Karrad's eyes trailed up and down each twin in turn, making Mikoneh's flesh crawl. "I know Queen Feresse is eager to meet with you as well. How shall I include our names on your schedule?"

"Speak with me," Hilker said.

Karrad's thin smile flickered. "Ah. Wonderful." He took a step back. "I'll inquire of the queen when she would like an audience, and we shall discuss our possibilities." He inclined his head and backed away with swift efficiency. Soon he vanished down the corridor.

Mikoneh narrowed a look on Hilker. "You have a special way with Mages, I see."

Hilker snorted. "That one, maybe. He doesn't like me—I don't like him."

"I find it odd that he's arranging the queen's schedule," Maya said.

"I noted that, too," Mikoneh said.

"Yes." Atlanse tapped his sword hilt with one finger. "Irritating, and rather alarming."

"I'll speak with the king if you like," said Hilker.

"No," Atlanse said. "You'd just end up arguing with Lord

Father again. I'll mention it to him, for all the good it will supply." His tone was a faint growl.

"Shall I handle the ambassador?" asked Minno.

Every eye rested on him. Silence prevailed for several heartbeats.

"That's not a good plan," Atlanse said.

"Not to be contrary," Hilker muttered, "but I think it might be brilliant."

Mikoneh studied Minno's non-expression. "How would you go about that?"

Minno's eyes narrowed marginally. "I have ways."

"We're not there yet," Atlanse insisted. "Master Minno, please refrain from doing anything within this castle beyond what Owenekiras has asked of you."

The gray boy's owl blink was even slower than usual. "No eating then?"

Atlanse's grimace became a scowl. "I think you can puzzle out the nuances." He tipped his head, then held out his arm. "Come, Latta."

The princess hesitated, then glided to her father's side. She glanced at Mikoneh and Maya. "Perhaps I'll see you for supper."

"Come to our suite," Maya said. "I'll request the food to be sent there."

Latta's smile deepened. "Thank you, Maya."

Father and daughter moved off, taking most of the crown prince's knights with them. Hilker remained behind, picking something from his teeth with his pinky nail.

"What was that about?" Mikoneh asked his twin.

She rolled her eyes. "Why are you men so thick? She wants to visit Akonn. I provided an opportunity."

"Oh." Mikoneh shrugged. "How you expect me to pick up on that from what you said..." He shook his head and strode toward the nearest passage, aiming for their suite. "I think we should forgo dance lessons today. I want to see Jensirin—we thick men should stick together after all—unless you're coming, too."

Maya snorted, then pranced after him. Hilker followed.

"Vomm won't like it," Maya said.

"I don't really care," Mikoneh replied curtly.

As they headed for their rooms, his mind sorted through the puzzle pieces he held so far. Latta's song, the Mage attacks, the castle politics... With everything, the picture was still vague. He didn't know enough to suspect anyone of spying. He needed to move around more—meet more people—even if that meant visiting the queen and her rather attentive foreign ambassador.

CHAPTER 23

RIDER AND DRAGON

"We know that spirit of spirit was the first of the Elemental types, and from it the rest were born. We know that the first wielder, one of the Five born first upon Sirinhigha, was crafted from the soul material of spirit essence. We know that the element manifests rarely, and only when the wielder is ready. Almost no Spirit Elementalist is born with the gift. It comes later, and thus, is almost always a secondary aspect."

- *A Treatise on the Magic of the Hidden Realm* by Sariolin the Solitary

Akonn was awake and speaking with Jensirin, who sat in a chair beside the captain's bed. Both shifted to rise when Maya poked her head inside.

Alarmed, she rushed in, flapping her hands. "Don't stand," she ordered. "Either of you."

They froze, then settled back.

Satisfied, she drifted to the foot of the bed to assess Akonn's color. "How do you feel?"

"Better, thank you."

"Still weak as a newborn phoenix," Jensirin said over him, "I think his wound tore in his sleep."

"I was afraid that might happen," she sighed. "I'll brew a tea that will help relax you." She glanced over her shoulder to find Mikoneh leaning beside the door, looking content to stay there and hold up the wall. "Make yourself useful and boil me some hot water, O Master Elementalist."

He snorted. "Not a *master*. Not yet." He shoved off the wall and moved to the bedroom hearth. Servants were good about supplying fresh water and herbs. Mikoneh swung a cauldron over the embers, and all at once the flames leapt up, eager to see their dragon friend.

A smile tugged at Maya's lips. She had Akonn lay on his side, then she shifted the bandages. Luckily, she'd been able to keep infection from setting in, and the captain's coloring *was* much better. Still, he wasn't recovering as fast as she liked.

She caught up her herb knife and sliced away the bandages to change them, then let her gaze slide to Jensirin. He watched her hand movements, his eyes intent. Her fingers fumbled, but she pressed her lips together and concentrated on her task.

"Did something happen?" asked Akonn, his voice muffled from the way he was laying. "You both seem more grim than usual."

"We were attacked last night on the road," Mikoneh said, brushing his hands off. "We weren't hurt—but the Mage and his puppet didn't fare so well."

Maya winced. "Neither did the castle guards." She bent close to Akonn's bare back to dab away the crusted ointment ahead of applying more. "We should send something to their families."

"I'll ask Crim to see to that," Mikoneh said. "He'll know what's appropriate."

Akonn cursed under his breath. "Two attacks in close succession. They seem desperate."

"Well," Maya said, "we spoiled their plans. They're improvising."

"True."

"Water's boiled," said Mikoneh.

Maya glanced at the roiling cauldron. "You know, you might actually be useful to keep around."

Mikoneh rolled his eyes, but he couldn't wipe away his smile entirely. That was heartening. He was coming out of himself.

"Could you—"

"Fill the teapot, I know." Ignoring the ladle, Mikoneh hefted the cauldron and skillfully poured water into the delicate porcelain container. He returned the cauldron to the flames, sniffed at the various dried herbs, and started stuffing them into the strainer.

Maya's eyebrows lifted. "I'm impressed." She turned back to Akonn to continue cleaning the wound. "You could make a decent healer, Mikoneh."

He scoffed above the clatter of a teacup and saucer. "Don't try to recruit me. I only know enough to get by."

"That's more than a start," Maya said.

Jensirin leaned forward. "You have healer's hands, Princess Mayanaleh."

She promptly dropped her cloth. Heat crept up her face. "Uh—thank you. That's... Thank you, Jensirin."

He nodded, then leaned back. His eyes shifted to track Mikoneh crossing the room, teacup rattling in his hand.

"I hope it's not too potent," Mikoneh said, setting it on the stand. "Or too sweet. I'm not good at measuring honey."

"That's true," Maya said with a grimace. "I hope you're as

patient as you look, Captain Akonn." The aroma coming from the cup *was* strong.

The wounded man chuckled. "We'll find out, I suppose."

Maya applied fresh ointment, then rewrapped the wound. Finished, she helped him sit upright, handed him the teacup, and sat down. A wind spirit swept a strand of hair from her face. Mikoneh had gone back to the table, to finish cleaning up the herbs, but now he drifted around the bed to join Jensirin.

"How are you?" he asked the dragon lord.

Jensirin glanced at Mikoneh, then away. "Better today."

"Good." Mikoneh brushed his fingers against Jensirin's shoulder, then drew back. "Do you want to teach today, or do you need more time?"

"I will teach." Jensirin rose and towered over Mikoneh. "Have you eaten?"

"Yes."

The dragon lord glanced at Maya. "Will you join us?"

"Certainly." She slipped off the mattress. "We should leave Akonn to relax."

Akonn bobbed a slow nod, licking his lips. "It's already working."

"Good." She plucked up the half-drunk teacup and set it on the stand. "Don't fight it. Let your body heal." She brushed her skirts straight, then moved toward the bedroom door. Excitement bubbled in her chest. She ached to learn more about her dragon traits, heritage, and—well, anything else. And she definitely didn't mind observing the teacher.

Jensirin and Mikoneh followed her into the common room.

"Are we flying again today?" Maya asked.

Jensirin shook his head. "We should discuss—"

"Bonds." Mikoneh's tone was firm.

The dragon lord hesitated. Then he nodded. "If you like."

"Please," Mikoneh said. "I think it's important. Minno seemed to think so, too."

"Very well." Jensirin motioned to the settee. "Sit."

"What were you going to teach us?" asked Maya, shooting her twin a reproachful glance.

"Dragon traits and tendencies," Jensirin answered, "since you will begin to notice them in yourself more and more, with your dragon blood awakened. But bond magic may be more essential." He eased himself into the nearest wingback chair.

The twins took the settee, and Maya adjusted her skirts around her feet. Mikoneh sat back, rigid, tense. His jaw was set in a hard line. Studying the haunted look that was bright in his eyes again, Maya's heart twisted.

Jensirin stared into the hearth for a long moment. When he spoke, his voice was barely above a whisper. "In the beginning, dragon bonds were formed for warfare, so that dragons and their human riders could communicate better in battle. As a result of that magical connection, the dragon and his bonded can also feel each other's pain and emotions."

Maya settled back to listen, trying to focus on the words rather than the tacit pain that swirled between Jensirin and Mikoneh. That they both felt it, she had no doubt. Just as she had no doubt that they would never address it directly. Not with her there. Their past with the Mages haunted them both.

The dragon lord launched into an explanation that painted pictures in her mind of dragons in air battles, belching fire and wind while men rode on their backs.

A bond was a special soul link between rider and dragon, allowing for a connection that protected and enhanced both. The human—or fae—could tap into dragon traits while the dragon was shielded from a type of magic that drove dragonkind mad. It was of mutual benefit.

"Those bonds were first formed through a blood link,"

Jensirin said. "They were appropriately called war bonds. From them, a new magic was born. In times of peace, bonds are still forged between those with compatible souls—but it has become rarer. Finding your true bonded is difficult."

"Minno said that female dragon bonds are different from male bonds," Mikoneh said.

Jensirin folded his hands on his lap. "Just as a brotherhood is different from a sisterhood, the two bonds are as distinct as your two sexes. That's not to say one is lesser than the other, or that they aren't in many ways similar—but females are more resistant to forced bonds. Without mutual affection, the bond frays and breaks. In the rare few cases where a successful female bond was forced—the dragon died almost immediately."

Maya's mouth fell open. "I could *die*?"

"Only if someone tried to force a bond—which is rare. The Mages ceased long ago to attempt the process. Male dragons are easier to subjugate and maintain. It is a...slower breaking. Though it usually ends in death or soul imprisonment all the same."

Maya's chest panged. "Like with you."

"Yes." Jensirin's voice was barely audible.

Mikoneh jumped up and began to pace, looking like a caged animal. Maya's pain dug deeper, rooting around the swell of helplessness in her stomach.

"It's so awful," she whispered.

"It doesn't have to be," Jensirin said in stronger tones. His eyes followed Mikoneh. "A bond in its natural form is beautiful."

"Can bonds be formed between a human man and a female dragon?" asked Maya.

"No. It is exclusive to gender—except for the matebond."

"Matebond?" Maya pressed her palms together.

"That is the common term for the romantic bond usually

formed between two dragons, but there have been exceptions —such as with your blood parents."

Maya's mind skittered to an image of Owenekiras and his deceased wife. Rathana. Mother. "They were matebonded?"

"Indeed. It is possible to matebond with a human. There is a kind of soul ritual involved. But the dragon has most of the say in that happening, so the Dark Mages struggle to exploit it. It has been forced, but the results were...unpleasant for the Mage. They haven't tried it since."

"Good," growled Mikoneh, twisting to pace the other way.

Maya swallowed. "What happens when...when the mate-bond ends? Like with Owenekiras's."

Jensirin fell still. "I do not know. Could he mate again? Perhaps. Will he? I cannot say. Your father's bond with Lady Rathana should have extended her life for many years, but it could not make her immortal."

The twins fell silent. Mikoneh moved back to the settee and flopped down. He reached for Maya's wrist, caught it, and squeezed. Maya swallowed hard. Speaking with those who'd known their parents—both the adoptive and blood connec-tions—brought a wave of choking emotions and a strange creeping chill. She ached to know more, to put together a picture of Rathana, happy with Owenekiras, in company with Jonatten and Seranni. All four of them—friends.

At the same time, her mind shied away from the image. Those days were gone. Only one of the four still survived, and he was almost untouchable.

Not forever. Maya was determined to come to know Owenekiras Rokahn, to see inside him, and come to love him as she did Fa and Mama.

Jensirin reached into his robes. He withdrew two *korta* fruits. "Eat."

Maya took hers, then hesitated. She'd drawn out wings, but

not claws. Focusing on her fingers, she sought out a sensation and—there. Claws slid over her human nails, black and deadly sharp. *Dragon.* She was a dragon. It felt so right.

Or is the better word dragoness? That was what Hilker called her.

Cutting into the *korta*, she basked in the sweet scent of the dragonfang fruit, then ate. Mikoneh did the same, and Jensirin stayed still, watching the dancing flames in the hearth.

Mikoneh finished his fruit first and wiped his hands against each other while he studied Jensirin. Maya passed her twin a handkerchief, and he murmured his thanks without moving his eyes from the dragon lord.

"Is it strange?" Mikoneh asked.

Jensirin stirred, meeting his gaze.

"Being alive," Mikoneh clarified.

Jensirin nodded. "It doesn't yet feel...real."

"It will," Maya gushed out, ignoring the flush that touched her cheeks. She leaned forward. "After..." Her voice caught, but she forced the words out. "After the fire that took Fa and Mama, I thought I was dead. I felt like it. Nothing was real— but eventually I came back to myself."

"I'm not sure that's the same, Maya," Mikoneh whispered.

"It's similar," she said. "I realize what you've been through is far worse, Jensirin. I—I can't imagine. But it *will* get better. I promise."

Mikoneh glanced at Jensirin, who was staring at Maya as though he'd never seen her like before. The flush deepened against her cheeks, threatening to melt bone. She wanted to shrink into the settee, but she refrained, instead holding his gaze with a fierce determination not to give him any room for doubt. Weak as she was, she'd come back from the abyss, and that meant *anyone* could. Especially someone as strong as him.

Jensirin searched her face for a long, breathless moment.

Only the pop and hiss of the fire filled the room. He shifted. Opened his mouth—

A knock pounded on the chamber door.

Maya jumped halfway out of her skin.

Mikoneh rose, set his hand against his sword belt, and prowled to the door. Cracking it open, he peered out, then swung it wide. Maya caught a glimpse of a man in bright colors with a jaunty feather on his cap, then Mikoneh murmured something and shut the door. He turned to face his two companions, and held up a folded parchment sealed with a large blob of wax.

"Looks like the queen wants to meet us sooner rather than later."

Maya's brows shot up. "I thought they were going to coordinate our schedules."

Mikoneh fingered the seal. "I think the king interceded on his wife's behalf. This looks official." He padded across the room, then sank into the cushions beside Maya. His scent wafted up: citrus, mingled with cedar, and a note of woodsmoke.

Mikoneh broke the seal, unfolded the parchment, and leaned close to let Maya read over his shoulder.

To Their Highnesses, the Prince and Princess of Rokahn,

You are hereby summoned to tea with Queen Feresse. Please arrive promptly at the fourteenth turn, dressed well, and ready for scintillating conversation.

Yours, etc.

The signature was a flourish of swirls too fancy to be legible. Maya read the invitation over twice. "What sort of official summons is that? It's ridiculous."

"The queen is obviously ridiculous," Mikoneh muttered. "What did you expect?"

"Restraint," Maya hissed. "But apparently anything that hails from Lintha can't be bothered with that virtue."

Her twin's mouth quirked up. "What about Lady Namirsha?"

"She's even worse than the queen." Maya stood up. "Mark you, I *like* her better, but Linthans do *not* know how to be subtle. Everything is a show."

He chuckled, but his mirth faded fast. "I don't think we can ignore this."

"Of course not." Maya folded her arms. "What we need is a plan."

"The plan is to collect information." Mikoneh tossed the invitation onto the nearby end table. "This isn't all bad."

"No, it's good." Maya fingered her borrowed gown. "But we're wading into deeper waters. What do we want to gain from this meeting?"

"Favor," Mikoneh said. "We need the queen to let us roam free. Maybe have you meet some of the ladies at court that are in her esteem."

Maya nodded. "Then we need a gift. Something she can't resist."

"Like what? She's a queen. She can get anything she wants."

"I know..." Maya sighed. "I'm not very good at intrigue."

"Now isn't the time to boast, Maya." Mikoneh slumped against the settee's back and stared into space. "We own nothing. Not even our clothes. We know of nothing we can safely give away. We have no friendly connections she'd crave. Even our elements are at least common enough not to draw comment."

"If only we could..." Maya glanced at her claws. She twisted to eye Jensirin. "Tell me about dragon scales. Hearth stories say they have special properties. Knights and dragonslayers are always seeking them out."

Jensirin's brows flew up, but he nodded. "Our scales are harder than stone, nearly impenetrable. The older the dragon, the larger the scales."

"Can they be removed individually?"

"Yes."

"Would removing one cause a weakness in the dragon's natural armor?"

"Not for long. Scales rapidly grow back unless the dragon is dead." Jensirin lifted his hand and drew back his sleeve. Green and blue gradient scales spread over his arm in an instant, then he plucked one free. The scale gleamed like deep water in the fire glow. Sure enough, another scale slid into place over the hole he'd made.

Maya's eyes widened. "That's amazing."

Mikoneh had drifted closer. "What are you plotting, Maya?"

She let herself grin. "We'll gift the queen a rare necklace made entirely of dragon scales." Her smile softened. "If you don't mind providing a few more, Jensirin?"

"Hold on." Mikoneh twisted to face the dragon lord. "Is it dangerous? Could her Mage *friend* use the scales against you?"

Jensirin shook his head. "Not if they are a gift. Once shed, they belong to whomever I allow to receive them—excepting if the recipient should invoke justice against themselves. That bears a consequence."

Mikoneh's shoulders eased. "And are you all right with gifting your scales to a spoiled, petty queen?"

The dragon lord nodded. "If it serves your cause, I'll give you my teeth." He flashed a grin that exposed his fangs.

Maya laughed. "I don't think we're there yet but thank you."

Jensirin caught her eye. His own sparkled. "Very well, but something to keep in mind: Dragon teeth grow back, too, just like scales. They are, however, much more dangerous gifts."

"Good to know," Mikoneh said.

"Shall we get to work?" Maya asked, beaming.

CHAPTER 24

OCEAN SCALES

"That leads well into a discussion of secondary elements."

- A Treatise on the Magic of the Hidden Realm by Sariolin the Solitary

Midafternoon, at the fourteenth turn, Mikoneh stood outside the queen's private parlor. He was being searched by her personal retinue of guards. Maya stayed close beside him, enduring a similar search, as though the twins were highwaymen. Mikoneh said nothing, though his mouth twisted in annoyance, and Maya slapped a guard's hand when he went to search above her knees.

"That's quite enough," she growled.

Mikoneh tugged his burgundy surcoat straight. "We don't have any poisons or daggers hidden away. Let us in before we're late."

The guard rubbed his hand, then tipped his head toward the door. "You may enter."

Mikoneh caught Maya's arm and escorted her into the

chamber beyond. It was bright, sunlit, and reeked of too many flowers arranged in dozens of vases.

There was no sign of the Mage Ambassador. Mikoneh relaxed a little.

Queen Feresse stood before the broad window, her sandy-blonde hair cascading down her shoulders in ringlets, her dark blue eyes sparkling. She wore a gown of white satin, with tiny glittering gems hemmed into the ermine fur-lined edges. The sleeves were voluminous, cuffed with more fur. She glanced up from her nails and smiled at the twins. "Ah. Welcome." Her voice was the sickly-sweet tones of a woman trying to sound youthful—which was pointless, as she couldn't be much older than Latta. She moved from the view of falling snow, trailing through the endless bouquets of flowers, her train hissing after her like a great snake. She proffered a slim hand toward Mikoneh, and he took it in a bow, kissing the air above her gaudy rings.

Maya curtsied beside him, murmuring, "Your Majesty."

Feresse extracted her hand, and moved toward a delicate table and chairs standing over an ornate Linthian rug. She used a handkerchief to wipe her fingers, as though to rid herself of Rokahnian germs.

"Please, sit." She moved to one of the dainty chairs, slipped into it, and smiled at the twins expectantly.

Mikoneh escorted Maya to her spot, helped scoot her closer to the table, then claimed his own chair. The fragrance of floral tainted the scent of tea—or perhaps the queen was one of those peculiar people who added flower extracts to their drinks. He stifled a grimace.

"I must say," Feresse said, "you're both more beautiful than I remembered from the feast." She gestured, and a servant peeled off from her place at the wall, unnoticed until now. The servant was young, perhaps fifteen, and dressed in muted grays that seemed to leech the color from her face.

"Pour the tea," Feresse said.

The servant obeyed at once, her movements deft and economical, as though she'd been trained to draw no notice to herself. As the girl set tea down before Mikoneh, he caught her eye and smiled sympathetically. She flinched away, almost slopping the tea.

Maya took that moment to drop the cake she'd plucked up, as though to divert the queen's attention. "Oops." She smoothed her skirt, not diving for the sweet. "I've always been so clumsy."

Feresse offered her a smile like oozing syrup. "It's no trouble, my dear. Though I do suggest you overcome that deficiency. Men do *not* like clumsy women."

Mikoneh kept his mouth clamped on his opinion of *her* opinion. Instead, he picked at the frosting on the cake the servant had given him. The fragrance of sugar mingling with the flowers threatened to send his stomach into tottering fits. How could anyone stand so much...*perfume?*

Finished serving, the young girl moved back to the wall and pretended to be a statue.

Mikoneh discarded the cake and risked a sip of tea. Floral flavor exploded across his tongue, destroying the notes of herbs and spices. *Revolting.* He nearly dropped his cup and had to resist slamming it against the porcelain saucer. Licking his lips, he hid his disgust behind a careful smile.

"What a unique blend, Your Majesty."

"Thank you," Feresse said, her smile turning gooey. "It's my own concoction."

Maya had just ventured to try the tea, and her eyes widened before she, too, set her cup down fast. "Oh. My. It's...so flavorful."

"Isn't it?" Feresse looked like a bird puffing up her plumage. "I always hated tea. So *green*, like drinking grass. So, I began experimenting. A drink is only worth sipping if it's sweet, as far as I'm concerned."

Mikoneh's stomach twisted. Even if she weren't consorting with Mages, he'd struggle to like such a honey-brained fool.

"I do enjoy sweet things," Maya offered.

Feresse eased back, perhaps deciding they'd passed some test. Maybe she wasn't consorting after all. Maybe the Mage just knew to gush about sweet things, too.

"How are you enjoying Simynshin?" asked Feresse.

"It's lovely," Maya said, "though I've always preferred the east. I get homesick for the bay between Oceana and Lintha."

Feresse's eyes lit up. "Ah, yes. I used to sail that bay. My family had an estate in Northern Lintha. So picturesque."

The two women chattered about the eastern scenery for a while, allowing Mikoneh to sit in silence and bless Maya for her diplomacy. She had a talent for turning a fight into a picnic, just like Fa. That friendly air. That ready smile.

He made a mental note to tease her about her flair for intrigue later.

"Latta tells me you enjoy riding," Feresse said.

Mikoneh tensed. Her eyes were on him. "I do," he said. "It's...fun." He nearly winced.

"He's very good," Maya said.

"I hate horses," Feresse said. "They smell, and they buck you off."

An almost irresistible urge to tease the queen—to really frighten her—trickled through Mikoneh, but he clamped down on it hard. "They can be dangerous." Well, he *mostly* clamped down on it. "Especially when they see snakes. I once saw a soldier fly half a yard and break in half when his horse encountered a water snake. It was near a moat."

All right, so he'd caved to temptation.

Feresse's eyes grew wide as saucers. "I *told* them. I told everyone. Papa never listens."

Maya coughed into her cup and shot Mikoneh a warning glare, then she set down her drink. "We brought you a gift, Your Majesty." She pulled the string of dragon scales from her dress pocket. Sunlight set the ocean scales off, and they flashed and rippled.

Feresse's eyes widened again, and her lips parted.

Maya had requested a silver chain and clasp to be sent from the tailor, and the man himself had come to oversee its use. His delight in helping Maya to craft the unique necklace was evident in the way he'd rubbed his hands together and murmured cheerily to himself. Maya had used her dragon claws to puncture holes in the scales and thread them through the delicate chain. While Mikoneh had never been fascinated by jewelry crafting before, somehow, while watching Maya and the tailor work, he'd been riveted.

Queen Feresse reached for the necklace. "What is—"

"Dragon scales," Maya said. "A rare gift, Your Majesty, for a rare beauty."

Hooked. Mikoneh leaned forward to read the greed and pleasure written like scrawl across Feresse's ooey-gooey face. She snatched the necklace, held it in the sunlight for full effect, and gaped.

"Exquisite," whispered the queen.

Even the servant's attention was fastened on the necklace.

It *was* lovely, but not utterly mesmerizing. Or perhaps Mikoneh couldn't understand the appeal because he wasn't human. Maybe he was immune to its effects.

We'd better have that lesson on dragon traits and tendencies soon.

Feresse shook herself, then barked out, "Well, help me put it on."

The servant girl scrambled forward, and draped the necklace around the queen's throat. A heartbeat later, it was clasped and hanging there like it belonged. Feresse ran her fingers across the scales.

"It's the most...it's such a..." Were those *tears* in her eyes? Feresse reached forward and rested her hand over Maya's on the table. "No one has given me anything better. Thank you, my dear."

Mikoneh should've felt relieved by that statement, but somehow, he felt like he and Maya had made a dreadful mistake. What would people do to get ahold of more dragon scales? What might they attempt to take the queen's?

Do we know what we're doing at all?

CHAPTER 25

SIFTING OUT GOLD

"While many scholars hold to the idea that every living soul may tap into an element through the Spirits Elemental, few believe that a secondary element will manifest in all wielders. Certainly, a secondary elemental type is more commonly recorded among the fae."

- *A Treatise on the Magic of the Hidden Realm* by Sariolin the Solitary

"The necklace is a gift. None can take it safely," Jensirin said. "Otherwise, they may invoke a dragon curse."

Mikoneh blinked where he stood before Jensirin's chair in the suite's common room. "The queen won't be murdered in her sleep, then?"

"Not by anyone but a fool."

There were plenty of those around, so that wasn't any kind of reassurance.

"What if people start hunting dragons to claim their

scales?" asked Maya, obviously clutching the same fears. She was perched on the arm of the damask-patterned settee.

Jensirin shook his head. "Ter told me that it's widely believed dragons died out in the Age of Dragons—"

"But the scales may prove otherwise," Maya interjected.

"Or they will assume they came from a sea monster."

"Sea monsters can exist, but not dragons?" Mikoneh's voice rose in his incredulity.

Jensirin shrugged. "Why do you think dragons developed the ability to transform into humans?"

"To make themselves more vulnerable to torture and death?" Mikoneh's tone was flat.

"To *hide*," Jensirin said. "Long before the threat of Dark Mages, those willing to risk a dragon's curse for the magic properties of scales, bones, and fangs became a rampant problem. Greed ran wild, and dragon hunters were in high demand. Therefore, dragons adapted."

"But people might still try hunting if they think they can find a dragon in human skin. What's to stop them from hurting Maya or me?"

"If you die as a human, your scales and fangs aren't accessible. And your bones lose most of their magical potency."

Mikoneh narrowed his eyes. "Potency for *what*?"

"Oh, various things," chimed in a new voice.

Mikoneh whirled toward the newcomer. Ter was sitting on the window seat, his legs swinging free.

"Where have *you* been?" Mikoneh asked with more sharpness than he'd intended. "I thought you were sticking around here, but I've hardly seen you."

Ter had the decency to wince. "I did slip away to assist Owenekiras with something for a spell, but I've been around the past few days, attempting to speak with a rather stubborn king. One of my least favorite kinds of dealings."

On that they could agree. "I assume you mean King Prettem."

Ter's ears drooped. "The same."

"What about?"

"The wisdom of treating with Mages."

Mikoneh's lungs pinched. "Did you have any success?"

"Not really." Ter dropped from the window seat and moved over to the cluster of furniture where the others stood. He flopped into an armchair. "I understand you had to deal with his wife."

Maya piped up. "She's a vain little thing. So much younger than I'd thought—but not as young as she thinks she is."

"Hmm." Ter steepled his hands. "Vain and young, perhaps, but not entirely feather-headed."

"Latta seems to think she's stupid," Mikoneh said.

"Perhaps more foolish than stupid," said Ter, "and foolish people are the most dangerous variety. She's only clever in a few matters, but one of those includes getting her own way. When that means manipulating the king of a country, her singular skill becomes rather alarming."

"Put that way," Maya said, "she scares me."

"She should," Ter said. "She's already convinced Prettem and over half the court that the Mages are misunderstood. That their past sins are no longer relevant. That by barring them, Simynshin is losing out on the wealth and prestige the eastern kingdoms already enjoy."

"Eastern—" Mikoneh choked. "How is Oceana's recent collapse in any way enticing?"

Maya cringed. "You knew—"

"I could guess," he snapped. "What else would happen after we toppled the castle and disgraced the nobility? I imagine men like *Lord* Drayve are swooping in to pick up the pieces, and the peasants are answering his call—or that of others like him—purely to avoid being trampled between warring provinces."

"Yes," Ter sighed, "and thus, the peasants are trampled."

"That's what Owenekiras is countering, isn't it?"

"Indeed. Things are rather bleak." Ter leaned forward, propped his elbows on his knees, and rested his chin on his interlaced fingers. "He's trying to prevent a blood bath."

"Will he succeed?" whispered Maya.

Jensirin stirred. "If anyone might, it is Owenekiras Rokahn."

Mikoneh glanced between the dragon lord and the Ephe'ahn. "You say that, but he's fighting on a *lot* of battlefronts. How thin can one man stretch?"

"He is not one man," Ter said. "He is like a banner, drawing just and noble souls to his side. He unites more than he divides, sifting out gold from the pebbles and sands of a river. The Dragon King reveals."

"You make him sound like a god," Mikoneh said.

"Some view him that way," Ter answered, "but to me he is… a friend. For my part, anyway." He plastered on a smile that seemed heavy. False.

Mikoneh arched an eyebrow but didn't push the childlike fae. "While I wish him luck, especially concerning Oceana, we have plenty of troubles right here. Our meeting with the queen was fruitful in its way, but it might've caused a few complications."

"Yes. The dragon scale necklace. I overheard. Though it may turn out well in the end." Ter's apologetic expression seemed genuine enough. "We'll bear it in mind and leave the matter alone for now. What you must presently focus on is—everything."

"Only that."

"Indeed."

Mikoneh sighed, and plopped down on the settee. "I realize spying is essential, but it feels so..."

"Futile," Maya supplied.

"Yeah, that."

"It is until it isn't." Ter's ear fluttered.

"But how are we supposed to find the leak feeding information to the Mages?" asked Maya. "The ambassador doesn't seem to *need* any help. Perhaps it's Feresse after all."

"Can't be," Mikoneh said. "She's a tool, not a source. And the ambassador remains too conspicuous. They need someone who can walk around more easily than either. Besides, Feresse isn't that smart."

"A servant, then?" asked Maya. "They walk around like wraiths. No one notices them or speaks to them. That servant girl nearly fainted when you thanked her."

"Noticed that," Mikoneh muttered. "But servants aren't generally educated—at least, not in Oceana. They wouldn't know what they were looking for. They wouldn't have the savvy to pull strings."

"But someone could infiltrate and pretend to be a servant," Maya said.

"Possibly," Mikoneh said, "but I'd wager on a lord or lady being the source. Someone with influence. Servants are *too* innocuous."

"I tend to agree with Mikoneh," Jensirin said. "Though that doesn't mean the leak isn't using servants to pass information along. It may be an entire network."

Mikoneh sighed. "Which means we need to cozy up to the nobility at the upcoming tourney if not before."

"Don't rule out the merchant class," Ter said. "Your tailor, for instance. Or your cobbler. The florist who delivers your daily bouquets. These citizens move regularly between street and castle corridors. They glean information and are gaining in popularity since Queen Feresse arrived. Remember, she came from the merchant class of Lintha."

The chamber door snicked open. Everyone tensed. Penn slipped inside, glancing at them from behind a new stack of tomes.

"Oh," Penn said. "You're back from Lord Crim's estate."

"Since this morning," Mikoneh said. "Have you been in the library all night?"

"Only since early this morning. I fell asleep reading a very dull report on tariffs." Penn tottered forward. He reached a table near the door, and dumped his books across its surface. After stretching his back, he took a seat beside Mikoneh. "How have things been?"

Maya laughed. "Since when? We've hardly seen you in *days*."

Penn's cheeks reddened. "Well, I...got caught up."

"By everything but reality." Mikoneh clapped his friend's arm. "We've had a few adventures." He launched into an explanation of the attack on the road, and the subsequent return and meeting with Feresse. Penn asked for a few points of clarity but was otherwise the perfect attentive audience.

"Next up is the Winter Tourney," Mikoneh said with a grimace. "At least we still have two weeks until then. Maybe we can still find the leak and get out of here beforehand."

Penn looked between the twins, then sighed. "I should've stayed in Relvin."

Mikoneh snorted. "And had your head chopped off. Good plan."

"It seems somehow safer than all of this," Penn said. "But since I'm here, I might be able to help. I've been rooting around in Simynshinian history. There's a great deal to unpack, and I won't bore you with trifles—"

"Thank you."

"—but I think I can understand why the king was *looking* to marry someone in Lintha. Perhaps he's fallen in love with Queen Feresse, but I suspect his original motives were less romantic."

Mikoneh tapped his finger against the settee's arm. "Let me guess. Money."

"Right." Penn collapsed against the settee's back. "Simynshin has been losing money at an alarming rate."

"How? They haven't been funding Father's army, have they?" asked Maya.

"Not as far as I can tell," Penn said, "though I don't have access to the royal treasury, obviously. Still, I've been discussing trade routes and deals with the library scholars. They're just intellectual enough not to realize my questions aren't purely academic. They've given me a wealth of information about Simynshin. Its crops dying. Blight setting in. The agricultural empire failing. It has nothing to do with Owenekiras's forces. The scholars are convinced he's funding his army by himself."

"That's crazy," said Mikoneh. "No one can fund an army of that size alone."

"A dragon can," Ter put in. "Easily."

Mikoneh scowled. "*This* dragon couldn't."

"You're young," Jensirin said. "You haven't begun building your hoard."

"Let me just get on that, then." Though Mikoneh spoke dryly, something swelled in his chest. A *need*. A *hunger*. He did his best to ignore it.

"My point," Penn said patiently, "is that none of the nobles were doing well. Not until they started finding Linthian wives or business partners with powerful connections. King Prettem and Lord Crim were among the first. And it worked. It stabilized a deteriorating economy. But now Simynshin is reliant upon a foreign power to stay afloat, and that foreign power insists on letting in Mage ambassadors."

"Did the scholars mention what caused the blight?" Mikoneh asked. "Is it still an ongoing problem?"

"No. The crops grew well this past season," Penn said. "No blight. No early winter."

"Imagine that."

"It's rather obvious when you know to look," Maya said.

"Hindsight," Ter put in.

Mikoneh drummed his fingers against his leg. "Holding an entire kingdom hostage using agrarian pestilence. How do we fend off an enemy like that?"

Maya shook her head, fine wrinkles gathered at her brow. "With Oceana in chaos, Simynshin has no real ally."

"Even if Oceana weren't in chaos, it was never much of one for Simynshin," Penn said, frowning. "Besides, the deep snows will set in soon. Armies won't be able to move. They'll have to winter wherever they are."

"Alas, you are right, young lord," Ter said. "War on the open field will cease until true spring breaks. That means what we accomplish here may decide the next season of bloodshed. On which side of this war will Simynshin ultimately stand?"

Mikoneh leaned on his elbows propped against his legs and scrubbed his face, a weariness wrapping over his bones. "Even if we find the leak, how do we convince King Prettem to listen to us? What if he's already chosen to side with the Mages?"

"Then we stop him." Jensirin's voice was hard as steel. "By whatever means may be necessary."

Maya jerked her head up from her own reverie while Mikoneh tensed, blood prickling.

"We cannot take drastic measures at this stage, my lord dragon," Ter said in soft tones. "Our priority is to learn what the Mages are plotting—"

"World domination, I think," Mikoneh muttered.

Ter's ear fluttered, but the Ephe'ahn spoke on smoothly: "—in more particular terms."

"You mean what they want with Latta," Maya said.

"That," Ter agreed, "and whatever other plans they've laid out for Simynshin."

Penn shifted. "It's safest to assume the Mages mean to block Owenekiras from every side. He's their greatest threat, isn't he?"

"Yes," said Ter. "But the *how* is our real question."

"Isolation," Mikoneh said. "It's how Drayve did things in Oceana. My parents—my...adoptive parents..." The words tangled on his tongue. He swallowed and tried again. "They had a growing force. New recruits joined their rebellion every day. So, Drayve had Sathe"—Mikoneh fought off a shudder—"he had Sathe kill them...and put the fear of fire into every dissenter's heart. Then Drayve *shamed* every rebel still working against him. Mocked us. Belittled our efforts. Punished the innocent and blamed us for the need of it." Mikoneh couldn't disguise the bitterness in his voice. "He made us small and powerless by carving out the heart of our rebellion."

Penn set his hand on Mikoneh's shoulder. "But we were growing again. You were bringing people back. They were starting to see the truth—"

"It's dead now," Mikoneh snapped, then winced. "Sorry."

"It's fine," Penn whispered. "I'm angry about it, too."

Why his friend's admission surprised Mikoneh, he couldn't say. Maybe it was because Penn was always so level-headed and calm. Always a voice of reason in the storm of Mikoneh's resentment.

Fluting out a breath, Mikoneh shoved off the settee and began to pace. "The Mages won't be silent, but they'll have to be subtle. They can't use the same blight now that they have a presence at court. It'd make them look bad. That's good and bad for us."

"Harder to spot their ploys," Penn said.

"But also harder for them to maneuver," Maya piped up.

"Right." Mikoneh halted and stared at the crackling flames dancing in the hearth. "Which makes things more equal, at least." He grimaced. "Let the games commence."

CHAPTER 26

DEEPER THAN WILL

"For my own part, it feels foolish to make broad assumptions about magic that manifests through the will and whimsy of sentient creatures."

- A Treatise on the Magic of the Hidden Realm by Sariolin the Solitary

As the Winter Tourney approached, fresh snows fell, frosting the world like a decadent dessert. So, too, Mikoneh's schedule over the next week was a storm of information crammed into his head. Dances, basic dragon facts, table etiquette, lordly decorum, the proper method of donning Rokahnian clothes—the tailor was appalled that Mikoneh had been strapping on his boots *before* brushing his hair—and the renewal of his fire lessons. There was barely a moment to breathe, let alone search out clues regarding the spy the twins had been brought to Elenth to sniff out.

The presence of Minno was an added annoyance, but the odd gray boy did know what he was talking about. When Lord Crim urged Mikoneh to draw a wreath of flame across the air,

Minno stepped from the far side of the open tower and caught Mikoneh's wrist in a surprisingly strong grip.

"Not that way," Minno said. "You'll waste your energy on superfluous motions. Your *will* matters more than your gestures. You needn't speak either. The fire spirits understand intention if you visualize it well enough."

Sure enough, visualizing turned out to be far more convenient and powerful than gestures and words. Mikoneh found himself conjuring up flames in various shapes before the lesson was over. He came very close to melting a single snowflake.

As a pleased Lord Crim led them toward breakfast, Mikoneh fell back to walk beside Minno. "Do the other elements work in the same way? Through imagery?"

"Yes, but it's stronger for fire because it's easier to picture than, say, wind. Gestures work best for that element. Your sister appears to have a good instinct that way." Minno kept his gaze forward. "Earth is fond of words. Water is...less consistent. It prefers a strong will." After a moment, he added, "All are about intention."

"What about spirit itself?"

"That one is deeper."

"Deeper than will?"

"Yes."

Mikoneh chewed on that all the way to breakfast.

Jensirin looked fitful. Mikoneh eyed him at tea ahead of their daily dragon lesson. If he wasn't already certain that the dragon lord's soul had been returned to his body, Mikoneh might fear the man would vanish like a wraith in moonlight.

Maya looked worried as well. She poured Jensirin extra tea and tried to get him to talk.

"Can we transform into full dragons today?" she asked after a third failed attempt at lighter conversation.

Mikoneh tensed, the memory of his own transformation clawing at his mind. Sathe had forced him to shift from his human shape into...well, a dragon, obviously. His mindset had changed. His outlook had altered. And he'd been tiny. Sathe had said it was because he was such a young dragon, but even the Mage had seemed surprised that Mikoneh hadn't become something far bigger and fiercer.

Instead, he'd been small, vulnerable, utterly at Sathe's mercy.

Jensirin set his teacup down. "You wish to transform?"

"Well, yes," Maya said. "Shouldn't we learn how?"

Mikoneh plucked up a delicate cucumber sandwich from the tray a servant had provided with their tea service. The castle staff had become acquainted with Mikoneh's aversion to sweets and seemed determined to provide him with scores of alternatives, like he'd personally challenged their head cook's honor.

Maybe Latta had told them.

He grimaced at his sandwich. Despite Prince Atlanse's reservations, Latta had invited Mikoneh for a ride after his dragon lesson today, and the crown prince had agreed to let them go. It made sense. They needed to be seen together often, but Mikoneh had his own misgivings about leaving the castle.

"Very well." Jensirin's voice was soft, but it jarred Mikoneh from his thoughts.

Maya leaned forward, sloshing her tea. "Really?"

"If you like." The dragon lord rose. "If you're finished, we can begin now."

Something tightened in Mikoneh's stomach. "Maya, it's not..." He trailed off. Not what? Safe? Impressive? Fun? He sighed and crammed the sandwich into his mouth. The flavor of cucumber, soft creamy cheese, and a sprinkle of herbs rolled over his tongue. He snatched another from the tray, then followed Jensirin and Maya to the open space between the furniture and the window seat.

Maya cast a look around. "Is this enough space?"

The faintest hint of a smile twitched at Jensirin's lips. "I assure you that it is." His gaze drifted toward Mikoneh, and a question hung there.

Mikoneh shrugged. He needed to face this now or later. Why not now, along with everything else? His transformation into a full dragon—even one the size of a large cat—had been the least of his torment at Sathe's hands. Maybe it was the place to start facing what had happened.

Jensirin inhaled as though he were bracing on Mikoneh's behalf. "To draw out your wings, you simply drive them from their hiding place within your body. But full transformation isn't the same. Instead of drawing from a space, you will revert *to* that space. Think of it like...like stepping from one room into another. Ah, no. Better still, think of it like curling back up in your warm bed after waking."

The shift started even before Jensirin had finished his directions—like Mikoneh's blood had been eager to change into his truest shape. The world around him grew while he himself shrank. Maya, still in her human skin, gasped and whirled toward him with her golden eyes wide.

Mikoneh's mindset shifted last, settling into a more comfortable, instinctual place. The pain was less here. The colors in the room—silvery-gold light from the midday sun, the prisms cast by crystal vases, the merry roar of the fire— snared his attention. The scents of food and flame sharpened. He stood on his four legs steadily and stretched out his wings. Blue scales glinted, and the fiery hues of his underwings sparkled.

Maya dropped to her knees before him. "You're so *tiny*." Her voice rose in a delighted squeak.

"You are very young dragons," Jensirin said. "It will be centuries yet before you reach the size of a dragon like Owenekiras or myself, unless...well, there are exceptions, but they are rare."

"I—I knew that," Maya stammered. "I mean, I knew we were young by dragon standards, but *this*." She stroked Mikoneh's wing. "You're *precious*."

He let out a protest that sounded like a squawk.

Maya giggled.

"You can speak, Mikoneh," Jensirin said.

He knew that, too, but he didn't feel inclined. The room beckoned him. There were so many places to explore. He brushed off Maya's hands, and shuffled toward the settee. Or, rather, *under* it. The cool darkness—relative though it was— beckoned to him, like some primeval instinct calling him home.

Maya stood up. "Me next."

Jensirin offered up a few more directions. Think small. Shrink. Step *in*.

Just shy of the settee, Mikoneh craned his head in time to see Maya bend and shape herself into a small white dragon with lightning blue webbing. Her mane was the same blue-black as his own. She was smaller than him, a tad slighter in her build, but the difference was negligible.

Maya opened her mouth and unleashed a chirp. She tilted her head on her long neck, then trotted toward him, her wings flapping around like a frenzied chicken—not quite used to them.

"Fold them in," Mikoneh told her.

She halted and obeyed, then caught sight of her tail. With another chirping noise, she spun in a circle, chasing it.

Mikoneh shook his head, then turned his attention to the settee a few short paces away.

The common room door opened, then closed. A familiar scent wafted across the room, stronger than usual.

"What in the name of all the glorious—" Penn's voice cut off. He stood beyond the settee, out of sight.

"They are exploring their bloodline," Jensirin said in quiet tones.

"They're—"

"Tiny, yeah, yeah." Mikoneh ducked under the fabric and wood, happy to reach the cool shadows beneath the settee.

"Can they get bigger?" asked Penn.

Jensirin launched into an explanation, and Mikoneh dismissed them. Something about being in the darkness stirred the fire in his veins. An urge to conjure flame shivered up his spiked back, but he shoved that down.

Not inside, another inner voice told him.

He glanced at Maya. Still chasing her tail. She caught it. Chomped. The white dragon squeaked and tumbled backward, rolling into a ball of white scales and lightning-shot wings.

Mikoneh snickered—which produced a puff of embers. He patted the scorch mark on the rug to put out the little fire. Maybe the servants wouldn't notice.

Something glinted in that whisper of flame. He tipped his head. Hunger swelled.

A gem.

He shuffled toward it, using the elbows of his wings to increase his speed. There, pressed against the front leg of the settee, a large cloudy blue gem glittered dully. Mikoneh snatched it up in his clawed hand—

And the world exploded into nightmares.

Chapter 27

To Find New Treasures

"The Spirits Elemental are sentient. That much we must acknowledge. Whether they feel deeply as humans or not, or whether or not they breed, we cannot deny that they are free-thinking creatures."

- *A Treatise on the Magic of the Hidden Realm* by Sariolin the Solitary

Maya massaged her tail carefully, her black claws sharp and glinting, signifying danger—like her teeth. She hadn't known her fangs were so sharp, but they'd chomped through her tail scales like soft bread.

Penn was laughing as Jensirin assured her that one small dent in a single scale wouldn't leave her vulnerable.

She opened her mouth to inform him that it still *hurt*—

Mikoneh's scream was like a knife to her heart.

Fear surged through her, and she darted toward the settee. Her dragon sight locked onto her twin. He was writhing, his claws clasped around something that glowed. Penn reached the settee on her heels, and he shoved the furniture aside.

"Do not touch him!" Jensirin shouted, freezing Maya in place. He stepped past her, a dagger in hand. For a wild moment, Maya feared he'd harm Mikoneh, but he merely knelt, wedged the blade between Mikoneh's scaly fingers, and popped a gem from his grip. The gem rolled back under the settee and flashed in a strand of firelight.

The dreamsnare.

She'd forgotten about Owenekiras's gift in all the chaos after Brentin's attack.

Mikoneh lay sprawled across the rug, limp, a tiny, scaled creature.

Maya lurched forward, willing herself to shift back into human shape—to gather him up in her arms. Her body obeyed, elongating, bones moving into new places, unfolding and expanding, until she knelt in her familiar form, blessedly still gowned. She reached for Mikoneh, then hesitated.

"It's safe," Jensirin said. "But do not touch the dreamsnare. It may still contain some of his nightmares."

She stared at the gem. "You mean..."

"He released them all at once when he touched it. They played out in his mind in a single instant. That is the danger of such a gem."

Shuddering, Maya tucked her hands under Mikoneh's warm scales and lifted him up into her arms. The blue sheen of his body rippled with firelight. He was so light and lifeless. His tail dangled, its spines glittering. Mindful of his sharp edges, Maya clutched him close to her chest. His tiny heartbeat reached her ears.

"Will he be all right?" she whispered.

For a long moment, Jensirin didn't answer. His eyes were narrowed on the dreamsnare, his brows low, mouth moving in a silent string of words. Then he blinked, twisted toward her, and offered up a smile. It was weak, tinged with worry.

"I don't know," he said.

"He will be." Penn folded his arms. He remained beside the settee, his eyes bright. "He's Mikoneh. Nothing keeps him down for long."

Maya nodded, trying to soak in her friend's confidence. "He doesn't lose. He pivots." Her twin was always saying that.

"Right." Penn flashed a grin.

Jensirin rested his slender hand on Mikoneh's side, closed his eyes, and muttered a few more words. His eyes slid open, his pupils narrow slits. "I don't think it damaged his mind."

"Was that a possibility?" Maya's stomach knotted tight.

"When dealing with magic, it's best to check," Jensirin whispered, turning away—but not before she caught a flash of guilt.

Maya caught his retreating hand. Jensirin hesitated, then met her eyes. "He'll be fine," she said. "And you're not responsible."

"I owe him my life."

"That doesn't mean you can always protect him."

"I mean to try." He pulled from her grasp and stood. "We should get him to bed. I don't know when he'll wake..."

"Can we change him back into his human form?" Maya unfolded herself to rise. Her skirts hung heavy around her bare feet. She'd kicked off her shoes when they'd entered the room for tea. Mikoneh was a ragdoll in her arms, unmoving, barely breathing.

"I do not recommend it," Jensirin said. "He'll have an easier time distancing himself from his nightmares in this form."

That made sense. Maya's mindset had taken a drastic turn when she'd transformed. The world had looked, felt, even smelled different. She'd been more animal than human, and young—so young. Ready for adventure. For exploration. For *play*.

She'd been a child again.

Adjusting her grip on her dragon twin, she moved toward his room to lay him down and let him rest—if he possibly could. Penn followed her. From the corner of Maya's eye, she caught sight of Jensirin drifting from the common room. His expression looked haunted before he disappeared out into the corridor.

She and Penn untucked the covers to make a little nest for Mikoneh, and she curled the dragon into himself. He remained limp. Maya stroked his warm scales, dazzled by the sparkles that made his hide look like the night sky.

"Penn," she said. "Will you stay with him? I think I need to follow Jensirin."

"Certainly." Penn perched on the edge of the bed. "Go do what you do best."

She paused. "And what's that?"

"Heal people," he said.

Heart swelling, she offered him a grateful smile, then hurried from the bedroom. At the door, she glanced back. Mikoneh looked like a little blue lump. Sending out a prayer, she left him to fight his demons. She'd done what she could, little though it was.

Crossing the common room, she stepped out into the castle corridor and halted. Two guards were stationed at the door, and they stood a little straighter at her notice.

"Which way did Jensirin go?" she asked.

"That way, Your Highness," one guard said, gesturing.

Maya thanked him, ignoring the squirming in her chest at the use of her formal title. She hurried up the corridor, the rustle of her skirts and slap of her bare feet loud in her ears. At the next crossroads she paused again. No one was there to ask directions.

She studied the gallery running to her left and right. She'd rarely gone this way. The left corridor ended at stairs leading up. That seemed a safer bet than the long, straight corridor on her right. Dragons liked heights.

She made her gamble, racing up the left corridor. A stray breeze swept a wind spirit into view. She smiled faintly, and reached out a hand. The wind spirit alighted on her palm, shifting into a translucent birdlike form to twitter at her.

"Did you see the dragon lord come this way?" she asked.

The opalescent bird tipped its head, then flapped its wings, lifting itself to ascend the stairs. Maya followed.

The stairs spiraled, then fell away at another set of corridors, one going straight, the other heading right. She glanced at the wind spirit hovering in the air, beating its wings.

"Any ideas?"

The bird chirped, then swooped down the right corridor. More wind spirits joined the first, leading a procession.

Ahead, the tall, dark-cloaked figure of Jensirin drifted moodily along the brightly lit corridor. His shoulders were hunched forward, like he carried the world on his back. Lonely. He was so lonely.

Maya's heart twanged. An urgency flooded her veins. She hurried toward him, skirts swishing, hair trailing behind her under the command of several of the wind spirits.

"Jensirin!" Her voice rang out, high and clear.

He tensed, whirled, and stared at her wide-eyed.

Maya neared him and held out one hand. "Wait for me."

His hand came up. Their fingers met. Maya halted, breathless, though she'd only run a few yards. Something urgent still rolled through her, and staring into his lavender eyes—full of loneliness and despair—she was glad she'd heeded her instinct.

"Let me walk with you," she whispered.

Jensirin opened his mouth, the tension in his face promising a protest, but he stopped himself. The world fell still around them. His hand closed over hers, and he slowly smiled.

"Of course, Princess," he said. "If you wish."

"I do," she said.

"What about your twin?"

"I'll be there when he wakes up."

Jensirin nodded, then extracted his fingers from hers. He motioned down the passage. "I have no real direction."

"I don't mind wandering." She tucked her arm through his, though he'd not offered to lead her. To his credit, Jensirin only missed a beat before he guided her along the corridor.

They walked in silence for a while, and Maya observed the lines of brooding that slowly drew themselves across his face. She cast around for something pleasant to say—anything to distract him. Then she scowled at herself.

"Do you need to talk?" she asked instead.

His foot stumbled, but he corrected himself at once. "About what?" His tone was level, but tension set in his jaw.

"You're suffering. I see it plain as day." She took a breath and rushed on. "I'm not trying to pressure you. If you'd rather not discuss your burdens, we can talk about being dragons instead. But I'm a very good listener—and sometimes you can unburden yourself a little by sharing the load with a friend." Her cheeks warmed at her own presumption, but she *did* count him as a friend, at least for her part.

For a long time, he said nothing. They glided along the empty corridor, a strange picture for anyone who might see them. He, a lordly and comely figure, marked by long centuries of torture. She, a peasant turned princess, with a silk gown, bare feet, and tangled hair flowing like a river behind her. Maya imagined they looked as though they belonged in a woodland kingdom in the High North, rather than within the civilized walls of Elenth Castle.

They reached a new crossroads. Broad muntined windows flooded the corridor ahead, painting the flagstones silvery-blue under the influence of storm clouds. Maya tugged Jensirin along. The subdued lighting brushed their clothes.

Jensirin paused to stare out at the view of Elenth Lake. Maya followed his eyes and found herself hypnotized. The surface was crusted in ice, glistening and smooth like a looking glass.

"I do not know how to live." His confession was soft, almost inaudible.

Maya held still, barely breathing lest she interrupt his reverie.

His eyes flicked to the sky, then back to the lake. "Your brother has given me a great gift—and I owe him everything. Yet I feel unworthy of it. I lived so long ago. I lived, loved, dreamed, fought. Now...I do not know how to go about those things again."

"You'll find them," she whispered. "Bit by bit."

"But I'm afraid to lose them again."

She studied his profile. The haunting pain was bright in his eyes.

"The fear of losing things is part of living," she whispered. "It gives us strength to fight for what we love."

"My strength wasn't sufficient last time," he whispered. "Will the same story repeat itself again? Will I gain all merely to lose it?"

"Maybe. I've lost everything before—at least, nearly so. Yet I've gained so much since then." She squeezed his arm against hers. "It doesn't fill the hollow spaces, but it soothes the pain of them. Though that's only possible if you choose to find new treasures."

He exhaled softly, then turned to study her. "I don't know if I can."

She smiled. "That's okay, Jensirin. You're not required to—and certainly not all at once. You don't pounce on a thing at first glance and decide to make it your gem. The people we meet, the memories we make, the dreams we carve out—these take time to discover and cherish. Take that time. Often, the journey determines the worth of the treasure."

CHAPTER 28

MIDNIGHT BLUE

"I met a so-called scholar who insisted that the Spirits Elemental are after-images of previous wielders, and therefore they do not have free will. That they are only memories of souls bound to the past. This is preposterous. We know from the Nijaal that these tenacious creatures existed before humans ever did upon Sirinhigha."

- *A Treatise on the Magic of the Hidden Realm* by Sariolin the Solitary

Upon returning to their suite, arm in arm with Jensirin, Maya stumbled to a halt. Latta had arrived. *Blast, I forgot about Mikoneh's promised horse ride!* The princess wasn't alone. Crown Prince Atlanse and Lord Crim were also present. All three were crowded in front of Mikoneh's closed bedroom door where Penn barred the way, looking harassed but determined.

"I'm sorry, but I can't explain," he said, then broke off to eye Maya. Relief softened the planes of his face. "Here's Maya now. Ask *her* what you want to know."

Maya smiled. Dear, loyal Penn. Suspicious of all and sundry for the sake of his friends. She swept fully into the common room, dragging a reluctant Jensirin with her. He still harbored a strong aversion to people.

"I'm sorry to have kept you waiting." Maya led them away from her twin's door. "I didn't know you were *all* coming."

"I came for a scheduled horse ride," Latta said, glancing with caution at her father.

"That much I knew." Maya relinquished Jensirin, then seated herself on the settee and smoothed her skirts around her legs. "But why are *you* here, harassing the viscount, Your Royal Highness? My lord?"

Atlanse and Crim had the decency to look sheepish. Jensirin slinked over to the hearth and stood with his back to the room.

"Someone said—" Crim began.

"That is," Atlanse spoke over him, "we heard—"

"—that your twin was attacked again."

Maya's eyes narrowed. "Heard where?"

They clammed up.

"I'd venture to guess they're spying on us," Penn said.

Atlanse fluted out a breath and drifted over to drop into the nearest wingback chair. "It's only precautionary, in order to better protect you. It felt warranted after everything."

Maya's shoulders threatened to slump, but she resisted. "If you're spying, you already know what happened to Mikoneh."

"Then something did happen." Latta stepped closer with a rustle of silk skirts. "Is he all right?"

"We don't know *what*," Crim said. "Only that something did. The guards report what they hear."

"Of course, they do," Penn muttered. "*Court* life."

"Mikoneh's fine," Maya said in a firm voice. "Just resting."

"What happened?" asked Crim.

Maya met the merchant lord's eyes. "Bad dreams."

He frowned. "The guards said—"

"She's telling the truth, my lord," said Jensirin. "He touched a dreamsnare containing his nightmares. It unleashed them all at once, which overwhelmed his senses. But he will recover soon."

Atlanse fell back against his chair. "Is that all?"

Maya stiffened but bit her tongue. Let him think it was nothing.

The crown prince dragged a hand down his face. The faint scratch of skin against fine bristles scraped over Maya's ears. Atlanse hadn't shaved this morning.

"I thought Owen was going to *eat* me," he muttered.

Crim drew close to his prince and rested a hand on Atlanse's shoulder. "It hasn't come to that yet, Your Highness." The merchant lord found Maya's eyes. "May we see him?"

"I don't think—" Penn began.

"That's fine," she said, "if it will put your minds at ease. He's only sleeping. Please don't disturb him."

"We understand." Crim started for the bedroom door. Atlanse rose to follow him.

Latta remained behind, twisting her ring. She glanced between her father, vanishing into the adjacent room, and Maya still seated on the settee. "*Will* he recover all right?"

Maya nodded. "He must. And Mikoneh always does what he *must*."

Penn stepped over to Latta's side, and gingerly set his fingers on her arm. "He's too bull-headed to do anything else, Your Highness."

The princess met Penn's eyes, then she smiled faintly. "He

is that." She turned back to Maya. "How is Captain Akonn?" At the question, Penn's hand retreated.

"Restless," Maya said. "He wants out of bed—I can see it in his eyes—but I won't have it. He's not fit to walk around yet. His wound is a bit infected, but he'll recover, of that I'm certain."

Latta's quiet smile bloomed a little brighter. "I'm sure he will in your care."

Atlanse and Crim stepped from the bedroom, conversing quietly. They strode over to the cluster of furniture.

"We're very sorry for disturbing you," Crim said. "When news reached us of another attack—"

"It's perfectly understandable," Maya said.

"Except for the spying part," Penn murmured.

"How did he seem?" she asked, shooting Penn a warning glance.

"Restful," Crim said. "I think."

Atlanse nodded agreement, though his gaze had settled on Jensirin. Firelight danced in his blue eyes. "You're the former Revenant, aren't you?"

The silence could drown a fish.

Maya rose, setting a hand against her collarbone. "Your Highness—"

"Yes, I am," Jensirin said.

Latta's eyes widened. Crim's hand fell to a dagger belted at his waist. Atlanse, however, remained stationary.

"I offer formal welcome," the crown prince said. "I apologize for not doing so weeks ago. Owenekiras mentioned you'd be coming, but with the tourney and everything else, I've been remiss."

Jensirin inclined his head. That was all.

"We should go, Crim." Atlanse turned to Maya. "I apologize again for our intrusion."

"That's not necessary. Thank you for your concern."

"If your brother requires anything—"

"I'll let you know," Maya said firmly. "Thank you."

The two men headed for the door. Before slipping out after his prince, Crim cast a lingering glance at Jensirin, his brows pinched. The door shut after him.

Latta had remained behind. "May I see them?"

Them. She wanted to see her captain as much as her betrothed.

Maya glided toward her twin's bedroom. "Certainly. This way."

Penn followed the women, his hand draped over his sword. His broken arm had mended well. Thank goodness for that. They needed all the able bodies they could muster—and even though Penn preferred books to fighting, he was an excellent swordsman.

The viscount had drawn the bed curtains around the four-post monstrosity where Mikoneh slept. Pulling them aside, Maya laughed. Mikoneh was still in dragon form. How had she forgotten? The Simynshinian princess drifted closer, and drew a sharp breath.

"Looks 'restful' indeed," Maya chuckled. "It must have been quite a shock, even if they do know he's technically a dragon."

Penn sighed. "That's why I was trying to keep them out."

"He's beautiful." Latta reached out a tentative hand, then brushed her fingers against the midnight blue scales. Mikoneh's wing shifted, and light rolled across the scales. "I always wondered..." She glanced at Maya. "Are you identical?"

Maya shook her head. "I'd assumed we would be, but I'm white rather than blue. Our hair is the same, though."

"Rokahnian royal hair usually is." Latta brushed the wing

again, scattering prisms across the coverlet. "I suppose he *does* look peaceful, in a reptilian way."

"I'm surprised," Maya said, "considering how awful his dreams must be."

"He thrashed about at first," Penn said. "Just after you left. Then he slowly fell still."

Maya moved around the bed and crawled onto the coverlet. She curled up beside her twin. "You may visit Akonn if you want, Princess Latta. I'm going to stay here for a bit."

Latta lingered a few heartbeats longer, then slipped away. Penn offered to escort her, perhaps out of politeness alone, but Maya suspected not. She found his interest in Latta didn't bother her.

Inching closer to Mikoneh's little body, she stroked her hand across the smooth, glittering scales, then shut her eyes. Weariness folded in around her, drawing her toward the shores of sleep. Overwrought, she didn't fight.

INTERLUDE III
FLY

- From the Corpse Poet's 32nd Sonnet

Nightmares pitched him into a dark ocean. He swam against the current—broke the surface—only to be flung back by another crashing wave of horror. He screamed, but the sound was lost in the depths of his subconscious mind.

One moment he was in human form. The next, the hands —his hands—clawing at the current were scaled, winking and flashing in the glow of a cold, distant moon. Sathe's voice, his arms, wrapped around Mikoneh—vast and smothering.

'**Succumb, Firebrand. You are mine.**'

He thrashed harder. He wouldn't cave. Not ever!

Help me! His cry was lost in the void. No one could hear. They never did.

Help! he called anyway.

Light flooded the black waters. What he'd thought was the moon drifted nearer.

No, *he* was moving toward a high cliff. Or a tree, perhaps.

Standing at the tor of the tall something, a figure reached for him.

"Fly."

His scaled hand broke from the water. His wings wrestled the current, mangled. Broken.

"I can't."

Despite the distance, he felt the lady's smile like it carried the warmth of midsummer. "You must. *Fly*, my shadow!"

With a scream, he flung himself from the ocean. His body was in dragon form. Dark waves shaped like hands groped for him, tearing at his wings—but he broke free.

And soared.

The lady held out her arms. He collapsed into them, pitching them both backward and onto a path made of water. The lady gently wrapped her arms tightly around him. He lay on top of her, quivering. Unshed tears blurred his vision. Could dragons cry?

The lady stroked his scales. Despite their hardness, he felt her circular motions, gentle and soothing.

"Must I wake up?" he choked out.

Her fragrance curled around him, sweet and ethereal. "Not yet, my shadow. Rest a while."

He tucked his head against her neck, nestling among the threads of her wheat-blonde hair. "Thank you."

CHAPTER 29

THE THORNS OF HIS DREAMS

*"Returning to the matter of secondary elements, it is especially
possible for dragons to manifest a secondary type—and rarely is
it a sub-element. I've seen a dragon wield fire and water
simultaneously."*

- *A Treatise on the Magic of the Hidden Realm* by Sariolin the Solitary

Moonlight drew Mikoneh from slumber. He tried to sit up, but found himself still in dragon form, with Maya—looking human—sleeping on his wing. No wonder he'd dreamed his wing was broken.

The rest of his nightmares were mere fragments. Everything felt far away, disconnected. He didn't fight for clarity. Instead, he tugged his wing free and changed back into human form. Clothes hung on his lean frame, heavy but welcome. Maya murmured something and shifted, then fell still. He waited a few moments, letting her slip back into a deep sleep, then he crawled out of the bed.

The moon was singing to him.

He padded to the window seat, and stared out at fat flakes of snow whispering across the wide, silvery sky.

"Beautiful, isn't it?"

He jerked around to find Minno standing in the gloom. The banked fire cast orange light across his face. Why was Mikoneh surprised? The gray boy's nighttime visits were becoming a habit.

"Please stop doing that."

Minno moved up next to him. "Doing what?"

"Coming into my room uninvited."

"Jensirin invited me."

Mikoneh grimaced, prepared to argue—but it was possible Jensirin had. He didn't know the Revenant that well. *Former Revenant, remember?*

The events of the past few weeks were jumbled. It was always like that after a sleep plagued by nightmares, but this time was worse.

"Dreamsnares are helpful until they're not," Minno said. He stared outside, one hand flexing like he'd wounded it.

"Dreamsnare?"

"You didn't know? It's a gemstone that collects nightmares. Your father left one for you a while back, but evidently it was lost in that scuffle with the stablehand. You found it, and like an idiotic baby dragon, you picked it up without a second thought. Your nightmares were unleashed."

"Explains why it was so unpleasant."

Minno made a sound of agreement, then sprang up onto the window seat in a lithe motion and unlatched the window. It swung open on a gentle breeze, letting in a few drifting snowflakes. One landed at Mikoneh's feet and melted into a glistening dot of water.

"What are you doing?" he asked the boy, caution tightening his voice.

"You need fresh air. So do I." Minno stepped up onto the windowsill, caught the casing with one hand, and leaned out.

Mikoneh's grimace slipped into a scowl. "I'd prefer to be sleeping right now."

"Would you? But you got up."

Mikoneh opened his mouth to argue, then sighed, and closed it. "Never mind."

"I usually don't."

"That much I did puzzle out."

Snow dusted the top of Minno's head, and the air grew colder. Mikoneh shivered, then blinked. Why did he feel the cold? He'd forgotten how the sensation felt after weeks of having a fire blazing in his core. He lifted his hand and drew warmth from inside him. Flames sparked, then caught above his palm, and the cold disintegrated. One last shiver took his frame. Minno's gaze had settled on him, and Mikoneh met those strange, flat eyes.

"What?"

"I thought you were going to bed."

Mikoneh opened his mouth again—then snapped it shut, feeling decidedly like a turtle. He brushed off threads of annoyance, then shrugged. "Did you come here for a reason?"

"Yes."

"Gonna enlighten me?"

"Do you really suffer from such a short memory?"

Mikoneh arched his brow, but the memories flickered across his mind, settling back down. Right. Minno had been sent to protect him. Owenekiras had asked.

"You come and go a lot for someone who's meant to—"

"Nighttime is my shift," Minno said. "Jensirin agreed."

"Great, now you and Jensirin are friends?"

"No. He said he would eat me if I betrayed you again."

Minno's tones never wavered, and his expression was its usual level of grimness.

"And is that a figurative threat, or more literal?"

"Literal, I think." Minno rapped a knuckle to his chin. "At least, I wouldn't put it past him. Once dragons taste of darkness, they are often compelled to accomplish dark things. Like eating people."

Mikoneh folded his arms, digesting those words. They rang inside him like a warning bell, but he shoved aside his fears for later. "Oceanians always believed all dragons ate people. In legends, of course."

"Oceanians also believe hanging your laundry out to dry on a cloudy day brings in mushroom fairies who curse the second-born daughter to become a spinster. Rubbish."

"A fair point." Mikoneh had always scoffed at hearthwives' superstitions. So had his parents. Maya had found the local customs charming in a silly sort of way. "Dragons don't generally eat people?"

"No. Only one type of dragon does, and it's a rare type."

"Wouldn't happen to be Linthian dragons, would it?"

"No. Lintha doesn't have dragons. They're too sensible to live there."

"Also fair." Mikoneh left his flame hovering in the air, and he sat down on the window seat. A dull throb was starting in his head. Minno possessed a talent for producing those. "Do you know anything about Rev—about Jensirin?"

"Yes." Minno dropped from the sill and positioned himself on the far side of the long seat.

Mikoneh waited, steepling his hands together, then he rolled his eyes. "Are you going to tell me?"

"Is it your business?"

"He's my friend."

"Then ask him."

"I—I don't want to pry." He grimaced again, feeling Minno's weighty gaze on him. "I know, I know. This is prying, too. I just don't want to cause him pain."

"No pain you might cause could be worse than what he has already experienced," Minno said.

"I know that, too." Mikoneh raked a hand through his hair. "Believe me."

"I do."

Mikoneh glowered at his hands. "Why are you so infuriating?"

"Practice."

"Oh, so it's not inborn?"

"No. I was once a sweet, innocent, lovable child." Minno's impassive voice made it impossible to tell if he was being sarcastic. Either way, Mikoneh had a hard time imagining Minno being sweet, even with a few inches shaved off.

"Sure you were." Mikoneh leaned back and stared into the floating flame. A fire spirit had taken up residence there and was coaxing the flame higher. "Don't light anything on fire."

"Don't feed it any bad ideas," Minno said. "Fire is mischievous. Almost as much as wind."

Mikoneh scrubbed at his eyes. Sleepiness was leaking back into his thoughts, but he resisted. He preferred the gentle cast of moonlight to the thorns of his dreams. His hand froze. Moonlight? But it was snowing. He craned his head to stare out at the lit-up sky. No moon peered through the heavy cloud cover, and yet something was glowing—and singing. A bird? "Is that...?"

Minno glanced over his shoulder. "Oh. Yes. That's mine." He held out his arm. The bird flew inside and perched like a hawk on Minno's sleeve, its silvery wings bright and shining. The warmth it emanated was definitely from spirit of spirit.

It was a duck.

Mikoneh tipped his head to one side. "Your spirit manifestation is a duck?"

Minno blinked at the bird. "Yes. Obviously."

"But...why?"

"Because it makes me...well, I won't say happy."

"Good. Because I wouldn't believe you."

Minno turned his slow blink on Mikoneh. "Perhaps it does make me happy."

Was the boy trying to be contrary?

Mikoneh rubbed at his eyes again, swallowing his irritation. He shouldn't let a child get his dander up—no matter how old Minno really was. "I'm going back to bed." He started to stand.

"Are you?"

Mikoneh slumped back down. "No. I don't want to sleep." The memory of crushing waves rumbled in his ears. He scrubbed at his face again. "Maybe...maybe you could teach me about spirit of spirit." The words tumbled out. He froze, then sighed.

Minno was blinking at him like an owl again. "Are you sure?"

"No. But do it anyway."

"Very well." Minno reached into the tiny pocket of his gray tunic and withdrew Duck. The tangible, non-glowing one, who was much too big to fit inside such a cramped space. The boy set the fowl on the stone floor, patted the mallard's green head, then settled back on the window seat. The spirit duck remained perched on his arm, undisturbed. "Hold out your hand."

For a breath, Mikoneh wasn't sure Minno was speaking to him. Then he shook himself and held it out.

"Palm up."

Mikoneh flipped his hand.

The gray boy rotated his arm and dumped the spirit duck

onto Mikoneh's palm. The duck fluttered its glowing wings, and Mikoneh flinched, but the creature's weight was, while not feather-light, certainly not as heavy as a real duck. The sense of substance was more suggestion than actual mass. The silvery duck poured a warmth into him, chasing away the last tendrils of his dreams.

"Reshape it."

Mikoneh jerked his stare from the duck's black eyes. "What?"

"What form does it take for you?"

"Um, this one's yours."

Minno shrugged. "I summoned it, but it isn't my core. It is the material of divinity, inhabiting all things."

"I thought that was the Void and Hollow."

"Those are the corridors of Mithrinn—the Universe—born from old magic. Spirit is what flows within the walls of those corridors to keep them vital, so that they in turn can keep *us* vital. It's symbiotic. Especially with the...the death of the *Complété*." The boy dropped his gaze to Duck on the floor. Did Mikoneh imagine the lines of grief etched around Minno's eyes?

The boy drew a breath. "Mold the spirit essence you're holding. Give it new shape."

Mikoneh had used spirit of spirit before against Sathe. He'd stolen the Mage's name and commanded him to kill himself using this power.

Is that why I'm hesitating?

No, it wasn't that. He'd been resolved to end Sathe, and spirit of spirit had been a tool, like a sword or arrow taking down an enemy. He wasn't traumatized by his newfound abilities.

I'm just traumatized all around. His lips twitched up. Why did that strike him as amusing? *I've really cracked, haven't I?*

He settled his attention on the duck-shaped spirit patiently nestled on his palm. Wisps of silvery aura drifted off the duck's feathers, curling like smoke before slipping away—but the wisps didn't disintegrate. Every instinct whispered that. They slipped *away*, into another plane.

"The World Between." Minno's voice was its usual monotone. "That's where it goes. You cannot use spirit of spirit indefinitely. Its eldritch nature is unstable in the temporal world—our existence—which is also called the principal plane. Once spirit is summoned, it slowly bleeds away. If you use it in an active manner—to attack or to shield yourself for example—it breaks down faster. Spirit matter isn't intended to be corporeal or mortal. It doesn't die. It merely shifts."

"Good to know." Mikoneh stroked the duck's feathers. They were soft, tangible—but in a liquid way, like water. "What do you say, little fellow. Want to be something more majestic?" The duck tipped its head, then morphed into the shape of a dragon. Luckily, it maintained its small size.

"I thought you might choose that shape in your bias," Minno said.

"Bias?" Mikoneh scoffed. "I found out I'm a dragon less than two months ago."

"Yes, bias. Dragons always are. Most folk would consider a hart or an eagle to be majestic—but your kind just sees those animals as food."

Mikoneh rubbed the back of his neck. "I didn't tell the spirit what to become."

"Ah. So, your spirit essence is a sycophant."

"I don't know!"

Maya groaned and rolled over on the bed.

Mikoneh lowered his voice, glowering at Minno. "This is why I didn't want you training me."

"Because you have no discipline and can't control your temper? Makes sense."

Energy surged into Mikoneh's fist, but he set his teeth and held still, seething. Pounding the boy's face in would only prove Minno right. Instead, Mikoneh turned his glower on the silvery dragon still perched on his open palm. The wisps of aura were still bleeding away, though slower now. He stroked the dragon's tiny scales. It didn't look like a young dragon, but like a full-grown dragon in miniature.

"Is the bleeding slowed because I revitalized the spirit when it changed its shape?"

"Yes," said Minno. "Maybe you're not an idiot, after all."

Mikoneh ground his teeth, then shrugged. "Now and then I do produce my own thoughts. Thank the sands."

"If sand is the source of your intellect, you're in trouble." Minno rose and stooped to collect Duck. "Better not tap into your spirit essence more tonight. You've already taxed it a lot."

"By asking it to change into a dragon?" Mikoneh arched his eyebrows.

"No. Before that. When you slept. You..." Minno frowned at him. "You did something to stop the deluge of nightmares."

"*I* did?"

"So it would seem. I don't know what. I could find out, but that would be an invasion of your privacy, which neither of us wants. I don't care to understand how your mind works, when it does at all."

"Thanks a lot," Mikoneh said flatly.

"You're welcome. Goodnight." He started for the door.

"Wait. I thought you were here to guard me."

Minno glanced over his shoulder, not missing a step. "I am."

"But you're leaving."

"I'm stepping out. I will remain close. Goodnight." He

reached the door and opened it. A thread of firelight spread a crack of orange across the floor. Minno stepped out, then shut the door behind him.

"He's insane," Mikoneh muttered.

"So are you," Maya said from the bed. "It's a boy thing."

He scoffed but didn't argue.

"Are you going back to sleep?" asked Maya.

"Not yet." He settled on the window seat and stared outside. The snowfall was thicker, coating the world in sparkling white. The tiny dragon spirit swooped from his hand and landed on the sill. Together, they watched the crystals fall from the heavens.

Dawn stole in softly, a little later than normal.

CHAPTER 30

ON THE SHORES OF ELENTH LAKE

"Personally, I suspect that wielding a secondary element is a matter of one's mind. A disciplined person is more likely to awaken another type, whereas the casual user of the prominent element is unlikely to."

- *A Treatise on the Magic of the Hidden Realm* by Sariolin the Solitary

"Are you sure, Mikoneh?"

Mikoneh rolled his eyes at his twin. "Maya, I'm perfectly fine—and I need to be out in public more. We have a job to do, remember?" He tugged his riding gloves on and flexed his fingers. "Latta and I won't go too far."

"You'll keep to the grounds, then?" Maya's eyes flicked to the ice-crusted window in the common room where they stood. The fire crackled and popped in the hearth.

Mikoneh stifled a second eye roll. "I'm not going to stay cooped up. I'm not sick. It's only a little slick out there. And I can summon fire. We'll be fine. Besides, Prince Atlanse is sending an escort with us. Nothing is going to happen."

"Fatal last words," Penn said from the breakfast table. He crammed toast and jam into his mouth while he perused a hefty tome.

"You're especially good at those," Mikoneh shot back with a warning glower.

Penn shrugged and heaped more grapes onto his plate. Only Maya looked anxious, which had become her default setting in recent days. Understandable, perhaps, but still annoying.

Mikoneh glanced toward the hearth. Jensirin was seated in a chair near the flames, watching the twins from hooded eyes. He looked like he hadn't slept in a week. A pang of sympathy filled Mikoneh's chest, but he didn't know how to help his friend. How did someone heal from what the former Revenant had endured?

Sometimes, space is what I need. Maybe he needs that, too.

A knock sounded at the door. Mikoneh started for it. "That'll be Latta. I'm off."

"Please take care," Maya said.

He could imagine her wringing her hands, but he didn't glance back. Lifting his hand, he offered a dismissive wave. "Promise." Opening the door, he found the Songbird Princess beaming at him. "Good morning, Latta," he said with more cheer than usual. He welcomed any chance to escape Maya's fretting, even a ride with his betrothed.

"Good morrow, Mikoneh." Latta flowed into a graceful curtsey. "Feeling up for our ride?"

"Definitely." He proffered his arm, ignoring the uncomfortable flipping of his stomach. She slipped her arm through his, and they took off, letting the stationed guards shut the door. A dozen men-at-arms followed at their backs.

FRESH AIR CURLED around Mikoneh's face. He breathed it in, glad to rid himself of the last coils of his nightmares under the broad silver light of a cloudy winter day. All that remained was the ever-present hollow where Sathe's bond had been.

A path had been cleared to the bailey, where horses were already saddled and waiting. Mikoneh led Latta to Firechaser, then strode to Rook's side. He swung up into the saddle. The leather creaked under his weight, and the musty scent of the horses filled his nose.

Riding wasn't flying, but he still loved it.

The men-at-arms mounted their own horses, reins jangling, leather groaning in the cold. Latta glanced at them, then her bright eyes landed on Mikoneh.

"Ready?"

He grinned and nodded. Snapping his reins, he lunged forward under Rook's power. The horse was as eager to run as he was. Man and stallion outstripped Latta, but the princess only laughed. Firechaser took it as a personal challenge and picked up the pace.

Rather than use the main castle gates, they raced for the southside gate. Prince Atlanse had requested they not head into the forested areas, so instead, Latta had suggested a trip to the shores of Elenth Lake. Mikoneh had agreed.

They rode like thunder chasing lightning, the horses' hooves sure even on the drifts of snow. Piles of white crystal were knee-high in places. Swirls of fresh powder danced in the slate sky, but they were tiny and dry, hardly a threat to the beauty of the morning.

Ahead, the frozen lake gleamed like an enormous looking glass capturing the cold wintry light. At its whipped cream shores stood a large tent bearing the heraldry of Simynshin. Several horses were tethered to the pilings of a nearby dock.

Mikoneh slowed Rook. His stomach writhed. Was that King Prettem? Why would he come out here so early in the morning, especially in the wintertime?

Maybe it's Atlanse.

That would be less surprising than the king, particularly if he wanted to keep a close eye on his daughter.

Latta reined in Firechaser. Her scowl was deep. "Why is Queen Feresse here?"

Mikoneh jerked his attention back toward the tent. "How can you tell?"

"The ribbon beneath the pennant. It's coral. That's her color."

Sure enough, a silken coral ribbon streamed on the pole beneath the Simynshinian flag. Mikoneh's insides knotted up. His mind flashed to the dragon scale necklace.

"She's probably not here for us," he said. "Did she know we were riding today?"

"I've no idea." Latta nudged Firechaser forward.

Mikoneh followed on Rook, and they soon neared the tent. The men-at-arms remained close.

An unfamiliar handmaiden, bundled in a dark fur cloak, stood waiting. She inclined her head, then motioned them toward the tent. "The queen is expecting you, Prince Mikoneh."

He tensed, then shot a glance at Latta. She'd gone rigid in her saddle, and her eyes narrowed. A chill wind caught threads of her brunette hair and tossed them.

Mikoneh swung down, moved up next to Latta's horse, and offered his hand. "Come on, Your Highness. It's warmer inside."

She stared down at him. Then she took his hand, letting him hoist her to the ground. Snow crunched under her boots.

The servant's eyes were wide. "Your Highnesses, the queen didn't say—"

"Lead on." Mikoneh motioned toward the tent.

The servant cut a look at Latta, eyebrows pinched together, then she drooped, and turned to lead them inside. The men-at-arms remained outside on horseback.

Low braziers glowed within the interior. The flames brightened and fire spirits slipped from the blazing coals to wave their greetings. Mikoneh offered a nod back, then followed the handmaiden through the furnished room—replete with tables, lounges, and area rugs—and through a flap into a second chamber.

Queen Feresse was pacing the room, clad in a turquoise dress glittering with thousands of gems. She gnawed her knuckle, eyes lined with worry, aging her by a decade. The dragon scale necklace sparkled against her throat.

The handmaiden hesitated. "Your Majesty?"

Feresse whirled around, her eyes wide, almost wild, then they calmed. She glanced at Latta—and froze. "Why are *you* here?"

"Prince Mikoneh and I were riding together," Latta said coolly. "We are betrothed, after all."

An itch started at the back of Mikoneh's head.

Feresse's eyes narrowed. "Of course, dear Latta. The way you remind us daily of your upcoming wedding, I suspect the entire world knows by now."

Latta bumped up next to Mikoneh, tightening her hold on his arm. "Excellent. I would hate for anyone important to miss that fact."

The itch deepened. Mikoneh took a step forward. "You needed to see me, Your Majesty?"

Feresse glared daggers at Latta for a heartbeat longer, then whirled toward Mikoneh. The smile that bloomed on her lips was startlingly genuine. She turned and drifted toward a beige-colored chaise lounge, perched at its edge, and smoothed the layers of her skirts.

"Sit, Your Highness." She gestured to a round, plush seat that had no back. "Make yourself comfortable. May I interest you in a cup of *choiteni*? It's a kind of boiled chocolate drink from Cimin."

"Thank you, but I ate recently." Mikoneh stayed where he was, unwilling to sit when Latta hadn't been offered a chair. "How can I help you, Your Majesty?"

Feresse's lips puckered in a pout, then she sighed and picked at the fabric of her dress. "Leave us, Tryss."

The handmaiden bowed and retreated.

"Stop glaring at me, Latta," Feresse said. "I have no interest in seducing your dragon prince."

Latta snorted in derision.

Oh. The itch crawled across Mikoneh's frame. So, *that* was their game. "Good, because I have no interest in being seduced by anybody. What's this about, Queen Feresse?"

The Linthian woman studied him. "You're an odd one, but then, most Rokahns are."

He didn't bother to ask what she meant by odd. Weariness was already curling around his frame, and the day was still young. He hated politics.

The queen folded her hands together, sighing through her nose, like she bore the weight of Simynshin on her slim shoulders. "I need your help. I—I'm being blackmailed."

"You're being..." He stared at her. "Sorry to sound rude, but how is that my problem?"

Feresse stiffened, her lips turning down. "Don't you care that I'm in distress?"

"The world is in distress," he said. "You're just one person in it."

Tears welled in her eyes, and he felt his defenses crack. Blasted conscience. With a grimace, Mikoneh led Latta to the little round chair.

"Sit," he told her gently. When she obeyed, he turned back to Feresse. "Who's blackmailing you and why?"

"You'll listen to my petition?" asked Feresse breathlessly.

"Sure." He prayed it would offer insight into her mind, as well as information he needed.

She squirmed. "Lord Crim is blackmailing me."

"Crim is? Why?" Heat licked at Mikoneh's voice. While he didn't fully trust the merchant lord, he'd viewed the man as someone too honorable to prey on anyone defenseless. But was Feresse defenseless? Did Crim have a lot to gain from blackmailing the queen? Could the merchant lord be trying to eliminate the Mage influence at court through whatever means, even getting his hands dirty?

Or is he an enemy? Mikoneh hadn't ruled that out yet either.

Feresse was twisting the fabric of her dress. "He...may have information about me that's less than...flattering."

"Obviously," Mikoneh said, "or he couldn't blackmail you. What's he demanding for his silence?"

Feresse's eyes flicked to Latta, then away. "The king's death."

CHAPTER 31

A Path in the Snow

"Few elemental wielders ever become Master Elementalists for the same reason—a lack of discipline. It seems to me that the Spirits Elemental reward those who take the time to respect and befriend their kind."

- *A Treatise on the Magic of the Hidden Realm* by Sariolin the Solitary

The tense silence was broken by the pop of the nearest brazier.

Feresse slumped back on the lounge, openly pouting now. "I don't want to kill my own husband."

"Why not? You don't love him," Latta snapped.

"Of course not." Feresse straightened up. "But I do love being the queen."

A dull throb started in Mikoneh's temple. He rubbed it hard with his thumb. "So, Crim wants you to assassinate King Prettem, after which he'll destroy the evidence of your illicit affair with someone at court."

"Exactly—" She froze, then inhaled sharply. "How did—"

"Lucky guess." Mikoneh didn't bother to stifle his growl. Why was royalty so easy to predict? He glanced at Latta. Well, perhaps not all of them. "All right, Feresse. You have a big problem, that's plain enough. Why are you telling me about it?"

"I want you to stop Crim's plot."

"How, exactly?"

"Simple. Kill him."

He resisted slapping his forehead. His head was aching enough already. "Simple, is it?"

"He's your fire instructor, isn't he? You could make it look like an accident."

Mikoneh turned away to hide his disbelief. Was she really saying what he was hearing? Maybe he was still caught in the currents of his nightmares. Maybe...

Latta was eyeing him, her expression too complex to read. Was she worried that he might take Feresse's demand seriously?

He schooled his expression and turned to face the queen. "All right, you've explained the who and the why—but we haven't covered the *what*."

"You mean what's in it for you?" she asked primly.

"Exactly."

"Why, Latta, of course." Feresse's smile turned sharp and calculating. "Would you like her voice back?"

He fell still. The Mages had taken Latta's singing voice away long before anyone at court had dreamed that Mikoneh would wind up there. They couldn't have done it only to give the queen leverage for making him do what she wanted.

At least we now have evidence she's been colluding with Dark Mages.

Feresse leaned forward, her eyes catching the glow from the brazier. "As I said, it's simple. You kill Crim, the king stays alive, I remain queen, and your beloved has her voice returned to her. One life is a small price to pay for the prizes we keep."

"I can't believe I thought you were an idiot," Latta hissed. "Clearly, you're insane!"

Feresse scoffed. "You really think insanity drives me? Poor naïve girl. I know what I want, and I'll do what I must to keep it. That's all."

Mikoneh frowned at the swirling pattern on the rug beneath his feet. "There's a fine line between cold ambition and quiet insanity."

"Well?" asked Feresse.

He sighed. "Give me time to think."

"There's not much time left," the queen said. "Crim wants Prettem dead by the Winter Ball."

One week from now. That was all.

"Send the king away," Mikoneh said. "If he's gone, you can't kill him, and Crim can't expose your affair. Send him away for his health."

"He'd never leave before the tourney," Latta said.

"That's true," Feresse agreed. "It's his favorite event."

Mikoneh's mind raced. He curled his hands into fists. He needed to speak to Crim, but that meant exposing his knowledge of the blackmail, and the queen's contact with him.

"What proof does Crim have of your affair?"

"He won't tell me."

"But you believe him?"

Feresse's cheeks colored. "He knows the man's name."

"He's not just guessing?"

"He wouldn't have to," Latta said. "The king is...possessive. If any doubts were cast on his wife's activities, he might fly into a blind rage. It's possible he'd execute her."

Mikoneh scoffed. "I almost don't blame him. You're married, for sand's sake."

Feresse's face reddened more, and her eyes flashed. "Don't preach to me, Prince of Rokahn. We're not all so *pure* as your kind." She turned away to glare at the stand near her lounge. A cup of brown liquid sat there; if it held boiled chocolate, it was cool by now. "It gets lonely, you know." Her voice was a faint whisper.

"*You* chose to marry for a crown," Mikoneh growled. "Don't try to make me feel guilty because you ignored any chance for love until *after* you made a binding promise of fidelity." He turned back to Latta. "We're leaving."

"You won't help me?" asked Feresse.

"I told you to give me time to think. Goodbye for now, Your Majesty." He took Latta's arm, and they left the chamber behind. Feresse's quiet sniffles followed him out.

Crossing the second chamber, Latta squeezed his arm. "You're bold as gold, Mikoneh."

He snorted. "Timidity's never been my trouble."

"What is?"

"Knowing when to hold my tongue."

Latta laughed.

"Wait!" Feresse called.

Mikoneh halted at the flap, and glanced back.

"You'll say nothing to anyone. Right?" Splotches of red dotted Feresse's face. "Either of you. You'll keep my secret?"

Sighing, Mikoneh bowed his head. "I'll be as discreet as possible."

"Why would I ruin my grandfather's happiness?" asked Latta.

The queen looked so relieved, Mikoneh almost pitied her. Almost.

He stepped outside and let the cool air wrap around him, bringing the scent of more snow. The crispness was welcome after the heat inside. He stared at the frozen lake. Its surface gleamed beneath a ray of sunlight peeking around a cloud. His footprints from earlier carved a path in the snow, revealing tufts of yellowed grass beneath.

Why did everything have to be so ugly? Why couldn't snow stay white?

His shoulders hunched beneath an onslaught of memories —flashes of the village massacre, moments of Sathe's torture— but he wrestled them back. He needed to focus on the present, on spies, blackmail, stolen voices, and brewing wars. On Mages.

I should've asked Feresse more questions about Latta's voice.

He could go back inside. Demand answers.

But no. First, he needed to speak with Crim. The queen might be lying about everything. She might be a skilled actress manipulating events to suit her ends.

One thing's certain. She and Crim aren't friends.

It wasn't much, but it was something. Of the two, he was more inclined to trust Crim—especially with the man's devotion to Seranni's memory—but Mikoneh wasn't stupid enough to take the merchant lord off his list of possible Mage agents.

"Want to keep riding or go back to the castle?" asked Latta.

"Keep riding," he said. "I need to collect my thoughts before I make any kind of move."

"For what it's worth," Latta said, "I don't want anyone killed just so I can sing again."

"It's more than that. The Mages, Latta. They want your voice for something, and it can't be for any altruistic purpose. We need to get it back."

"I know. But not at the cost of someone else."

Mikoneh sighed. "I agree. But I'm not sure it's that simple." As he swung into his saddle, he noticed a lone figure walking along the lake shore. "Is that Hilker?" he asked, squinting under the sun.

Latta glanced at the figure. "I'm not sure. Your eyesight is better than mine."

Mikoneh almost called out to the man, but he wasn't in the mood for Hilker's quips, and he wasn't ready to discuss what he'd just learned with anyone. Not until he spoke with Crim. He hated to suspect a new friend, but Mikoneh wasn't going to blindly trust anyone at this point.

Perhaps never again.

CHAPTER 32
A Game of Fang and Claw

"Perhaps most peculiar and admirable of all is that the Spirits Elemental are not wild. Mind you, they are not tame either. The nearest I can come to a comparison in nature is the songbird— but I believe the Spirits Elemental feel much more deeply than even those sweet animals, despite what scholars may say to the contrary."

- *A Treatise on the Magic of the Hidden Realm* by Sariolin the Solitary

Mikoneh and Latta rode back to Elenth Castle for lunch. They left Rook and Firechaser at the stable, then Latta guided Mikoneh to the northeast side of the castle, where a lavish room had been set aside for their meal. Half their contingent followed them while the rest moved off to perform other duties. One guard positioned himself behind Mikoneh's chair, and a second guard stood behind Latta's.

"Nice being alone." Mikoneh spooned up some beef stew.

Latta grinned. "Indeed. Very cozy."

The prince and princess sat at an oaken table laden with braided breads, stews, cheeses, a hot pudding, and a bowl of ripe fruit. Mikoneh assumed an Earth Elementalist kept the fruit healthy out of season. An area rug warmed the floor in lieu of a fire. Heavy curtains hung over the window to combat the chill. Sconces lined the walls, and fire spirits danced among the flames. Several waved at him, but Mikoneh ignored them.

He skimmed the tapestries on the walls depicting forest scenes abounding with animals, including a few mythical beasts. His gaze settled on the depiction of a white unicorn peeking around a tree. If dragons existed, what other myths were real? His lips curled up. He'd known so little back in Relvin.

I still know almost nothing.

His thoughts wrenched back to Queen Feresse and Lord Crim. Political intrigue was something he'd detested all his life. Now he was caught in the cankered center of it all.

"Do you know if Crim is at the castle this morning?" he asked.

Latta's spoon froze halfway to her mouth, and a droplet of stew sauce dripped onto the table. "He's busy with preparations for the tourney, so he might be anywhere."

"Because of the merchant part of his title, right?"

"Yes." Latta lowered her spoon. "He and his wife"—her tone strained on the last word—"won the bid to supply most everything for the event."

"I can't help but notice you really don't care for Lady Namirsha."

Something flashed in Latta's eyes. "She's a lovely person."

Well, that told him exactly nothing. He scooped up another mouthful of stew, chewed longer than he needed, then swallowed to try again. "You don't trust her, then?"

"She's Linthian" was Latta's curt answer.

The guard stationed behind the princess grunted, then shifted to disguise his agreement.

Mikoneh shrugged. "She's also married to Crim. Do you trust him?"

"I—" Latta frowned at her bowl. "I'm inclined to."

"Aren't he and your father old friends?"

"Yes. They met in their youth when Crim's family first came to court."

"Then his family wasn't always in such high standing?"

"No, Crim's ancestors served the Mages in the Age of Dragons." Latta shrugged her hand at his expression. "Simyn-shin has a long memory."

"I'll say." He dipped buttered rye bread into his stew. "What changed their standing?"

"Gold."

"Figures. In what way?"

"Crim's father bribed King Prettem." She ripped a grape from its stem. "It never set well with Crim, though, and he's worked hard to prove his loyalty to crown and country. That's why the queen's *request* surprises me. This doesn't strike me as something Crim would do."

"Agreed."

"How will you proceed?"

"Talk to Crim," Mikoneh said. "Nothing else for it."

The guard sniffed his approval. Mikoneh resisted a smile. He'd always wondered how guards could remain so stoic during all the complicated, embarrassing, or amusing conversations they were privy to. The lower castes were highly underestimated.

Neither royal dared to discuss Feresse's demands in further detail, well aware that any one of their contingent could be spying. Mikoneh soaked up the last drops of his stew with a second chunk of dark bread, then he washed his lunch down with a swallow of wine. Rising from his chair, he grimaced at the sweet undertone in the flavor.

"I need to excuse myself, Your Highness."

Latta dabbed her mouth with a napkin. "Do what you need to do, Prince Mikoneh."

He bowed, then strode from the room. The contingent split itself again, and half the guard followed him into the corridor. A nearby fire spirit crackled and tossed itself like an ember to land on his shoulder. Mikoneh didn't break stride, though he reached up absently to pat its fiery head. The spirit held a tiny human shape, its long hair flickering and popping. The imagery reminded him of Minno's nocturnal visit and the impromptu lesson on spirit of spirit.

His fingers prickled with light, but he shook off the sensation. Now wasn't the right moment to practice the rarest form of Elemental magic.

He glanced at the nearest guard stationed on his heels. "Any idea where Lord Crim might be?"

"Setting up the tourney ring on the grounds would be my guess, Your Highness."

"Thank you. Mind leading the way?"

The guard inclined his head and quickened his pace to lead out. They took corridors Mikoneh hadn't explored before, and here, crowds of aristocracy were in plenty. Caught up in his own issues over the past few weeks, he'd forgotten how stuffy they all looked. The guards were careful to keep Mikoneh flanked so none of the clustered nobles could approach. He'd never been so grateful for an escort.

The irony of the last few months didn't escape him. Not long ago, Earl Drayve's guards had unceremoniously thrown Mikoneh, Maya, and Penn into Relvin's rotting dungeon.

They'd nearly been burned at the stake. Now, they were privileged guests of the Royal House of Chenta in a respected country far removed from Oceana and Drayve's petty tactics.

Sathe had also been part of that world. Before his death, Sathe had been forced to tell Mikoneh what he knew about the Mage Queen's plans—including her interest in Prince Atlanse and Princess Latta. He'd also dropped another tidbit. One that sent chills through Mikoneh.

Someone was stalking Mikoneh. Someone who wasn't a Mage, and who had a personal vendetta against him. It didn't make sense. He'd lived in Relvin since his early childhood, and except in his fight against Drayve, Mikoneh had made no enemies.

Yet Sathe hadn't been lying. With his true name in Mikoneh's control, he couldn't lie.

What am I missing?

Something to root out later.

"Prince Mikoneh!" The voice was a deep rumble.

Mikoneh craned his head to search a crowd of men gathered in an adjoining corridor. Dozens of eyes stared at him, some openly hostile, others bright with curiosity. Standing at the rear of the throng, a tall man dressed in motley blues, reds, and purples doffed a feathered cap and bowed his head.

"Who's that?" Mikoneh asked, his step faltering.

"A player," the guard said. "His troupe will be performing at the Winter Tourney."

"He knows me?"

"Everyone knows *of* you, Your Highness."

They moved beyond the corridor, away from the crowd.

"Enough to recognize me?"

"Yes, Your Highness. News of your likeness has spread across Simynshin. Yours and Princess Mayanaleh's. Crowds are gathering faster than usual. Even representatives from Cimin are said to be on their way."

Mikoneh's nerves tautened. "Why?"

"You're one of the lost princes, Your Highness. And you've come back."

"One of them?"

"Yes, Your Highness. Your father and uncle are lost princes. And Cimin also lost one ten years ago."

"Right. I'd heard about that." Mikoneh rubbed his thumb against his sword hilt. "What's the crowd doing in that hallway?"

"Awaiting their audience for approval to participate in the tourney. Everyone there is either a performer or a warrior. They'll be screened most thoroughly. We can't be too careful about intruders these days."

Mikoneh nodded, rubbing his sword hilt harder. "Who approves them?"

"Sir Kalet. He's head of the Valor Knights."

Mikoneh knew of the Valor Knights, as well as their leader. Sir Kalet was as strong as he was vicious—and yet, strangely, he was also a poet renowned across Sirinhigha. The village women of Relvin Province had coveted his verses and dreamed of Sir Kalet riding through town, romancing them, and taking them along on his latest quest. Even Maya—even traitorous Kevva— had been entranced by his eloquence. Never mind that the poet also had a reputation for slaughtering whole villages if the whim took him.

Something about his darkness is as appealing as his artistry. Mikoneh would never understand that.

Still, he looked forward to meeting the knight. Fa had made a point of dissecting the man's battle strategies, pointing out their flaws and strengths. A game of Fang and Claw would be a welcome challenge against Sir Kalet.

Mikoneh quickened his step to come level with his guard guide. "By chance, do Simynshinians play Fang and Claw?"

The guard's smirk was answer enough, but the man responded anyway. "Certainly, Your Highness. Legend claims that a dragon princess founded our great kingdom. Fang and Claw is as much a tradition here as the Snow Flurry Dance."

"Your royalty is descended from dragons?"

"No, Your Highness. 'Tis just a legend, and besides, our founding House had no blood heirs. They adopted children. The Royal House of Chenta comes through that line."

"Makes sense." Mikoneh barely cared, but he archived the information for later. Everything he learned about Simynshin might be relevant. More intriguing was the implication that Fang and Claw originated from dragons.

He kept his silence until they reached a door leading out into a courtyard laced with ice and snow. Slumbering trees and broad-leafed blue holly stood sentinel before high outer walls where the delicate bones of dead ivy clung to the stones. A wooden gate guarded the way out of the small courtyard at the end of a path carved through the white crystals.

Crossing the courtyard, Mikoneh inhaled the crisp air. More snow was on its way—he could smell it. His steps were easy on the icy path. Since his dragon blood had stirred, his balance was better than ever.

Nearing the gate, Mikoneh's eye caught on the vibrant red holly berries peeking out from among glossy leaves veined with thick frost. He brushed his fingers against the nearest shrub. The fire spirit dove toward the berries, but Mikoneh batted it off. Flickering into ember shape, the spirit drifted out of the gate ahead of him.

The green was flat and long on the western side of the castle. It was also presently white rather than green. Under a gray sky, gusts of wind rose to toss crystals into the faces of men and women setting up tents, pavilions, and lists. Braziers dominated the borders of the tourney grounds, chasing off the worst of the wind chill with plumes of smoke. Dozens of colorful tents billowed and puffed like the workers milling around them. Voices rose in a cacophony that throbbed against Mikoneh's skull.

Along one side of the grounds, hammers pounded the air. Stalls were being set up for food and wares. An old crone stood at the nearest stall—already assembled—and was throwing colorful scarves over the wooden planks holding her rickety booth together. One scarf slipped from her gnarled fingers, dancing overhead in a strong wind. Mikoneh darted forward and snatched it. His claws unsheathed, puncturing the silky material. He winced.

The crone tottered toward him. "Thank ye, young master, thank ye—" She froze, then teetered backward. "R-Rokahn fiend!"

The nearest hammers ceased to pound. The babble of voices cut off. Heads lifted. Eyes searched and found him. Their expressions ranged from curious, to anxious, to antagonistic.

Mikoneh sheathed his claws and proffered the shawl. "I'm sorry I snagged it. I can pay for—"

The crone had caught her balance, and she shook her head. "Keep it. Celes preserve me." She whirled and tottered back toward her stall.

Mikoneh set his jaw. Striding after her, he fished for the coin pouch tied to his belt. The tailor had supplied each twin with a similar pouch, along with Simynshinian money. He'd assured them that Owenekiras had approved the money exchange, and had briefly lectured them on the worth of each bronze, silver, gold, and platinum stamped coin. Mikoneh dropped a few bronze pieces onto his palm.

"How much?"

The old woman batted away a wisp of gray hair. "No charge, Lord Rokahn."

"I insist."

The lead guard plucked a bronze coin from Mikoneh's palm. "It's fine, good woman. He's not with the queen."

It took Mikoneh a heartbeat too long to realize the guard didn't mean Queen Feresse. The man meant his aunt, the usurper: Queen Elayorah. He shook his head. "No, I'm definitely not."

Where he'd eventually stand on Rokahnian politics, he couldn't say. Not yet. But he didn't relish building his nest in *that* woman's branch until he understood the nuances of his family tree.

The crone eyed him, then wobbled forward, and snatched the bronze coin from the guard's hand. "Thank ye kindly." She bobbed a doddering curtsey, then shuffled behind her stall to offer Mikoneh a glower from the proper distance.

Seemed crones were alike the world over.

Mikoneh dumped the remaining coins back into his purse and turned from the stall. Eyes snapped away. Hammers pounded with added vehemence. The guard motioned to the stomped down aisle through the snow, and Mikoneh followed at a quick pace.

This Rokahn hasn't done anything to any of you, he thought. He curled his fingers into fists and marched at the guard's back, tromping harder than necessary just to focus his irritation on something he couldn't damage.

The din around him filled his senses, slithering at the edges of his vision, taunting his steps. Hammers struck—until they faltered at the sight of him. Voices dropped. Whispers hissed like snakes on his heels.

One bold fellow spat on the ground near Mikoneh's boot.

The Dragon Prince halted, turned his head, and eyed the man with a quiet challenge. The boldness disintegrated, and the man staggered backward, then fled behind his stall.

"Ah, Your Highness!" Crim's pleasant voice boomed over the air, slicing through the tension. "I wasn't expecting you out here."

CHAPTER 33

LULLING THE WORLD TOWARD SLUMBER

"The nature of an Elementalist's relationship with its spirit type is not like a dragon bond, but it does put one in mind of the same."

- *A Treatise on the Magic of the Hidden Realm* by Sariolin the Solitary

Mikoneh pried his glower from the man hiding behind his wares and managed a limp smile for the merchant lord. Crim was striding toward him, arms outstretched, perhaps a bit more theatrical than usual. Mikoneh's smile deepened. Crim arrived, caught his shoulders, and sized him up.

"Looking a little pale still, but you're one tough fellow." Crim wrapped an arm around Mikoneh and dragged him deeper into the tourney grounds. "Don't mind the riffraff. Some of these merchants hail from Southern Simynshin, and they've gotten a stronger whiff of Rokahn's recent tyranny than most. Half are angry at Queen Elayorah, the other half hate your father. Next week, don't be surprised when the brawls break out after the ale makes a few rounds."

A child darted out in front of them, waving a hasty apology. A woman caught the child at the corner of a booth and muttered a stream of warnings. She glanced up, smiled brightly at Crim, then froze when she spotted Mikoneh.

He looked away, too weary to try for a smile that she'd misread.

"Ready for the hullabaloo?" Crim asked.

"Not really." Mikoneh batted off a wisp of hair. "But I realize my presence is necessary. I just don't know how to avoid causing fights."

"You can't. People fight. You just have to inspire them to fight for the right things."

Crim's words ate at Mikoneh's heart. He *liked* Crim. He needed to be able to trust him. With a grimace, Mikoneh dragged his eyes from the path back to the merchant lord.

"We need to talk. Do you have a little time?"

"I can spare half a turn, I think." Crim glanced around. "Eddan! Where are you, my fine fellow?"

A scrappy-looking man raced around a stack of barrels at the end of a platform under construction. He was dressed in fine threads, but they'd been worn often enough to tote stains and snags. His face was framed by a tousled mess of straw-colored hair under an obnoxious hat.

"Yes, m'lord?" Eddan swept into a dramatic bow.

"See to Tarl's wagon mess. I'll return soon."

"Yes, m'lord," said Eddan, then loped off.

"Sorry to interrupt you," Mikoneh muttered.

"Not at all. I needed a respite anyway." Crim motioned to a yellow-and-silver-striped tent. At its peak, a cluster of colorful, patterned pennants made a stand against order and sense. "We'll find privacy in here, elusive as she is."

Mikoneh followed the merchant lord into the relative gloom. The guards stationed themselves outside. Crim dropped the flap into place, plunging Mikoneh into deeper shadows. His eyes adjusted fast.

The merchant lord moved across the interior, weaving between opened crates spilling out their packing straw. Crim leaned over one and dug around until he produced a bottle of wine.

"Thirsty?"

"No, thank you," Mikoneh said. "I just ate."

Nodding, Crim rummaged around for a goblet, and upon finding it, opened the bottle. "What's this about?"

"Feresse." Mikoneh watched carefully for any flash of guilt —or any other emotion.

Crim looked up, an easy smile on his lips. "What about her?"

"Blackmail."

Crim's brows creased. "Is she blackmailing you?"

Mikoneh stiffened. Was the man ignorant or lying?

"Or are you planning to blackmail her?" Crim poured red wine into the goblet, then set the bottle aside. He plucked up the drink, swirled it, and took a sip. A flicker of satisfaction crossed his face. "Excellent bouquet."

Mikoneh took a step toward the crate. "Crim, she claims that *you're* blackmailing *her.* That you know about an illicit affair, and you're demanding the king's death for your silence."

Darkness gathered on Crim's face. "Me, demand the king's death?"

"That's what she says. She asked me to kill you first. I'm not sure if she's crazy or—"

"Extremely manipulative?" Crim set his goblet down. "It's a wonder she thinks she can get away with it." He frowned. "Do you believe her?"

"Honestly? I don't know what to believe—though I *want* to trust you over that faithless hag."

Crim's lips quivered up. "I thank you for that, and I appreciate your caution. This is quite a world you've stumbled into, and you're doing a fair job. Hilker and I were discussing that only this morning. Jonatten and Seranni raised you well."

Warmth spread over Mikoneh. "Thank you, Crim. But what do I do now? She claims you're blackmailing her, and you claim to know nothing about it. You both seem sincere."

"Perhaps..." Crim drummed the rim of his goblet. "I wonder if one of my representatives is compromised. Maybe someone is acting in my name, drawing the blame away from the real culprit. That'll be blasted hard to trace down."

"No jest there," Mikoneh muttered. "Can I help somehow?"

"You've already helped more than you know," said Crim. "Really, Mikoneh. Thank you. Especially for not killing me." His eyes gleamed.

Mikoneh snorted. "I'm not much for assassinating people."

"Oh, no? Well. We all have our specialties." Crim took another drink, then tugged his doublet straight. "I have things to do, so I'd better get a move on."

"I told Feresse I'd think about my answer. She said you've given her until the Winter Tourney to kill King Prettem."

Crim's frown deepened. "Well, we could let this ride out and see who comes forth with word of her affair—but then, she'll probably prepare other agents, in case you decline her *kind* invitation." He waved his hand. "I'll speak with Hilker. If anyone can track down the plotter in all this, it's him."

"Who is he, really?" asked Mikoneh.

Crim blinked. "You don't know?"

"Nope."

"Ah. He's the king's brother-in-law. The deceased first queen's blood relative. Which makes him Atlanse's uncle. I shouldn't be surprised he hasn't said anything. He's rather a pariah at court."

"Why, because he speaks his mind?"

"Exactly." Crim shrugged. "Politics."

Mikoneh offered a derisive snort in answer.

"It's ugly, but it's your new life, Your Highness."

"I don't have to like it," said Mikoneh.

"No, indeed. Never trade your soul for the elation of power. It's like Ciminian *renemm* powder: costly, addictive, and terribly harmful."

"Yeah, I've seen the effects of both." Mikoneh moved to the tent flap, and peeked outside. A troop of soldiers in gleaming armor tramped past, their stoic expressions cracking under the haze of anticipation. The aroma of smoke and meat clung to the air. Festival time. Drink, games, blood sport, thieving, whoring, cheating—all the good and bad that came with the quadrupling of a populace.

"I should head back," Mikoneh said.

"Leave this to me for now, Prince." Crim came up to stand beside him. "Say nothing to Feresse until I've contacted you. Again, I appreciate you letting me know."

"Hilker's training Maya this morning," Mikoneh said. "You'll find him in our suite until our dance lesson."

"Not surprising. He promised to help me here, but he's always slacking. Drives Sir Kalet crazy."

"They work together?"

"Often. Kalet is his son."

Mikoneh's eyebrows jumped. "*Hilker* is the Corpse Poet's *father*?"

Crim's expression froze, then melted into a torrent of emotions, mostly horror and amusement. "Corpse Poet? How fitting. I bet even he'd appreciate the title. Oceanians dubbed him that, did they?"

"Yeah." Mikoneh had to rearrange his mental image of the dreaded Valor Knight with Hilker as a contributing parent. Instead of the stoic non-expression, Mikoneh drew in a sardonic curving of the lips, a tilt of the brows, a haughty lift of the chin. Honestly, it suited the man's reputation far better than Mikoneh's former imagery.

He shook himself free of his reverie. "Where are the lists?"

"Keep heading down past the stalls," Crim said, "and you can't miss them. Want a peek ahead of the competition?"

Mikoneh shrugged. "The other combatants have competed here before. I haven't. I need to lessen their advantage with a glimpse at the terrain, especially with this weather."

"I'm happy to hear you're competing. You might also enter the Elementalist competition."

Mikoneh huffed a laugh. "I hardly think I'm ready for that."

"It's split into categories, from beginner to advanced. Wielders are judged by their unique approach to magic more than anything—and *you* tend to think beyond the map, as they say. I suspect you and your sister would do splendidly."

"Something to consider."

"I hope you will." Crim clapped his arm. "Off with you, young pup. I'd best get back to my business or risk the king's wrath—which frightens me far more than Feresse's lies."

Mikoneh drifted out of the tent, trying to dislodge the weight keeping his nerves taut. Crim was worried—and he should be—but he was hiding it well. Still, Mikoneh had done all he could, and his mind was at rest in one regard: of the two, he was still more inclined to trust the merchant lord, and that was a relief.

The guards flanked Mikoneh. The hostile glances from

onlookers resumed. Mikoneh ignored them as he made his way to the lists. He had much bigger troubles to ruminate on than the ignorance of people who didn't even know him.

Let them have their rumors and legends. He needed to prod at real dangers.

THE COMMON GREEN ended where a small wood began. After Mikoneh inspected the slushy grounds where the tourney would commence, he wandered toward the leafless trees several hundred yards from the half-constructed stands. Most of the trees were beech, alder, and ash, with the occasional rowan tucked in among the towering sentinels. The wind creaked through the naked boughs, beckoning him. The woods promised a solitude that didn't frighten him.

Glancing at his guards, Mikoneh gestured to the wood. "Give me a little space? Just for a few moments."

The lead guard hesitated, then nodded. "Please stay within sight, Your Highness."

"Sure."

As wide-spread and bare as the trees were, that wasn't hard to do. Mikoneh stepped into the woods. Snow crunched beneath his boots while the soft *tink* of tiny snowflakes pattered against his head and cloak.

The farther he moved into the woods, the quieter the world grew. The hammers and shouts faded into peaceful stillness. Mikoneh halted, still within sight of the green, but removed enough to pretend he was alone. Only the flutter of a cardinal's wings broke the silence. Mikoneh watched the little red bird climb into the cloudy sky, and his heart soared with it.

Closing his eyes, he dropped his chin. The crisp air filled

his nostrils. The quiet creak of the trees was like music lulling the world toward slumber. He ached to join it in rest.

If only he could feel safe. If only he could escape the phantoms of his soul, the hollow where Sathe's touch had bored into him, the fear that clung to his chest and crafted shadows in his periphery. If only he could feel unsullied, unmarred by the violation of his captivity, and the horror of slaughtering that village.

Tears pricked at his eyes. Mikoneh inhaled.

Please, God, send me a sign. Show me I'm not past mending.

A twig cracked. Mikoneh's eyes snapped open. Breath clouded before his mouth. He stared into the wooded gloom, hackles rising. He snatched his sword hilt, ready to unsheathe his blade, but the stillness remained peaceful. The wind died.

Something approached from deep in the woods, bringing a light with it. Snow whispered, not crunching. Mikoneh found himself stepping toward the light. Was it a lantern?

No, too bright for that. The light before him was soft like moonlight, but warmer than the winter sun.

Mikoneh faltered. His jaw fell. Within that radiant glow, a unicorn walked. It was neither horse nor deer, though reminiscent of both. Its coat was silver, and its mane was whiter than the drifting snow. The being's eyes shone gold, as did its horn and hooves. Its gaze was fixed on him, and under that stare, Mikoneh felt something inside him crack, spilling forth warmth and joy, softening the pain, the shame and sorrow, the fear, until he felt nearly whole.

Tears spilled down his face. He reached out to the unicorn. The graceful creature tossed its mane, horn sparkling in the thickening snowfall. It came nearer, leaving no mark along its path. Mikoneh blinked. The unicorn was walking *on* the snow. It—*she*—touched her nose to his bare fingers.

A sob fell from Mikoneh's lips. Every story he'd ever heard

concerning unicorns spoke of their aversion to taint and evil. Yet she'd touched him.

His tears flowed faster. "Thank you."

The unicorn held his eyes a moment more, then she turned and dashed off into the trees, vanishing in the growing gloom of the mounting storm. The light disappeared with her retreat. Mikoneh stood transfixed, then lowered his hand and curled his fingers over the lingering sensation of the unicorn's silken touch.

He turned at last toward the green, wiping his face dry. Upon leaving the woods, he met the lead guard's worried expression.

"Did you see her?" Mikoneh whispered.

"See who, Your Highness?" the guard asked, snatching his sword hilt.

Mikoneh hesitated. "Never mind. I must've been daydreaming." He knew that was a lie. The warmth in his chest was real. So was the memory of cool silk against his fingertips. He hadn't dreamed that up.

All the way back to the castle, he smiled, ignoring the chilling glares and curious whispers of the workers chasing his back. They didn't matter. He wasn't beyond healing. That was all he needed to know.

Sathe didn't break me.

Chapter 34

Always a Dragon

"There is no singular spirit that attaches itself to the wielder, yet a bond does form between the adept Elementalist and the spirits that they can see. My own affiliation with earth is a remarkable and rewarding experience."

- *A Treatise on the Magic of the Hidden Realm* by Sariolin the Solitary

Wind spirits howled outside the glass panes of the common room. Maya shivered, though the cold didn't eat at her like it once had. Hilker had left in the middle of their wind lesson, after receiving an urgent message from Crim, giving Maya free time ahead of the twins' dance lesson.

With careful steps, she approached Jensirin, who was huddled beneath his crimson cloak at the fire, lost to the torments of his mind. He looked hunted and careworn, his lips pressed so tight they'd lost their color.

Maya knelt beside the crouched man, clutching the teacup

and saucer she'd prepared. Steam rose from the green-tinted liquid, along with the strong aroma of mint and honey. She cleared her throat and waited.

Jensirin maintained his vigil over the flames, unflinching.

She tried again. "My lord?"

He whirled, knocking the cup and saucer from her hands. The porcelain shattered against the flagstones. Shards skittered over the floor. Maya sat stunned, only a fragment of her mind noting the dark stain seeping into her silver skirts.

"Oh. Mayanaleh." His voice was tight with regret, and breathless with relief. "Forgive me. I—I—"

"I'm so sorry I startled you," she said, and rose at once. "I'll clean it up." She hurried over to the table where the tea things were laid and grabbed up a few cloth towelettes. Returning to the hearth, she found several pieces of porcelain resting in Jensirin's outstretched hand. His finger oozed blood.

"Forgive me," he whispered.

"Nothing to forgive." She knelt and looked him in the eyes. "Accidents happen all the time, Jensirin. You're allowed."

His lips pinched tight again, but he nodded.

Maya plucked up the shards, set them on a towelette, and used another to dab at his finger. "You looked cold. I thought you might like something hot to drink. There's plenty more. I'll bring you another cup once I've tidied up."

"You don't need to." His voice was still faint.

"I want to," she said firmly.

The cut wasn't deep, and the bleeding stopped with a few more dabs. She gathered the remaining porcelain shards, then mopped up the spilled tea with the red-stained towelette. Rising, she returned to the table to make a fresh cup.

"Will you join me?" asked Jensirin with a voice like liquid.

She cast a smile at him over her shoulder. "I'd love to, thank you." After heaping honey into two cups, she moved to the fire gingerly, trying not to rattle porcelain on porcelain. A few drops escaped from her cup, but she ignored that and offered one cup and saucer to Jensirin. He accepted it with murmured thanks.

Maya eased herself to the floor and took a sip of mint tea while she gazed into the fire. "It's always amazed me how beautiful and necessary fire is—but it's so destructive, too."

"Like dragons."

She glanced at him. "Are dragons necessary?"

He nodded. "Dragons are justicers. Not just on Sirinhigha, but among the stars. Dragons demand, seek out, and maintain justice."

She fingered the rim of her saucer. "That would explain a lot about my brother. He's always such a stickler for rules."

"He's the Dragon Prince—Owenekiras's heir—protector of every dragon across each world in all of Mithrinn." Jensirin smiled faintly. "The weight of that responsibility would crush a lesser soul."

Maya took another sip of tea. Licking her lips, she asked, "What am I?"

"As the Dragon Princess, you bear the same duty. You, too, protect dragons, promote justice, and maintain order. During the Age of Dragons, so many of our kind went into hiding. The ripple effect extended beyond the borders of our world. Dragons have always been hunted, but after the first war against the Mages, hatred and mistrust spilled over. Many of our brothers and sisters across the universe have vanished. With the Mages awake again, we must find our kin before our enemy does."

"Dragons took human form, right?"

"Most often, but there are other ways for a dragon to hide. Some shifted into a stealth form—those with the knowledge and talent for it. Others still slipped into the Cores of their worlds, protected by special guardians. Many more sleep within hidden vales and dens." He sipped his tea. "It is my hope to return dragons to the glory days of yesteryear, when we roamed free, and were valued as the poets and sages that we are."

"Are dragons poets and sages?" Maya laughed.

"Certainly."

"But they're so—well, *fierce.*"

"Yes, as you can be, Dragon Princess. But are you not also gentle, compassionate, and prone to whimsy?"

She shifted, uncomfortable. "Well, yes. I suppose. It's just…"

"You assumed you were different because you were raised by humans, and because your birth mother was human?"

"Yes."

"Born a dragon, always a dragon. There is no such thing as half or quarter. You are a dragon true, my lady. We are as varied and unique as any human."

"But we're not human," Maya murmured. "Yet I *think* like a human."

"You're not a beast if that is your worry," Jensirin said. "Dragons are mighty, fierce, strong, and—after a few centuries —quite massive. But we think and feel, just like any sentient soul."

"But birds and squirrels don't feel in *quite* the same way as people," Maya said.

"True. They rely on instinct. I believe the difference lies in knowing right from wrong—though I'm no philosopher. Whatever the case, we are much like humans, but we aren't human."

"Because we're dragons."

"Yes."

Staring into the flames, Maya sipped her tea. "It's so strange to be something I've always been, yet never knew it. It's like I don't quite fit into my own skin."

"Nothing has changed," Jensirin said gently.

"Sure. Just everything."

He fell silent.

Maya swished her tea, then watched the fragments of herbs float back to the bottom of her cup. The aroma of mint curled around her face. "Thank you."

"For what, Princess?"

"For listening. For guiding me and Mikoneh. I can't imagine what you've been through, and what you're wrestling with right now, but I do know it's tremendously hard on you. Yet you're bearing it all so well." She risked a glance at him and smiled. "I admire your strength, Jensirin."

He was staring at her, his lips parted, his eyebrows drawn together. "I'm...not strong, Princess."

"Really?" She tipped her head to one side. "And yet you're here, after being a *Revenant* for—for who knows how long. And you're trying. I see it. You look pale and lost, you're grieving, but you're not hiding like the other dragons. You're not a puddle of melted snow on the ground. To me, that's remarkable."

He looked away, color dusting his cheeks. "It isn't... I simply..."

"You're simply trying, and that's amazing." She rested her hand on his arm. "I don't mean to make you feel uncomfortable. I tend to do that to people and I'm sorry. But I need you to acknowledge your efforts, Jensirin. Even before, as a cursed and tormented Revenant, you helped my brother. We were terrified of you—and you still aided him."

"He's my prince," whispered Jensirin.

"Yes. And you fought against a Mage's chains to help that prince. Give yourself what credit you're due, my lord." She squeezed his arm. "You're stronger than you believe. Someday, I'll convince you." She leaned back and took another sip.

The fire popped and hissed, a dribble of sap sizzling on a log.

Jensirin set his cup down with a faint *clink*. "Thank you, Mayanaleh."

"You're quite welcome, Jensirin. After all, I'm a justicer—and that means speaking the truth."

The door to the common room swung open, and Maya turned in time to see her twin standing there, a handful of guards behind him. He thanked one of them, then slipped inside and closed the door.

Maya climbed to her feet. "Everything okay?" She searched his face, surprised by the color there, along with his faint smile.

"Yeah." The single word curled with warmth. "I am. I think I'll take a nap before we head for our next lesson." He started for his room. Something in his step was lighter.

Maya's heart swelled. She hugged herself, drinking in renewed hope. Mikoneh slipped into his room, scattering light behind him. Maya whispered a soft prayer of thanks. He wasn't healed, but he'd taken a step toward mending. That was more than she'd expected so soon.

Settling back down by the hearth, Maya studied the brightened flames. She imagined fire spirits dancing in the embers. "You know, Jensirin. I'm coming to love fire. No matter how low it burns, it can always be rekindled."

THE QUEEN'S GAME

"As I said, no single earth spirit prefers me, yet there are a handful of these sweet beings that come each morning to my window and leave ripe berries on the sill."

- *A Treatise on the Magic of the Hidden Realm* by Sariolin the Solitary

Five days later, the last dance lesson was over. Vomm had washed his hands of the twins, though the prim smile he wore told Mikoneh that the man was secretly pleased. That had to mean something. Maybe Mikoneh wouldn't maim Princess Latta's toes during their first dance together, like he had in his dream the night before.

Striding with Maya toward their suite, a contingent of soldiers at their backs, Mikoneh allowed his thoughts to wander to the next day's events. The Winter Ball. The tourney. The queen's demands—not yet answered. Crim hadn't contacted Mikoneh about what he and Hilker had learned, which didn't bode well. In fact, Crim had been absent all week, doubtless caught up in festival planning. Hilker had been distant and grumpy, so Mikoneh didn't dare ask him about any progress.

With all the preparations in and around the castle, the twins hardly left their rooms. Latta visited a few times before other duties kept her away. Ter popped up once to inform the twins he had been called away for a while, and Minno had vanished. Mikoneh was left on his own to train his element, and he did what he could in the common room. Frustration bubbled up in his chest every time he thought about the time he was wasting studying magic and etiquette rather than searching out the leak. But there was nothing he could do about it.

"You look pensive," said Maya. "Fretting over your first royal dance?"

"Something like that."

"You'll be fine. You didn't stomp on my toes once today."

"Don't tempt me."

She laughed, shaking her head.

"There you are!"

Crim's voice brought Mikoneh's steps up short. He whirled. The merchant lord was traipsing up the adjacent corridor, Hilker at his side. They looked nonchalant, despite Crim's tousled hair and the Wind Master's wrinkled clothes.

"Do you have a spare moment, Your Highnesses?" asked Crim.

"Absolutely." Mikoneh gestured toward their suite still several turns away. "Join us for afternoon tea?"

"We'd love to," Crim said.

They moved up the corridor, and Mikoneh's thoughts shifted back to Feresse's request. What had Crim learned? What was he planning to do? Hopefully Crim had made progress where the twins hadn't.

Mikoneh quickened his pace. The rest kept up.

When they reached their suite, Latta was just stepping out of the common room. Her eyes widened. "There you are."

"Here we are," Mikoneh said, shrugging his hands. "Do you need a word, too?"

"Yes." Her eyes flicked to Crim. "Perhaps concerning the same matter." Latta's eyes were ringed with shadows. She looked like she hadn't slept in days. Mikoneh could certainly relate to that. After the incident with the unicorn, he'd napped peacefully and rested well the following night, but once her gifted warmth gradually wore off, his nightmares had returned.

He caught the door and gestured. "Come in and be welcome, all."

"Thank you," said Minno inside the room. "I already am. In, that is."

Mikoneh blinked at the gray boy, then sighed. Why not? His nerves were already on edge one day before the Wintertide events began. What was one more complication?

The company seated themselves near the fire while the guards remained outside the common room. Jensirin was absent. Worry pricked at Mikoneh's chest, but he ignored it. One issue at a time.

"Who wants to go first?" asked Mikoneh, taking a seat on the floor before the hearth. He crisscrossed his legs, folding them in front of him.

Crim glanced at Latta, then Minno. "Perhaps..." He nodded at Minno. "Should you start?"

"I'm only here for the bread." Minno held up a cucumber sandwich. "Duck is partial to it." He dropped broken bits of crust onto the floor, and Duck nibbled at it like a starving thing.

"Ahhh." Crim shifted in his wingback chair. "Well. Then perhaps you can take a few more of those sandwiches and go away?"

"I'd rather stay," said Minno.

"It's fine," Mikoneh said. "He's here by Owenekiras's leave."

Disbelieving eyes turned toward Minno, then quickly away.

"Right." Crim glanced at Latta. "Perhaps you, then, Your Highness?"

"I suspect our motives are related," she said. "This is regarding Queen Feresse's demand, right?"

"So it is," said Crim. "Very well."

Maya was seated on the arm of the settee, watching with mute interest, her eyes bright and sharp. Mikoneh hadn't told her about Feresse. He hadn't wanted her to fret until he knew more, then when no information was forthcoming, he'd felt it was too late to tell her casually without angering her. In retrospect, he should've trusted her with the information everyone else possessed.

She doesn't need to be protected. She needs to be trusted.

Mikoneh resolved to confide everything to her, even the unicorn, after the others left.

He shifted. "What have you learned, Lord Crim?"

"Nothing."

"Nothing?"

"Nothing *yet*."

"You haven't located the agent using your name," Mikoneh guessed.

"Right. If there is one. If this isn't the queen's game meant to rattle our collusion."

Mikoneh nodded. "I'd considered that."

"She seemed sincere to me," said Latta.

Crim blinked. "You were present, Princess?"

"Yes. Mikoneh and I had been out riding."

"This happened that long ago?" asked Maya, her gaze settling on Mikoneh.

He dropped his eyes to study his hands. "Yeah. I should've mentioned it."

"Yes," she whispered. "You should have."

His face burned. He cleared his throat and forced himself to look up. "What's the plan?"

Crim sighed and flung up his hand in a helpless shrug. "I'm open to ideas. Hilker and I have both poked and prodded, but we can't find answers or a path ahead."

Maya leaned forward. "I need to know what happened."

Latta launched into an explanation, sparing Mikoneh. He stared at the floor, listening, his mind churning with possibilities. What could they do? Feresse had offered to give Latta's voice back, but only under an impossible condition. He could never kill Crim.

Mikoneh froze. "Wait."

Every eye found him.

"We could bluff."

"How?" asked Crim.

Mikoneh's lips quivered toward a dry smile. "How do you feel about being dead, my lord?"

CHAPTER 36

PLAYING IGNORANT

"If the Spirits Elemental have family units or clans amongst a single type, I cannot tell. They tease and squabble like birds over a worm, but they appear to exist in harmony. If only people could do the same."

- A Treatise on the Magic of the Hidden Realm by Sariolin the Solitary

Shouts broke the silence of middle night. Mikoneh was sitting at the window seat in his bedchamber, a book propped on his lap, its words unread. The scent of snow wafted in from the open window. Mikoneh snapped his book shut and darted into the common room. A guard stood in the open doorway, letting torchlight stain the floor from the corridor beyond.

"What's going on?" asked Mikoneh.

A bedroom door flung open behind him. Maya, judging by her windswept scent.

The guard shook his head. "I was sent to keep you safe.

That's all I know." Beyond him, armor rattled in the corridor. Guards raced past. Panic sparked in the air.

Maya moved up to Mikoneh's side. She was clad in her pink robe, and her hair was tousled—though a faint breeze worked hard to unravel her snarls. "Did something happen?"

"The guard doesn't know." Mikoneh glanced toward the hearth. No one stood before the banked coals. Mikoneh's insides knotted, but he forced himself to breathe. In. Out. In.

Maya took his arm. "Do you think everything's all right?"

"Gotta be," he said. *Please let it be.*

"I'll make some tea." She slipped from Mikoneh's side, and moved toward the table where the tea things were always in readiness. He followed his twin to boil the water.

He didn't want tea. He didn't want distractions. He wanted to know whether the plan had worked, or if something had gone wrong. Time passed, and no one came to deliver any news. Minno and Jensirin never appeared. Dawn crept into the common room, gilding the furniture, glistening against nature's frosty scrollwork ornamenting the windowpanes.

Maya had provided the guard at the door with a chair, then brewed him some tea. He was a young man, all smiles for the pretty princess serving him. Mikoneh was too agitated to drink anything, or sit, or sleep. He paced, wearing down the damask rug beneath his bare toes. Every nerve was taut as a lute string. His mind whispered about failure—but he blocked it out. His instincts were coiled up and ready to spring loose, but he held himself together.

Wait. Just wait.

The rattle of armor in the hallway brought Mikoneh to a halt. He spun toward the door. The guard flung himself from his chair beside the exit, coming to full attention just as the door swung open. A sea of people poured into the room. At their fore was Crown Prince Atlanse, with Latta on his arm, and tumbling in behind them—red-faced and rumpled from a sleepless night—was Queen Feresse.

Atlanse glanced at the guard, then Maya, then pinned his sights on Mikoneh. "Have you been in this chamber all night?"

"Yes," Mikoneh said.

"You've not left?"

"Not once."

"What's going on?" asked Maya, stepping closer. "We heard the commotion last night, and we've not been able to rest."

"Lies," said the young queen. "Servants saw you leave last night, Prince Mikoneh, in company with Lord Crim. And now he's dead."

Mikoneh froze, the apparatuses of his mind turning. *So, that's your game.* "I don't understand. Dead? Where? How?"

The queen's cheeks flushed brighter. "Don't play ignorant."

A tall, muscular figure pushed through the crush of guards and nobles. "Excuse me, Your Majesty. I must come through." At his deep, rumbling voice, most people parted, but Queen Feresse shot the man a withering glare.

"Don't just bob there like a lily pad, Sir Kalet," she said. "Seize the heir of Rokahn. Arrest him."

Mikoneh's eyes narrowed. So, this was Kalet, eh? The Corpse Poet in the flesh. Looking the man up and down, his contradictory reputation made sense. Power and grace aligned in Kalet's frame. He was a comely man in a rugged sort of way —if Mikoneh was any kind of judge of male beauty. But his eyes set Mikoneh's teeth on edge. They were dark and glittering in the common room's gloom, reminding Mikoneh distinctly of Sathe.

"I don't think we should do anything in haste," Sir Kalet said.

"Good idea," said Hilker from somewhere in the throng. "Owenekiras may not appreciate his son being falsely accused and imprisoned."

Murmurs rose at that, and Queen Feresse's face pinched.

"But Lord Crim is dead," someone said.

"And the Rokahnian prince and princess have been here all night," another countered.

"What about their lackeys?"

Maya shot a glance at Mikoneh, her eyebrows hanging high.

He shrugged. *Who do they think are our lackeys?*

Minno's deadpan voice cut through the muttering debate like a Ciminian blade. "What if I said I killed Crim?"

The nobility parted like wheat under a scythe. Standing behind them in the corridor, Minno held up his hands. They were bloody. At his feet stood Duck. The bizarre image of a child covered in gore, accompanied by a harmless animal, was disconcerting, even to Mikoneh who knew Minno was broken.

Sir Kalet shoved back shoulder-length locks of pale blond hair, then strode over to Minno, a hand settling on his sword hilt. "You admit to murdering Crim?"

"I asked a question," said Minno.

Kalet's fingers tightened on his sword. "This isn't a game, Master Minno. Did you or didn't you kill Crim?"

"Is Crim dead?"

"Yes," Kalet said.

"Then I am responsible."

Mikoneh's stomach heated. What was the dunce doing? This wasn't the plan. Maya glanced toward him, panic dancing in her golden eyes.

"As close to a confession as we're likely to get," Hilker said. "Arrest him, Sir Kalet."

The Valor Knight nodded and set a hand on Minno's small

shoulder. "You're under arrest for murder. Stay your tongue until the trial if you wish to have any chance before King Prettem's court." He motioned, and two guards moved forward to seize Minno.

"Ah," said Minno. "But I have no intention of entering Prettem's pet dungeons." Anger flashed across his face like steel. The guards set their hands on his shoulder, and Kalet relinquished his grasp. In the next breath, the two guards stiffened, then slumped forward. One let out a dull "quack" and began to waddle in an exaggerated impression of a duck. The other echoed him and tried to flap his arms like wings.

Minno scooped up the real fowl, then turned and fled down the corridor. "Arrest me if you can, Kalet." His steps were fleet across the flagstones.

"W-wait!" called out Kalet, staggering forward—but the ensorcelled guards waddled into his path.

Mikoneh's jaw had fallen. Emotions brimmed within him; a strange pattern of mirth and disbelief surged toward hysteria. Maya threw a hand to her lips and choked down a giggle. The nobility shrank inside the common room. Several traced symbols over the air as though to ward off evil. Maybe they had cause.

Hilker threw his head back and cackled. Kalet tossed his father a disapproving glance, then barked orders at the remaining guards. None heeded him. No one chased after Minno.

Mikoneh slipped into the corner near the window where dawn hadn't yet chased away the shadows. The din of panicked voices weaved through him, charging his nerves, prickling his skin.

A hand fell against his shoulder.

Mikoneh yelped and spun.

Jensirin.

"You." Mikoneh grabbed at his pounding chest. "That... don't do that..."

"Apologies," whispered the dragon lord. "You looked... unwell."

Mikoneh tipped his head. "Just, you know, panicking a little. That stunt of Minno's was crazy."

"Yes." Jensirin looked troubled. "It should wear off. He merely planted a suggestive memory of being a waterfowl."

"Oh. Merely that?"

"Minno is a Keeper of Memory—the first and the best. He —well, he is what one might call a loose catapult."

"I can see that." Mikoneh tried to shrug it off. "How did everything go?"

"As planned." Jensirin's eyes followed the crowd. Mikoneh glanced over to find Sir Kalet rounding up the nobles and leading them from the room. Several guards were herding the two waddling men. Prince Atlanse remained inside, with Hilker next to him. Feresse stood out in the corridor, glowering at Maya who was speaking quietly with Latta. The Simynshinian princess twisted her ring around her finger over and over, glancing occasionally at Akonn's door.

The last noble was shooed away, and Feresse strode forward to speak heatedly with the Corpse Poet. Kalet's expression was unyielding, and Mikoneh felt a tug of respect for the Valor Knight. He'd assumed the man would kiss up to the queen, not repel her games.

"Prince Mikoneh?" Atlanse's voice was close and low.

Nearly jumping from his skin, Mikoneh scowled at the Crown Prince. "Yes, my lord?"

Atlanse stiffened, then his lips slanted into a sideways smile. "I didn't mean to startle you."

"Well, you did." Mikoneh shook his hands to stop the

tingling in his fingertips. "It's fine, Your Royal Highness. I'm just on edge."

"That only makes sense." Atlanse's expression softened. "Crim was my friend, as he was yours. I understand your grief."

Mikoneh weighed the man's words. Was Atlanse acting, or had Crim not informed the Crown Prince of their scheme. His distressed mien looked genuine.

"I suspect your grief is deeper," he whispered. "You've known him for years."

Atlanse considered the floor and nodded, then turned away, hiding his expression and any hint of what he might know. "He told me that you intended to enter the lists. I'll understand if you prefer to back out now."

"No, I'll fight. He would want me to."

Atlanse nodded, setting his eyes on the coals in the hearth. "And the Elementalist challenge?"

"Maya and I will both participate."

"Good. Excellent." The Crown Prince turned toward the door. "I'll see that everything's arranged." He sighed. "After I escort my stepmother back to her wing."

"That's not necessary." Mikoneh caught the man's arm. "I think I need to discuss her accusation, here, now. I promise to maintain my temper and stay diplomatic."

Atlanse huffed a laugh. "A Rokahn, diplomatic? Pah." But he strode away, not arguing. "Come, Latta. We must send word to Namirsha—and she may need your friendship in her grief."

Latta hesitated, frowning. She cast a questioning glance toward Mikoneh, then let her father pull her from the room. After a brief word, Sir Kalet left with all the royals but Feresse.

She stepped into the room, her ocean-hued dragon-scale necklace glittering. Feresse glanced at Maya, then turned back to Mikoneh. If she noticed Jensirin in the corner, she didn't reveal that fact.

"I honestly didn't expect you to succeed," she said.

"On the other hand," Mikoneh said, "I did expect your treachery following on the heels of your affair."

"Then why follow through?"

He shrugged. "Call it a calculated risk. I want Latta's voice back."

"I'm sure you do—but I can't help you with that."

"Oh, no? So, you lied?"

She offered her own shrug. "Call it a calculated risk. I needed Crim gone, and you wanted something in exchange. Let this be a lesson in politics, boy. You can't trust people in power."

"I never have. Especially not royals who are unfaithful to their marriage vows. Your infidelity disgusts me."

Her eyes narrowed. "Yet you played along."

"I did, yes."

Feresse's eyes darted to the nearest bedroom door. "Who's here? Who's listening in?"

"Oh, no one special." Mikoneh allowed himself a grin. "Just the king."

The door to Akonn's room clicked open and swung aside. There, a silhouette loomed. "Hello, Feresse." King Prettem's voice was a low rumble, full of power despite his age.

Mikoneh's grin stretched wider while the blood drained from Feresse's face.

Caught.

CHAPTER 37

ONE OF US

"There are no children and no adults among them. They simply exist. If the Spirits Elemental are born, grow old, and die as a consequence of age, I cannot see the signs—though I have witnessed an earth spirit use its life energy up to spare a wielder. It was the greatest heartbreak I have ever felt."

- *A Treatise on the Magic of the Hidden Realm* by Sariolin the Solitary

Mikoneh had taken a big risk in dragging the old king into the issue with Feresse. Crim had advised against it. Penn had gone pale. But Hilker had laughed. Maya had supported Mikoneh's decision, eager to put the ordeal behind them with as little fuss as possible.

At first, King Prettem had been dismissive. Mikoneh hadn't dared mention the particulars, especially not anything of Feresse's affair. Instead, he'd led Prettem to believe that his beloved wife was in danger.

It wasn't technically a lie.

Prettem at last agreed to hide in Akonn's room and wait.

He's assured Mikoneh he was a light sleeper, and whatever commotion occurred, he'd be awake to listen in. "Anything for my beloved wife," he'd declared.

Mikoneh had wrestled away his guilt. The king deserved to know the truth—hopefully he would be rational about it, rather than foist the blame where it didn't belong. Hilker had warned that his brother-in-law could be hot-tempered.

"Do this right, though," Hilker had offered up, "and you'll make a true ally of Simynshin."

Mikoneh intended to do just that.

Feresse had made one critical mistake in her calculations: Mikoneh Rokahn didn't play games—he crushed them.

Prettem strode into the common room. He was dressed in yesterday's clothes, and though they were rumpled from a night spent sitting in a chair, his fur-lined cape and sparkling crown set him apart. His white beard was trimmed. His eyes—fastened on his wife—glittered like rime.

Feresse trembled, then raced forward. "Whatever you heard, my pet, it's not true. I've been entrapped!"

"Trickery is part of the game," Prettem murmured. "You lost, my dear."

Feresse's eyes widened. "Beloved—"

"Don't." The king shook his head. "Your disgrace is evident enough. I see the lie in your eyes. Every denial will worsen your punishment." He turned from her to find Mikoneh. Prettem's gaze could shred through steel. "A clever move, Your Highness. Bold but meticulous. Proof of your heritage, that's certain."

Mikoneh's cheeks warmed, though he couldn't determine if he felt pleased or shamed by that association.

Prettem turned to the chamber's main door. "Come in, Sir Kalet."

The Valor Knight entered, and bowed his head. "My liege?"

"Take Queen Feresse to her quarters. See she's kept under guard there until her trial."

"As you command, my liege." Kalet marched across the room and caught Feresse's arm. "This way, Your Majesty."

Feresse blinked back tears. "You can't do this to me. What of trade with Lintha? You would risk open war?"

Prettem sighed. "Questions you should've asked yourself before you betrayed me, my wife. If war is upon us, be it on your head—not mine."

She blubbered but didn't struggle against Kalet as he led her toward the door.

"Wait," said Prettem. "One last question. Who is the man who led you astray? His name if you please."

Kalet paused to let Feresse turn around. Her eyes glistened with tears, but a hardness blazed there. "Never. I'll never betray him."

Prettem nodded. "I'll discover him on my own, then. Take her from my sight, Sir Kalet."

Guards met them in the hall, and Feresse was led away before someone reached in to shut the door. King Prettem stalked to the hearth. He stirred the coals with the iron poker, then tossed a log over the sputtering flames.

"Owenekiras returns later today," Prettem said without turning around.

Fire spirits nibbled on the log.

"Just in time for the Winter Tourney," Maya said.

"Indeed." Prettem turned around at last and cupped his hands behind his back, beneath his cape. "He has long warned me of Lintha's treachery."

Mikoneh held still, unwilling to provoke the king. Maya

must've had the same sense. She tugged at her robe ties, staying silent.

"Do you agree that Lintha has been seduced by the Mages?" asked Prettem.

"Yes," Mikoneh said.

"Your reasoning?"

"First," Mikoneh said, "Oceana always mirrors Lintha's actions, and I've witnessed the Mage influence *there* firsthand."

"And second?"

"Your lady queen's close association with the Mage ambassador."

Prettem nodded, fingering his trimmed beard. "Any other reasons?"

"Instinct," Mikoneh said, then hesitated. He knew what he needed to say, but it would sting to speak aloud. *Do it anyway.* "And fact. I...met one of the Mage Generals, Your Majesty. He told me they mean to conquer the civilized world. Infiltration has been their method. Even if Queen Feresse had nothing to do with their presence here, I'd never trust them to remain benign."

The king grunted and turned away. "I'll discuss this matter with your father once he arrives."

"As you please, Your Majesty."

The king sighed. "I should thank you for this...but I can't bring myself to feel any gratitude." Prettem left with a flourish, sweeping his cape out after him. Guards flanked him in the corridors, and they marched away with a clatter of boots and rattling armor. Penn slipped inside after them, dripping wet. For once, he held no books.

"They wouldn't let me in. Now I can see why." Penn arched his brows. "How did everything go?"

"Not too badly." Mikoneh moved to Akonn's room and knocked. When a voice invited him inside, he entered. Near a lit candle on the nightstand, Crim was sitting in one of two chairs. In the bed, Akonn sat propped against an army of pillows. His infection had been staved off, but he still looked weak.

"It worked." Crim's eyes were bright. "You're a good tactician, not that anyone should be surprised by that. After all—"

"I'm a Rokahn," Mikoneh sighed. "I get it. But in my family tree, there must be a halfwit somewhere, and if I ever find them—well, I'll celebrate. No family is superior to any other, my lord."

Crim's smile slanted sideways. "Akonn mentioned you dislike nobility, but you'll need to overcome that prejudice somehow. You're a prince, Mikoneh. You're one of us."

"No man should be defined by his blood rather than his character," Mikoneh said. "Some of the most worthy, honorable people I know are farmers and blacksmiths."

"Yet you disdain all nobility as a rule." Crim shrugged. "Believe me, I harbor my share of hypocrisy, but I urge you to check yourself, my friend."

Mikoneh scowled at the floor, letting his shame roll through him. "I know you're right, Lord Crim. I...I'll try."

"I know you will." Crim stood up. "Well, I think it's time I rose from the dead, eh? King Prettem asked me not to dawdle—and poor Minno is liable to get himself hurt for that stunt of his if I don't present myself soon."

"Doubt it," Mikoneh scoffed. "No one's gonna catch him."

"Maybe not."

"Definitely not. He made two guards think they were ducks."

"Are you serious?" Crim asked.

Akonn's face went blank. "Really?"

"He's not lying," said Maya, standing just inside the room behind Mikoneh. "I witnessed it, too."

"Jensirin said it won't last. Probably." Mikoneh scrubbed at an itch on his arm. "Of all the strange things I've seen since leaving Relvin Province, that might be the oddest of all."

Maya hummed her agreement.

"Remind me not to annoy that one," Akonn muttered.

"Likewise," Penn said in the doorway.

"Well." Maya batted at a yawn. "I'm going back to bed for a few turns. You boys do what you want." She slipped from the bedroom.

Looking glassy-eyed and still dripping water, Penn found his own room.

Despite the weariness from a sleepless night, Mikoneh resisted the call of his bed. The Winter Tourney was only one day away, and he had fire to master, sword training to brush up on, and an estranged father to speak to.

"What will you do?" asked Crim, watching him closely.

"Spar." Mikoneh shrugged. "After your morning business, mind giving me a fire lesson?"

"I'd be glad to," Crim said. "Let's meet at the west tower in two turns."

AFTER AN INTENSE SWORD bout with Master Donivan in the training hall, Mikoneh made his way toward the west tower.

Around him, servants bustled along the corridors, hanging holly wreaths, placing fresh candles into wall brackets, stringing garlands made of evergreen boughs and cinnamon sticks, and arranging bundles of fragrant pinecones in clever little baskets. Spices clung to the air, stirring up childhood memories of Snowcrest, the winter fete back home. During the darkest night of the year, Fa and Mama always prepared mulled apple wine, drank a toast to the slumbering world, and sang and danced with the twins until dawn. The following morning, they'd all given gifts to each other.

Mikoneh's heart pinched, but he breathed in the perfume of cloves, cinnamon, nutmeg, and ginger, mingled with the spice of freshly cut pine. Homesickness was welcome on the heels of the night's stress. He'd rather feel a familiar sense of pain from love and loss than wallow beneath the press of his trauma and fear. He would never regret knowing Jonatten and Seranni.

"Your Highness?" called a rich, familiar voice.

Mikoneh turned and spotted Sir Kalet approaching along the corridor. The man's face held lines, though from worry or anger Mikoneh couldn't tell. Kalet's presence was commanding, but his hand wasn't on his sword. Halting, Mikoneh waited for the Corpse Poet to reach him. The knight paused to let a servant scurry past, then ate up the last stretch of ground on his long, powerful legs.

"Forgive me for interrupting you," Kalet said. "I realize you're on your way to your Elementalist lesson."

"I have a spare moment." Mikoneh tacked on a diplomatic smile. His instincts were tense, ready for any unexpected provocation. "Did you need something, Sir Kalet?"

The knight blinked. "You remembered my name?"

"You're a legend in Oceana."

"Ah." Kalet shifted, looking uncomfortable. "Legends are rarely what we make them."

"Modesty from the Corpse Poet?" Mikoneh folded his arms and stared the man up and down. "Didn't expect that."

Did Kalet actually blush? "Ah. Corpse Poet. It's been a

long time since I've heard that moniker." He winced. "But I suppose people aren't quick to forget."

Doubts crept into Mikoneh's head. He'd had a half-grown suspicion that this man was the queen's secret lover. Somehow, the image of a fierce and bloodthirsty man with a penchant for spouting poetry lent itself well to the image of an illicit affair—but this knight...he wasn't what Mikoneh had expected. Searching Kalet's eyes, Mikoneh found regret and...gentleness?

"Are you not the great warrior people make you out to be?" asked Mikoneh.

Kalet's mouth crooked. "I'm an excellent swordsman."

"But?" Mikoneh blinked, startled by his own question. "Never mind, Sir Kalet. It's none of my business. I apologize."

The tall man shook his head. "If I'm a legend, it's natural you would be curious. I, too, am curious about you. Imagine my shock—not a full turn ago—to learn that Lord Crim is indeed alive, and that you are the mastermind behind revealing the queen's unfaithfulness. It was a brilliant if reckless plan."

"More desperate than brilliant."

"Modesty, Your Highness?" A twinkle caught in Kalet's eye.

Mikoneh's lips twitched up. What kind of man was Kalet? Modest, deadly—he had his father's dry wit—but perhaps it was too soon for Mikoneh to read the stranger. He was accustomed to hasty assumptions on a battlefield, but this kind of combat was different. Mikoneh needed to learn the new terrain, and fast.

"Did you seek me out to satisfy that curiosity," Mikoneh asked, "or was there another reason?"

Kalet's shoulders squared. "Actually, I wished to speak with you regarding your entry into the tourney lists."

"Is there a problem?"

"No. Not at all." Kalet tipped his head, sizing Mikoneh up.

"I was hoping to begin the sword challenge with you as my opponent. The king wishes to start the tourney off with a high precedent to give each contestant the proper motivation. In the past, performances have been lackluster. Many of the youth are unwilling to put their all into fighting, for fear they'll be drafted into the war."

"You don't even know how well I fight, Sir Knight," said Mikoneh. "Wouldn't Master Donivan be a better opponent to face off against?"

Kalet shook his head. "You carry your skill as openly as you carry that sword of yours. Every movement tells me you're a warrior. Besides, Master Donivan is hardly something fresh. Surely, his skill is excellent, but he and I always face off to open the tourney. You bring something new to the field—and that will send the message we need."

"What message, precisely, are you going for?"

"That we Simynshinians and Lord Rokahn are allies, and we ought to join him in this war against the Mages."

"But if we're opponents, won't that say the opposite?"

Kalet offered another headshake. "You've never entered a tourney before, have you?"

"No. In Relvin, politics didn't allow for much sport, and besides, I wasn't a knight."

"Ah, Relvin. Isn't that Lord Drayve's province? Petty tyrant, isn't he?"

Something in Mikoneh's chest twisted. "Yeah. Petty. Though not long ago, he was my greatest enemy."

"By my spymaster's last report," said Kalet, "Drayve's estate was burned to the ground, and he fled into the forest. Most Oceanians suspect he died, others say he's hiding out in a little cove beyond the wood. I don't recall the name offhand."

"Bone Cove." Mikoneh shuddered, recalling his own

escape from Drayve, through the woods and into the caves of that lonely cove. There, he'd fallen into Sathe's hands.

"Yes," Kalet said. "That's the one."

Mikoneh shook off the fingers of cold trying to prod at his mental wounds. "I'll accept your offer, Sir Knight. I trust your judgment on this matter more than my own. I'm afraid I'm a small fish in a vast sea here."

Kalet's teeth flashed in a disarming smile. "You're a Rokahn. You'll find your footing in no time. And for the record, you're nothing approaching small. The weight of your name alone is enough to topple kingdoms. Best you learn to use that, Your Highness. Now, if you'll excuse me, I'll take my leave. I don't want to make you late for Lord Crim's lesson." He bowed. Mikoneh returned the gesture, then the knight strode away, parting the crowds.

One female servant dropped her bundle of pinecones as he passed.

Mikoneh stooped to help her pick them up, then mumbled farewell and retreated toward the tower. His mind churned. His instincts hummed. The games of Simynshin were even more complex than he'd expected—but Kalet was right. Mikoneh wasn't a little fish anymore. Wherever he moved, he'd make great waves.

He couldn't forget that.

CHAPTER 38

THE HOLLOW IN HER HEART

"More than one colleague has disapproved of my choice to leave my people in pursuit of a solitary life—but I wouldn't trade living among the Spirits Elemental for anything else."

- *A Treatise on the Magic of the Hidden Realm* by Sariolin the Solitary

During breakfast, Maya left Jensirin to his thoughts. She'd tried speaking with him, but he didn't seem to hear her, and she didn't want to make him feel cornered by pushing.

She'd seen many soldiers suffering from trauma after bloody engagements back in Relvin. Even her surrogate parents —so confident and strong—had wrestled with inner demons some days. Especially Fa. He'd witnessed things, Mama often said, which no living being should see.

With Jensirin, that darkness, that troubled countenance, ran deeper.

She ached to help him, but experience had taught her that sometimes the best help came with silence. She'd tried to sleep, but her full mind wouldn't let her, and she'd abandoned the attempt and instead ordered food. He knew she was nearby, breakfasting alone, patiently waiting. The dragon lord remained in the darkest corner near the window. He'd been pivotal in convincing Queen Feresse's spies that Lord Crim was dead. Jensirin had assured the twins he could handle the task, and after a few careful questions about maintaining the safety of the castle staff, Mikoneh had agreed to let him. In short, no real bodies were to be used. Jensirin had cracked a smile at that —a small one, yes, but still a smile.

Maya ate her berries and cream with relish, determined to make up for a sleepless night with some good nourishment. She pushed away thoughts of Jensirin and focused instead on the upcoming Winter Ball. She'd grown very fond of dancing, which came as no surprise to anyone who knew her. But more than that, she'd grown quite skilled at it. Even so, she was worried that all that practice would fly out the window once she was surrounded by gawking strangers. The same thing had happened in the village dances back home. She wasn't bad on her feet—until people were watching.

A knock cut into her fretting.

"Come in!" she called.

Latta poked her head inside. "Hello, Maya."

"You didn't go to Lady Namirsha's?" Maya beckoned her friend to the little breakfast table.

"No." Latta drifted inside and shut the door behind her, but not before Maya glimpsed Latta's new bodyguard stationed outside. "It seems Lord Crim magically rose from the dead. It's quite the miracle." Her eyes sparkled.

Maya laughed. "Yes, my brother has some unusual skills."

The Songbird Princess folded herself into the opposite chair from Maya's, and plucked up a raspberry. "He certainly likes to start fires. Most appropriate."

Maya nearly snorted but stopped herself. She was certain ladies didn't snort—publicly. "Did you come here to chat or for some other reason? Either way, I don't mind."

"Thank you." Latta twisted her golden ring. It flashed in a strand of daylight. "I just wanted company."

"Are you sad?"

"No." Latta smiled. "Quite the contrary. Feresse is going to be put on trial. Her days of—well, of bullying me—they're done."

"Was she terribly cruel?"

"Not more than most court women of my acquaintance, but she had the rank to do more about it. She would say what she thought out loud—not in any way that could be considered improper—but in a way that hurt. It's rather a game to most courtiers. How sly can one make one's insults? How passively can one be mean-spirited? I doubt it's different with village women. You've dealt with it, too, I dare say."

Maya shook her head. "Not really. My mother was a soldier. Seranni, I mean. She put most women off, so they largely left us alone. It wasn't until I met Kevva that I understood how vicious women could be while appearing nice. She felt like my kindred friend—until I learned she was using me to get to Mikoneh. Then she betrayed our rebellion's position to Lord Drayve purely to spite my brother when he rejected her."

Latta stiffened. "What a nasty vixen."

"Indeed."

"What happened to her?"

"She was at our execution," Maya said. "Mikoneh nearly torched her. I don't think he meant to, but I've never asked. She'd become Drayve's mistress from the look of things, drenched in emeralds and pearls. He's a lascivious man."

"Is he handsome?" asked Latta.

"No. He's rather pointy."

Latta snorted.

Maya blinked. Perhaps she'd been wrong about ladies, or maybe Latta felt comfortable around her.

The princess poured herself a goblet of water, and her ring flashed again.

Maya's dragon impulse kicked in, and she nearly snatched for the golden band. "You're always wearing that ring. Is it special to you?"

Latta's face softened into an expression of fond sorrow. She ran a finger across the plain gold band. "It was my mother's. I found it amongst her possessions last summer, and I took it for my own. I hadn't expected it to fit, but it seems I have one thing in common with her after all."

"You must miss her a great deal," Maya whispered. The hollow in her heart resonated with Latta's.

"I do, every day, though I don't know why. She didn't care for me. I—I think she loved me in her way, but I was an inconvenience. Everything about her life here in Simynshin was, especially my father. I doubt she thinks of us, or her time here, except with relief that she's gone."

"But isn't she disgraced in Cimin?"

"Yes, but Ciminians have so much pride in their heritage, she likely feels more at home there—even in disgrace—than she ever did here, lavished in finery and affection."

"Yet you love her," Maya said. "Enough to wear her ring."

"I can't bring myself to abandon her like she abandoned us. I can't do it." Latta sighed. "When I fell ill, this little trinket comforted me. It feels like the ring is a piece of my mother I never witnessed. It stayed with me in my illness like she never would have." Latta stroked the band again. "Maybe it's because I can't imagine her wearing this ring. It's too simple, too plain. It's the piece of her she rejected and left behind for me."

Maya reached across the table and took Latta's hand. She

squeezed the princess's fingers. "Don't belittle yourself, Latta. Some people don't see the treasure before them, no matter how beautiful it may be. But people *can* change. Perhaps, if not now, someday she'll realize what she lost."

The princess dropped her eyes, took a breath, then squeezed Maya's hand back. "Thank you, my precious friend." She looked up. "But tell me—what happened after Mikoneh nearly singed Kevva. Did she run away screaming? Was proper dragon justice done during your escape?"

"Alas, no," Maya sighed, retracting her hand. "She likely remained at court and pleased Drayve at his whim. Maybe that's enough punishment."

"Hardly." Latta scowled. "Her actions were inexcusable. I hope she's been driven from Drayve's court in shame, and that she's out there in the cold right now, in some hovel. Is she pretty?"

"Yes," Maya grimaced. "Too pretty."

"That's good."

"How so?" Maya laughed with surprise.

"It tells me something important about your brother. He's not taken in by beautiful, shallow women."

"That almost sounds like jealousy."

Latta stiffened, then sighed. "I suppose I've harbored *some* feelings for your brother since our childhood. I think the little girl in me rather expected that we would fall in love and fulfill the vows of our betrothal. It seemed a romantic notion."

"And then you met Captain Akonn?"

A pink hue feathered Latta's cheeks. "Yes, well, that's more impossible even than marrying your twin. Akonn is a mere captain, whatever his personal qualities. My father—and my grandfather—would never approve."

"Does Akonn share your regard?"

Latta twisted her ring. "I don't know. He's very careful. I—

I did tell him of my feelings, which was profoundly foolish. He thanked me but said nothing more. It was then I realized how impossible our connection could ever be."

"I'm sorry." A flicker of movement caught Maya's eye, and she tensed.

Jensirin. He was still in the corner. How could she forget all about him? And having this of all conversations!

She deliberately didn't look toward the window and prayed that Latta wouldn't notice the cloaked man in the corner.

"It's not your fault, Maya," Latta said. "Don't be sorry."

"I know… I just…understand what it's like. I've had feelings for someone before, unreciprocated, and then…" She stared at her bowl of berries. "Then he died." The words cut. She had never told anyone about the man she'd loved and lost. Not even Mikoneh.

Latta caught Maya's hand. "That's so sad."

"War always is." Maya blinked away the sheen of tears, and her smile deepened. "It's all right though. I don't regret loving, no matter what form it takes. I'd rather love and lose someone than not love at all. That feels much lonelier."

Jensirin's eyes skewered her. He was listening intently.

Latta squeezed her hand. "You're a very wise young woman, Maya. I'm so glad we're friends. Please promise that won't change."

Maya met the princess's brilliant blue eyes. "You have my oath. Now and always."

CHAPTER 39

FEND OFF GREED

"But how, some have asked, can I study what I cannot see? They never stop to consider that perhaps they are the blind ones, not I. There's so much to see beyond what our eyes can tell."

- *A Treatise on the Magic of the Hidden Realm* by Sariolin the Solitary

Owenekiras Rokahn arrived in the afternoon at the head of a contingent of armored men. Horns blasted at the gates to announce them, and Mikoneh looked down on the procession from the west tower, with Crim at his side. They leaned over the parapets.

Crowds gathered outside the castle walls. Some cheered. Others booed and hissed their disdain.

Crim shook his head. "Nothing like small-minded simpletons to complicate a war."

"I hope you're not lumping the villagers and peasants into one category and leaving out the nobles who bear the same sentiments." Mikoneh glanced at Crim.

The merchant lord snorted. "You mistake me, Your Highness. I'll take the vitriol of the rabble down there over the simpering pettiness and malice of the merchant and noble classes. Each is ugly, but one stems from ignorance and the other from greed. The former is far easier to cure than the latter."

"I appreciate the sentiment, but that so-called rabble isn't as ignorant as you think, and is just as prone to greed and malice. They're people, Crim, and people are disposed to the same defects of character regardless of their birth origin."

"I didn't think *you* would have that view."

"I may not like nobility as a rule, my lord, but I like to think my prejudice runs deep for reasons less superfluous than a stereotype. I disdain the idea of rulers and human chattel."

"You're so much like her." Crim sighed. "The Rokahn visage may be your outer birthright, but you carry Seranni's heart."

Mikoneh's chest panged. He didn't risk turning toward Crim. Instead, he kept his focus on Owenekiras in the court-yard below. The Dragon King dismounted from his black horse, and his men mirrored his actions. Mikoneh had expected to see Ter among them, but the Ephe'ahn was nowhere in sight.

"Even so." Crim cleared his throat. "You're a prince of Rokahn, dragon-born, and destined for a throne. You might not like government, but someone's got to rule, Mikoneh."

"Yeah. Just...not the way Drayve does."

"That perspective, along with your bloodline, puts you into a perfect position, doesn't it? You can change things."

Mikoneh snorted. "Right. Because I know all about government. Oh, and let's not forget that I'm heir to a kingdom I can definitely stroll into at any point to begin reformation."

"While I'm a man who appreciates sarcasm, timing is

important, Your Highness. Don't sell your influence so short." Crim shifted his weight on the parapet. "I need to warn you about something."

"What now?"

"I—and several others—have worked hard to reduce your level of interaction with the nobility of Simynshin during your stay at Elenth Castle, but at the ball and tourney, we won't be able to deflect them."

Dread closed Mikoneh's throat, so he simply nodded.

"I'll do what I can to stay at your side and introduce you. We can use a few subtle signals to communicate who is an ally and who is..."

"Malicious?"

"Quite." Crim sighed. "Frankly, you don't have many allies —but perhaps the queen's disgrace will course correct a few unthinking fools."

And enrage others. Mikoneh fingered the rough stone he leaned against. Below, Owenekiras was conversing with King Prettem. Prince Atlanse stood beside them. A few long weeks ago, he'd not have been able to see who was who from this height. Dragon sight certainly had its advantages. "You know, I don't really blame people for protesting war. Most just want to avoid bloodshed. I hate the idea of drawing a blade—or claws —against my fellow creatures. If only it were easier to sort out differences and fend off greed with words."

"Humans—and, well, dragons—sentient folk, I suppose..." Crim shrugged. "We're complicated. Varied. I see no method as brutally honest as warfare. It takes loss and suffering for us to see reason. Maybe that's a cynical view, but I stand by it. I've tried peace talks at court. I've pled for understanding. But I'm also part of the merchant guilds of Simynshin and Lintha. I've seen the greedy sods of society haggle and steal, all while wearing a smile and pronouncing their greatest enemy to be their dearest friend. People are ugly, Mikoneh. We only become beautiful through pain."

The horses below were led toward the stables. King Prettem motioned Owenekiras inside the castle proper, and the Dragon King's contingent followed.

"I didn't expect that philosophy from you," Mikoneh murmured.

Crim chuckled. "No one does."

"Crim." Mikoneh turned to lean one arm against the parapet and leveled a look at the merchant lord.

"Yes, Mikoneh?" Crim met his gaze.

"I—I want to trust you. That's hard for me these days, after everything..."

"Understandable. I can't even imagine what that Mage put you through."

A shudder wracked Mikoneh's frame. He shut his eyes against the swirling force of memories, swallowed hard, and inhaled a steadying breath. "Regardless...I don't want Sathe to win. I need him *not* to win. That means forcing myself to trust —within reason. I want to believe you and I are friends."

"I agree," said Crim.

"So." Mikoneh shuffled his feet. "I'm trusting you. To be my friend. To be an ally. I—needed you to know that."

The merchant lord searched his face, then offered a gentle smile. "Thank you, Mikoneh. Please know I respect how hard-won your gift is. I cherish it—and you have my oath you won't regret that trust." He stepped forward, and clapped a hand to Mikoneh's shoulder. "Now relax, knowing I have your back— and that I appreciate you having mine."

Warmth flooded the cold chambers of Mikoneh's soul. A terrible vulnerability gnawed at his instincts, but he elected to ignore it. He had to start trusting again. Had to defeat Sathe's silent voice. Had to prove to himself that the world wasn't so broken that it was beyond saving, just like him.

That started with stepping out of hiding.

"Now." Crim slapped the nearby parapet with his free hand. "Shall we go greet your father?"

"All right." A puff of vapor appeared before Mikoneh's lips in the cold. Thick snow fell silently from the heavy coverlet of clouds. As they moved toward the trapdoor, Mikoneh couldn't help but feel he was walking into a goblin's den.

Chapter 40

What Justifies Revolution

"I have spoken to the earth spirits about the other spirit types. I have listened to the wind, watched water, and felt the sting of fire. We all have a soul within us, connecting us to spirit of spirit. But there are other ways to learn more."

- A Treatise on the Magic of the Hidden Realm by Sariolin the Solitary

Crim led Mikoneh to a large banquet hall, where Owenekiras sat at a long table with King Prettem. Joining them were Crown Prince Atlanse and an assortment of nobles Mikoneh vaguely remembered from his welcome feast weeks ago. The princesses, Latta and Maya, were also present, sitting together, whispering. Penn was once again absent.

I really need to talk to him about that.

Penn had a bad habit of feeling helpless, and he tended to push himself past his limits to make up for some self-conceived lack. Beyond that, Mikoneh missed his friend and their conversations.

Crim led Mikoneh along the side of the hall, and the aroma of seafood dishes guided Mikoneh to a chair. His stomach rumbled with appreciation. Owenekiras looked over from a quiet conversation with Prince Atlanse, but King Prettem was the first to speak up.

"Ah, welcome, young tactician. Pull up a chair. Come, Lord Crim. Eat, eat."

"Thank you, sire," Crim said with a grin. "Don't mind if we do."

The king's about-face was a welcome change, Mikoneh decided, even if it punctuated how dismissive Prettem had been at first. Progress was progress, and Simynshin *needed* to enter the war as Owenekiras's ally.

Mikoneh claimed a velvet chair and tucked into a meal of smoked fish, clam soup, and buttered toast, with the usual cup of *tiassana* tea, until Latta caught his eye. She smiled at him. Her color was good—better than it had been since he first met her. Perhaps news of the queen's disgrace was responsible for the improvement.

"How was training?" asked Maya from her seat directly across from him.

"Good," Crim answered. "Your brother's instinct for fire is impressive. If I didn't know any better, I'd say he learned the element in a past life."

Mikoneh snorted. "I don't think I'd like the trade-off. Who wants to live life after life after life, just for a little more power?"

"Me," answered King Prettem. "The older you get, the less abstract the finality of death becomes." He plucked up his goblet and drank deeply from it.

Mikoneh speared his fish, trying to block the image of his soldiers slaughtered by Drayve's knights, but that only welled up the village massacre. He hunched against the guilt. He knew the concept of death all too well.

"I should think living forever to be a dreadful prospect," Prince Atlanse said. "Sirinhigha deteriorates yearly. I hate to consider where the world may be in one hundred years."

"It changes less swiftly than you might think." Owenekiras's voice was a soft rumble. "Life is a cycle: war, peace, and revolt. A faction rises to make change—whether good or bad—and challenges the former regime. War inevitably breaks out. People die until all are sick of death, and then one faction or other gives up their stance to preserve life. Peace follows—but only until another dreamer seeks reform. Thus, it has always been. Thus, it will always be."

"Surely, the cause isn't so meaningless as your philosophy suggests, Owen," Atlanse said, prodding the air with his fork. "The *why* is what justifies revolution. Freedom from tyranny, for instance, is crucial. Oppression must never stand."

"Ah, but what is your definition of oppression?" asked a diminutive voice at the end of the table. Mikoneh whirled to find Ter seated there like he'd been part of the group the whole time. No one else, save Maya, seemed surprised by his presence. Ter smiled at Mikoneh and continued. "To some, security is found in having their lives controlled. In every facet regulated. In others, oppression is *any* rule imposed. Any imposition made. No matter where you stand on a view, someone else will oppose it and shout 'Tyranny!' War is perhaps justifiable, but it is always lamentable."

Atlanse skewered Ter with a long look. "You make me feel about two inches tall."

"And yet, I am shorter than you." Ter chuckled, his ears twitching.

"Enough of this depressing topic," Crim said. "Let's discuss the Winter Tourney. I hear-tell"—he glanced at

Mikoneh—"that a certain Rokahnian heir is taking on our very own leader of the Valor Knights in the tourney's opening."

Every eye slid toward Mikoneh.

He sipped his clam soup, swallowed, then dabbed at his mouth with a cloth napkin. "It's true."

Crim rubbed his hands together. "I, for one, am delighted to watch Simynshin's best warrior take on Jonatten and Seranni's privately trained sword pupil. Even Master Donivan is struggling to decide on whom to place his wager."

"When was this decided?" asked Maya.

"On my way to the tower this morning," Mikoneh said. "Sir Kalet found me."

One gaze lingered longer than the rest. Mikoneh found his father's eyes and held them. Owenekiras didn't look away, but his expression was as guarded—as impenetrable—as a fortress. At last, the Dragon King turned back to his food.

Mikoneh chewed on a bit of smoked fish, letting his thoughts drift from familial connections, toward the tourney. If only he didn't have to dance first.

CHAPTER 41

THE SAME MOUNTAIN STONE

"I've traveled among the hidden dragon caves and lost fae vales of Sirinhigha. I've traversed the high peaks of the North and explored the deep tunnels beneath the ground. By visiting the ancient peoples and places of this land I have come to understand how little I know—and how much the Spirits Elemental understand."

- *A Treatise on the Magic of the Hidden Realm* by Sariolin the Solitary

Minno turned up at the castle on the evening before the Winter Ball. With supreme reluctance, the guards admitted him, and he found his way to the Rokahn suite—in company with a handful of knights.

Mikoneh looked up from his game of Fang and Claw and sighed. Penn sat opposite him while Jensirin and Owenekiras looked on quietly. Crim, Maya, Latta, Prince Atlanse, and Ter were also present. Akonn had tried to join them, but Owenekiras had ordered him back to bed with a warning that he wasn't to move until the tourney, or the Dragon King would strip him of his rank and sword.

"Forgive the interruption," the lead knight said in the doorway. "Minno claims one of you will vouch for him."

"I will," Owenekiras said from where he stood near the game table. "Come, Minno."

The gray boy entered, clutching Duck and looking particularly disheveled and forlorn. "I suspected my name had been cleared by now. I'm not sure what all the fuss is about."

"I dunno," muttered Mikoneh, "maybe the fact you had blood on your hands and confessed to murder?"

"Yet Crim is clearly alive." Minno pierced the merchant lord with a steady look until the man shifted and coughed.

"Yeah, but the blood remains a compelling mystery," Mikoneh said.

"It was my own." Minno slumped down in an open wingback chair. "Where else would I get it?"

"You hurt yourself?" Maya stood from the settee where she'd been teaching Latta about common Oceanian herbs.

"I'm fine." Minno pressed deeper into his chair. "Don't touch me."

Maya set her jaw and marched toward his chair. "Don't even consider making me think I'm a duck. Fowl or not, I'll still treat your wound. Show me."

Mikoneh expected indifference, but Minno stared at Maya with surprise—and was that fear? After a heartbeat, he held out his palm. It was badly bandaged, and deep red stains smeared the outside edges. Maya set to work untying the strips of cloth.

"You're unexpectedly fierce, Maya," Latta said from her place on the settee.

"I've known her all our lives," Mikoneh said, "and she still takes me by surprise."

"She gets it from her mother," Atlanse said. When both twins looked at him, he shrugged. "You pick which mother, I suppose. Rathana and Seranni were built from the same mountain stone."

That adage was new to Mikoneh, but he understood the gist of it. He smiled. "If you mean they had the same stubborn qualities, I wouldn't be surprised."

"Indeed. Fierce, capable, and loyal to their cause to the bitterest end," Atlanse said. "I had the privilege of knowing both of them."

"More importantly," Crim said, "they were strong yet also gentle. Seranni was always rescuing birds from the stray cats near the market squares in Elenth, or feeding feral dogs, or leaving out leftovers for whatever poor creature."

"She did that in Relvin, too," Maya said, applying an ointment to a gash along Minno's palm. "She inspired me to become a healer."

"Rathana was quieter than Seranni," said Atlanse. "But she carried that same fierce protective instinct."

Mikoneh scooted a captain piece across the gameboard to protect a village. While Penn deliberated over his next move, Mikoneh risked a glance at Owenekiras standing close by. The man was as stoic as ever, his silver eyes pinned on the gameboard, the muscles of his face firm but not taut from suppressed emotion. If he felt anything at the mention of his dead wife, he offered no hint. Nothing.

Drawing a bracing breath, Mikoneh shifted in his seat to face his father. "Was Rathana quiet with you?"

A single beat was all the hesitation Owenekiras had. "No." Another beat. "She spoke quite a lot." His voice held its usual restraint, but a thread of something else wove through it.

Impulse muzzled Mikoneh's reflex to avoid painful subjects. "Do you miss her?" The question was insensitive. He knew that even without Maya's disapproving glower or the humming silence of the common room.

Owenekiras remained impassive. "Every day."

The answer soothed something within Mikoneh, even as he acknowledged an ache to recall a woman he'd never known.

But I did know her. Why don't I remember anything?

Pain flared up, filling his mind, tensing his muscles. His vision wobbled. Mikoneh clutched his knees until the fit passed.

Owenekiras's gauntleted hand brushed his shoulder. "Mikoneh?"

"I—I'm just tired, I think." Did he think that? Or was this a Mage attack—or something else entirely? His panic attack in Elenth had been extreme. "I didn't sleep last night."

"We could all use an early night," Penn said. "Tomorrow is a full day."

That was true. The Winter Ball would commence at sundown, but before that the twins must have their final fittings for each outfit they would wear for every festival event, then at noon they must join the Royal House for a parade through Elenth.

Mikoneh stood up. "I'll finish destroying you tomorrow, Penn."

Penn sighed and set his jester piece down near the village—his last poor defense against full-on invasion. "I think I'd rather concede tonight. Otherwise, I'll just dream about your finishing moves."

"Coward." Mikoneh managed a grin.

"Because I have the grace to know when I'm beaten?"

Mikoneh snorted and leaned over the board. "You still had a chance here if you'd moved the gryphon to the mountaintop. Its healing tears would give your jester one extra move. Humor can be crippling."

"Oh." Penn studied the board. "I hadn't remembered the tears... That's quite good." He sat down to reexamine his plays.

"Goodnight, everybody." Mikoneh started for his bedroom, then paused and turned to study his father. "Goodnight, my lord."

"Safe dream paths to you, Mikoneh," said Owenekiras.

Entering his bedroom, Mikoneh locked his door, barred his window, and changed into silken pajamas. He'd stopped sleeping in just his smalls after Minno's several impromptu visits. He slid into his blankets, and sighed—until a wash of dizziness broke over him again. He slumped against his pillows. Fingers of darkness groped at his mind. The room tipped sideways. He clutched at the coverlet, and set his jaw until the world settled upright again.

Steady. You're just exhausted. Go to sleep.

He squeezed his eyes shut...

...and tipped into dreams at once.

INTERLUDE IV
SILVER ACROSS THE DARK CLOUDS

"Memory fades into ageless silence, but a true heart will always remember."

- From the Corpse Poet's 8th Sonnet

"You don't want to remember." The lady stood at the same cliff ledge overlooking a stormy sea. Her wheat-blonde hair lashed in the wind, and her white cloak whipped and thrashed at her ankles. "The storms come to drive back the memories."

He moved to her side. His long dark ponytail flung into his face, and he dragged back the tresses to peer out at the sea. "What memories am I avoiding?"

"Those of Rathana."

The name struck Mikoneh like a blow, though he didn't know why. "Who is that?"

The woman turned to him, her emerald eyes full of gentle chiding. "You know already."

Mother, said a voice deep in his soul.

"She died," Mikoneh whispered. "Didn't she?"

"Yes. That much you know. But you don't remember."

He leaned out to stare down at the roaring breakers. "Isn't it enough to know?"

"It might be—but the storm says differently. What is it, precisely, that you do not wish to recall?" The lady's steady eyes were trained on him. "Her death? Or what caused it?"

Mikoneh tensed. "I don't know."

"You mean you won't answer."

"Yes," he admitted.

"My shadow friend, you are the bravest soul I know. I will never doubt that. Nor do I doubt that you will come to terms with your pain."

He bowed his head. "I've lost so much already."

"Yes. That is so—including *her*. Do not lose the love that came before her loss in an effort to avoid pain you already feel. Give that pain meaning."

He swallowed, tasting brine. The storm lit the heavens, painting silver across the dark clouds. "I know you're right."

The lady stroked his cheek. "And I know that you will *do* what is right, no matter the cost to yourself. You always have."

"How do you know?" he whispered.

She leaned in, bringing the scent of flowers in springtime. "Because I—"

Chapter 42

Of All the Puzzles

"I cannot wield all five elemental types. I am not even granted a secondary element. Perhaps I lack the discipline. But still, I see them in the hidden moments, the pauses between the heartbeats, the silences between thought. If you look without looking, maybe you'll see them, too."

- *A Treatise on the Magic of the Hidden Realm* by Sariolin the Solitary

Mikoneh jolted upright. Someone was pounding on the door.

"Up, sleepybones!" Maya called. "The tailor's here."

Dismal light streamed in through the half-drawn curtains around Mikoneh's bed. He groaned, and nearly rolled over to find sleep again, but a stab of anxiety slid between his ribs. The parade and ball were today. Somehow, he'd rather fight a Mage.

Don't be dramatic.

Fine then, a goblin.

Those might be real.

He sighed and sat up, conceding defeat against his mind. Better face the day and conquer it—or at least survive it.

He flung aside his coverlet, climbed out of the monstrous bed, and slipped on his robe. Padding into the adjacent chamber, he found the tailor smiling at him, holding out a Rokahnian-style surcoat glistening with gold piping and tiny black gems. The ensemble was nevertheless tasteful.

"You look far too pleased with yourself," Mikoneh grunted.

The tailor chuckled. "I've surpassed my own genius, Your Highness. Black diamonds from the mountains of Northern Cimin. See how they sparkle?" He waggled his fingers, and the light set off the diamonds like tiny rippling flames. Mikoneh was mesmerized by the sight.

He shook himself. "You can't take credit for the work of nature."

The tailor shrugged. "I take credit for knowing best how to put nature's work on display. You and your sister will outshine the House of Chenta."

"Is that a good idea?" asked Maya, stepping from her room, dressed in a gown made to match Mikoneh's, from its deep blue fabric, to the red and gold accents, to the glistening black diamonds. She spun in a circle to show it off, and the gray morning light from the window struck the diamonds and scattered sparkles across the walls and floor.

"Ah, radiant." The tailor looked smugger than ever. "And it's absolutely a good idea. Crown Prince Atlanse wishes for you both to be front and center. Everyone must see you, recognize you, and accept you."

Mikoneh studied the tailor a little closer. "Are you personally in favor of fighting the Mages?"

"Personally"—the tailor motioned for Mikoneh to strip off

his robe—"I'm in favor of melting their bones with dragon fire and throwing the ashes into Pae'Tal's volcano."

"So, nothing extreme."

The tailor snorted. "Most folk in Simynshin have been shielded from the effects of the Mages for decades. Many don't believe the emissaries sent here even come from the same roots. The distinction between a Dark Mage and a common sorcerer are lost on them."

"Are sorcerers common?" asked Maya, turning around to afford her twin some privacy.

"The barely talented sort, yes."

Mikoneh dropped his robe onto the nearest armchair, then slipped a gray silk blouse on. "Ter explained to us that these Mages—the dark kind—are a breed unto themselves. Like a separate race of humans with special magical abilities."

"That's so," said the tailor, helping Mikoneh into the surcoat. Once it was straight, he hummed to himself, tucking pins into several places. "Nearly perfect."

"Are you not Simynshinian?" Mikoneh asked.

"Not by birth," the tailor said. "I'm Rokahnian—though not of the old blood. My parents fled to the mainland from Rokahn with my brothers and me during the coup that gave your vile aunt the throne in Vorsah."

Vorsah. Mikoneh pictured the Rokahnian capital city as it had appeared on Fa's maps. At the time, it'd been just one more faraway place, one he'd likely never visit. Now it was his birthright and home of his blood. A once self-reliant empire now caught under the blade of Mages.

"That's why you're so good at Rokahnian clothes." Maya turned to face the two men again. "You really *are* brilliant, Tayvin."

The tailor laughed. "Thank you kindly, my lady. I live to

please the true line of Rokahn. Indeed, having you here is a dream I never dared to grasp. The last shreds of my modesty have fallen away under the power of your praise." He swept into a bow, then straightened, and pinned Mikoneh's sleeve cuff with a flourish.

"I see you've made a friend out of him," Mikoneh told his twin.

Maya's eyes sparkled. "Tayvin's a dream. I want him to be my personal tailor."

Tayvin chuckled again. "I'm flattered—and I accept. Please discuss the arrangement with your father."

Mikoneh glanced between them warily. "Is this a business arrangement or a marriage proposal—and are you joking or serious?"

They both broke into laughter.

"I'm half serious," Maya said. "But it's strictly business. Tayvin is happily married."

"'Tis true," said Tayvin. "My wife is fair as sunshine and sweet as a thornbush."

"Sounds...dangerous." Mikoneh didn't know what else to say.

"Oh, she is," agreed Tayvin. "But I thrive on danger."

"Oh, yeah? Yet you fled Rokahn."

"Touché. Though in my defense, my parents aren't so stout-hearted as myself, and I was but a tyke at the time. My penchant for danger has grown across the years, and I think being employed by the ancient House of Rokahn would satisfy my desires perfectly. As a bonus, dressing the two of you in traditional Rokahnian attire is the pinnacle of my career. There's no higher place to rest my laurels."

The man certainly liked the sound of his own voice. Mikoneh smiled and shook his head. "Whatever makes you happy, I suppose."

If Tayvin had a response to that, he couldn't offer it up, for his mouth was now full of pins. He proceeded to tuck away for several breaths, then helped Mikoneh shrug off the surcoat. Maya excused herself to try on another dress. Tayvin helped Mikoneh into a few more surcoats and vests.

When the tailor was at last finished pinning and tucking the twins' various outfits for the various festival events, he opened the door to the suite and allowed a fleet of servants to whisk away the half-finished wardrobe pieces.

"I'll have your first outfits ready well before the parade." Tayvin offered a last bow, then trotted from the room.

Heaving a sigh, Mikoneh sank into the nearest chair. "He's a wonder."

"Isn't he?" Maya poured a goblet of wine and offered it to Mikoneh, who took it with murmured thanks.

Breathing in the bouquet, Mikoneh grimaced. He really didn't care for wine, especially the sweet kind. He set the goblet aside. "I could use breakfast."

"It should be here soon," said Maya. "They're being thorough in checking any food that's brought up. I think the staff is concerned about poisonings, especially now that our father is here."

Our father. The phrase felt heavy, but not entirely foreign now. Nor unwelcome.

"Have you seen Owenekiras this morning?" Mikoneh asked, glancing toward the bedroom designated for the Dragon King's use.

"No, but he always seems to get up earlier than me, no matter what time I drag myself from bed. That, or he doesn't sleep." She shrugged. "He's probably already down in Master Donivan's training hall, or meeting with Prince Atlanse."

"Probably." Mikoneh pushed himself from his chair. "I feel like we should be doing something, too. I hate all this waiting around just to be on display."

"Haven't you been training?"

"Yeah, but Crim's too busy today—"

"I'll train you," said Minno in his usual monotone voice. The twins jumped. He stood at the window like he'd been there the whole time, but surely the twins would've seen him. Minno stepped closer to them. "You need another lesson in spirit of spirit before the Winter Tourney begins, I should think."

Mikoneh sized the gray boy up. "You know, of all the puzzles I've run into since leaving Relvin Province, you're the one I'm having the most trouble with."

"That stands to reason," said Minno. "Do you want another lesson or don't you?"

"I'll accept." It was something to do, and besides, Mikoneh did want to understand his spirit element better. Against Sathe, it had been his only real defense. "Now?"

"I don't see why not."

Maya settled into a cushy armchair, cradling a cup of herbal tea, content to watch while she used wind to levitate Penn's stack of books and restack them. Mikoneh moved with Minno to the floor near the window, where gloomy daylight stained the flagstones. Minno instructed Mikoneh to sit cross-legged on the floor, then sat before him in the same attitude.

"Summon a spirit of spirit, in dragon form if you can," said the gray boy.

Closing his eyes, Mikoneh tapped his center, where the flickering silver light nestled. A spirit elemental slipped from his fingertips, and he stared at it, smiling faintly. It had adopted a dragon form again.

"Good," Minno said. "Now, will it into flame."

Mikoneh hesitated. "Can I do that?"

"A spirit flame, not fire-flame. Don't tap your fire element just now. You can learn to use the two in tandem once you master each individually. Otherwise, you'll lose control and hurt someone."

Mikoneh pushed the image of fire into the dragon spirit, and it flickered and shifted into a living flame, still silver in its hue.

"Good. Spirit of spirit appears to respect you. That is an essential foundation. Hold that shape for several breaths."

"Yippee." Despite needles of satisfaction in his chest, Mikoneh found himself unwilling to show much enthusiasm before Minno. The boy rubbed him wrong, and no amount of training together was likely to change that.

The spirit flickered, almost losing the shape, and Mikoneh set his jaw.

"Just a little longer," Minno said. "But talk about something now—it will help you practice splitting your focus."

Mikoneh nodded, latching onto the first topic that popped into his head. "Can I ask what's with your duck obsession? I get having one for a pet, but why use your talent to manipulate people into believing they're waterfowl?"

Minno offered up his slow blink. "Why not?"

"Frankly, it feels almost silly, yet you're the least funny person I've ever met."

"I don't find it silly. It's appropriate."

"I think it's funny," said Maya. "And rather entertaining."

"Entertaining isn't the same as being witty," Mikoneh said. The spirit's form broke, and the silver light vanished.

Minno sighed through his nose. "Concentrate on your lesson."

"Guess the talking's over then?"

Minno didn't answer.

As Mikoneh tried to resummon the spirit of spirit, a knock sounded on the door. A servant entered, followed by several more, each carrying trays of steaming food. The aroma of meat wafted over the air. Mikoneh snuffed out the silver light, and rose to fill his growling stomach. Minno joined the twins at Maya's invitation, and once the servants left, they tucked into a meal of fish, eggs, bread, and seasoned olive oil for dipping, as well as tangerines.

"Is Penn awake?" Mikoneh asked through a mouthful of poached egg.

"He left early for the library," Maya said with a faint thread of annoyance in her voice. "I worry he isn't taking proper care of himself. He seems obsessed."

"I'll talk to him," Mikoneh promised, though he wasn't certain how soon that would be. According to Crim, the twins' schedule was packed.

Halfway through the meal, Jensirin stepped from Akonn's chamber and joined them without a word.

"Good morning, Jensirin," Maya said cheerily. "Were you watching over Akonn all night?"

Mikoneh lowered his fork. "Is there a reason to?"

"His wound tore a bit last night," Maya said, peeling her tangerine. "I think he'll be fine if he learns to stop pushing himself. He was trying to prove to me he was healed enough to protect us during the parade today."

"Idiot."

Jensirin nibbled on a bit of fish. "He's angry enough at himself without our judgment."

"Still a foolish thing to do," Mikoneh said.

"Let's not take stock of all the foolish things *you've* done." Maya grinned at him. "We'd be here for the rest of the year, and possibly into the spring."

He rolled his eyes but didn't argue. He knew better than that. Maya had a memory like an historian when it came to him.

Jensirin cracked a smile. "The captain will be fine, I'm confident."

Mikoneh eyed the dragon lord, taking in his pale complexion and tangled white hair. "And you? Are you all right?"

"I am."

"*Convincing.*"

That smile twitched wider. "Truly, I'm well. Today is a good day. I have not participated in a festival in centuries. The fragrance of pine, spices, and the coming feast are stirring wonderful old memories." He took another bite of fish. "I am not confident I will do well in crowds, but if it's possible..." he glanced at Maya "...I had hoped to reserve a dance with you tonight."

She lit up like a torch. "I would be delighted, Jensirin. Thank you!"

As they finished their meal, Penn arrived with a new stack of books. He greeted them all cheerfully, even Minno, and grabbed a tangerine before settling in near the fire with a heavy tome.

Mikoneh shook his head, unable to stamp out a smile. "I knew you liked books, Penn—but I didn't take you for a fanatic. Tell me you're still making headway in your research."

The viscount huffed a laugh. "I like to think so. Don't discourage me."

"Aren't you joining us for the parade?"

"Sands, no. I hate drawing that much attention to myself."

Mikoneh pinned him with a flat look until Penn snorted.

"I realize you hate it, too, but all this spectacle is about you. So, let me do my part, and you do your part—and we'll laugh about your suffering later."

Mikoneh stomped over to the chair, and rapped his knuckles against Penn's skull. "That's for your callousness."

Penn laughed harder, causing Mikoneh to grin, but he sobered a breath later.

"Seriously, Penn, don't push yourself too hard."

The viscount let his smile fade away. "I won't. But I *must* do my part, Mikoneh. Please don't stop me."

"I won't unless you give me reason to yank those books from your fingers because you're wasting away. Got it?"

"Says the one most likely to get himself hurt. I'm fine, Mikoneh. I'm making headway."

Studying his friend, Mikoneh noted the dark circles under Penn's eyes, but those brown eyes were brighter than they'd been since fleeing Relvin Province. In the morning glow they almost rippled like ocean waves, full of purpose and determination.

"All right, idiot, do what you feel called to do," Mikoneh said, relenting.

Penn's smile returned. "You showed me how."

Chapter 43

The Spirit of Simynshin

"I have been asked by several young wielders, after seeking me in the wilds of Sirinhigha, how they may become masters. The fact is that the term master is a misnomer by its common use. You cannot master the elements. They are untamable, and what you tap is the mere crust of earth hiding a caldera. All you can do is master yourself."

- *A Treatise on the Magic of the Hidden Realm* by Sariolin the Solitary

Dressed in Tayvin's fine threads—including new fur-lined cloaks—Mikoneh and Maya joined the Royal House in the castle bailey. Swirls of frost embellished the paving stones and outer walls wherever the snow didn't cling. Mikoneh's breath appeared in a cloud, though he didn't feel the frigid cold.

After swinging into his saddle, he glanced toward Maya. The wind moved her hair in its own mild breeze, and her nose wasn't red. Atlanse, Hilker, and Crim, likewise looked warm compared to King Prettem's ruddy cheeks. Latta huddled deep in her cowled cloak.

Shifting the other way, Mikoneh spotted Owenekiras seated atop a black charger. He always looked cold and removed, though with his mastery over all the elements, it was unlikely he felt a modicum of the nipping wind.

Fat snowflakes floated from the cloudy sky while liveried men and women moved along the line and shifted the royals and nobles around, organizing them for the parade. Mikoneh was placed beside Latta while Maya rode with Owenekiras, just behind them. King Prettem and Prince Atlanse took the lead. Where Crim and the others fell in, Mikoneh couldn't tell from where he sat.

At last, the servants scuttled back. The cavalcade rode through the castle gates, and across the moat, toward Elenth. Soon, buildings loomed on either side of the frozen road. Simynshinians hugged the edges of the thoroughfare, waving small flags or handkerchiefs. As the king passed, the lined-up people moved in a ripple, craning their heads to catch every detail. Whispers hissed and slithered around the Rokahnians. Several citizens were brave enough to glare at Mikoneh and his kin. Others looked torn between interest and fear. A boy in the crowd caught Mikoneh's eye, offered a broad grin, then pointedly dropped his admiring gaze to the Dragon Prince's battered sword.

Mikoneh grinned back, heartened. War hadn't crushed the spirit of Simynshin like it had Oceana's. There was still time to turn the tide here, to make a stand and rescue a world on the cusp of subjugation.

That's the real reason we've come to Elenth. Don't forget it.

It was too easy to forget the bigger picture by losing himself in lessons and politics. He'd come here to stop Sathe's kind from infiltrating. That's why he'd agreed to the betrothal farce.

Why he'd played Queen Feresse's game. Why he still put up with vitriol and suspicion.

Larger buildings rose around the parade. Onlookers spied them from around corners while crowds thickened at the borders of the main road. Someone tossed frost-bitten flowers at the king's horse. The knights flanking the procession clutched their swords close, ready for any sort of trouble.

"Long live King Prettem Chenta!" came a shout near a stone church.

A deep voice rolled over the first. "Down with the Rokahns!"

Mikoneh stiffened, his nerves humming. Rook's ears flicked. Perhaps the black stallion sensed his tension. One knight inched his horse closer to Mikoneh's. Sir Kalet. With one lingering glower, the knight silenced the murmur of grumbles flowing through the crowd.

"Don't they know we're not affiliated with Rokahn's present ruler?" asked Maya softly.

Mikoneh's sharp ears caught her question, and Owenekiras's response.

"Whether I serve the current steward of Rokahn or not, many fear me and my kin."

His kin. Mikoneh's knuckles tightened on his reins. Kin.

Lifting his head, Mikoneh willed his nerves to loosen and his anxiety to roll away. Whatever the reputation of the House of Rokahn—or of Owenekiras specifically—he and Maya would carve their own standing.

"Maya," Mikoneh said. "Keep smiling. Wave to them."

He conjured up his own smile, more reserved than his twin's, but still warm. If part of winning the war required winning over the masses—proving to them he wasn't some dismissive royal—Mikoneh would aim for that. He'd won people over to his cause in Oceana by being himself. He could do it again.

Latta's eyes settled on him.

He glanced at her. "What is it?"

She smiled. "You look very handsome and strong, Mikoneh Rokahn."

He laughed, taken off guard. "Thank you, I guess." His grin widened. "Let's keep talking—without neglecting the crowds. If I'm more at ease, it'll be easier to win them over."

She blinked. "Ah. More the politician than I'd suspected."

"Not really. I just want them to know I'm not an enemy. You're their princess, and they love you. If you show approval of my character, it'll go a long way toward helping me."

Her smile deepened. "I'll gladly show them that."

"Thank you."

She pointed out more of the buildings and explained a bit of the ancient history of Elenth. Mikoneh joked with her, making her laugh. Maybe it was only his imagination, but the people seemed to respond. Glowers and nervous glances melted into curiosity. Mikoneh flashed a few smiles into the crowd, and some even smiled back.

Maya was doing even better. She waved and called out to the people, and even tossed her pale pink handkerchief at a little girl near a street corner. The girl lit up like the dawn.

Ages later, the procession reached the far edge of the city and looped to join a new street that would eventually lead back toward the castle. Mikoneh scanned the crowd, seeking any hint of a threat, but Prettem and Atlanse had tightened security enough that any attempts to attack the march would be foolhardy.

He continued to speak with Latta, and occasionally turned around in his saddle to converse with his twin and father. Owenekiras was responsive, though not outgoing, but Maya's bright eyes and catching smile seemed to melt the wintry air around her. Or perhaps she was manipulating the wind, making it warmer. However it happened, she encapsulated springtime.

"She's a wonder," said Latta fondly.

"She is that." Mikoneh's heart swelled. Not so long ago, she'd been a mere shell, broken by grief after Fa and Mama's deaths, but now she was vivid and bright. New life had poured into her veins.

He would never let that spirit die again—not while he drew breath.

AT LAST, the parade ended, and the royals dismounted in the castle bailey. Maya caught Mikoneh's arm and dragged him toward their suite for their last fitting and an afternoon nap. In a few turns, the Winter Ball would commence.

Mikoneh's nerves were taut as lute strings.

Forget battles, Dark Mages, even goblins. His greatest hurdle might lay just ahead.

CHAPTER 44

HIS GREATEST ALLY

"There are two known methods to tap into the elements. The first is to reach out into nature and grasp it. The elements are all around us, beneath us, above us. The second is to tap the aspect within. The elements are there as well. The first method is the most common, for it is least taxing."

- *A Treatise on the Magic of the Hidden Realm* by Sariolin the Solitary

Crystals and diamonds flashed and sparkled. Music floated over the air. Mikoneh stood at the precipice, outside the wide-open door to the ball-room. The temptation to run was strong, but Maya clutched his arm, likely sensing his hesitation.

Chandeliers were drenched in a thousand lighted candles, and myriad fire spirits seemed determined to spread the wafting scent of beeswax around, to mingle with the fragrance of perfume, wine, sweat, and cinnamon. Beneath the lofty ceiling, crowds of people swayed and skipped to a jaunty tune while still more bodies were crushed together at the edges of the spacious room.

So many people. It was like a battlefield, sans the blood. Instead of swords or spears or maces, eyes roved the room, glinting with malice or humor or nerves. Voices rose in a cacophony of faux laughter, hissing whispers, and idle chatter.

Near the side entrance where the twins stood, the king sat on a throne upon a shallow dais. Two chairs stood to either side of him, both empty. The fact that a fourth chair was absent spoke volumes about Queen Feresse's predicament.

Nearby, a cluster of musicians stood upon a second platform, plucking, piping, and fingering instruments to create the cheery music floating through the air. They wore matching apparel. Their feather caps bobbed to the music, their doublets glinting faintly with jewels.

Someone cleared their throat behind Mikoneh. He twisted around, taking Maya with him since she wouldn't let go. Latta stood beside her new protector: a tall, lean man with an ugly scowl made more severe by a prominent scar on his cheek. The Songbird Princess was dressed in white and silver set with tiny diamonds sewn into snowflake shapes. Against the dark brown of her long hair, and the blue of her eyes, the effect was stunning. Mikoneh stared, breathless. Maya nudged his boot, and he shook himself.

He waved Maya off and offered his arm to his betrothed. Latta took it with a sincere smile. Mikoneh shoved down a flash of panic, and they entered the ballroom together. Some part of Mikoneh hated to leave his twin behind, but protocol demanded it. He glanced back, hoping Penn had arrived to escort her.

Someone had come, but it wasn't Penn. Mikoneh grinned.

Jensirin was leading Maya into the vast chamber, his expression serene, his frame straight. He'd shed his crimson cloak and wore a black surcoat, breeches, and boots, all with dark green trim. At his waist hung an ornamental sword in an ornate sheath of black and silver. Freed of his cloak and standing under the flickering flames, Jensirin looked taller, stronger, and lordlier. His slitted lavender eyes gleamed with pleasure as he leaned down to hear something Maya murmured. A smile crossed his lips, and his quick reply brought laughter to Maya's eyes.

Maya wore an ice blue gown trimmed with delicate white pearls and silver piping. Her full skirt swished with every movement—and she beamed like a blazing star, aware of how pretty she looked in the masterpiece. To keep the twins affiliated with each other, Tayvin had crafted a matching ice-blue damask-patterned surcoat and breeches, accented with silver, for Mikoneh.

Behind Maya and Jensirin strode Owenekiras Rokahn. For once, the man didn't wear his armor. Like Jensirin, he still wore black, but it was in a decidedly Rokahnian fashion. A damask-patterned cape floated behind him, and his ornate broadsword was belted to his waist.

Twisting straight again, Mikoneh found himself smiling. He might dread the frivolity of the affair, but he could bask in Maya's happiness, and he would do his part to win over the Simynshinian nobility. He squared his shoulders and hoisted his chin, not letting his smile falter. Confidence—but not arrogance—would be his greatest ally.

He and Latta reached the dais, followed by the others, and King Prettem rose. The music faded, the dancers floated to a halt, and every eye settled on the prominent folk of the Houses of Rokahn and Chenta.

"My dear subjects," said Prettem, lifting his hands. "I stand before you a humbled man."

Mikoneh shot him a surprised look before he could school his face.

The king continued. "Like some of you, I had begun to scorn Lord Rokahn's forces harbored on our lands. His war seemed a distant, pale, trembling thing. The Mages were no longer as they had once been. If they sued for peace, why would we not answer in kind? People change over time, no?" He heaved a sigh. "While I continue to hope for a future removed from the tethers of warfare, my hopes for peace ties with Mage-kind have proven to be naïve. It is thanks to the heirs of Rokahn—the rightful heirs, mind you—that our kingdom has been spared a great calamity."

He bowed his head, but not before a flash of grief crossed his face. "My own beloved wife, a woman whom I deeply cherished, has betrayed me. Because of her, I embraced the tempter in our midst. The Dark Mage ambassador has thence been thrust out into the cold. He can no longer spread his vile words among my people. I barely discovered the queen's plot in time —and she will shortly stand trial for her crimes. How did I discover her treachery? Through the quick actions of Prince Mikoneh Rokahn, the betrothed of my dear granddaughter, Princess Latta."

Mikoneh studied the throng. Astonishment flickered across most of the nearest faces, but scorn or guilt twisted others. Someone pushed through the crowd, away from the king's speech.

"Let it be known henceforth," Prettem continued, "that Simynshin will side with Owenekiras Rokahn in this war—for war it is, and we cannot pretend otherwise. Shall we not fight against tyranny, my people?"

A ripple of murmurs answered. No one knew quite how to respond. To bring up a divisive issue at a festive party was a bold move.

Mikoneh spotted Crim among the nobility, standing near his wife. They were clad in matching green velvet with gold accents. The merchant lord smiled encouragingly at Mikoneh. Near them, Hilker stood conversing softly with Master Donivan. Mikoneh hadn't been certain whether the sword-master was of high birth or not, but obviously he was someone of consequence to attend this gathering.

As though sensing his eyes on them, both men glanced in his direction. Hilker offered up a crooked smile while Donivan frowned.

"At this winter festival," the king went on, "we come together to celebrate the heritage of our ancient land. Simyn-shin has stood the test of famine, disease, and war for centuries. But we did not do so alone. It is through our friendships with other countries that we have weathered these countless storms —and they likewise have done so through our aid. Now is no different. And so, as we lift toasts to our good fortune, let us also remember to band together with those who seek the common welfare of folk in all the wholesome places of this wide and wondrous world.

"Bearing that in mind, I urge you to welcome our Rokahnian guests, to come to know them, and to acknowledge our common goal for what it is. A merry festival to you all!"

Chapter 45

Like a Spell

"I mention how taxing tapping the elemental aspects within yourself can be, but bear in mind one thing. Even as an element can drain your energy, there are ways to use that same trait to revitalize yourself."

- *A Treatise on the Magic of the Hidden Realm* by Sariolin the Solitary

Relief rippled through the throng. Goblets lifted in echoing wishes of a pleasant holiday, and the music struck up again. Mikoneh had rarely seen a crowd retreat so hastily, and it told him all he needed to know. For one reason or another, these people didn't share their king's enthusiasm for this reforged alliance with Owenekiras Rokahn. Be it fear, prejudice, or some other view, they would prefer not to support the war effort.

A surge of heat wrapped around Mikoneh's chest. For one white-hot moment, he imagined himself willing the candles and torches to burn brighter—to seize the attention of the whole—and slap them in the face with reality by detailing his harrowing captivity. How dare they harbor sympathy for such wicked, despicable monsters? How dare they ignore the plight of Oceana? The greed of Lintha? The friction in Rokahn? Did they not see that they were as aloof and uncaring as the tyrant emperor of Cimin?

He took a single step but jerked to a halt. Latta's arm, looped through his, grounded him.

Tantrums don't help. Reasoning isn't enough. They need proof, not claims.

He set his jaw, turned to Latta, and smiled. "Care to dance?"

She searched his face, perhaps reading the remnants of his inner conflict, then she nodded with a radiant smile. "I would be honored, Mikoneh Rokahn. It's something I've looked forward to since our early childhood. You once promised me a dance."

"Did I?" He ignored the pang of fear surrounding his lost memories. Instead, he led the princess from the dais, took her in his arms, and sent up a quick prayer: *Let me not trip and make a complete fool of myself.*

He found the music's timing and swept Latta into the next steps. At first, the press of the other couples threatened to throw off his movements, but he recalled Crim's advice—pretend to be flying—and the masses melted away. Latta was an exquisite dancer. Where Maya moved like the light and airy wind, Latta was water, fluid and graceful. Each step poured into the next in an effortless flow. Her eyes sparkled with pleasure, then she shut them, apparently trusting Mikoneh to keep her from plowing into anyone.

He steered her around the dance floor, making certain not to remain in one place. Though he tuned out the Simynshinian nobility, he meant to stay visible. No one would conveniently ignore him, his family, or their cause—not on his watch.

The music ended at last, but Mikoneh didn't release Latta. As the first strands of a new, slower song played across the air, he grinned. "Care for another?"

"Please," said Latta, leaning toward him, her eyes open again. "If I didn't know any better, I'd have thought you were born dancing."

His grin widened. "It's not unlike flying."

She sighed. "How I wish I could tread the clouds like you do."

"I could take you." The invitation fell from his mouth before he thought it through. He hesitated, then shrugged. "If you want."

"I would love that!"

They drifted into the new dance movements, and Mikoneh found the slower pace reminiscent of gliding across sun-touched clouds. "When I tap into my dragon blood, my strength increases enough that I don't think I'd struggle to carry you."

The princess snorted. "Are you calling me heavy?"

He almost missed a step, and heat crawled up his cheeks. "Um."

She laughed. "I'm in jest, my dear friend. Don't fret so."

He relaxed, and his movements loosened.

The dance carried on for a quarter-turn, and they chatted and laughed together, spinning and gliding. When at last the music faded, Mikoneh escorted her toward a refreshment table. Halfway there, a conversation reached his pointed ears.

"He's handsome, I suppose," a woman said.

"He looks just like his father," another woman answered.

"Let us hope they're not alike in other ways," said a man with a nasal tone.

"Whether they are or not," said the first woman, "I hate to

see him so near Princess Latta. How dare he touch her—Rokahn filth."

Mikoneh quickened his step until he reached the table. Crim joined them, with Namirsha at his side.

"You're a winsome couple," the merchant lord said. "I think even your most strident enemies would have to admit it."

Smile tight, Mikoneh handed Latta a glass of chilled juice. "Let's hope it buys me a little goodwill." He ignored a nobleman's pointed glower as the man marched past. "I didn't realize the Winter Ball would live up to its name in frigid manners."

"It's not all aimed toward you," Latta said. "My mother's actions, and my father's unapologetic alliance with your father, have likewise made me a target of derision."

"I also have my own collection of enemies for various reasons," Crim said. "Not everyone here is fond of Linthians."

"That actually does me some good to hear," Mikoneh said, then glanced at Namirsha. "No offense."

"None taken," the lady replied, smiling. "I well understand why Lintha is disliked in other parts of the world."

Maya and Jensirin reached the table. The Dragon Princess was practically glowing. Near a second refreshment table, Hilker stared into his goblet like he'd rather be anywhere else than a ball. He didn't seem to be listening to the chattering man standing next to him, gesticulating dramatically. Where Donivan had gone, Mikoneh couldn't tell.

"Have you ever seen anything so beautiful as this?" Maya breathed, snaring her twin's attention.

"Yes," Mikoneh said. "*Serielias.*"

She blinked at the mention of the Nijaalin Wood in the High North. "A fair point. But this is still enchanting."

"Maya, you find most things enchanting."

She opened her mouth to protest, then snapped it shut and shrugged. "I think finding beauty in all I can is a gift."

"I agree with you." He sipped his juice and was pleasantly surprised to find it tart. "Have you seen Penn yet?"

"I haven't." Maya glanced around. "Do you think he got lost on his way here?"

"With that big brain of his, no chance. He might've skipped on purpose."

"I'll wring his neck if he did," Maya said. "He promised me a dance."

"And one for me," Latta said. "I hope he's all right."

So did Mikoneh, but he only said, "He probably lost track of time. When he gives himself over to a book, he has difficulty escaping."

Latta chuckled. "I wish I were that devoted a reader."

"It doesn't promise a long life. Half the time, he hardly remembers to eat."

"You're one to talk," said Maya. "Mikoneh gets lost in a book oftentimes himself. Or, he used to, when he actually read."

Mikoneh shrugged. "There hasn't been a lot of time lately for hobbies."

"What do you enjoy reading?" asked Latta.

"History and strategy mostly." He shrugged, then paused as he noticed Sir Kalet approaching. The Valor Knight's dark eyes were pinned on him. Mikoneh lowered his goblet. "We have company."

As the knight reached the group, Latta smiled, the glint of mirth in her eye. "Hello, Sir Cousin."

"Princess." Kalet dipped into a bow, then glanced at Maya. "Would you introduce me to your sister, Prince Mikoneh?"

"Oh, sure." Mikoneh gestured to his twin. "This is Mayanaleh—princess of Rokahn, I guess."

She rolled her eyes, laughing. "You guess?" She smiled at Kalet. "I saw you briefly the other day in our suite, I believe."

"He's the Corpse Poet." Mikoneh kept his tones casual. "Meet Sir Kalet, son of Hilker."

Maya's expression flickered from shock to confusion before settling on wonder. "Oh. Well. It's lovely to meet you, Sir Kalet."

He took her hand, stooped to kiss her knuckles, then straightened up. "I'm honored to stand before a lady of the House of Rokahn. I once met your mother, Lady Rathana. She was as lovely as a sunset. You bear her countenance."

If nothing else, Maya certainly bore the *colors* of a sunset across her cheeks. Mikoneh stifled a laugh.

"Well, Sir Kalet," he said. "You've definitely left a lingering impress—"

"Thank you, Sir Knight!" Maya kicked Mikoneh's boot without exposing her slipper beneath her skirts. He kept his expression schooled.

Sneaking a glance around him, Mikoneh found people watching with marked interest. It seemed that the celebrated knight's presence—and the casual nature of conversation—had eased the tension coiling across the chamber. A few brave souls inched closer. One man sidled up next to Kalet.

"Hello there," the newcomer said, then drained his goblet. "Are you going to introduce me, Kalet?"

"Yes, of course. This is Count Teev."

"A pleasure." The count gave Maya a long look that set Mikoneh's teeth on edge. "You're a lovely creature, Princess."

"And you've had too much to drink," Kalet said. "Off with you, my lord." He gently shoved Teev away.

Others trickled over, and Mikoneh lost any chance of remembering their names and titles, though he tried. Kalet's presence was like a spell, drawing over the curious, and making the hostile at least tolerant. They came in twos and threes, bowing graciously, often commenting on how comely the twins were, or how lively. It made sense, Mikoneh supposed, that people would be surprised by their approachability. He glanced toward Owenekiras several times, but the man never moved from his place standing on the dais. Meanwhile, King Prettem and Prince Atlanse took turns speaking with him or dancing with various ladies. The Dragon King remained an impenetrable fortress of ice and stone, surveying the room but never engaging.

At one point, Maya leaned close to her twin. "What are you watching?"

"Our father," whispered Mikoneh.

She tracked his gaze and frowned. "He looks miserable."

"Does he?" Mikoneh couldn't read one iota of emotion in the man.

Maya nodded, then turned to Jensirin, who had remained faithfully stationed at her side between dances and whispered something to him. Maya had been asked by several men to dance, and she'd accepted each invitation. Now, though, she gently turned one man down, squared her shoulders, and glided along the edge of the room, toward the dais.

Mikoneh set his drink aside and studied his twin with growing admiration. The woman was undaunted. She reached the dais and gracefully cut into Atlanse's conversation with Owenekiras Rokahn. Extending her hand, she spoke. Though he couldn't hear her in all the noise, Mikoneh could imagine her words easily.

"You look lonely up here. Shall we dance?"

Surprise flashed across Owenekiras's face but the expression was gone almost at once. He took her hand, tucked it around his arm, and guided her to the dance floor. Swirling couples faltered, then tripped away to allow a path for the Dragon King and his daughter. The music stuttered, too, then found its rhythm again. They reached the center of the chamber, and

Owenekiras slipped his arms around Maya. They stepped into the movements without hesitation, flying across the floor.

"She's a wonder," Jensirin said. "The bravest soul I've ever known."

Mikoneh grinned. "Yes. She is."

No one else danced. Mikoneh nearly asked Latta, but some instinct told him to hold off. This was important. It was... humanizing. An irony, considering the nature of Rokahn blood, but crucial, nonetheless. If people feared Owenekiras Rokahn, this would do much to crack the false reputation that bound such fear to him. Was he dangerous? Yes. Was he a maniac? No.

"She's like a healing balm," Latta whispered. "I'd forgotten how much I loved your sister like she was my own." She rested a hand on Mikoneh's arm. "Promise me the two of you will never vanish on me again."

He kept his eyes on the dancing pair. "I vow it, insofar as I have any control over the matter."

"Fair enough."

When the song ended, Owenekiras swept into a graceful bow. Maya curtsied.

The Dragon King straightened—and the room flinched back. He was *smiling*. It was a soft, frail thing, not at all cruel or cold. Seeing how the man looked at Maya—with affection and gentleness—something inside Mikoneh shifted. A longing welled up, desperate as a starving man. He wanted that connection. Wanted to receive the same sort of smile from this cold man.

Maya didn't allow Owenekiras to retreat to the dais. She led him to the table where her twin stood, and the crowd scattered like fallen leaves in the wind, leaving only the handful of those willing to stand beside Mikoneh: Latta, Kalet, Jensirin, Crim, Namirsha, and their guards.

"I love balls," Maya said, breathless and beaming. "Do you want something to drink, Father?"

Crim proffered a goblet of chilled juice. "It's got an excellent flavor, my lord. Unless you want something stronger?"

Owenekiras took it. "This will do."

"Do you enjoy dancing, my lord?" asked Sir Kalet, his tone cautious.

"Yes," Owenekiras said. "Though I don't enjoy the crowds."

Maya caught Mikoneh's eyes and said in a carrying voice, "I've realized something important tonight."

"What's that?"

She grinned. "Father is shy."

Chapter 46

In a Wasteland of Snow

"How to rejuvenate your core magic varies by element, and in that I have no knowledge beyond earth. Few have found the way to do this at all, and of those who do, they will say nothing. I think that is because words are useless against such an instinct."

- *A Treatise on the Magic of the Hidden Realm* by Sariolin the Solitary

On the heels of her statement, stillness fell over the group. Latta nearly choked on her drink. Crim was stifling laughter while Kalet looked horrified. Mikoneh risked a glance at Owenekiras, but his face remained unreadable. Whether Maya was teasing the man, or if she was convinced of her words, Mikoneh wasn't sure.

Crim cleared his throat. "Well, Princess Maya, would you care to dance with me?"

"Certainly." Maya released her father, and glided off on Crim's arm.

Mikoneh glanced at Latta. "Want to dance again?"

"Yes." A sly smile played at her lips. "But not with you."

She practically pounced toward Jensirin. "Come along, my lord."

Jensirin stiffened, then let his shoulders relax. Latta led him to where the dancers were gathering for a circular set that required a lot of weaving and hopping. Mikoneh hadn't enjoyed learning that one, and he was glad he'd escaped a public display.

Sir Kalet set down his goblet. "I should find my mother and offer her a dance. If you'll excuse me." He dipped his head, then walked off.

Lady Namirsha gave Mikoneh a brilliant smile, and for one terrifying breath he feared she'd rope him into the dance after all, but she merely curtsied and moved off to speak with a woman nearby.

Soon, father and son stood alone at the refreshment table, apart from two guards, watching the dancers bob and weave. Mikoneh tried to get the knots in his stomach to loosen. Feeling uncomfortable around Owenekiras irritated him. Whatever the Dragon King's reputation, he was still only a man—well, a dragon, anyway.

Ha. Only *a dragon.*

Mikoneh cracked a smile. For the thousandth time, he marveled at the vast changes in his life.

Stop stalling and talk to the man.

Fingering his goblet, he glanced at his father. Owenekiras was studying him back. Rather than look away, both men locked eyes and stared on.

"Are you doing better?" Owenekiras asked. "You have more color in your face."

"Yeah. I'm doing much better."

"Minno reported on the incident with the dreamsnare."

"Ah. Yeah. That was kind of unpleasant." He shuffled his feet.

"You're fortunate it did not break your mind or trap you in your dreams. A weaker person might even have died from the shock."

"Are you serious?"

Owenekiras turned his eyes to the dance floor. "A dream-snare is harmless to those with less...potent pain. But yours was extreme."

"That's a risky sort of magic."

"All magic carries risks. I did warn them not to let you touch it again."

"It fell under the settee in the skirmish with Brentin. I didn't know what it was, so..."

"Yes, I know."

Mikoneh's mind flashed to the gray boy reporting on his well-being. "May I ask you something?"

"Of course."

That straightforward answer was surprising, but Mikoneh wasn't going to question it. "*Why* do you trust Minno so much after the stunt he pulled with the Mages?"

"Minno is a complex person with a complicated worldview. He has few known weaknesses—but—"

"You're obviously one of them."

"Yes. In the sense that he is rather..."

"Jealous of anyone coming near you?" Mikoneh suggested.

"Perhaps so."

"No perhaps about it." Mikoneh set his goblet aside to fold his arms. His chest hitched at the memory of Sathe. "Minno tried to destroy me just to keep me out of your life—for some reason."

"It isn't my story to tell." Owenekiras sipped his juice. "I will say this much, and no more: your sufferings have been great, even harrowing. But Minno's are much weightier and of a larger quantity. Judge him gently if you can."

Mikoneh shifted to argue, then clamped his mouth shut. Why debate something he hardly understood? Yes, he'd suffered at Sathe's hand in unspeakable ways...for a single month. Jensirin had been the prisoner of Dark Mages for centuries—and Minno was old, despite his youthful appearance. How could Mikoneh pretend to understand the torment of souls so ancient?

I'm a child in their eyes, whining because I scraped my knee.

He exhaled and let his gaze drift across the room. "I'll try to give him the benefit of the doubt. But even if he hadn't betrayed me to Sathe—I'm not sure I'd trust him. He's too... odd. What's with the duck, anyway?"

A fleeting smile brushed Owenekiras's lips. "A childhood pet."

"A— Wait. How old is that duck?"

"Nearly as old as Minno. Millenia."

Mikoneh's jaw dropped. "You're kidding."

"No." Owenekiras took another sip. "I rarely kid."

"But—how?"

"The duck was cursed."

Mikoneh chewed on that, torn between asking what kind of curse led to such long life and how a *duck* got itself cursed in the first place. The music ended. The onlookers applauded while Maya and Crim made their way back to the table with Latta and Jensirin right behind them.

"One thing is certain," said Crim. "Your sister is a *much* better dancer than Seranni ever was."

Maya blushed a brilliant red. "Thank you, my lord."

"Not at all."

Hilker slipped up. "Excellent. My turn, student. Unless you're too tired."

Maya's beaming expression could scatter a storm cloud. "I'm not a bit tired."

Off she went again. Crim positioned himself at Mikoneh's side.

"Not dancing? I thought you might ask my wife."

Mikoneh's grimace resurfaced. "Not a chance. I only dance when I'm obligated."

"Well, don't forget to dance with your twin. Show the room how marvelous you both are. Maya won't forgive you if you don't—I have that on the best authority."

Mikoneh winced. "I believe you."

He resigned himself to the next dance, whatever it may be. Glancing around the room, he spotted Kalet speaking with an older woman. The Corpse Poet's mother, judging by their similar noses and mouths. She carried herself well, gowned in deep red and matching rubies.

Crim started up a conversation with Owenekiras about the welfare of Oceana, and Mikoneh was grateful for the shift in topic—until they mentioned Drayve.

"Relvin Province is decimated," Owenekiras said in neutral tones. "Most of the farmers have fled to the surrounding provinces. Kelpa, mostly. Of Drayve himself—or any of his house—there has been no sign."

Kevva flashed across Mikoneh's mind. Had she fled with Drayve, or had the sniveling lord abandoned her in his haste? Were they caught in the winter storms, miserable in each other's company? Kevva had never handled discomfort well. A piece of Mikoneh welcomed the thought of her suffering—but another part of him flinched with guilt. She was a fool, and she'd been the cause of so many deaths, but once she'd been a friend.

True friends don't betray each other.

Stifling a sigh, he sipped his juice. Owenekiras and Crim turned to matters in Nauttia, capital of Oceana. It sounded grimmer there than in Relvin. The castle's literal collapse, the disgrace of the Royal House and noble echelons, and the exposure of Mage corruption, had left little for the people there to use as a foundation for government.

"Right now, it's all squabbles," Owenekiras said. "Qualified and unqualified alike are vying for control in a wasteland of snow. A victor will likely surface in springtime, and then we will better know whether Oceana serves the Mage Queen. As it stands now, we can go no deeper into the kingdom. The leak here likely warned the Mages of my army's passage eastward, and they fled before the snows grew worse. With full winter setting in, even winged beasts will struggle to fight the snow at this stage. The fate of Oceana is out of my hands for the time being."

Those words stung. Mikoneh stared into his goblet. Memories tugged at his heart, but he pushed them back. As much as he wanted to fly straight for the country where he'd been raised, he couldn't do more for Oceana than he'd already tried—and certainly not as much as Owenekiras and his armies had done. Swallowing, he looked up. Owenekiras was watching him, his silver gaze bright under the influence of so many candles.

"I am sorry," said Owenekiras.

"I know." Mikoneh rubbed his thumb along his burnished goblet stem. "You did what you could. Sathe is the real reason Oceana fell. Him, and King Nilo—the old fool."

"Speaking of Oceaneans," said Crim, "where is Lord Penn?"

Mikoneh shook his head. "Probably in the library." He frowned. "Although I'm surprised he reneged on his promise to dance with Maya. It's not like him, book or no book." Needles crawled up his arms. "D'you think something might've happened?"

"We'd better find out if only to reassure ourselves." Crim

motioned to a nearby guard who extracted himself from the wall. "Find Lord Penn. Check the library first."

Mikoneh set down his goblet. "I'm going with him."

"Is that wise?" asked Crim. "You have work to do here."

"Wise? Couldn't say." Mikoneh followed the guard toward the nearest exit. A new song began, the piping notes high and chilling. He glanced back to find Maya approaching the table, her eyes fastened on him. Her brow was furrowed.

He offered her a reassuring smile, then stepped from the bright chamber, out into the dim corridor. The fragrance of pine and cinnamon tugged at his nose. Footsteps fell behind him, and he turned again. Sir Kalet was coming toward him fast. Mikoneh caught the door.

"Leaving, Your Highness?" asked the Corpse Poet.

"My friend hasn't arrived. He might've gotten himself lost."

"Ah. Allow me to escort you." He waved the guard off. "You're dismissed."

"Yes, Sir Kalet." The guard bowed to them both, then moved back into the ballroom. Kalet let the door close behind the man.

"Where to first, Your Highness?"

"The royal library."

They took the passages at a fast clip, saying little. At a crossroads, Kalet paused in a shaft of moonlight flooding through tall, muntined windows. Snow feathered down from the sky. They'd reached the second floor and were nearing the library.

"Is your friend absent-minded?" Kalet asked.

Mikoneh stared out at the snowbound world. Great drifts had invaded the bailey below, and servants were working hard to clear pathways along the cobblestones and outer wall parapets.

"Not usually. It's more likely he fell asleep. He's not been getting much of that these days."

"Is he a great reader?"

"When he needs to be." Mikoneh moved beyond the windows. "He's trying to understand more about the politics of Sirinhigha. Oceana had a skewed view."

"A scholar, is he? I respect that."

They moved to the great double doors leading into a grand chamber laden with towering shelves that sprawled up several stories. Ladders and spiral stairs framed the great room. Dust, ink, and leather perfumed the air. Seating areas were spread across the floor atop damask rugs, and desks and tables were burdened beneath scrolls and tomes, inkwells, and lanterns. Despite the late turn, librarians roamed the room, stacks of books in arm. All was quiet, but for the faint patter of feet moving hither and thither.

Kalet strode to the nearest man seated at a table, bent over a scroll. Mikoneh followed close. The scholar's quill scratched at the parchment, his handwriting a steady flow, cramped yet legible.

"Excuse me, Gredd," Kalet said.

The man looked up, a pair of pince-nez clamped to his nose, the lenses magnifying his eyes. He was a dusty old man, paper thin and withered, with wispy hair of silvery gray. "Ah, Sir Kalet. Come for new reading material? We just got in a rare find." He started to rise.

"Hold a moment, Gredd. Have you seen Lord Penn?"

Gredd blinked. "Penn? Ah, the inquisitive young man. Yes, yes. He was here a turn or so ago, but I dare say he left. Said he needed to attend the Winter Ball."

Mikoneh's chest pinched.

"Thank you, Gredd," said Kalet. "I'll return for that rare book tomorrow."

"You'll enjoy it. Dragon poetry."

Kalet stilled, then glanced at Mikoneh. "Perhaps you should read it first, Your Highness. You'll enjoy it immensely."

Gredd eyed Mikoneh for the first time. "Ah, the Rokahn prince. It's an honor to meet you."

"Gredd is the head of the Guild of Words in Simynshin," Kalet said. "But we've not much time for introductions. We'll come again later, Gredd. Thank you for your help."

"Anything at all for the hero of Elenth."

CHAPTER 47

FRAGRANCE OF THE FLAMES

"Even so, I will try to explain how to restore one's energy. With earth, it comes from grounding. The humor in that statement does not escape me, but it remains true. Even as I tap the earth's strength to grow a tree, if I am grounded—centered—it will renew me in return."

- *A Treatise on the Magic of the Hidden Realm* by Sariolin the Solitary

As they left the library, Mikoneh studied Kalet from the corner of his eye. They maintained a quick pace, heading straight for the Rokahn suite. Mikoneh sent up a prayer that Penn would be in the common room, asleep, drooling on the pages of some dusty old tome.

"So," Mikoneh said, rounding a corner, "dragon poetry. Is it any good?" He needed to keep his thoughts level, to stave off the panic attack mounting in his chest.

Kalet stumbled but caught himself. "Any g— You've never read the poetry of your kind?"

"Never."

"That is perhaps the saddest thing I've ever heard. Tomorrow, we must get that rare volume from Gredd. Dragons are among the greatest poets and artists in the world."

"That seems odd to me." Mikoneh flexed his fingers, recalling the feel of his scaly dragon hands tipped with claws. "Can dragons even paint?"

Kalet snorted. "You're more apt with metalsmithing, as a rule. But I've seen some of the great paintings and murals your ancestors created. They're wondrous."

They turned yet another corner, nearing the suite.

"*You* believe in dragons, Sir Kalet?"

"Certainly. My father serves Owenekiras Rokahn. I'd be daft not to heed the legends. I've also seen a fairy ring and spotted a unicorn high up on a ledge."

Mikoneh's eyebrows shot up. "Near here?"

"No, farther north. There are no unicorns here, alas. It was perhaps the most singular experience of my life. I wish I could've touched her."

Mikoneh recalled the soft, almost cool sensation of the unicorn's silvery coat. He yearned to see that being once more, to stare into her ancient eyes, to feel whole again.

The suite lay just ahead. The two men slammed the common room door open. Mikoneh darted into the gloom first, but the Corpse Poet was right on his heels.

They stumbled to a halt at the eerie sight before them. The broad bay window was wide open. Snow dusted the window seat. Spread out across the cushion—pale as death—lay Penn. Faint clouds of breath misted before the viscount's face: the only sign of life.

Standing in the window's opening, a cloaked figure loomed against the night. A hissing laugh escaped from under the cowl. "I knew you would come for him, Mikoneh Rokahn."

Chills nipped at Mikoneh's skin. He took a step back, every instinct screaming at him to flee. Run. Don't think.

Kalet's sword scraped free of its sheath. "Stand down, maggot."

The cloaked figure chortled. "Does the Valor Knight think he can take on a full Mage?"

"Yes," Kalet said. "It isn't the first time."

Kalet's calm was grounding. Mikoneh exhaled a low breath, centering himself, drawing on the warmth in his core.

Penn. You need to rescue Penn.

Flexing his fingers, Mikoneh summoned fire. Hot flames burst across his hands, dancing, sparking. The fire in the hearth answered, leaping into life, casting orange light across the dim chamber.

The Mage's laughter deepened. "I'm not so pathetic as Sathe was. You can't defeat me. Surrender yourself, Dragon Prince, and enter the Mage Queen's service."

Sathe hadn't been pathetic, but Mikoneh didn't feel like arguing the point. He took a step forward, shoving down his panic, ignoring his mind's cry to run.

"I don't really care how powerful you are," he ground out. "I want my friend—unharmed." Lifting his hand, he let his element grow higher and hotter until it flashed white. The fragrance of the flames curled around his face—a kind of airy, bright, cleansing scent, unlike anything Mikoneh had smelled before. He tore his gaze from the fire, setting his sights on the Mage.

Did the man flinch back?

Mikoneh took another step. "Release Penn and I *might* not rip you apart."

The Mage's laughter was weaker than before. "You're a novice. An infant. You don't frighten me." He lifted his hand. An orb of violet light flickered into life.

"Then you're a fool." Kalet's voice was taut.

Mikoneh glanced at the Corpse Poet. Kalet eyed him warily.

Mikoneh fastened a glare on the Mage. "You don't frighten me either." It wasn't a complete lie. Mikoneh's fury had eaten away the tendrils of terror around his heart, purging him, until his focus was hot as a smithy's forge.

The sound of fire filled his ears, roaring like it had on the night his parents died. Calm descended like a veil around him, snuffing out all but his need to protect Penn. He took another step, held his palm out before him, and unleashed his flame.

It streamed forth, blazing hot, thunderous, swallowing the violet light, then slamming into the Mage. Another flash of Hollow flickered, then died. A scream filled the air. The fire burned on and on and on and on...

Then it cut off. Mikoneh slumped to his knees, spent.

Kalet raced forward, leapt over Penn's prone form, and leaned out over the window.

"He's running away."

Mikoneh gasped for breath. "Anyone chasing him?"

"Archers are letting loose their arrows."

That would hardly be enough, but Mikoneh had nothing left to use in a fight. He shoved himself to his feet, staggered, then inched his way toward Penn. Kalet jumped down from the sill and leaned over the sleeping man.

"Alive."

"Can you wake him?" asked Mikoneh.

Kalet checked Penn's eyes, then shook him. "Out cold. Possibly by magic. We need a healer and a Magery expert. Fortunately, your sister and father fit those requirements well."

"Mind getting them?" Mikoneh slumped down beside the window seat.

"I won't leave you alone. That Mage might have been

pathetic—whatever his claims to the contrary—but he could return and finish you off in your weakened state."

"He'd be more likely to capture than kill me."

"That hardly makes me feel better." Kalet gave Penn another look over. "I don't want to move him. It could upset whatever spell might be upon him." The knight marched to the door, flung it open, and stared out into the hall. He let out a soft curse that carried to Mikoneh's sharp ears. "Not one guard. This lapse in security concerns me."

Mikoneh gripped the edge of the window seat and pushed himself to his feet. Every muscle groaned. "This was planned. Maybe that Mage was only meant to weaken me. He gave up too easily."

Kalet snorted. "Perhaps, but you didn't see your face. I'm accustomed to battle—and you singed my blood with those eyes of yours."

"Not sure how to take that, but thanks for the intriguing imagery." He glanced down at Penn. "You can't leave me, and I won't leave him." He twisted around to size up the Valor Knight. "It's a risk, I know, but will you carry Penn to the ballroom?"

Kalet adjusted his grip on his sword. "You can't possibly defend yourself, let alone three of us. Nor do you have the strength to carry your friend. We must remain here, unless we can awaken Master Penn and he's well enough to walk."

Mikoneh stopped. "Wait. Akonn." He pointed to the Captain of the Sword's room. "He's in there. Can you check on him?"

Kalet crossed in a few quick bounds, snipped the door open, and peered inside. "Hello, Captain."

A voice answered, too low and soft for Mikoneh to catch the words. Or maybe he was too tired to tap into his dragon hearing.

"...heard nothing?" Kalet's voice was disbelieving. "Either you're a sound sleeper or your room was bespelled."

Another answer, indistinct.

"Mage attack," Kalet explained. "I have Mikoneh with me, as well as Penn. If you're up to it—"

"I can manage," Akonn said, louder.

Kalet nodded and left the door ajar, then crossed back to Mikoneh. "He will be aiding us."

"I can't believe he heard none of that."

"They probably cast a spell to keep him from hearing anything. Akonn is a fae, and Captain of the Sword. Mages prefer not to engage them in combat."

"He's also injured."

Kalet's lips twitched up. "I would still personally avoid upsetting his kind."

That statement twisted Mikoneh's gut. Despite Akonn's reputation, someone had risked wounding him before—almost fatally. Who would dare if both a renowned knight and Mages avoided it? Akonn hadn't seen his attacker, which gave Mikoneh exactly zero clues regarding who it had been.

I hate fighting blind.

He turned back to Penn, and gently cuffed his cheek. "Penn. Hey, Penn. Now would be a good time to wake up."

A rustling came from Akonn's door, then the captain stepped into view, clad in his repaired uniform and gripping his unsheathed sword. He still looked pale, but his eyes were bright. "Reporting for duty, Your Highness."

"Thank you, Captain." Mikoneh tapped Penn's cheek again. "I don't suppose you know any magic to wake him up?"

"Not my area of expertise, I'm afraid." Akonn strode across the chamber. "Normally, Princess Latta could use her voice to wake him, but..."

Mikoneh frowned. Yet another motivation to restore her song. "I don't think it's wise to remain—"

He felt the biting cold before he glimpsed the violet light.

Kalet shoved Mikoneh aside, even as the malevolent glow spread its fingers across the room. Glass shattered. Mikoneh struck the floor, then rolled over in time to find a half dozen robed figures pouring through the broken window.

Kalet shouted at Akonn, who was already in motion. The captain's sword flashed in the Hollow's glow. He caught one figure, tearing through the robe. The cowl fell back, revealing a half-dead face, mottled flesh hanging from exposed bone. The Dark Mage's leering grin seared into Mikoneh's mind.

Can't. Can't go back there.

He huddled into himself, bone weary, gripped by a fear that paralyzed every limb.

Can't go back. Please.

Kalet was shouting at him. The words couldn't penetrate his mounting terror.

A black-robed figure knelt at his side.

Akonn thrust his blade through its back, and the figure lurched forward. Cold, wicked eyes gleamed when they met Mikoneh's.

Its voice was harsh like steel on steel. "You will not—"

Akonn lopped its head off. The head rolled toward the settee.

More Mages flowed into the window, walking on the air. Their cold magic crackled and flashed. Kalet stumbled backward, caught in a blast of Hollow.

Akonn's sword flashed again, and Mikoneh caught a wisp of blue light across its tip. Void. Akonn was tapping into Hollow's opposite to fend off the enemy. How Mikoneh saw it —how he understood it—he didn't know.

He tried to rise, but his arms and legs still felt frozen. He gritted his teeth. Penn lay helpless across the window seat, beneath the band of Mages invading the chamber. For every lesser Mage Akonn took down, three more poured in. Kalet was less effective against them, but he still fought well. If Mikoneh survived to face off against him tomorrow, it would be a close fight.

Move, Mikoneh. Summon fire!

The flames in the fireplace answered, bursting into a raging inferno, leaping out of the hearth to singe the rug. Fire spirits took to the air, riding embers.

'Attack,' Mikoneh mouthed.

They crackled their understanding.

He couldn't tap the heat in his own body, but he could still employ an army.

The fire spirits leapt at the Mages, catching their robes on fire. One Mage let out a scream. Others flinched back, beating at their attire. Akonn decapitated another. Kalet tripped up one in retreat, then rammed his sword into its eye socket.

Flames ate the area rug, crawling closer to the furniture. Mikoneh wrenched his arm up, and found his voice. "Don't let the room burn!"

Two fire spirits scooped up the wild flames and tossed them at the nearest Mage.

A robed figure leaned over Penn, the flash of a dagger catching Mikoneh's eye. "Desist, Firebrand," hissed its chilling voice.

Mikoneh jerked forward. "Don't touch him!"

"Surrender. Come with us, and your friends—all of them —will live."

Mikoneh trembled, caught between his protective instinct and a writhing fear. He couldn't go back. Not ever again. But Penn...

"Don't heed him, my prince!" called Akonn, blocking

tendrils of dark magic with his sword. "Mages cannot be trusted. He'll kill Penn the moment you're taken!"

That was likely true, but the Mage would kill Penn if Mikoneh refused to obey.

What should I do? What can I—

The door to the corridor burst into splinters.

Owenekiras Rokahn stood in the doorway.

CHAPTER 48

STRANDS OF LIGHTNING

"I can only guess what the other elements require for such a recharge. It took me a long time to realize that I didn't have to deplete my resources at all, and by then, my days of fighting were long over."

- *A Treatise on the Magic of the Hidden Realm* by Sariolin the Solitary

Lightning crackled up the walls, swallowing the room in white-blue light. Owenekiras's eyes glowed blazing silver—almost molten. Behind the Dragon King, Jensirin stood with his ornamental blade drawn, fury dancing in his countenance.

The Mages fell back toward the window. Mikoneh choked on a sob of relief.

Lightning spidered over the ceiling, blindingly bright. Mikoneh flinched.

Someone screamed.

Another crack and roll of thunder.

Another scream.

Someone hastily shouted out something in a language Mikoneh didn't recognize—but he could imagine its meaning: *Retreat*.

"I don't think so," Owenekiras rumbled.

More lightning crackled. Thunder clapped.

Another scream followed.

Mikoneh shielded his face with his hands, then risked a look. A Mage crumbled to dust. A black cloak billowed to the floor. The scent of charred bones and flesh was acrid in the air.

Two Mages escaped through the window, plunging toward the ground. An arrow whistled across the air, followed by others, clattering against the castle wall.

Lightning speared the final Mage attempting to retreat. He turned to ice rather than dust. His mouth gaped wide, his eyes bulging with terror. This one wasn't a lesser Mage—he still had skin and hair. Encased, he stood frozen, glistening in the last strands of lightning before they flickered out.

Owenekiras strode across the common room, his eyes still blazing. Jensirin darted around him and flung himself to his knees beside Mikoneh.

"Are you wounded?" asked the dragon lord.

"N-no. Just taxed. Used too much fire."

Jensirin looked him up and down, skeptical, then he nodded as though he were satisfied. The dragon lord turned to Owenekiras, who had positioned himself between Mikoneh and the ice-swathed Mage.

Kalet approached, wiping a string of blood from the corner of his mouth. "Is he dead or merely captured, my lord?"

"Captured." Owenekiras brushed his gloved fingers across the ice. "I was careful."

"Good. I'll arrange for him to be taken to the dungeon."

"No." Owenekiras pointed to his bedroom. "He will spend

this night in company with me. I have several questions for him."

Mikoneh's gaze slid to the frozen Mage, and he shuddered. Despite the man's immobility, something of his essence leaked through the shield of ice, prickling Mikoneh's skin, reminding him of Sathe's foul touch...

The room spun. The edges of his vision darkened.

Firebrand...

"Look at me," Jensirin whispered. "Ignore his memory. He can't hurt you now. Breathe."

With a jolt, Mikoneh realized his lungs had failed him. He drank in a breath, then another. The room fell back into place. Jensirin rubbed his back, whispering encouragement and instruction: Take another breath. That's right, keep breathing. You are doing fine.

Shame burned Mikoneh's cheeks. He drew up his knees and slumped against them while trying to banish the mental comparisons his mind had drawn between him and Jensirin. They weren't fair to either of them.

We each handle suffering differently.

The dizziness subsided. His vision brightened, and he lifted his head. Jensirin had moved from his side and was helping Kalet gather the robes from the ground. Piles of ash remained behind.

"W-where's Maya?" Mikoneh whispered.

"Still at the ball." In trembling hands, Jensirin clutched a charcoal gray robe.

With a pang of sympathy, Mikoneh pushed to his feet, but his muscles protested, forcing him to slump back down at once. "Let someone else do that."

Kalet, seeing the exchange, approached the dragon lord and gently pried the robe from his fingers. Wordlessly, the Valor Knight moved off to the next pile of Mage remains.

Movement snagged Mikoneh's attention, and he turned in time to see Owenekiras leaning over Penn. The Dragon King murmured something, too low for Mikoneh to catch, and placed his palm across Penn's face. Owenekiras mouthed a few more words, and Penn's hands twitched. His chest rose and fell faster. He inhaled a sharp breath.

Owenekiras straightened up, removing his hand. "Take a moment, Penn. If you try to move too swiftly, you will fall over."

Mikoneh scooted himself closer to the window seat and set his hand on Penn's shoulder. "You okay?"

"M-Mikoneh?" Penn turned his head toward him, blinking slowly. "What happened? W-where..."

"Take it easy. Give yourself a moment to remember."

Penn fell still, his eyes shifting as he took in the room. He drew a long breath and sat up. His skin was still deathly white, and he shook with the effort of moving. "I don't u-under-stand... Where are we?" He glanced toward Owenekiras and gulped. "Who is that?"

Mikoneh tensed. "You don't know him?"

"N-no."

"What *do* you remember?"

"Uh..." Penn dragged a hand over his face. "Running away...from my father's castle. A-after he tried to execute us... We were—You—" His eyes widened. "You summoned fire!"

Alarm slashing at his insides, Mikoneh twisted toward Owenekiras. "Will he get his memories back?"

Owenekiras nodded. "The loss is likely due to the magic used on him. My guess is someone didn't want him remembering their face. We should have Minno take a look."

"I haven't seen Minno tonight."

"He went for a walk," said Jensirin. "He told me he dislikes dances."

Mikoneh nearly snorted, but then sobered at once. Minno was capable of manipulating memories. Was it mere coincidence that he was nowhere in sight when Penn had been attacked and part of his memory taken?

He glanced at Owenekiras. "Do you still vouch for Minno?"

The Dragon King frowned. "I do, yes. He gave me his word."

"Is that all it takes to trust someone?" Mikoneh couldn't fight the bitterness in his voice.

"Not always," Owenekiras said, "but with Minno, yes."

That answer stunned Mikoneh. How could this man take Minno at his word after *everything*? Heat surged through his blood. His hands curled into fists. He choked on a desire to shout out his disdain, his fury.

Don't lose control. Don't make a fool of yourself.

He bowed his head, letting the heat burn through him. His muscles loosened. Flames sparked on his fingertips. His elemental core had recharged. He laughed, too startled to stop himself.

My anger fuels my power. Handy to know.

"What's wrong?" asked Penn warily.

Mikoneh held his palm up, willing the flames into full life. They danced across his hand, banishing shadows, filling the room with warm orange light. His anger melted into the flame.

Penn stared, mesmerized. "You really can summon fire."

"Yeah," Mikoneh said. "Which you'd gotten used to. You've just forgotten. We're a long way from Relvin Province, Penn." He grinned at his friend. "We're presently guests of the Royal House of Chenta, residing in Elenth Castle in Simynshin. Oh, and I'm a dragon."

CHAPTER 49

SIE-DRAYA

"Yes, it is true. Once I was battle-hardened. I used my earth talents to lay waste to battlegrounds and uproot forests. It sounds histrionic now. If only that was all it was, but I barely sleep at night when I recall the past carnage I wrought."

- A Treatise on the Magic of the Hidden Realm by Sariolin the Solitary

It was Jensirin who had softly insisted something was wrong—and Owenekiras who'd asked Maya to stay behind to keep the ball goers occupied. She'd agreed, though every instinct hissed at her to follow them.

It's Mikoneh. I know he's in trouble.

Thankfully, Crim had taken it upon himself to escort Maya around to meet the numerous nobility. His wife, Namirsha, joined them for some introductions, but not others. Maya guessed that had a lot to do with Linthian sympathies. Even Crim steered clear of a few openly hostile glares, dancing around them to call out to milord so-and-so or milady such-and-such.

Crim was generally well liked, which didn't surprise Maya in the least. His easy smile and pleasant voice were enough to turn female heads. Namirsha's smile tightened whenever glittering court ladies pressed closer to fling a witty remark or two toward the merchant lord.

Maya was asked to dance by lords young and old alike, and she accepted all of them, determined to do her part in bringing Simynshin around to help in the war against the Mages. Some lords refrained from discussing more than the recent weather and how the deep snows kept them from good hunting. She tacked on a smile during such exchanges, pretending to enjoy listening to their explanation of butchering helpless animals.

She was a dragon and craved meat now like she never had before, but she didn't have to relish the kill.

Fortunately, the younger dance partners appeared eager to discuss the war with her. One man—a wide-set fellow called Lord Fontinn—broached the subject without preamble.

"Do you agree with your father's view on the necessity of this war, Your Highness?" His blue eyes were large and keen. His gold buttons glittered under the bright candelabra.

Maya welcomed his straightforwardness. "I do, Lord Fontinn. While I deeply lament the lives lost in battle, I've seen what the Dark Mages are willing to do. Oceana's present chaos is entirely on their heads."

"I've heard rumors," Fontinn said, "that your brother, Prince Mikoneh, toppled Nauttia Castle, crushing King Nilo and all his court in his fury, after he discovered they'd sided with the Mages."

Maya tensed. "Certainly not!" She bit her lip, flushing at how far her voice had carried.

Fontinn shrugged. "'Tis only a rumor, Your Highness. May I ask what really happened?"

Mind churning, Maya let Fontinn lead her through a series

of complicated steps. How much should she say? Who knew about her twin's captivity? Studying Fontinn's eyes, she read cleverness and perhaps open-mindedness.

Should she risk telling him?

The facts will come out, now or later.

She took a bracing breath. "One of the Mage Queen's generals captured my brother and dragged him into the tunnels underground. Lord Owenekiras and several allies—along with myself—worked to rescue Mikoneh. Unfortunately, he was tortured for weeks before we succeeded. During his captivity, he was taken to King Nilo in Oceana. It was there we mounted our rescue by conjuring up a hurricane. Lord Penn—an Oceanian noble—as well as Captain Akonn of the Sword, and Ter N'Avea sneaked into the castle ahead of time. They helped most of the court to escape before the castle collapsed."

"Did the hurricane bring down the castle?"

"No, the Mages brought it down to hide their retreat. That castle has withstood hurricanes for centuries."

Fontinn weighed her words, then nodded. "I'm sorry to hear about your brother's captivity. I've read about Mage torture. It's incredibly inhumane. He appears to be recovering well."

"He's the strongest person I know."

"Thank you for telling me, Princess Mayanaleh. I listen to rumors and try to glean what truth from them that I can, but it's always best to trace them to their source where possible. I've had strong doubts about the Mage ambassador's overtures, and with the king's denouncement of Queen Feresse—along with your brother's harrowing experience—I'm prepared to pledge my knights to your father's cause." He tipped his head to one side. "One last question, fair lady. Do you know why the Mages were determined to imprison your brother? Was it to hold him hostage to secure Owenekiras Rokahn's surrender?"

"Partly." Maya steeled herself to deliver what might be too far-fetched. "It was also to bond with him and turn him into a weapon."

Fontinn's hold on her tightened, then he blinked and loosened his fingers. "Then it's true?" He searched her face. "The royal line in Rokahn—you're really dragons?"

"Yes," Maya said. "We are."

His gaze danced between her eyes, and his throat bobbed as he swallowed hard. "I see. Yes, that makes sense. I've always half believed..." The music ended, and he brought Maya to a graceful stop. "You've given me a great deal to consider, Your Highness. Thank you for a stimulating conversation. You're a superb dancer."

Maya's cheeks warmed. "Thank you most kindly, Lord Fontinn. Especially for your open mind."

He bowed, then strode away.

Crim came to collect her, Hilker at his side.

"That seemed to go well," the Wind Master said. "I'm impressed. Fontinn is a very reserved man."

"Maya could charm a bad-tempered crab," said Crim.

Her flush deepened. "You flatter me, my lord."

"The truth is rather flattering on you," he said.

Embarrassed, she batted that away. "Lord Fontinn seems inclined to pledge his knights to our cause."

Crim and Hilker blinked, then exchanged a glance.

"That's excellent news," Crim said. "He's always appeared to be a strict pacifist. His knights are among Simynshin's most skilled, but since inheriting his father's estate, Fontinn's been opposed to any fighting. His men have been restless and prone to violence in Elenth as a result. They went from revered to useless, and that goes poorly with warriors. Several have turned into drunkards."

"That's a pity." Maya watched Fontinn walk across the ballroom. "I don't think he's so much a pacifist as extremely cautious. How did his father die?"

"Assassin," Hilker said. "Two years ago. Lord Dalter had a lot of enemies at court. He was a staunch supporter of Owenekiras, and had no talent for tact."

They reached the nearest refreshment table, causing several court ladies to flit away. One woman in pale pink tossed Maya a frigid glower, then jerked her head around and stormed off.

Probably one of Feresse's sycophants, now in disgrace by association.

A strange sort of satisfaction foamed up in Maya's chest at that thought. She'd always been an outcast in the village circles back home—but now roles were reversed, and those with the biggest egos and smallest brains were being put in their place.

Just don't get a fat head yourself, Maya.

She accepted Crim's proffered wine goblet with a smile and a thank you. She only sipped at the heady red liquid. She had no intention of getting tipsy while Mikoneh and Penn remained gone. Once the mulled drink had steadied her nerves, she set it aside.

Latta approached the table with a worried glint in her blue eyes. "Any news?"

"None," Crim said. "But I'm confident that Owenekiras and Jensirin can handle most matters."

Most was small comfort. Maya fiddled with her embroidered cuff.

Hilker downed a full goblet of wine, then set it aside. "I think I've had enough of frivolity for one night. I'll take my leave."

"What about your son?" Maya asked.

Hilker sniffed. "That one can take care of himself. I ain't worried." He strode off, looking grumpier than usual.

"Ah," said Crim in low tones, seizing Maya's attention,

"here comes Lord Tikar. He's a foreigner and honorary ambassador from the Isles of Kwilaj. Cimin conquered his people generations ago. What Cimin does in this war, the isles will do. Even so, your influence could sway their decision."

Maya turned her smile on the ambassador. He was a dark-skinned man with glittering eyes the color of amber. His black hair was slicked back and glossy in the lighting. He wore baggy clothes, muted in hues, except for the exquisite gems lining his cuffs and hems. His build and presence suggested that he was a man in his fifties, but his flawless skin made Maya second-guess that.

Crim bowed his head, then spoke to Tikar in a musical language. The ambassador responded in kind, gesturing toward Maya.

"Lord Tikar, I present Princess Mayanaleh Rokahn. My lady, this is Ambassador Tikar of the ancient Isles of Kwilaj."

Tikar extended his hand. Not knowing what to expect, Maya offered her own. Tikar took her fingers, gently twisted her hand around, and dropped a garnet into her palm.

"Accept my gift, *Sie-Draya,* I beg thee." Tikar's voice was low and soft.

Maya stared at the garnet, transfixed. "Thank you, Ambassador Tikar."

He released her hand and backed away, then straightened. "You are as lovely as your ancestors, with their strength and wisdom. Long have the Isles of Kwilaj awaited the return of *Priea Sie-Draya.*"

Maya cast an inquiring glance at Crim, but the merchant lord avoided her eyes. Instead, he addressed Tikar.

"The garnet is the finest I've ever seen, my lord," he said. "A worthy gift."

Tikar inclined his head. "I shall take my leave now." He

backed away, then pivoted on one heel, and strode toward a cluster of men and women near the musicians.

Maya turned toward Crim. "The return of *what*?"

"The Princess She-Dragon, I think," said Crim. "Kwilaj once worshiped dragons like gods—especially the females. You're a sign to them, Maya. Soon, Kwilaj may defect from Cimin."

The blood drained from her face. "Did I just start a *war*?"

"No, no. You merely escalated one."

She resisted an urge to throw her goblet at him. "Well, that's so much better, isn't it?"

"Rokahns move things, Princess. You can't help yourself. But then, that shouldn't surprise you. Dragons are awfully big as a rule."

"*I'm* not."

"Your spirit is, dear princess. I assure you."

She had nothing to say to that, so she turned to the table and selected a delicate red-and-white swirled confection. It smelled of peppermint. A commotion started at the nearest set of doors. She whirled, then gasped with relief.

Mikoneh strode into view, followed closely by Sir Kalet, Owenekiras, and Jensirin. They all looked perfectly put together—though Maya noted that Mikoneh had changed back into his parade attire. Dark circles edged his eyes, but that was normal these days.

She dropped the candy onto the tablecloth, but kept the garnet clutched close, and swept toward her twin. King Prettem met him first, and Sir Kalet moved to speak in the king's ear. Mikoneh stood by, listening, interjecting now and then.

Maya reached them. "What happened? Did you find Penn?"

"Yeah. He's fine. Just a little confused." Mikoneh clutched

Fa's sword strapped at his waist. "We were attacked by Mages, but they're gone now."

She inhaled, then searched his face. "Are you all right?"

His crooked smile was answer enough. "I will be."

At least he didn't try to lie. He wasn't good at it—not with her, anyway.

Prettem glanced at the twins. "Should tomorrow's tourney be canceled, Sir Kalet?"

"No, I think not, Your Majesty," the Valor Knight replied. "We ought to show the Mages that we're not so easily rattled."

"Agreed," said Mikoneh. "Besides, you and I have a bout, Sir Knight."

Kalet grinned. "So we do."

Mikoneh turned to face the room and Maya followed his gaze. Though the music pressed on, few people were dancing. Most had stopped dead on the floor, now whispering while observing the Rokahns clustered around the king. Mistrust gleamed in dozens of eyes.

Maya tucked her arm around her twin's. "I'm glad you're back. I—"

"Want a dance." Mikoneh heaved a sigh. "I know, I know." His voice was weary, but the light in his golden eyes assured her he was only teasing.

They moved to the center of the ballroom and fell into step with the music. As they twirled, Maya let her fears roll away. They'd remain close, lurking at the edge of her soul, waiting to strike again. But for now, for this moment, she would pretend she and her twin were safe, the world was at peace, and Mages weren't tainting Sirinhigha, one kingdom at a time.

Chapter 50

Ethereal Death

"It is only now that I regret tainting the earth spirits. No, they aren't warped because of my actions. They are still innocent and pure, and somehow, they still love me. Yet I cannot overcome the guilt of using them as I did."

- *A Treatise on the Magic of the Hidden Realm* by Sariolin the Solitary

Despite the strangeness of the night before, morning carried the jubilant energy of festival time. The air was charged with anticipation. The ball had ended near dawn, and Mikoneh had somehow managed to keep his feet until Crim assured the twins they could retire.

The tourney wouldn't begin until midafternoon, allowing all the nobility and gentry to catch up on their rest. Mikoneh slept deeply, though his dreams were even more unsettled than usual. He woke remembering nothing about them except mottled hands clawing at his flesh.

Dragging himself from bed around noon, he bathed in the tub prepared for him, willed the fire spirits to dry his hair, then slipped into the dark gray leather armor provided by Tayvin for the tourney proper. The armor was surprisingly flexible, and he sat down to a light brunch without difficulty.

Jensirin was awake and joined him for the meal in the common room.

"Has Penn stirred yet?" Mikoneh asked between mouthfuls of stewed tomatoes and fluffy buttered bread. They tasted like ash.

"Not yet."

"Any sign of Minno?"

"None."

Mikoneh skewered a slab of cold roast beef and chewed it while he pondered the gray boy's absence. "I don't like not knowing where he is."

"Nor do I," Jensirin said.

"Do you think he's betrayed us again?"

"I hope not." Jensirin prodded at the tomatoes with a faint grimace, then pushed them aside. He focused solely on the roast beef. "Your father did not return last night. I would guess he went looking for Minno ahead of his interrogation session."

"He seems convinced that Minno's not part of last night's attack."

"Owenekiras is a careful man. He wouldn't make that assumption lightly. There are oaths that are magically binding. Perhaps that is what he meant about Minno's word."

"I hope so." Mikoneh tore off a bite of bread. He didn't feel hungry, but he needed to eat before he fought. "Are you all right, after everything?" He glanced up to read the dragon lord's expression, but it was closed.

"I will be."

The words, echoing his own from last night, sent a pang across Mikoneh's chest. "Thank you for coming to find us," Mikoneh said.

The ghost of a smile touched Jensirin's lips. "I will always find you. I owe you that much."

"Again, you owe me nothing. We saved each other."

"You brought me back from an existence far crueler than death. I will owe you for the rest of my days."

Mikoneh pushed a tomato around with his fork. "That's really not necessary."

"Even so." Jensirin ripped a section of roast beef with his teeth and chewed with vehemence.

Maya's door swung open, and she staggered out, wearing her nightgown and robe. Her hair was a tousled mess, though the wind seemed determined to remedy that. "G'morning," she mumbled, and half-fell into her chair.

"Morning, sleepyhead," Mikoneh said.

Jensirin smiled at her. "Good morning, Princess."

She offered the dragon lord a sleepy smile, rubbing one eye. "What time is it?"

"Midday, give or take half a turn," Mikoneh said.

She grunted, then piled tomatoes onto her plate. "When are the Elementalist battles?"

"Day after tomorrow." Mikoneh had spent the last full turn of last night's dance picking Kalet's brain concerning the tourney proper. "The first two days are focused on traditional weapons, beginning with sword, then archery, maces, knife-throwing, and ending with polearms."

She gave another grunt, then stuffed her mouth with tomatoes.

Mikoneh placed a thick slab of roast beef on her plate, and buttered some bread for her. "No more late nights for you."

She sighed dreamily. "It was so wonderful, Mikoneh, with all those candles, and the flowing dresses, and the smells! I never realized how much I love pine." She sighed again. "Best of all was the dancing."

"Liked that bit, did you?" He winked at Jensirin.

"'Course I did," Maya said. "As you *well* know."

"Yeah, yeah." He finished his last hunk of meat, then set aside his fork, and pushed away from the table. "I'm going to check on Penn."

Maya snapped awake. "Oh. Penn." She started to rise.

"Stay down. Eat your food. I've got this." He hurried to Penn's room, slipped inside, and crossed to the bed.

Penn was curled into a ball under the coverlets, his breaths even, his face untroubled. Mikoneh hesitated, then shook him awake. Penn uncurled himself at a snail's pace, stretching and yawning, like he'd had the most beautiful sleep in the world. Mikoneh nearly cuffed his head for that.

"Morning, Mikoneh." Penn offered another yawn while he brushed back his long blond hair.

"Sure is. How're you feeling?"

Penn blinked at him, then stiffened. "I had the *oddest* dream you called yourself—"

"A dragon? I take it your memories are still absent." Mikoneh sank onto the edge of the mattress. "Drat it all. I'd hoped you could tell us more about last night, but I guess not."

"Sorry."

"It's fine. Once we locate Minno, we can get you a bit more up to date."

Penn gazed around the room. "Are we really in Elenth Castle?"

"Yep."

"Amazing. I'd love to take a tour."

"You already did. And you met Princess Latta—whom you're very taken with."

Penn colored. "A-am I? But Maya—"

"Is rather taken with someone else, as usual. There's a bathtub in my room, Penn. I'll make sure the water's still warm, then you can scrub up. There's also some food out there. Help yourself."

Penn was studying Mikoneh with a frown. "You've lost weight."

Standing up, Mikoneh turned his back on the viscount. A humming started in his head. "I'm heading out. Gotta check on someone else." Panic clawed at his lungs.

"Have you been ill?" Penn persisted.

"I—Yeah. But I'm better now." He retreated from the room and went immediately to Akonn's chamber, so he didn't make himself a liar.

"How is Penn?" asked Maya.

"Sleepy." Mikoneh stepped into Akonn's dark room and shut the door with a snip. He leaned against the wooden barrier, drinking in deep breaths until his panic subsided. The humming went mute.

Why am I so afraid? The truth dawned on him slowly. Mage. There was a Mage in his father's room. So close. No wonder his dreams had been so potent. But surely, the captive Mage couldn't escape. Owenekiras was too thorough for that. *Get ahold of yourself, Mikoneh!*

"Are you all right, my prince?" asked Akonn from the shadowed bed.

"Fine. Just...needed a moment."

Akonn said nothing. Mikoneh closed his eyes and let the last dregs of his panic drift away.

"You're not weak because it's hard."

A smile cracked Mikoneh's lips. "Am I weak for some other reason?"

The Captain of the Sword chuckled. "I'll leave you to decide that." The coverlets rustled. Feet padded across the tapestried area rug, and Akonn's herbal scent drew closer.

Mikoneh peeled one eye open. "Should you be getting up?"

"Already done. Besides, I'm allowed to join you at the tourney today." Standing in the gloom, Akonn shrugged, then rested a hand on Mikoneh's shoulder. "You don't think me weak for staying in bed after nearly dying."

"No, but—"

"There are many types of death, Your Highness, and I think the physical sort may be the least painful or harrowing." Pain flickered in Akonn's pale green eyes. "Mind you, I'm not diminishing the suffering of the innocent or the soldier in wartime. I've lost my share of comrades. Murder and massacre are egregious sins. But I hold to the idea that mental or emotional death is still worse. *These* we can suffer a hundred—a thousand—times before our final breaths. Worse still are the pains we suffer that should result in a kind of ethereal death— yet somehow, we survive, bruised, traumatized..." He sighed. "Your wounds need time to heal, just as mine did. Give yourself grace."

Mikoneh swallowed hard, looking everywhere except at Akonn. "I'll...try. Thanks."

Akonn patted his shoulder, then released him. "Is that food I smell out there?"

"Oh. Yeah."

"Good. I'm hungry."

Mikoneh stepped away from the door, giving Akonn passage. The aroma of food was drowned out by the memory of mineral rock, stagnant water, rotting flesh, and hot blood. He squeezed his eyes against the recollection, then shook himself, and followed Akonn into the bright chamber beyond.

Don't focus on that. You're free. Today's the tourney. Just think about dueling Kalet.

CHAPTER 51

A DOVE'S FEATHERS

- A Treatise on the Magic of the Hidden Realm by Sariolin the Solitary

Sunlight glittered on the crusted snowbanks circling the tourney grounds. Puffs of air escaped Mikoneh's mouth, and the crunch of powder under his boots mingled with the din of hawkers, tourists, and horses.

The scent of roasting fowl, pork, and venison; meat and fruit pies; fresh braided breads; gingerbread candies; mushroom pasties; roasted corn-cobs—and a hundred other delectable foods—clung to the air around the food stalls. The bouquets of ale, mulled wine, and hot cider, whispered around them, wafting from further down the aisles.

A cluster of village women had descended upon the old

woman's scarf stall. Several glanced toward Mikoneh, Maya, Owenekiras, and their entourage as they passed. A pretty lass beamed at Mikoneh, her rosy cheeks brighter than the red scarf clutched in her hands. Her friend grunted her disdain and elbowed the rosy girl, clearly less enthusiastic about Rokahnian royalty.

Mikoneh hurried on, his fur-lined cloak rippling out behind him.

The crescent-shaped stands surrounding the lists rose high and proud. Akonn—finally allowed to do his job—guided the Rokahns toward a row of private boxes opposite the stands. A flash of Drayve's box before the execution block in Relvin seared Mikoneh's mind, but he shoved that back. This wasn't the same. These sturdy boxes on stilts were for sport, not unjust sentences.

Behind the Rokahns, Penn—looking pale—as well as Crim, Hilker, Sir Kalet, and four more Valor Knights in glittering bronze armor, followed the royals up into a roomy box littered with plush chairs, blankets, and a roaring brazier.

"Princess Latta will join you after our bout, Your Highness." Kalet grinned at Mikoneh. "Settle in for now. I'll fetch you in plenty of time for the match. First, the king has his speech to make." He bowed and stepped from the box, leaving the four knights behind to guard the stair.

The twins glanced at each other. Would King Prettem again announce his newfound support for Owenekiras's cause, this time for the masses? It might risk a riot—though perhaps Prettem hoped people would be too full of food and drink to upset their seating arrangements.

I wouldn't count on that.

The day was perfect. A cloudless sky gaped over the stands, cold but bright and windless. The crowds bumped and jostled each other on their way past the lists. Nobility and gentry had comfortable seating near the field while the common folk stood in the openings between the stands and royal boxes. All were dressed in festive colors, rich red, green, and blue hues in stark defiance against the cold white wastes surrounding Elenth Castle and the gleaming, icy lake.

An assortment of pennants hung limp on the tops of poles —garishly colorful—boasting the various Houses represented on the field throughout the coming games.

Maya didn't bother sitting. Instead, she leaned out over the box's rail to study the milling throngs. She drank in a deep breath. She was gowned in burgundy trimmed with silver, complementing her plaited hair and rosy cheeks. The tailor, Tayvin, had finished off her ensemble with a white cloak lined with silver fur.

"The wind spirits are beside themselves," she said.

Hilker laughed. "They're a bunch of gossip-mongers, that's certain."

Mikoneh arched his brow. What did the wind have to gossip about? Surely not fashion or politics.

Joining his twin, he spotted hundreds of fire spirits flitting from brazier to torch to spit. They looked almost drunk, whizzing about, toppling into one another. He grinned, shaking his head. "Fire's enjoying the festival, too." He scanned the crowds and glimpsed a pickpocket darting away from a shouting nobleman, with knights in pursuit. "Have you ever seen so much humanity?"

"Isn't it wonderful?" said Maya.

He wasn't sure he agreed, so he said nothing. As a rule, he liked people. Just not so many, all at once. Leaning out further, he found the Simynshinian Royal Box on the right. King Prettem was standing below, next to the stair, a knot of guards surrounding him. He was speaking with Kalet and a nobleman Mikoneh didn't recognize.

"Oh, look. It's Donivan."

He twisted away from the king to follow Maya's finger. The swordmaster was standing at the center of the tourney field, examining the ground. Despite the heavy snowfall of the previous night, the field was clear. No one would be slogging through snowdrifts to win a sword bout after all.

Hilker sidled up next to Mikoneh. "Thought you ought to know something I'm confident my son failed to mention."

"What's that?"

"The opening match. It's meant to be a spectacle. Apart from death, it's no holds barred. Savvy?"

Mikoneh blinked. "You mean…"

"Right. Magic's allowed. Fire, flight, sword—a combination of all three."

Mikoneh's brows rose. "And Sir Kalet *failed* to mention this?"

"He's rather absent-minded. Just give him an extra kick for me. Singe his hair. Something."

A laugh escaped Mikoneh. "Not a very loyal father, are you?"

Hilker winked. "My eldest son's a fine man, but his ego has inflated over the past few years. I'd like him pushed down a peg or two."

"And you think I—"

"Certainly. You're a Rokahn, aren't you?" Hilker slapped his back, then sauntered away to speak with Owenekiras.

Shaking his head, Mikoneh turned back to watch Donivan's field examination. He began reformulating his dueling strategy. If magic was allowed, did that mean Kalet was an Elementalist? If so, which kind?

Earth and spirit were the rarest types. Meanwhile, Hilker was wind. Did an element pass from father to son? Chances were slim that Kalet was a Fire Elementalist, or he'd have been offered up as a potential candidate to mentor Mikoneh—that or Kalet wasn't good at teaching. The final possible element was water, the direct foil to fire.

If Mikoneh considered the odds, he'd probably wager on water. Certainly, if he braced for that, he'd find any alternatives less challenging.

"There's Latta," said Maya, pointing.

The Songbird Princess and Crown Prince Atlanse had moved next to King Prettem. Over the din of the assembling masses, Mikoneh's sharp ears couldn't pick up their conversation, but Latta looked grim and paler than ever.

"What do you think's wrong?" he whispered.

Maya shook her head. "Give me a bit." Her brow creased in concentration, and she leaned further out over the box rail.

"What are you doing?"

"Asking the wind to funnel their conversation this way. Now, hush."

He obeyed, straining his ears as though that would somehow help Maya. The result was a dull headache, nothing more. The hum of the crowd, the soft tones in the box behind the twins, and the faintest breeze stirring around Maya caressed Mikoneh's senses, until—

King Prettem's voice rolled into the box, as clear as though he were standing right in front of the twins. "...not a good idea."

"I don't see why we can't try it," Kalet was saying. "What could it hurt?"

"Latta," the king answered tersely.

"I'm prepared to take that risk," Latta said.

Hilker, Crim, and Owenekiras stepped up to the edge of the box.

"That was cleverly done." Hilker beamed at Maya.

"Though eavesdropping on the king is somewhat alarming," added Crim.

Maya managed a sheepish smile but didn't bother to undo her wind trick. She turned back to the House of Chenta below and tipped forward more.

"You're gonna fall," whispered Mikoneh.

"Shh."

He rolled his eyes but left her alone. She was a dragon, after all, perfectly capable of flying if required.

The king twisted toward his son. "What say you, Atlanse?"

The Crown Prince sighed, rubbing a gloved hand across his jawline. "Once Latta makes up her mind..." He shrugged. "I say let her try."

Prettem exhaled, letting his shoulders relax. "I appreciate your willingness, Latta—but no. I think not."

Hilker shifted on Maya's other side. "Wish we knew what they were talking about."

"Shh." Maya glared at her mentor.

He clapped a hand over his mouth, eyes twinkling.

Latta moved closer to her grandfather. "I want to help if I can. It's important." Her voice was firm, but she looked as delicate and weightless as a dove's feathers. An impulse swept over Mikoneh to leap over the rail and catch Latta before she floated away, but he resisted it. She was stronger than she looked.

"No, Latta," the king said. "I'm sorry. I can't allow you to expose yourself like that. I won't risk anyone else I love."

"But if—"

"My word is final." The king turned and moved toward his box. "Sir Kalet, with me."

The king and Valor Knight moved toward the stairs and away from Atlanse and his daughter. Their footsteps faded from Maya's funnel.

"I don't understand, Latta," Atlanse said. "You said your voice was stolen."

"It was," she whispered, though her voice carried clearly through the funnel. "But I still wanted to try."

He set his hand on her arm. "There are other ways to persuade people, without using magic. Let the king try his way."

"His ways never work." She pulled away from her father and headed for the royal box. Atlanse stared after her, then followed, his steps slow.

Maya leaned back. The din of the gathering crowd filled in the space around them.

"That was odd," she said. "What does it mean?"

Mikoneh shook his head. "I wish I knew."

Chapter 52

Raining Flames

"If they have no defined concept of death, then why do I feel guilty that I've used the earth spirits to kill other people?"

- *A Treatise on the Magic of the Hidden Realm* by Sariolin the Solitary

Clouds moved in toward the stadium. The crisp taste of snow clung to the air. Mikoneh studied the threatening storm, then turned back to the grounds. Donivan was moving off the field, alongside several other officials. The stands were packed to bursting. The House of Chenta had gathered into its box.

The games would begin any moment now.

Trumpets blared. The hubbub from the spectators began to fade. A few stragglers darted toward their seats. A knight's horse tossed its head and stamped a hoof.

One last blast of trumpet notes filled the air, then all fell still.

Prettem appeared at the window of his box next door and

lifted his hands. "Good people of Simynshin, the Winter Festival is upon us!"

Cheers tore across the air. Hands waved tiny banners featuring the different noble houses of the kingdom. A few flashed dragons on them. As the noise died down, Mikoneh braced himself for Prettem's speech about refortifying alliances—but it never came. Prettem's next words were brief.

"I know you're all as eager as I am to begin the tourney, and so, I will not delay with fancy speeches. Let actions speak for me! I'm delighted to declare the tourney begun!"

The roar of the crowd was deafening. Chills raced up Mikoneh's flesh, and his stomach tied in knots. He'd dreamed of entering the lists all growing up, but this was something different. The stakes were higher than proving one's strength against other men. This was about kingdoms. This was about war.

Drawing a breath, he tried to steel his nerves. He hated spectacle. Despite his youthful dreams, once he'd joined Fa and Mama's rebel force to contend with Drayve, he'd come to understand that the glory one earned in a tourney meant nothing.

Still...if he were completely honest with himself, despite the mounting pressure to win over Simynshin's masses, he was looking forward to dueling Kalet.

Just do your best. Show them your prowess and *your resolve. Hopefully it will move them to see you're not a monster.*

That meant not turning into a dragon—even a miniature one.

Though maybe they need to be reminded that dragons are real.

He stifled that temptation at once.

The king was waving the crowd into silence again. At last, the noise subsided. With joy in his voice, Prettem went on.

"And now, lords and ladies, folk from near and far, to start off the tourney in proper Simynshinian fashion—"

Sir Kalet had descended from the other box and was waving Mikoneh down rather animatedly. Mikoneh made for the stairs leading down from the box while the king continued his introduction. It seemed Kalet had expected the speech to go on longer than it had, too.

"—I bring you Sir Kalet of House Terath!"

The roars rolled like thunder across the field. Mikoneh reached the ground and marched toward Kalet, choosing not to run and make a fool of himself. He took the opportunity to warm up his muscles instead, each movement deliberate and long.

Kalet approached.

The noise from the stands faded away.

"And facing our famed Valor Knight, I bring you Prince Mikoneh of House Rokahn, heir of the legendary Owenekiras!"

The cheers were less warm, but the air crackled with anticipation.

Kalet reached Mikoneh, his smile crooked. "Leave it to King Prettem to change things up in order to surprise the people."

"What happens now?" Mikoneh asked, winded despite pacing himself. His nerves were tight.

"Now, we select our weapons of choice"—Kalet glanced at Mikoneh's sword—"and face off."

Still no mention of anything other than physical weapons. What was Kalet planning? Or had Hilker been playing Mikoneh to get him to break a tourney rule? He didn't strike Mikoneh as the sort to cheat like that, but anything might be possible. Mikoneh's trust in these people was parchment thin.

"I'll use my blade," Mikoneh said.

Kalet eyed the weapon with mild skepticism. It wasn't anything fancy, but Mikoneh didn't care. The steel was well forged, and the weight was familiar. He'd never put much stock in appearances.

Kalet grasped his own sword. "And I, mine."

That statement was some relief. A sudden fear had gripped Mikoneh that if only one type of skillset was allowed, Kalet might announce his element as his pick, leaving Mikoneh with a physical weapon against magic.

Let's see what you're up to, Sir Corpse Poet. Your move.

Kalet led Mikoneh to one side of the tourney arena, then motioned for him to stay there. Kalet then paced out twenty steps, spun, and drew his sword. Mikoneh drew his own.

They stood before the breathless crowds, waiting.

King Prettem motioned from his box. The trumpet blared again.

Sword flashing under the sunlight, the knight charged. Mikoneh remained still, reading Kalet's stance. *Going for a low angled cut, huh?* Mikoneh dropped his blade—caught Kalet's sword in a half-circle guard—lunged. Kalet deflected.

The crowd roared. Mikoneh fell into the familiar motions, pleased that he kept pace with Kalet. Reading the man's movements was easy. Mikoneh had learned every sword movement by the time he was six. Fa had raised him on tactics, long before he could lift more than a wooden sword. Still, he'd feared he'd have a disadvantage against a Simynshinian knight—especially after his captivity—but he was keeping up even with his recent malnourishment.

Don't get overconfident, dolt. It'll make you sloppy.

He shifted to offense, forcing Kalet back a few steps. They parried. Thrust. Cut. Blocked. Mikoneh spotted an opening and stepped in for a battering attack. He managed four strong hits before Kalet deflected, forcing Mikoneh off course. Kalet seized his chance and thrust. Mikoneh repelled the attack, slipping back into defense.

Kalet's footwork was excellent. His shifts were flawless. Mikoneh found himself pushed back across the field. He grinned. He'd not faced such a skilled opponent in ages!

He lunged, blades crossing, until his sword fort met Kalet's feeble.

"You're good," Kalet ground out, using a whirling technique to deflect. Mikoneh had anticipated the counter, and he disengaged before he lost his weapon.

"Thanks. You, too."

"Shall we up the stakes?"

"If you please," Mikoneh said.

Kalet fell back, sword gleaming, his eyes bright. "Let's give the crowd something to *really* talk about." The ground rumbled.

Mikoneh glanced down. *Earth. He's earth!*

The ground cracked, and a fissure ran before Kalet, toward Mikoneh.

Mikoneh flung himself left, but the fissure followed him. Thorny vines sprang from the gaping earth, sailing toward him like thick green ropes. On instinct, Mikoneh leapt into the air, pulling forth his dragon wings—which slipped through the tailored slits Tayvin had sewn into his leather armor.

People screamed. Others cheered.

Mikoneh didn't have time to worry about his reputation. The vines shot up to attack. Maintaining his grip on his sword, he summoned fire. Answering flames crawled across his sword, engulfing the blade. He cut through the vines, then swept right, away from another barrage.

Below, Kalet laughed. "Your arsenal is most impressive, Your Highness."

"So's yours. Didn't mention using elements, though, Sir Poet."

Kalet shrugged. "I wished to test your mettle."

That was a poor excuse for an ambush, but Mikoneh didn't bother to argue. Hilker, at least, had given him proper warning.

Time to counter.

He drew a breath, gathering his thoughts. He knew little about earth, but it couldn't be hard to understand. Fire wasn't the most effective force against green plants—they wouldn't burn well, especially surrounded by snow—and setting foot on ground would be a great disadvantage.

He'd need to stay airborne, and he'd need to find earth's weaknesses.

Surely, growing green plants in the wintertime takes its toll. Earth is slumbering. He can't keep up an aggressive pace forever.

Then again, neither could Mikoneh. *Or can I?*

From his vantage point, he glimpsed a cluster of torches. A brazier. The smoke rising from the food stalls. He was surrounded by fire—he didn't need to rely solely on his own body heat. More grateful for Crim's and Minno's lessons than he'd been before, he allowed himself a grin.

Let's see what your lessons have done for you, Mikoneh.

He gathered heat into his palm.

Kalet flung more vines at him.

Mikoneh unleashed a stream of fire from his hand.

Vines met flame. Light flooded the field. Snow melted.

The crowds roared their approval.

Kalet retreated, slipping across the slushy ground. His vines writhed, blackened by fire. But the knight was still smiling.

Mikoneh lowered himself toward the ground, his wings beating the air. He drew on the nearest source of fire—a large brazier at the edge of the arena—careful not to tax his blood. Not yet. He hadn't mastered recharging himself yet.

He conjured up a swirling ball of flame and chucked it hard toward Kalet. The knight shot his hands up, still clutching his sword. The ground at his boots broke apart. Before him, a wall of stone and mud slid upward. Mikoneh's fireball smashed into the slushy rock and fizzled out.

Earth was a versatile element.

Mikoneh's grin widened. He summoned another fireball and veered around the earthen barrier. Kalet was waiting with a tangle of vines. They lashed out. Mikoneh flung his fistful of fire, willing it into a blazing wreath. The vines flinched back, but more broke through the frozen earth behind him.

Mikoneh whirled, cutting them with his sword.

More still erupted from the ground. Mikoneh threw himself higher into the sky, raining flames past his feet.

Kalet laughed. The ground rumbled and shifted. Fist-sized rocks pelted the air, chasing Mikoneh further aloft. He dodged and spun away from the onslaught, then brought himself to a hovering halt upon the air. Still grinning, adrenaline pumping through his blood, he tracked Kalet running and slipping across the field. Vines trailed him, rising like vipers guarding his flank.

The crowds continued to roar, caught up in the action.

Interesting. Mikoneh wondered if this would lean sympathy toward Owenekiras's cause or not.

Does that mean I need to lose or try to win?

He was paying for his aversion to politics now. But surely Fa and Mama had instilled a few lessons into him on the sly, especially with his heritage.

They'd always known he was a prince, and Maya a princess. Remarkable, then, that they'd never treated the twins as anything other than their own children. Somehow, that was touching to contemplate, even as a deep ache stabbed at his heart.

He shook himself. *Focus!*

Fire spirits had taken to the air and were circling him. One crackled a non-verbal question.

He lifted his hand. The fire spirits swelled around his open palm, marshaling, absorbing into a single attack. He willed the spirits to form into a spear of flame. Kalet had reached the boundary of the arena, a trail of vines and grass cutting diagonally along the muddy field in his wake.

How do I defeat you, Corpse Poet? Considering his limited experiences with the Spirits Elemental, he had no idea what might be required to bring such a duel to a close. Surely, it wasn't to the death—no one would risk either of them like that, not so boldly at least.

How do I pin him down and make him yield?

Mikoneh knew himself too well to consider feigning defeat at this stage, politics or not. It was hard enough being treated with contempt and suspicion, but it would be harder still if he had to deal with it while also living in failure. He wouldn't do that to himself, to his twin, or to their newfound House. If Rokahn was to win this war and take the Dark Mages down, they needed to reveal their resolve and strength.

Sorry, Kalet. That means you've got to lose, like it or not.

The knight was eyeing him from among a writhing mass of vines, his dark eyes keen and steady. He didn't look like someone prepared to lose. So be it.

Mikoneh hefted his flaming spear. Aimed. Spread his will into the minds of his fire spirit army.

He launched the spear.

Kalet held up his sword, thinking Mikoneh was aiming for him.

Wrong. Mikoneh smirked.

The spear fell far short of Kalet's position, sinking deep into the muddy earth. The spear appeared to melt, vanishing. Some in the crowd jeered, thinking Mikoneh had miscalculated. Let them. He didn't care.

He could *feel* the fire spirits beneath the ground, sinking deep, deeper, stirring up their sleeping brethren far below the arena, where the earth was still warm. The fire spirits then crawled upward, seizing the roots of the vines.

Turning a grin on Kalet, he saw the knight's eyes widen. He'd understood Mikoneh's plan—too late.

Mikoneh closed his fists. Flames shot up from the ground and crawled along the vines, blazing hot. They ate at the tendrils, making them writhe. A twinge of guilt twisted in Mikoneh's chest.

Am I hurting the earth spirits?

He nearly drew his flames back but stopped himself. If dueling between Elementalists was common, and the Spirits Elemental willingly aided them, surely the attacks weren't fatal to the little creatures. Could the spirits even die?

Another question to ask later.

He urged the flames to burn hotter and faster. Kalet retreated from the inferno, and the ground rumbled, far removed from Mikoneh's nest of fire spirits underground. The Dragon Prince spun to face new vines, but rock shot up below his feet, and stone shaped like a giant's hand snatched at him.

Mikoneh somersaulted in midair, dodging the massive hand. It closed its stone fingers on air.

The hissing slither of vines filled his ears. He wheeled, slicing his fiery sword across the air. The vines retreated, thrashing. He spun back around, searching for Kalet in the debris of the field. Dust sparkled in the dimming sunlight, hiding the knight from view.

Find a heat source.

New vines shot up below him. At the same time, a cracking sound filled Mikoneh's ears. Someone screamed. Maya?

He spun.

A crossbow bolt tore through the membrane of his under-wing, puncturing between the outer scales.

Mikoneh cried out and flinched into himself. One wing tried to hold him aloft, but he tumbled toward the ground, his wound burning. The muddy earth rose to meet him, and he squeezed his eyes shut, bracing for impact.

CHAPTER 53

SCALES

"I have asked the earth spirits whether they hate my past misdeeds. They appear not to remember to what I am referring. Likely they weren't the earth spirits that were present during my past campaigns, but I will never know. It is impossible to distinguish one earth spirit from another by appearance."

- *A Treatise on the Magic of the Hidden Realm* by Sariolin the Solitary

A thick covering of spring grass caught him. Mikoneh rolled across the green-smelling cushion, wing throbbing, nerves raw. Chaos filled his ears. People in the stands were shouting, jostling, pushing. He lay upon the grass, huddled into himself, trying to comprehend what had happened.

Boots splashed through slush, approaching. An overwhelming desire to stay still and ignore whoever was coming swelled up—but that was stupid. Swallowing, he pushed himself into a sitting position, just as Sir Kalet's scent reached him through the swirling snow crystals. Had Maya conjured wind to give him shelter?

The Valor Knight slipped through the windstorm and climbed the mound of grass that he must have conjured to catch Mikoneh. He still held his broadsword. He raced to Mikoneh's side, his eyes bright with concern.

"Someone in the crowd aimed that crossbow at you. We need to get you to shelter."

"Maya."

"She's fine. No one would dare attack her so near your father."

Mikoneh shook his head. "No. I mean...she's a healer. She can tend my wing."

Kalet eyed the limp appendage. "Right." He wrapped an arm around Mikoneh's waist. "Let me help you."

They stood up, and Mikoneh found himself trembling. Shock, probably.

"That was quite the battle," Kalet was saying, leading Mikoneh through the snow crystals toward the royal boxes. "I'm sorry it was interrupted."

"Seems like someone wasn't enjoying it," Mikoneh muttered.

"We anticipated possible attacks. I just didn't expect one while you were airborne. Few knew you could go aloft."

Mikoneh frowned, trying to picture which direction the bolt had come from. It was all a blur. He hadn't been aware of his direction at that moment.

"Did anyone catch a glimpse of the attacker?"

"Probably not, in that sudden wind. But the bolt came from the westside stands. I'm almost certain. I have knights looking for witnesses."

Mikoneh nodded. Not from the direction of the boxes. That eliminated his first wave of suspects—unless, of course, the attacker had been acting under orders. That would make more sense, wouldn't it?

It's what I would do.

Snow stung his eyes, but he peered ahead until he could make out the box before them. A figure moved below the box, lifting something. Instinct prickled. Mikoneh threw himself on Kalet, knocking them to the ground, just as the crack of an unleashed crossbow bolt flooded his ears.

There's more than one attacker.

He jumped to his feet, flames tickling his fingers, illuminating the shadows under the box. He didn't know the man's face, but the assailant was indisputably human. Mages didn't need crossbows to attack.

"Who sent you?" asked Mikoneh, watching the man load his weapon.

The man sneered, his blue eyes glittering in the firelight. Kalet shifted, setting his palms on the frozen ground. The man with the crossbow glanced at his feet, his eyes widening. Vines burst from the earth, wrapping around him. His crossbow went off, and the bolt buried itself in a snowdrift that hadn't melted in Mikoneh's fire show. Yelping, the man was turned upside-down, and dangled, clutching his bow.

Shoes pounded down the box stairs. Hilker, Crim, then Maya appeared, rounding the stairs to stand beneath the box. Owenekiras came down last, his cloak billowing behind him. Maya eyed the captured assailant, then raced toward Mikoneh, throwing her arms around him.

"Are you all right?" She sounded breathless.

"Mostly. Close call, huh?"

She pulled back to search his face, her gold eyes blazing with fury. "I think that's the end of your display at the tourney —if the event goes on at all."

"A good point," said Kalet, rising and brushing himself off. "I should find King Prettem and learn his intentions. The crowds are in such panic, we may not be able to carry on." He glanced toward the cluster of men, all of whom were considering the dangling man like he was lunch. "I'll leave that one to your interrogation skills, shall I?"

Crim nodded, the only one who might've heard the Valor Knight.

Maya had brought her herb kit—of course she had—and ordered Mikoneh to follow her back up into the box where Penn and Akonn were waiting. He followed, keeping his wing curled forward. Blood dripped across the snow-packed path. That wouldn't do with Mages nearby. Willing flame to devour the blood trail in his wake, he started up the wooden stairs behind his twin. The faint hissing of fire on snow tickled his sharp ears.

They entered the box where Penn gaped at him, still looking too pale—perhaps more so now. That wasn't surprising. He couldn't have anticipated Mikoneh sprouting wings and taking to the air, throwing fireballs all the while.

"Hey, Penn," Mikoneh said with a grin. "Okay?"

The viscount shook his head. "You weren't jesting. You—you really are..."

"Yep. Scales and everything." He stretched out his good wing, and the midnight blue scales rippled with light. Movement beyond the box caught his attention. He turned toward the stands. They'd mostly been emptied, but knights and servants strode up and down, as though seeking out more assailants.

Maya caught Mikoneh's wrist and led him to a cushioned chair. He sank against the pillows and spread out his wing to let her have a good look.

"Think you can treat it?"

She shot him a patient scowl, then prodded the fire-hued membrane around the wound. "Certainly, I can. It's like treating a lizard."

He snorted, and her lips trembled upward. Stooping, she rummaged in her herb kit, clinking several jars of ointments together, before she drew one out.

"Penn, please get me a handful of snow."

He hurried off without question.

"You should've seen his face when you took flight," said Maya.

"I can imagine."

Akonn moved around the chair to watch Maya examine the hole. "How does it look?"

"Bloody."

"Fair enough." The captain reached into a pouch at his belt and withdrew a silver, broad leaf plant with red veins. "Wet this thoroughly, Princess, then stretch it over the wing once you stop the bleeding. It acts like a patch, so your brother can still fly in a pinch."

Maya snatched the leaf and stared at it. "Is it magic?"

"It's called *jarsui* in Fae Common. *Flight leaf* in Sirin-highan Common. Be warned: it doesn't work on magically inflicted injuries, but this appears to be a normal bolt wound."

"Thank you," Maya said. "It's perfect."

Penn trotted up the steps, stomped bits of snow from his boots, and rushed over with a snowball. "Will this do?"

"Yes. Hand it to Mikoneh."

He accepted the snowball from Penn and, anticipating Maya's need, melted the snow just as she held up a handkerchief. He poured the hot water over the cloth, and she set to work at once cleaning the wound. Mikoneh set his jaw and endured the flaring pain. Then she lathered on a pungent-smelling ointment while Penn fetched more snow at her command.

With the second helping of snow, she thoroughly soaked the flight leaf then stretched it across the wound. It adhered like a film and stuck fast.

She leaned back on her heels. "Seems to work well."

Akonn grunted his agreement.

The wing might be patched, but Mikoneh knew flying would still hurt. "Maybe I should just tuck my wings back inside, let it heal? I don't think it'll do any damage."

She chewed the inside of her cheek, then nodded. "My instinct agrees with you."

He pulled his wings inside his back, feeling the skin close over the slashes where the wings slid out. The pain was still there, but duller now.

Penn sank into the seat next to Mikoneh, shaking his head. "If I hadn't seen it for myself…"

"Let that be a lesson in trusting my word," said Mikoneh, grinning.

Footsteps pounded the stairs. Crim appeared, with Kalet on his heels, both looking pale and alarmed.

"Princess Maya," said the merchant lord in a rush, "we need your help. Princess Latta collapsed."

Maya shot to her feet, herb kit in hand. "Lead the way."

Mikoneh followed. So did Penn and Akonn. When they reached the bottom of the stairs, Mikoneh glimpsed Hilker leaning toward the upside-down prisoner, muttering threats that sounded distinctly gory. Close by, Owenekiras glanced over his shoulder to eye his twin children, a crease between his brows. He didn't follow them.

Snow crystals swirled around Mikoneh. "Can you do anything about this wind?"

Maya shook her head. "I didn't summon it. Neither did

Hilker. He said someone powerful must be behind it—probably working with whoever shot at you. The wind spirits won't listen to me at all."

Nodding, Mikoneh let his worry stew next to his concern for Latta. She'd been looking so much better last night...

They reached the royal box, climbed the steps, and entered a space as lavishly furnished as the Rokahnian box. The fragrance of pine and orange peels clung to the air, coming from the festive wreath hanging against the back wall. It glittered with ice, despite the warmth radiating from a brazier on the far side of the interior.

Prince Atlanse knelt on the floor near the box's rail, and Latta rested in her father's arms. Maya moved to their side with a rustle of skirts, knelt, and began her examination. Mikoneh inched closer, and Penn stayed near.

"What happened?" Mikoneh asked the crown prince.

Atlanse looked up. "She'd been acting odd all morning. Almost angry. Which isn't like her at all. She was also exceptionally pale, and complained of being dizzy. Earlier, she argued with the king about singing for the crowds, despite having lost her voice. I think she hoped to sway the crowds in favor of Owenekiras before the king's planned speech. My father said no."

Mikoneh scanned the box. "Where is King Prettem?"

"He was moved to a secure location in case the attack was meant to include him." Atlanse lifted an eyebrow. "I'm surprised you and your sister weren't removed as well."

Akonn inched forward. "He and his sister are safest near their father."

"True." Atlanse dropped his eyes to his daughter. "Is Owenekiras joining the manhunt?"

"We caught one of the attackers," Mikoneh said. "The Dragon King is interrogating him."

"Ah." Atlanse glanced at Kalet. "You failed to mention that."

"Apologies," said the knight. "I meant to before the princess collapsed."

"Did she do anything unusual just before she fainted?" Maya asked. "Penn, more snow?"

"I'll get it." Akonn moved down the stairs, one hand on his sword hilt.

"She was worried about you, Your Highness," Atlanse said, glancing at Mikoneh, "and wanted to go find you—which I wouldn't allow. Not under the circumstances. She sat back down at my orders, so that she wasn't in the line of fire, and she grew very quiet. Kalet arrived and reported that you weren't badly wounded. Then she—she spasmed and let out a small scream. She turned pale as the snow itself. And..." Atlanse squeezed her shoulder "...she slipped out of her chair. Kalet caught her before she struck her head."

"Good thing." Maya checked Latta's eyes. "I can't find anything physically wrong. She's merely unconscious. I only wish I could detect magical attacks—"

"Allow me." Ter stepped into the box with Akonn at his back, the latter clutching a snowball. Ter loped forward, and Akonn veered around him to hold out the snow to whichever Rokahn twin needed it. Maya took it, wrapped a fresh handkerchief around it, then dabbed at Latta's face. Meanwhile, Ter knelt on Latta's other side and leaned close to examine her.

"Where have you been?" asked Atlanse, his tones carefully controlled.

"I was called away urgently," the Ephe'ahn said, one long ear twitching. "I understand things have been very active around here."

"Oh," Maya said with a shrug, "just a false death, a Mage

attack during the Winter Ball, today's assassination attempt, and now this. I'd say it's standard for us of late."

Ter chuckled, searching each of Latta's eyes for himself. "Hmm. Well, I see nothing wrong beyond whatever is siphoning her voice."

"That's an interesting word choice." Atlanse frowned. "It hasn't been stolen?"

"Perhaps not." Ter sat straight. "Difficult to say, especially in her present state. My best guess is that she was resisting something—perhaps the magical thief—and that is what made her faint. Whatever happened, I would submit that she has not yet lost whatever battle wages inside her—but she is growing weaker."

Mikoneh studied the woman's pallid face, his lungs tightening. "How can we help, Ter?"

"Give her reasons to keep fighting, as you have been. And keep searching for her assailant."

"Is it a Dark Mage, Ter?" asked Atlanse.

"Perhaps so, but whoever it is, they are using magic that isn't Magery. A clever move. We might be dealing with a sorcerer or a fae as like as not. That's a broad field to search."

Atlanse sighed, looking older than his years, and very weary. "Thank you for looking."

Ter patted his arm. "Take heart. The fight is not won, perhaps, but nor is it lost."

"Right." The crown prince didn't look heartened at all. "Thank you."

Ter clicked his tongue, then stood up and moved to Mikoneh's side. "And how is that wing of yours?"

"Sore."

"You're nothing if not resilient."

Mikoneh shrugged, indifferent to his plight. At least his

enemy had a face and the chance of being defeated. He could handle that far better than a phantom attacker stalking helpless prey. The memory of Sathe's claim that someone *was* stalking him flickered over his thoughts, but he couldn't deal with that right now.

Latta groaned. Her eyes fluttered open, then widened, and she shot upright.

"Relax," Maya said gently. "You fainted, but you're all right now."

Latta opened her mouth, then coughed, clutching her throat. She jerked her head around until she found Mikoneh, her nails digging into her skin.

Cold washed through him. "Your voice. It's gone?"

She nodded, trembling. Tears welled in her eyes.

Mikoneh swore under his breath. His fingers curled into fists. "I thought you said the magic wasn't stolen, Ter. Is the fight lost, after all?"

"Not entirely," said Ter. "She still lives, and the core of her magic remains with her."

That statement smothered the group like a pall. Atlanse had gone still. "Is that the end result, Ter? My daughter's life?"

The Ephe'ahn's ears drooped. "I am afraid so. If whoever has borrowed her magical talent endeavors to keep it, they must employ one of two tactics: either maintain her life in this half-state, at the great risk of having the magic taken back, or draw out every last drop of magic using a special set of spells, and then end her life so that the magic does not trickle into its rightful heir through their magical connection."

"So," Mikoneh said, "her magic wants to return to her."

"Naturally," said Ter. "It belongs to her. It has her print upon it."

"Can't that be traced?" asked Akonn.

Ter's ears fluttered. "That is what I have been attempting to do. Even Owenekiras has tried."

"But I haven't." Akonn's voice was firm.

"So you haven't. Yet I would caution you, Captain. It is a tricky bit of tracking magic."

"Which I excel at if conditions are right." Akonn squared his shoulders. "Which must be why someone attacked me from behind. They knew that."

"What sort of conditions do you need?" asked Penn.

"My magic relies on the moon," Akonn answered. "A waning moon gives me little strength to cast the tracking spell and see its trail. Now that the moon is waxing, it shouldn't be difficult."

"Impressive," Penn murmured.

Mikoneh frowned. "But no one attacked you during that Mage ambush last night. That seems odd if the Mages are behind this."

And they were, weren't they? Hadn't Sathe told Mikoneh that Latta and Atlanse were their targets…

Have I foolishly been placing every fact into a single chest?

"Mages aren't privy to my skills," Akonn explained. "Only people who know me personally understand my magic to any degree, which does narrow the field of our search a little, thinking about it in hindsight. My attacker likely knows me well."

Mikoneh nodded absently. That made sense, assuming the attacker hadn't just been getting the Captain of the Sword out of the way. The urge to interrogate every single soul in Elenth swelled inside him, threatening to choke, but he pressed down on the feeling. Now was the time for control. He couldn't risk alienating the people after the progress they'd made. And Akonn was right. Few in the capital knew who the captain even was. That did narrow the field of their search considerably.

Mikoneh studied Latta's frightened face. He'd come here to protect her, but she was being attacked all the same. What could he do? How could he get her voice back, and prevent anyone from taking it again?

Her eyes found his. The fear in her blue depths was bright as fire, but strength still held on. She hadn't given in. He moved to her side, knelt, caught her wrist, and smiled.

"I won't let it end this way. That's a vow."

Her hand trembled, icy cold under his touch. Her golden ring flashed, arresting his attention, but he shoved back his dragon impulse to tug it off her finger. *That* was an instinct he needed to discipline himself against.

"What do we do now?" asked Penn.

"I'll try tracking down the source of Latta's magical drain," Akonn answered, "while everyone else protects the royals from assassins and Mages."

"Sounds simple on one's tongue," Crim said. "If only…"

Footsteps tromped up the stairs. They all turned as Owenekiras and Hilker reached the landing and stepped inside.

"Any luck?" Crim asked.

Hilker scowled. "Same trick as with that stableboy. When we started to question him, he foamed at the mouth and keeled over, figuratively speaking. He was just a pawn, that's sure."

Mikoneh's stomach churned. *Who can treat fellow humans as disposable like that?*

He knew the answer. He'd seen Lord Drayve and his minions treat others as inferiors all his life. He'd fought against that tyranny alongside his parents. And hadn't Mages once been human before they gave themselves up to their power?

Just remember not all humans are scum.

He squeezed Latta's hand.

Some are kind, brave, and virtuous.

The woman before him was of the second kind, and her

voice was being taken from her by those of the first variety. He wouldn't stand for it. Not because he was in love with Latta. He wasn't. It was simply the just and kind thing to do, and whether or not he was a human, he'd been raised by them. He loved them.

He would never let tyranny stand while he drew breath.

Chapter 54

Wounded Child

"I have asked the earth spirits whether they have any regrets of their own. They appear not to understand the emotion I've described."

- *A Treatise on the Magic of the Hidden Realm* by Sariolin the Solitary

The tourney was canceled. Even if King Prettem had insisted on continuing it, regathering the masses and convincing them that all was well was impossible. Already, rumors were flying that the Dragon Prince had been killed.

Maya sat beside her twin at the fire in their shared suite, gripping his hand, trying not to relive the moment he'd been struck by that crossbow bolt. He didn't seem to be shaken up by it, but she certainly was. Studying Mikoneh's profile, she marveled at his self-control. Whatever lay beneath the surface of his thoughts, he gave no hint of fear or anger. He stared into the fire, his gold eyes reflecting the flames, almost glowing.

They weren't to leave their suite. King Prettem had

commanded it. Crim had insisted on it. Sir Kalet had stationed guards outside the door and below the window to ensure it. They were virtually prisoners. She expected Mikoneh to start pacing any moment, but he merely sat in silence, the cogs in his mind turning.

Jensirin had seated himself nearby when they'd first arrived, and he'd listened to Maya's explanation of the morning's events. Since then, he'd kept silent and observed the twins as though waiting for one or both of them to crack. Penn had slipped into his room after mentioning a bad headache.

Everyone else was gone. Hilker and Crim had joined Owenekiras for the manhunt, combing the castle and grounds. Akonn had gone off with Ter to get Latta safely to her room and to try tracking her magical connection. Minno was still missing.

After the roar of the stadium, the silence of the common room was almost eerie. Only the pop and hiss of the fire and the faint breaths of Maya and her two quiet companions filled the spaces of the darkened room. She'd drawn the curtains, shutting out the winter light. She felt safer with no chance of prying eyes beyond the bay window. The glass had been replaced again, which helped with her sense of security.

Mikoneh shifted, recapturing her focus.

"Need something?" she whispered.

"No."

"Are you hungry?" She wasn't sure she was, but she'd try to eat if he did. "We can order some of those cucumber sandwiches you like so much."

"Not really hungry."

Jensirin rose from his chair. "I will have food brought just the same. Please try to eat it." He moved off to tug the bell pull, and Maya smiled gratefully after him.

Mikoneh's gaze settled on the fire again. "We can't let them win, Maya."

She could guess who he meant, but she was desperate to talk, so she whispered, "Who?"

"Whoever's working with the Mages."

Nodding, she squeezed his hand.

Mikoneh drew a deep breath. "Latta's helpless. I hate seeing that. She's so strong, but they've chained her."

An image of Mikoneh, too thin and tattered, flashed across her mind. He'd been half himself after being rescued from Sathe's grasp. Doubtless, he resonated with Latta's plight on a torturous level. Even now, he was still too lean, still haunted, still trying to mend.

"We'll save her," Maya whispered.

Mikoneh scowled at the flames, and they rose higher. "We must."

"We *will*."

Jensirin returned, seated himself, and said nothing. His eyes were trained on Mikoneh, his pale irises flickering in the firelight.

"Father will find those responsible," said Maya. How she felt so confident about a man she'd met only a short time ago, she couldn't say. She could only trust her instinct.

"I want to help." Desperation threaded Mikoneh's voice. "I can't just sit here."

"But they're after you, too."

He jerked his hand away. "So?"

"So, we could make matters worse by involving ourselves."

"Why did we come here, then?"

"To—to get Simynshin to reforge their alliance with our father. To find the spy—"

"To protect Latta," Mikoneh said. "Why else agree to this

fake betrothal? Sathe's information sent me here, and if I'm useless, he wins." His tones ended in a low growl.

Maya caught his hand. "That's not true. It's *not*. He's dead. You defeated Sathe. He's gone forever."

Mikoneh hunched forward, shoulders trembling. "I wish I believed that."

"Give yourself time." She rested her free hand on his back. "You let me heal. Allow yourself the same grace."

He inhaled a shuddering breath. "I know... I *know*. But I..."

Jensirin sat forward with a rustle of his robes. "Mikoneh?"

He lifted his head. His eyes were dim with pain and fear. "Yes, Jensirin?"

"We will save her. You and I." He stood up. "We must go now."

Maya's lungs hitched. "Wait, what do you intend to do?"

"Sneak out." Jensirin glided to the window, peeled aside the curtain enough to peek outside, then turned to face the twins. "Come with me, Mikoneh."

"I—" He hesitated, staring between Maya and Jensirin. "What's your plan?"

"To track down a Mage."

Maya shot to her feet, heart pounding in her ears. "Out of the question. They're seeking Mikoneh—and they can't mean you any good either. It's far too dangerous for either of you. We need to stay here."

Jensirin considered her. "Come with us, Maya."

She flinched. "No. No one is going *anywhere*."

"Yet we cannot sit here." Jensirin cast a look at the room, panic ringing his eyes. "We are trapped."

Understanding dawned. Maya moved across the room, her heart settling back into her chest. "That's what this is about, is it?" She caught Jensirin's wrist. "It's all right. We're not prisoners, I promise."

"But—"

"Maya's right," Mikoneh whispered. "We can't risk ourselves. Come here, Jensirin. Please."

The dragon lord hunched forward but allowed Maya to guide him to Mikoneh. She released Jensirin, and Mikoneh reached out. Slowly, gingerly, he pulled Jensirin into an embrace. The dragon lord stiffened, then melted into the hug until his chin rested against Mikoneh's shoulder. Mikoneh held him like he was a wounded child, and whispered words of comfort.

Looking on, Maya's heart throbbed. If only she could help both of them to stave off the trauma. To feel safe again. But only time would manage that miracle. That and a refuge they wouldn't find in Elenth Castle.

On impulse, she stepped forward and wrapped her arms around both men, swallowing them up in her love. It was all she could do, and she prayed it was enough.

Unsurprising to Maya, Mikoneh disentangled himself first, and moved to stoke up the flickering fire. It didn't take him two steps before the flames shot higher, but he still fed more logs into the hearth.

Food came soon afterward. Maya helped the maid set the little table and lay out the dishes. Cucumber sandwiches had made a reappearance, alongside smoked salmon, chicken breast, and an assortment of seeded breads, cinnamon butter, a creamy sauce that smelled of oranges, a warm pudding, and Mikoneh's pot of red leaf tea. Maya thanked the maid, who blushed and curtsied. As the girl's hand swept out, she knocked a fork off the table.

Mikoneh stooped to pick it up and offered the maid a grim smile. "Don't worry about it," he said over her apologies. "I can't count the times I've dropped a sword in training."

"That's certainly true," Maya winked. "Or me with my

herbs—priceless ones included. Don't worry, we won't tell a soul."

"Thank ye kindly, Yer Highnesses," the maid gasped out, backing her way toward the door. "Yer ever so kind." She tripped her way from the room, rammed into the armored guard, and bolted off with her empty tray.

The guard shut the door.

Maya burst out laughing. "Well, Mikoneh. You've a way with women."

"Shut up," he grumbled. "She was just nervous because we're Rokahns."

"Ah, but she didn't run until you smiled at her."

He rolled his eyes and snatched up a cucumber sandwich. "Stuff your mouth, won't you?"

Still chuckling, Maya obeyed, discovering she was actually ravenous. Tucking into her seat, she filled her plate with a little of everything and found she savored the pudding most. Mikoneh stuck to his cucumber sandwiches, meats, and steamed vegetables. Jensirin joined them and picked at his food, looking pale and absent.

"Try this," Maya said, offering him a spoonful of pudding.

He blinked at it doubtfully, then took a tentative bite. "Oh."

"Disgusting, isn't it?" Mikoneh skewered a bit of salmon.

"No, it's...very good."

"Traitor." Mikoneh scooted the pudding closer to the dragon lord. "But I guess it won't get wasted between the two of you."

Jensirin devoted himself to roast chicken and pudding after that, and Maya was pleased by his improved appetite. At Mikoneh's insistence, he tried a cucumber sandwich but wasn't nearly as taken with it as his friend. Maya beamed at them. The mood had lifted, the gloom banished for the afternoon.

She sipped her wine, content, until her worry for Latta crept back in. What were they going to do to get the woman's voice back?

A knock sounded at the door.

"Forgive the intrusion," said Crim, stepping into the chamber, "but we have a new problem."

The twins stood, and Jensirin mirrored them.

"What's happened?" asked Mikoneh.

Crim looked between Mikoneh and Maya, fear evident in the crease of his brow. "It's...difficult to explain. Mikoneh, you'd best come with me. Maya, please stay here with Jensirin."

She glanced at her twin, then back to Crim. The merchant lord looked pale...almost in pain. "Crim, are you hurt?"

He shook his head. "No, just tired." His voice sounded strained.

Mikoneh brushed his hand against Maya's arm. "I'll be back—and I'll be careful." He flashed her a grin, then moved toward the door. Crim stepped out, and Maya glimpsed the guards stationed outside. Mikoneh followed the lord, and the door shut after them.

Sinking back into her chair, Maya drew a long breath and stared at the remnants of her meal. "I wonder what's going on."

Jensirin remained standing, his eyes fastened on the door. "As do I..."

"What's wrong?"

"He didn't look right, did he?"

"No. He looked like he'd been injured."

Jensirin made a non-committal hum, then started for the door. "I don't like it."

Maya shot to her feet. "Wait. Should I come?"

"I think so."

They strode out into the corridor. Crim and Mikoneh were already out of sight.

A guard moved to block their path. "Lord Crim insisted that we keep you here for your safety, Princess Mayanaleh."

She frowned. "I'm with Jensirin. I'm perfectly safe, and this is important. But rather than argue the point, come with us. It does as much good as guarding the door." She summoned wind spirits, and they stirred her hair around her legs. "Or I can incapacitate you. Do you enjoy hanging upside-down?"

The guards exchanged harassed looks like they dealt with stubborn Elementalists often and had long since given up arguing with them. They tightened their holds on their spears and stepped aside. One motioned up the corridor.

"Lead on, my lady."

She glanced at Jensirin, who gave the guards a suspicious look then marched along the passageway. Maya looped her arm through his, determined to keep close. The guards likewise kept up the swift pace.

As they rushed along the cold stone corridor, Maya's nerves twisted. She didn't know what Jensirin was worried about, but her gut urged her to hurry all the same.

CHAPTER 55

ANOTHER PAWN

"Yet I know they feel, and deeply. I've seen an earth spirit weep after fire has ravaged a forest. I've felt the fire spirits rage as they consumed those trees. I've heard the sorrowful music of wind. And who doesn't recognize the many moods of the sea? Spirit of spirit, most of all, must feel deeply, for it is the material, the very essence, of eternity."

- *A Treatise on the Magic of the Hidden Realm* by Sariolin the Solitary

Crim led Mikoneh away from the main passages of Elenth Castle. Instead of going up, they went down, but not toward the main castle entrance.

"What's wrong, Crim?" he asked for the third time along their route.

The merchant lord shook his head. As they passed a lighted torch set into a sconce, beads of sweat glistened on his face. "I can't explain."

"Is it about Latta?"

Crim sighed. "Isn't everything?"

Mikoneh shrugged. "Do I know?"

"Down here. Not much further."

They'd reached a stairwell leading down into dank darkness. Mikoneh hesitated, glancing at Crim. His gut screamed against continuing.

"I think that's as far as I'm going without an explanation."

Crim grimaced. "I've already said I can't—"

"*Try*, Crim. I want to trust you, but this is..." He glanced at the darkness and shuddered. "This is strange. I don't like it, and I don't like how you're behaving."

The merchant lord's grimace cracked into a faint, pained smile. "I respect your reluctance, Mikoneh. You're wise to hesitate. But I'm bound to this course." His voice swooped lower than usual. "I have...no choice..."

"What does that mean?"

A blade flashed in the light of a nearby torch. Crim lifted a dagger to Mikoneh's chest, an amethyst glittering on its ornate silver hilt. "Don't make me use brute force, please."

"Crim." Mikoneh leveled his eyes on his friend's. "Is this magical manipulation, or is someone holding your wife hostage?" His chest throbbed. "Or is your wife behind this?"

Crim's eyes widened marginally, but he nudged his chin toward the stairwell. "Go down, Mikoneh. Please."

Casting a glance behind him, Mikoneh hoped against hope that a guard or a servant would come into view, see the problem, and sneak off to sound the alarm. But nothing stirred in the relative gloom. The castle felt deserted.

Nearly everyone was on a manhunt.

Had that been part of some bigger plan?

He breathed in, turned toward the stairwell, and started downward. Despite a month spent underground, and every bad dream since, he felt numb to the threatening shadows and dank scents like he was cloaked against the darkness. Crim kept the dagger raised. Its tip was a cold breath near Mikoneh's spine. Every nerve in his body tingled.

If I'm about to uncover the truth, it's not a waste.

The stairwell gave way to a landing, then turned and plunged into deeper blackness. Mikoneh's eyes adjusted, and he stared into a wide space full of covered furnishings. A storage area. The patter of retreating rats whispered in his ears. The smell of mildew, dust, and stagnant water assaulted his nose. He couldn't smell or see anybody.

They reached the level floor, where a door hung off its hinges.

"Are you locking me in here, Crim? 'Cause that might be a problem." He fingered the broken door.

"Not quite." Crim edged around him. "Stay there."

Mikoneh obeyed, trying to puzzle out the purpose in this. Was there any kind of exit down here? A window or a trapdoor? A faint scent twined through the putrid air. Was that snow?

Crim was rummaging among the furnishings, shifting things, stacking them...

"What are you doing?"

"Hush a moment, Mikoneh."

Scowling, Mikoneh flexed his fingers. He could take Crim on. Incapacitate him while his back was turned. But that would answer none of Mikoneh's questions. He didn't relish torturing the man, especially if Crim was another pawn—or worse, controlled by Latta's voice. How powerful was her ability? If she could charm the birds, or influence the masses like she'd wanted at the tourney, what could her magic turned evil do to an individual?

"Crim?"

"A moment, please."

"I can't just let you do this, whatever your reasons. I'm sorry."

Crim conjured flame. He held it aloft to study Mikoneh. "You can't stop me. It's already in motion."

"Tell me why."

"I...can't."

"You're not allowed, then?"

Pain flickered in the man's eyes. That was enough for Mikoneh. He stepped forward.

"Is Namirsha in danger?"

Hesitation. Confusion. Crim didn't know.

"Is she behind this?"

Was that doubt or anger?

Mikoneh took another step. "Let me help you."

"Y-you can't..."

"I'm going to anyway."

Crim dropped his handful of fire onto the stack of furniture. Fire spirits sprang up to consume the wood. Mikoneh summoned his own flame, drawing the spirits' focus.

"Stop," he said.

The spirits glanced between their meal and Mikoneh, reluctant.

"It won't do you any good," said Crim, and more fire poured off his frame, lighting other covered objects on fire. "You'll need to knock me out, or I'll keep—"

Footsteps rang down the stairwell.

"Mikoneh!" Maya's voice.

Jensirin came into view, followed by Mikoneh's twin. The dragon lord eyed Crim's dagger haloed in flame. Jensirin's slitted eyes constricted.

"Hold fast!" Mikoneh held out his hand. "Something isn't right."

Jensirin bared his fangs. He looked a bit unhinged.

"Maya, keep him back." Mikoneh spun toward Crim and concentrated on willing the flames to cease. During his lessons, it hadn't been hard, but this time he was fighting Crim's will. The wall of resistance was strong.

Crim's jaw was set, his eyes narrowed on Mikoneh. Flames kept pouring off him.

Fighting fire with fire wasn't ideal. Mikoneh blinked. "Maya!"

"Got it," she answered.

The air in the room thinned, and the flames shrank down. Fire spirits crackled in protest, but they faded to a mere outline. Mikoneh's lungs screamed for oxygen, but he kept his guard up.

"Want to snuff out, then keep fighting my will," he told the fire spirits in firm tones.

They hissed a final protest, then vanished, taking the flames with them.

Wind rushed through the room, thickening the air, purifying the acrid smell.

Crim chuckled. "Rokahns. Too quick for us common folk."

"You're the one who taught me," said Mikoneh.

"So I did." Crim wavered, as though he were about to pass out. "All for naught." He lifted the dagger to his own throat. "I miscalculated a lot of things, Mikoneh, and for that I'm deeply sorry."

"Don't!"

Wind roared past Mikoneh, and the dagger flew from Crim's hands. His legs were wrenched out from under him, and he swung upside-down, mouth hanging open.

"I don't think so," said Maya, striding forward. "We need answers."

Crim sighed. "Don't you understand? I'm already a dead man."

Memories of the stableboy's seizure flashed across Mikoneh's mind. He whirled around the room. No one was present. How could they know if Crim had succeeded or failed to carry out their plot?

Would that matter to them?

He spun back toward Crim. "It can't end this way!"

Crim was smiling at him. "I regret it too, my friend. I wish —" He began to thrash.

"No, no!" Mikoneh raced forward. "How can I save you?"

Maya reached his side, knelt, and crammed a plant into Crim's mouth. "Swallow. Swallow now!"

His thrashing continued. Foam leaked from the corner of his mouth. Maya lowered him to the ground, where he choked on the plant.

"Crim—please!" shouted Mikoneh. "Not this way!"

The merchant lord spat out the plant. "M—Mikoneh, t-trick. Don't—trust—" He gasped, and his body convulsed more violently. His eyes rolled into the back of his head. Foam poured from his mouth. He fell limp.

Maya turned away with a sob.

Mikoneh stared at his friend. The numbness returned, growing in his mind, pooling down into his body. Dead. Crim was dead.

Someone had controlled him—intending to frame him—and then cut his life short. Why? What was the point in any of this?

Anger flared, eating up the numbness, giving Mikoneh the energy to move.

Gently, he closed Crim's hazel eyes, then stood. "Jensirin, let's go." His voice was low.

"Where are we going?" asked Maya in a small voice.

"To *end* this."

"How?" She climbed to her feet, and though tears still shimmered in her eyes, determination set her jaw. She looked ready to tear warriors apart.

Mikoneh reached out, and she followed suit. Their hands linked.

"Latta's the key in all this," he said.

"Do you think Akonn has tracked down the magical thief?"

"We should check, but if not, there are other methods to get information."

She searched his face, then nodded. "I trust you."

"Good." He turned toward the stairwell. "I'm afraid we'll need to leave Crim here for now."

"It's cold down here," Maya said. "He'll...be preserved for a bit."

They moved toward the stairs, passing Jensirin, who fell into step behind them. Something of his senses had returned, though he still looked murderous. That was good. That emotion was usable.

Climbing the stairs, Mikoneh's footfalls were heavy, firm. His heart hung like a wilted flower in his chest. Crim had been his friend—an ally—a link to Seranni. Someone had robbed Mikoneh and Maya of that link. He would never forgive them.

They would pay. Dearly.

CHAPTER 56

SIDE WITH RIGHT

"Knowing that they feel—and perhaps with more depth than we do—I have asked myself why they show no sorrow in death. The answers I have divined bring me some comfort."

- A Treatise on the Magic of the Hidden Realm by Sariolin the Solitary

Two guards stood at the top of the stairwell, their eyes bulging with fear. It appeared Maya had scared them into submitting to her will, and who could blame them? Mikoneh ordered them to follow him, and they obeyed readily. The small group moved along the channels of Elenth Castle, aiming to find Latta.

"I don't understand what just happened." Maya spoke over the scuff of their feet on stone.

"I think Crim's control was an experiment," Mikoneh said, relieved to voice his suspicions aloud. That way he could sort through them better and catalog the points of his wrath. "Whoever's been tapping Latta's magic needed to see how far they could push a person against their will. I'd guess it didn't work as well as they wanted. Obviously, Crim had been prevented from explaining anything—but that took up too much power, and the control slipped. He didn't fulfill whatever task he was meant to: perhaps my death, or more likely, framing himself as the perpetrator in all this."

"But that falsehood couldn't last long," said Maya. "Even if you'd been provoked into killing him, Latta's power would still be taken. We'd know Crim wasn't the culprit by simple deduction."

"It might've been timed alongside her death to make it look like neither survived when I killed him. Like I was responsible for a tragic accident. After all, the perpetrator *wants* her dead in order to keep her song, but not until every ounce of her magic is stolen."

"That's horrible," Maya whispered.

"Yes, it is."

"But it didn't work, right? Latta isn't dead?"

"I doubt it," said Mikoneh. "The real thief doesn't have as much power as he thought. Crim's death is proof of that, at least." The words stung, and he clung to that hurt, forcing himself not to become numb again. He couldn't hide from this. He needed to feel the weight of Crim's loss. It would give him strength and clarity.

"I hope you're right." She looked ahead. Mikoneh heard the distant storm of footsteps approaching at the same time. Armor rattled.

Guards. A dozen of them, at least.

Mikoneh's instincts bristled. He caught his sword hilt, glad he hadn't bothered to change from his leather armor. Fire spirits in the nearby torch bracket perked up, sensing his tension. One floated over to light upon his shoulder. It crackled a question, but he had no answer.

Jensirin moved up to stand beside Maya.

The guards appeared in the passage, two in the fore clutching torches, the rest with swords drawn. Between the torch-wielding guards stood Sir Kalet, frowning.

"Mikoneh Rokahn, you have been accused of attempting to assassinate King Prettem. You must come with me."

The absurdity of the man's statement nudged Mikoneh's lips toward a smile, though he found none of this funny.

"When?" he demanded. "Just now? Or was it around the same time I supposedly killed Crim several days ago?"

"We are not in jest," said Kalet, marching toward him. "Please come quietly and let us sort this out. The king himself accuses you and showed me the wound you are said to have inflicted."

Mikoneh's eyebrows shot up. *What are you playing at, Prettem?*

"I'll come," he said aloud. "Let's get this sorted quickly."

"Where is our father?" Maya demanded over him.

Kalet hesitated. "We've sent someone to fetch him. Believe me, we don't want to cause any unnecessary friction, especially after reforging our alliance with Lord Owenekiras."

"A wise move," said Jensirin in a low rumble.

Maya tightened her hold on Mikoneh's hand. "I'm coming along."

Kalet opened his mouth, then clamped it shut. He nodded. "This way, please."

The twins and the dragon lord followed the armored procession up the corridors. Their door guards followed in silence. Soon the company reached levels where the wide windows let in cold light from the growing storm. Even if Mikoneh's match against the Corpse Poet hadn't ended prematurely, it seemed the tourney was doomed. The thick snow prevented him from seeing the castle walls or the grounds beyond. The procession turned south, but the fat white flakes hid the frozen lake from view.

The spice of cinnamon and pine wafted across the air. Mikoneh eyed the festoons of garlands and wreaths, but no remnant of the festive atmosphere remained in his chest. Crim was dead, Latta had lost her voice, Penn's memories had been taken, Minno was missing, and Mikoneh had been framed as a would-be assassin.

Maya squeezed his hand again, sensing his mood. He squeezed back, reassuring her. Somehow, things would work out. He hadn't survived execution and enslavement only to face a human king and be condemned.

We came here to help, not get mixed up in all this.

They reached a pair of double doors, and sentries pushed them open to reveal a warm salon lit by a massive hearth. The scents of smoke and mulled cider filled the air. Fire spirits chirped a greeting. King Prettem sat heavily on a wingback chair which was covered in a thick brown pelt. A healer bent over his arm, tying off a wad of bandages. The iron taste of blood pricked at Mikoneh's tongue. The doors shut heavily behind the company.

"Ah, here he is." Prettem waved off his healer, glowering at Mikoneh. "I'm surprised you didn't put up a fight."

"I'm not guilty," said Mikoneh.

"He's been in our suite with me," Maya interjected. "Ask your guards." She pointed to the two that had followed her and Jensirin.

Prettem glanced at the guards, then turned away. "You question my own eyes?"

"*Yes,*" said Maya.

Mikoneh tugged on her arm to quiet her. "We don't know what you saw, Your Highness. I've come to hear the facts."

The doors burst open, and in trotted Crown Prince

Atlanse. "What's this madness about accusing a prince of Rokahn of attempted murder?"

"It's the truth." Prettem rested a hand on his bandages. Red seeped through to stain the outermost layer. "He broke through my window." He turned toward the nearest window, where shards of glass riddled the stone floor, sparkling in the firelight. "In my surprise, I reacted too late. He cut my arm. When I shouted for help, and my guards responded, he fled at once. But I know what I saw."

"Me?" Mikoneh scoffed. "*I* just burst in here, cut you up, and fled back to my room? When was this?"

"Half a turn ago. Maybe longer. Plenty of time to return to your room and play innocent."

"That's preposterous," Maya cried. "He was with Crim."

Mikoneh tugged on her arm again. "You saw my face clearly, Your Majesty?"

"Yes. And I wasn't the only one." Prettem turned his head toward the shadows beside his chair. "Make your statement."

Hilker stepped from the shadows. "I'm afraid it's true."

Maya's eyes widened. "B-but—"

"Hush, Maya." Mikoneh squeezed her hand, then turned his attention to Hilker. Unease tightened his chest. "You saw *me*? You're certain?"

Hilker nodded grimly. "Afraid so. Now, I recognize this could still be a mistake. If some magic fooled our eyes—"

"It must be that," Maya burst out.

Mikoneh tightened his grip, and she fell still.

"Is such magic possible?" he asked.

"Yes," said Atlanse. "Difficult to conjure, but not impossible."

Mikoneh nodded. "Are there any other possible explanations?"

"Yes, you could've been controlled," Hilker said. "Perhaps by Mages, or—or someone else."

"Latta's attacker," said Mikoneh, nodding. "That's true." He drew a breath. "Crim was controlled not a quarter turn ago. He...tried to warn me but couldn't explain in detail. Then he died, just like that stablehand and just like the man we caught on the tourney field, foaming at the mouth."

Silence rang across the salon.

"Crim is dead?" whispered Atlanse.

"I'm afraid so," Maya whispered.

Mikoneh swallowed a lump. "Despite being controlled, I think he was trying to lure me away so that I had an alibi during the attack against Your Majesty." He locked his eyes on Prettem. "His body is in a lower storage room near the northeast tower."

"It's true," Maya said. "Jensirin and I saw—"

"Your word means nothing here," Prettem snapped. "I was a fool to trust Owenekiras or his heirs. Those with the blood of Rokahn will plunge the world into darkness, isn't that what the royal soothsayer said?"

"Sure," said Hilker, "but the royal soothsayer also said your marriage to Feresse would be a long and happy one."

"Father." Atlanse stepped forward. "Don't make the greatest mistake of your reign. We need this alliance with Owenekiras and his heirs. It's all that stands between the Mages and Sirinhigha as a whole. Oceana has fallen. Lintha has bowed to our foes. If we don't—"

"Enough." Prettem's voice rolled over the chamber like thunder. "You're weak, Atlanse. You've always been led by Owenekiras and his—his *ilk*. Have some pride in your own people. Simynshin has stood against all our enemies for millennia—"

"But that won't last if you abandon this alliance," Atlanse shot back.

"Atlanse, don't be foolish," Hilker warned in a soft voice.

Prettem rose from his chair and loomed, his eyes charged with fury. "You would side with *them* over your own king?"

"I would side with right against any man!"

"Treason!" Prettem swayed as though he might faint, then he caught his sword. "Guards, seize Prince Atlanse, along with the Rokahn heirs. We will hold them—"

Atlanse drew his sword, and Mikoneh followed suit, tapping into his fire at the same moment. Imprisonment wasn't an option. Wind stirred around Maya, and Jensirin turned to face the handful of guards before the double doors.

"Let's none of us be hasty," Hilker said. "We need to think this—"

"Silence, Hilker," Prettem barked. "You've always been a sentimental fool. Either you side with me now or join them in the dungeon."

"You think the dungeon will hold us?" Jensirin asked in a soft, dangerous voice that nonetheless carried to every corner of the room.

Hilker sighed, running a hand down his jaw. "A fair point. I suppose..." He drew a breath through his nose, then opened his mouth, and began to sing.

Mikoneh's mind turned foggy, and every sense whispered at him to obey the words of the song, though he couldn't hear what Hilker was chanting. That wasn't important. He needed to fight. To kill King Prettem—and Atlanse. That was most important.

Defend yourself. Fight the Simynshinians.

Something about that rang false, but he couldn't fathom why. They were going to kill him, weren't they? He willed fire to crawl along his blade and turned toward Atlanse. The

Crown Prince of Simynshin charged him, and their blades met with a thud. Sparks flew. Wind hissed. Their eyes met. Atlanse looked strangely detached, like he was sleepwalking.

Focus on the fight, you fool, thought Mikoneh, irritated.

The clash of weapons sounded around him. Others were fighting. Hopefully Maya would be okay.

None of this is okay.

Where that thought came from, he couldn't say. It didn't matter. It couldn't—

Lightning speared the room. Mikoneh froze, dazzled, along with everyone else. The flames dancing on his blade dulled. Glass shattered. He spun toward the noise. Splinters of glass littered the floor from a second broken window, and curtains billowed in a raging wind.

Standing in the freshly broken window frame, a dark figure loomed, silhouetted against another flash of blue lightning behind him. As the light died, Owenekiras Rokahn came into focus and stepped into the room, retracting his lightning-shot wings. In one arm, he held Penn up by his waist. The latter looked alert and worried. Owenekiras set the viscount down while scouring the chamber with his cold silver eyes.

Under the influence of that gaze, Mikoneh's senses fell back into alignment. He jolted, then spun toward Hilker.

"It's *you*," he growled. "You're the traitor!"

Chapter 57

The Nijaals' Own Luck

"Though they are slow to die, if die they do, the Spirits Elemental appear to understand loss—as evidenced by the tears for a ravaged forest. This means that death, in its basic sense, is understood. Yet they don't react to human and animal death. Is it because, unlike a forest that takes time to heal and regrow, our souls move on?"

- *A Treatise on the Magic of the Hidden Realm* by Sariolin the Solitary

"Forgive me for being late," Owenekiras said in rumbling tones. The words sent a chill across the room. Mikoneh shivered, despite his fire element. "I was delayed," the Dragon King went on, "by my rather hasty interrogation of the Dark Mage I captured last night. I regret that I ever trusted you, Hilker."

The Wind Master backed up a step. "Surely, you don't believe that monster! It's not what you—"

"Save your breath," Owenekiras said. "Penn recalls your attack clearly."

"It's true," Penn said. "When I left the library and returned to the suite to change for the Winter Ball, Hilker was waiting for me. He said I was getting too close to the truth. I'd seen him wearing a plain gold ring. It was identical to Latta's, and I'd asked him about it. He'd said that style was a Simynshinian tradition, but later Maya mentioned that Latta's ring belonged to her Ciminian mother. It felt off, so I went to the library to research traditions of Simynshin..."

Mikoneh's eyes widened. He spun toward Hilker, who was twisting the ring on his bare finger.

"There's no such tradition," Atlanse said. "Nor did my wife own any such trinket. She despised plain jewelry."

Hilker's gaze darted between them. "It's not—"

"Don't try to defend yourself," Jensirin growled. "The truth is written upon your guilty face."

King Prettem was staring at his brother-in-law like he'd never seen him before. "He...lied to me. Manipulated me. Made me think..." He turned toward Mikoneh. "You didn't try to kill me. *He* did."

"No!" Hilker backed up. "I only meant to frame him!"

"How is that better?" demanded Maya, marching forward, her eyes blazing, her hair lashing around her like livid snakes. "Why betray us, Hilker? Why—"

Hilker threw his mouth open, and music poured out, loud, deafening. Mikoneh's mind went blank. He watched through a film as Hilker darted for the open window.

"I don't think so," Owenekiras growled. Ice sparkled and stretched across the floor, painting cascades of torchlight across the walls and ceiling. Hilker sprang through the nearest broken window, narrowly avoiding the ice. He raced across the air.

Wind Elementalist.

Mikoneh jolted awake again. Hilker had stopped singing.

He killed Crim. He stole Latta's voice. Get the ring!

Fury roared through Mikoneh's limbs. He raced to the window, slamming his sword back into its sheath. "Maya, find Latta. Get her ring off!"

"Right!"

"Mikoneh, wait!" called Owenekiras.

Mikoneh flung himself through the closest window. A shard of glass nipped at his hand, but he ignored it. Wings sprouted from his back, propelling him forward. The flight leaf held like Akonn had said it would, though pain radiated up his wing as he tore through the air.

Hilker was running across the air like it was solid ground.

More wings beat behind them. Mikoneh glanced back. Owenekiras and Jensirin were both tailing him, gaining fast.

Join me, but don't stop me!

He jerked his head back around. Hilker was racing toward the northern woods.

Watch out for Mages, Mikoneh told himself. This could be a trap. He didn't know whether Hilker was working with the enemy or—

It's the only thing that makes sense. Mages attacked us after Penn had been put to sleep. Hilker must've let them in.

Mikoneh couldn't understand why Hilker had betrayed them—especially since he'd seemed to like Maya. He'd been proud of her as a student. Was this purely about gaining power to control the Simynshinian throne? Had something shifted in the man after Hilker's sister, the former queen, had died? Had the Mages promised him something in return for betraying humankind? Or was he some sort of zealot determined to bring about the full reemergence of his dread masters?

Whatever the case, Mikoneh couldn't find any reasoning that would excuse Hilker's actions. Crim was dead. Latta's magic had been siphoned and sullied. Akonn and Prettem had been wounded. Penn had been attacked and his memories repressed.

What if someone is being held hostage? Doesn't he have a large family?

The wrath burning in Mikoneh's chest reared higher, unwilling to give Hilker any excuses—but he needed to know. He *must* understand Hilker's motives.

First, I need to stop his flight.

Mikoneh conjured a fireball and threw it at Hilker's back. Predictably, wind knocked it off course, and Mikoneh had to snuff the flame out before it struck the trees below. He conjured more, commanding the fire spirits to deliver the deadly flames at different angles. One flame coughed and sputtered, smothered without oxygen.

Growling, Mikoneh stilled his fire and instead flew faster. His wings beat the air hard, but wind flung itself against Mikoneh, bringing swirls of snow. He was losing Hilker in the storm.

You can't have it both ways. Hilker couldn't keep sending wind if he wanted to avoid bolstering Mikoneh's element.

"Stop running!" Mikoneh shouted.

Mustering heat, he shot out both hands and sent blasts of fire streaming from his palms. A jet of flame grazed Hilker's arm. The man wheeled around, eyes wide. Ice struck him in the chest, sending him careening toward the forest below.

Owenekiras reached Mikoneh's side. Jensirin shot past them, racing toward Hilker's falling form.

"No!" Mikoneh adjusted his wings and followed fast on Jensirin's heels. Bloodlust curled off the dragon lord's frame. "Jensirin, stand down!"

He wasn't listening.

Owenekiras's voice rolled across the open air, deep and

commanding. "Jensirin, cease! We need him alive to reclaim Latta's voice!"

The dragon lord pulled up, letting his blue-green wings lift him on a current. Mikoneh caught a flash of Jensirin's dismayed expression as he passed, then Mikoneh turned his sights back on Hilker.

The man had caught himself on a cushion of air above the trees, nursing his chest. He stood facing Mikoneh and Owenekiras. A sneer stretched across his mouth.

"Leave me be!" Hilker yelled.

Mikoneh pulled up, letting his wings hold him aloft. "Give me back Latta's voice."

Hilker scoffed. "No. My allies need her gift."

"Meaning Mages?" asked Mikoneh, folding his arms.

"That's not your concern."

"I think it is," Owenekiras said, hovering nearby. "Why did you sell yourself to their cause?"

Another scoff. "You think this is a recent betrayal? I've *never* been your ally, Owen. You're a fool—and a powerful one. That's the worst kind, you know." Hilker's mouth quivered toward a smile. "My only real regret is that all this will hurt Maya. I like her. She's genuine. Sweet. And rather clever."

Mikoneh shook his head. "I don't understand. Why go to all this trouble now? Why help rescue me from Sathe if—"

"The Mage Queen didn't want Sathe bonded to you." Hilker shrugged. "When I informed her of what he'd done, she ordered me to get you out of there. That's why I helped mount your rescue. You did a great job cleaning up, by the way. Sathe was more trouble than he was worth to our cause. Too independent."

Owenekiras shifted, snaring Mikoneh's attention. The look on his face was surprisingly vulnerable. "I am saddened by the confirmation of your allegiance to darkness, Hilker, though Minno warned me."

"*That* nuisance. Well, he'll be no more trouble. I caught him snooping, and pushed him out a rather high turret window."

"Yes, I know," said Owenekiras. "I found him this evening. He helped restore Penn's memories to offer a more reliable eyewitness account. I was reluctant to believe Minno or the Dark Mage straight away. I thought you might have been framed."

Hilker frowned. "Impossible. Minno couldn't have survived—"

"He did, though his recovery will be a slow one." Ice crackled across Owenekiras's fingers. "Surrender, Hilker."

The man's eyes darted to the snowy ground. "No. I'd rather not face interrogation and dragon justice. I'll take my chances with the Mages instead, hm?"

Movement flickered below. Mikoneh tensed, and fire sparked on his fingertips. In the flash of orange light, he glimpsed shadows moving among the tree trunks. The air had turned colder, and he tasted rime on his tongue.

Dark Mages.

Fear bloomed in his chest, pressing against his lungs. He needed to leave. Now. Right now. He couldn't be captured again.

Hold your ground. Owenekiras is nearby.

The Dragon King eyed the figures below as a cat might consider an ant crawling near his paw. He wasn't worried, nor entranced. His silver eyes slid back to Hilker, and the human's assured smile slipped.

"Did you think we did not anticipate a trap?" asked Owenekiras softly.

Hilker shuddered. "You can't possibly fight so many."

The numbers kept coming. Shadows stretched under the tree boughs, promising a veritable army of Mages—against three dragons.

How many could they take between them?

Mikoneh had seen Owenekiras take on hundreds in Tesh-Relle not so long ago.

We have a good chance.

Hilker puffed up like a plumed bird. "They've come to end this pointless war. Don't you see, Owen, that *you're* the one standing in the way of peace? Sirinhigha groans under the endless violence of the ages, and all the prejudice of humankind. Do you have any idea what it's like being quarter fae in a human kingdom? The harassment and bigotry I've faced just for having strange eyes? Once the Mages gain power, all that will cease!"

"Don't play the victim," snapped Mikoneh. "Harassment doesn't justify mass slaughter and enslavement—which is what the Mages *want*. And don't you *dare* try to claim Crim's death was for altruistic reasons. Time to take off the mask, Hilker!"

Hilker shrugged. "I'll be well rewarded, it's true. The throne of Simynshin and my beloved Queen Feresse will truly be mine, and the looming threat of Rokahn—and of you fiendish dragons as a whole—will be gone for good. I can shake the shackles of my former life and be reborn to watch this world find peace once and for all! I call all that a great prize indeed!"

"Scared of dragons, are you?" Mikoneh smirked. "Fear's a dangerous ally, Hilker. Misleading, too."

Owenekiras spoke. "So then, you're the one Feresse has been unfaithful with. It will be good to clear the others we suspected."

"Even if you got King Prettem out of the way," Mikoneh

interjected, "there's still Atlanse. He's the rightful heir. How did you intend to take him out of the succession?"

Hilker scoffed. "You don't think he'd do anything for his precious daughter? He cares more about her than he does Simynshin. She's the perfect hostage."

Atlanse's weakness.

Mikoneh shook his head. "Greedy little beast, aren't you?"

"So he is," Owenekiras agreed. "It will be necessary to explain all this to your sister. She looked very hurt and confused by Hilker's betrayal."

"You don't seem to understand." Hilker gestured to the gathering shadows. "You're not getting out of this. You are both destined to become servants of the Mage Queen. She's eager to introduce herself to your son and heir, Owen."

Violet light sprouted below. The Dark Mages were charging their magic.

Mikoneh inched closer to his father in the air. Trying to stave off his fear, he focused on Hilker again. "Why did you kill Crim? He couldn't pose that much of a threat."

Hilker sighed. "Actually, he was one of my greatest problems. That's why Feresse tried to get you to kill him—but it was a flimsy attempt. I told her so. It was foolish of her to reveal our love affair to a Rokahn. She's...not very bright. Beautiful, mind you, but not very bright. Luckily, you mopped things up pretty well. But still, Crim remained an issue."

"In what way?" asked Mikoneh.

It was Owenekiras who answered. "His connections to Lintha. His wife, Lady Namirsha, has a great deal of influence in that country, and her adoration for her husband swayed her opinion on the war. In turn, sympathies were leaning away from the Mages in some corners of the Linthian merchant guild. Crim was successfully undermining Feresse and Hilker's efforts to isolate the Rokahn banner."

"That's true." Hilker shook his head. "And, at the same time, the presence of your children was swinging sympathies here in Simynshin. To think, *your* children—the heirs of a man built from ice—could change Prettem's mind, as well as half the court. One dance and Maya managed to enchant the hard-headed Lord Fontinn enough to throw off his pacifist act and promise his men to your cause. Between that and the crowd's response at the parade, I knew...I *knew* I must act, even in haste. I led Crim to Mikoneh, attempting to get them to duel. Killing Crim would incriminate him. But the blasted merchant fought my hold, and I was forced to frame your son for attempted murder of the king instead."

"Why did you steal Latta's song?" Mikoneh demanded. "Was that to try to control us or her father?"

Hilker grimaced. "Turns out controlling dragons through her song is rather difficult—it requires extreme concentration and close proximity, and I had to practice on human targets while I siphoned her magic. Even then, Latta's resistance was impressive, making any long-term control over anyone impossible. But her power has still come in handy, as you've seen. It will be even more so in the hands of the Mage Queen. She knows how to break wills."

"Since you're so chatty, there's something else I'd like to know," said Mikoneh. "Did you stab Akonn?"

"Aye, that was me. Wind is useful that way. He never saw the airborne dagger coming as he fended off my mercenaries."

"And at the tourney," Mikoneh said. "Were the mercenaries who tried to kill me there yours as well?"

Hilker shrugged. "If you were killed by Simynshinians, I'd hoped it might be enough to strain the new alliance between Owenekiras and Prettem. But you have the Nijaals' own luck." His eyes narrowed. "Well, you *did*. That ends today."

On cue, violet light exploded across the air, blinding Mikoneh. He threw up a wall of flame around himself.

Someone yelped.

The crackle of ice followed.

Peeling one eye open, Mikoneh found Owenekiras glowing with the blue light of Void. Ice clung to the trees like giant glistening spiderwebs, and Mages below scrambled for cover. Hilker was trapped in a thick gauze of ice. Jensirin winged into view just as Hilker opened his mouth.

"Look out, he's gonna sing!" Mikoneh yelled.

CHAPTER 58

A TORCH IN THE FRIGID WORLD

"Do the spirits understand, far better than we do, that life is but a fleeting moment between other spaces?"

- *A Treatise on the Magic of the Hidden Realm* by Sariolin the Solitary

Maya raced down the corridor, Penn at her side. Ahead of them, torches set at intervals lit the flagstones, guttering. Wind spirits followed, some resembling birds or butterflies, others wearing a dragon shape. They whistled a question.

"I need to reach Latta before it's too late," she explained. "Find Akonn. Let him know we're coming!"

Penn glanced at her, then looked ahead. Maya didn't waste breath on speaking. They kept running, following the familiar path she'd learned from her earlier visits with Latta. Almost there.

Her step faltered as Akonn hurried from a side passage, looking alarmed and angry. He relaxed the sword clutched in his hand. "Your Highness—"

"How's Latta?" asked Maya, breathless and heartsick.

"She's not well," the captain said. "She's hardly responding to anything. I've been working my tracking magic, Princess, and I'm afraid—"

"I know about Hilker. Take me to Latta," Maya ordered.

Akonn led the way to the Songbird Princess's suite at the end of the secondary passage. They entered a bright bedroom filled with braziers and torches set in sconces. A fire roared in the hearth. Forest tapestries hung on the walls. Festive wreaths conjured the scent of pine forests and spiced wine. Two healers stood near the four-post bed draped in silken coverlets, where Latta lay still. Her face was as white as death.

Maya strode forward, sat on the mattress edge, and drew Latta's hand from under the covers. The golden ring glittered on her finger, so innocent looking, yet so malignant. Maya started to tug it off.

A healer lunged at her, knocking Maya off the bed. She struck the area rug, and wind spirits chirped their indignation.

"Not so fast," said the healer.

Chills nipped at Maya's arms. She stared into the familiar face of Queen Feresse, dressed like a healer, but wearing the same simpering arrogance she'd always possessed. Releasing Maya with one hand, she groped for something. A dagger flashed in her fingers.

Maya's eyes narrowed. "You should've led with that."

She summoned wind. Feresse screamed as she was flung backward. She crashed into a sconce, knocking it over. The torch hit the flagstones and rolled. The second healer scrambled after it, but Penn reached it first and held it out like a sword to stave off the woman.

Akonn, meanwhile, had drawn his sword and set it under Feresse's chin. "Don't move."

Sitting up, Maya untwisted her skirts and climbed to her

feet, then hurried back to the bed, ignoring her throbbing skull.

"Don't you dare!" Feresse screamed.

Maya didn't spare her a glance. Plucking up Latta's limp arm, she tugged at the ring. It didn't budge. Panic surged in her chest. "How do we get it off?"

"It must be done simultaneously," answered Ter from the doorway. He loped inside. "That will prove tricky with you in here, and Hilker out in the woods."

"What can be done?" asked Akonn. "Must we...cut off her finger?"

"That would instantly kill her while Hilker still wears his ring. Though, short of killing her, we have very few options." Ter drew near the bed. "Luckily, you and Mikoneh are twins, my dear dragoness."

She stared at him blankly. "Meaning what?"

"Dragon twins have a special bond, meaning you may communicate with one another beyond the average connection shared between human twins. If you can open a channel with Mikoneh, you might manage to pull off the rings concurrently."

She stared at Ter. A flash of past silent communications between herself and her brother flitted through her mind—especially sensing his pain during his recent captivity—but she shoved all that aside for later. "How do I open that channel?"

Ter's smile gentled. "I commend your faith, Mayanaleh. Close your eyes and reach out. Try to sense Mikoneh. Ignore the wind, feel beyond its influence."

She obeyed, stretching her senses past the windows, into the snowstorm, trying to ignore the tug of the wind spirits delighted by her attention. And there, more *in* than *out*, she felt the familiar warmth of her twin blazing like a torch in the frigid world.

"I've found him."

"Good," said Ter. "Grasp that presence."

She did. The connection sprang up around her, and she could feel his distress, his fear, and his fury.

"I—I'm grasping it. I think he's in trouble."

"No doubt," Ter sighed. "Luckily, your father is also there. Trust them. Now, try to impress upon your twin the importance of taking the rings off together."

"Right."

In the bed, Latta moaned, startling Maya who wrenched her eyes open. Her channel with Mikoneh faded. Slamming her eyes closed, she tried to strengthen the connection again. The cord between them tightened.

Good. Very good.

She shoveled Ter's guidance across the cord, imagining the message carried like a light along its length.

It reached Mikoneh, and something brightened in his countenance. An understanding flooded him, and warmth surged back to her. Acceptance.

Maya caught Latta's hand and waited.

CHAPTER 59

THE JUDGMENTS OF A MAN

"I choose to believe they do, rather than think the Spirits Elemental simply have no compassion or remorse toward mortalkind. Indeed, they appear too happy and fond of humans and animals alike to dismiss us as irrelevant."

- A Treatise on the Magic of the Hidden Realm by Sariolin the Solitary

Menacing music poured from Hilker's mouth. At the same time, the Dark Mages shot threads of Hollow at the dragons. Owenekiras swooped down to block their violet magic. The music gained power, slithering through Mikoneh, trying to encourage blind panic.

He hurtled forward, curled his hand into a fist, and slammed his knuckles against Hilker's face. The music cut off. Hilker's head jerked sideways.

On contact with Mikoneh's touch, the icy gauze around Hilker cracked—then exploded. Wind shot shards of ice in every direction. Mikoneh dodged, weaving side to side. Hilker dropped out of his imprisoning web, then raced across the wind and into the high boughs of the pine trees.

"Not happening," growled Mikoneh, winging after him, away from Owenekiras's fight against the Mages below. Lightning struck the air, painting the world blue. Violet lights answered, crawling across the air in crackling streaks.

An awareness crept over Mikoneh—a sensation of light trickling through his veins, cocooning his heart. Maya. The feeling persisted. Weakened. Then expanded, bringing a sense of knowing.

The rings. They needed to remove both at the same time.

Mikoneh's wings beat the air. He picked up speed, evading trees, ignoring the pine needles that bit at his cheeks and hands. Hilker was just ahead. Mikoneh was catching up.

Glancing back, Hilker's eyes widened, and he tried to double his speed, but the wind was slowed by the forest. Mikoneh gained more ground. He was almost on the traitor. Almost close enough to tackle him.

Hilker dropped down, nearly touching the forest floor. Winter birds exploded from a thicket, their cries indignant. Mikoneh narrowly avoided them, the beat of their wings pounding in his ears, a counterpoint to his hammering heart.

Not daring to employ fire among the evergreens, Mikoneh angled his feet, and shoved off an old trunk. He careered toward Hilker and slammed into the man. They fell to the shadowed ground, pine needles deluging them. The tang of pinesap filled Mikoneh's senses. He wrestled with Hilker, scrabbling for his hand. Hilker fought him off, grunting and kicking.

"Get off!" the man cried.

"Give me the ring and I will!"

They rolled through the crunching snow. Bits of white crystals clung to their faces, hair, and backs. Both panted for breath. Adrenaline pounded through Mikoneh, hot as fire, willing him to fight with his all.

He grasped Hilker's wrist. The man sank his knee into Mikoneh's abdomen. Coughing, Mikoneh doubled over, and Hilker stood up. He backed away, clutching his ringed hand to his chest.

"Don't be a fool, Mikoneh. If you take this ring off, Latta dies."

"Better than you getting her power," Mikoneh gasped out. The pain ebbed, and he staggered to his feet. "Don't mess with me, Hilker. I'm ready to melt your flesh from your bones."

The man chuckled. "So fiery. So much like Rathana."

"Don't even *mention* her name like you care!"

"But I do." Hilker's eyes softened. "It's your father I take issue with, not Rathana. She was a great lady, worth ten of any Rokahn. But she fell for Owenekiras, and look what that got her."

"I'm not gonna listen to a man who chose another man's wife over his own family." Flames played across Mikoneh's hands. "Just tell me one more thing, Hilker—before I end your miserable life."

"What's your question?" asked Hilker, his mouth twitching upward.

"Is Kalet in on your plot, or is he an innocent bystander?"

"That fool boy? His integrity would be the undoing of the world. Isn't it funny? His reputation paints him as the villain. You suspected him, didn't you?"

"At first, but not for long. He's not the type to cheat."

Hilker snorted. "Any man will cheat if he's given the chance. Don't think King Prettem is immune—or your own father." He backed his way toward a dark gap in the trees.

Mikoneh's lip curled. "Didn't you just say your son wouldn't do what you've done. Which is it, Hilker?"

The man chuckled. "Fair enough. I suppose idealists will always attempt to change the world, but like Owen said, it only makes the cycle continue. Your efforts for peace and fidelity will lead to war just the same as the killing of a king. The only way to prevent it is to alter the present flow."

"And that's where the Mages come in?" Mikoneh inched forward. Snow crunched beneath his boots.

"That's right." Hilker reached the gap. His face fell into shadow. "I'll do what it takes to prevent war ever again. And yes, my means may be selfish—but at least I'm honest with myself. You dragons, on the other hand, are hypocrites through and through. You demand justice, but never ask it of yourselves. You're frauds. Liars. Cheats."

"I'm not gonna take criticism from the likes of you," Mikoneh growled. He'd covered half the space between himself and Hilker. The man was going to run any moment.

But Hilker only smiled.

Mikoneh took another step.

"Got you."

Before Mikoneh could move, violet light encircled him. A Mage circle. The array half-blinded him. Pain flared across his bones. He screamed. Chains wrapped up his limbs, invisible, but imprisoning all the same.

No. No. NO!

He tried to leap out of the circle, but his wings were dragged down by the magic.

Caught. *Caught again.*

"Mikoneh!" Jensirin's voice broke through the thrum of Mage magic.

"Stay back! Jensirin, don't you *dare* step inside the spell!"

Hilker was laughing. "You could've been a willing party in all this, Mikoneh, and it would've spared you the chains. Too bad. Be sure to say hello to the Mage Queen on the other side of this circle for me."

Jensirin roared.

"STAY BACK!" Mikoneh screamed. The ground was pulling him in, sucking him into the dark abyss of slavery and despair. He fought with everything he had, tried to wrestle against the cords of Magery wrenching at his soul.

They dug deeper, deeper.

He screamed.

Pain shattered the world.

Everything was going black.

A hand fell on his shoulder. His eyes snapped open, and he jerked his head around. He was kneeling in the transport circle, shuddering under the clawing, ripping magic.

He expected to find a skeletal guard ready to lead him to the Mage Queen, but amid the violet swirls, Minno stood at the center of the circle. His expression was bland, despite streaks of dry blood on the side of his head. His free arm hung like it was dislocated.

"Wha—" Mikoneh began.

Minno shook his head. "No time. Tell Owen—tell him I'm sorry." He shoved Mikoneh with twice the strength he should've possessed in his tiny body. The chains of light gave way.

Someone outside the swirling array was shouting. Hilker, probably.

"Wait, Minno!" Mikoneh twisted around.

"Go." Minno's eyes narrowed, and a burst of wind flung Mikoneh from the array.

"W-wait!"

The light closed over the circle, swallowing Minno up. With a last bright burst of Hollow magic, the circle vanished.

Mikoneh stared at the empty space. Even the snow had vanished.

Minno was gone.

CHAPTER 60

TO DEAL OUT JUSTICE

"If so, what do they know about the Realms below, between, and beyond, which we can only wonder about?"

- *A Treatise on the Magic of the Hidden Realm* by Sariolin the Solitary

Snow fell in the silence, the crystals faintly pattering as they landed on Mikoneh's shoulders and head. Reality settled in around him, and he realized the sounds of a fight came from his left. Wheeling, he found Jensirin struggling against Hilker, trying to take the ring.

The ring.

Latta.

Mikoneh snapped into action. Flames sparked at his fingertips, and he drew his sword, then marched toward Hilker and Jensirin grappling among the trees.

"Hey, Hilker!"

The man's eyes flicked toward him, and he scowled.

"What d'you think the Mage Queen is gonna say when

Minno appears instead of the Rokahn heir? Think you'll be punished?"

Hilker wrenched from Jensirin's grasp. "Meddling—conniving—insolent—"

Mikoneh flung out his arms. "I'm right here. Come and get me." Adrenaline scoured his insides. A reckless weightlessness flooded his body. He grinned, backing up. Somehow, Minno's sacrifice angered him. Deeply. How dare that child-sized creature do the noble thing after all Mikoneh's suspicions.

And then there was Crim, who'd dared to show Mikoneh that not all nobles were selfish cowards. Then he'd up and died.

None of it was fair.

Hilker took the bait, staggering toward him. The man drew a dagger. It glinted in the forest gloom, catching the glow of Mikoneh's fire sparks.

Jensirin stared between them. "Mikoneh?"

"It's fine. Time to end this one way or another. No more casualties."

Hilker snorted. "One more. Just that."

Mikoneh tapped into his connection with Maya. She was still there, warm, bright, and waiting. Bless her for the good woman she was.

He had no plan. No time to formulate one. Only a need—to rescue a friend from the plot of a monster in human skin. To end this ordeal before anyone else died. To deal out justice.

Hilker lunged, wind howling. Mikoneh threw up a wall of fire.

Wind choked out the flame.

Mikoneh slashed his sword, catching Hilker's dagger. The dagger spun away and vanished in a thicket. Hilker swore, backing off. Wind tossed his hair and tugged at his tunic.

They stood still, letting snow collect on their heads and

shoulders. Mikoneh waited, sword clutched in his hand, untouched by the cold.

He can counter my fire with ease, unless I can trick him into fueling the flames. That's unlikely. He's a master. What else can I try?

If Mikoneh were a much larger dragon, this engagement might be over already. Wasn't there another dragon nearby?

Not Jensirin. He's not ready to take full dragon shape.

But there was Owenekiras.

Think it through.

If Mikoneh tried to lead Hilker toward Owenekiras, chances were high the Wind Elementalist would flee instead, taking the ring and any hope of saving Latta with him. Mikoneh couldn't risk that. He wouldn't fail one more person —not today.

What do I do?

He gripped his sword tighter. No matter Hilker's wind magic, he was still a man. Well, so was Mikoneh, after a fashion. It would come down to their skills, man against man. There was nothing else for it.

Fire leapt up his blade, and he sprang at Hilker. Wind tried to choke the flames, but Mikoneh only sent up more. He couldn't afford to conserve his strength, so he wouldn't. Hilker slashed out his hand like he held a sword—and Mikoneh's blade met something solid.

A sword made of wind.

Mikoneh found himself grinning. His gaze locked on Hilker's. A similar grin stretched across the man's face. They danced over the frozen ground, fiery blade against wind blade. Their strikes thudded in the snow-laden air, muffled by the trees circling them like silent spectators.

Jensirin watched, not stirring from his spot. He held his side as though he'd been injured. If so, Mikoneh would add that to the list of Hilker's offenses. The man would pay dearly for each.

Hilker feigned a right step, then—summoning a second wind sword—he swept inward from the left. Mikoneh saw it in time to block the blow. Grimacing, he slammed his shoulder into Hilker's chest, then smashed his pommel into the man's chin.

Fire flared up from the hilt, racing toward Hilker's nostrils. The man smothered the flames, and curved away. Mikoneh snatched Hilker's right hand, and they struggled, tugging and twisting. Hilker scowled. The wind blades vanished, and invisible sickles sliced into Mikoneh, cutting his arms, his cheek, his leg. He staggered backward, throwing up another wall of fire.

The golden ring on Hilker's hand flashed in the light. Mikoneh squared his shoulders, refortified the flames engulfing his blade, and charged.

The man cursed under his breath, and wind sickles rose, slashing and biting. Mikoneh held his sword before his face, staving off the worst of the attack, willing fire to surround him. He bowled Hilker over, and they fell to the ground, rolling. Mikoneh singed Hilker's cheek. Hilker slammed an elbow into Mikoneh's chest.

Snow and flame danced around them.

Hilker gained the top position, seized Mikoneh's throat, and squeezed. Darkness crept into the corners of Mikoneh's eyes, and he gasped for air. Wind whistled in his ears. His flames weakened.

No. Not yet!

He shut his eyes, and mustered his anger.

Crim, Minno, Latta.

Fa and Mama.

Sathe's bond.

Drayve's tyranny.

Kevva's betrayal.

He let out every frustration, every loss, every doubt locked up in his chest. The flames roared. Even at the cost of his life, he would stop Hilker, take the ring, end the man's bid for power, and prevent any Rokahn from being sent to the Mage Queen.

Mikoneh wrenched his hand from under Hilker's knee and rammed his knuckles into the man's jaw. Hilker slumped backward, grunting. Mikoneh caught the ringed hand.

Maya, now! he cried in his mind, fumbling for purchase, hoping against hope the timing would be dead-on.

He caught the smooth band and yanked it off.

Hilker screamed. Wind raged, snatching the breath from Mikoneh's lungs.

Anger burned hotter, scoring Mikoneh's chest. He sprang to his feet.

End him. The voice might have been his own, though it seemed to come from somewhere far away.

He unleashed his fire. It exploded in a white-hot burst, singeing his fingers, his palms, his clothing. Every drop of his element rumbled out, scorching Hilker's flesh. Melting bone. Leaving nothing, not even a husk, behind.

Oxygen flooded Mikoneh's lungs. Wind stirred his hair, feeding the fire.

Dropping to his knees, Mikoneh's flames rose higher, higher, threatening to devour the forest.

Stop. Please stop.

A figure knelt beside him. Icy fingers caught his chin and turned his head until he stared into silver eyes. Owenekiras spoke to him, but the words were lost in the inferno roaring in Mikoneh's ears.

Another set of hands took his wrist. He glimpsed Jensirin.

The dragons seemed to be instructing him. He tried to heed them. Tried to read their lips.

Calm. Safe. Pull it back inside.

Shuddering, Mikoneh dropped his eyes and found a fire spirit—blazing blue with intense heat—standing on his leg. It raged, sputtering, indignant on his behalf.

"I'm okay now," he whispered hoarsely. "Please put the fire out."

The fire spirit tossed its head, disbelieving.

Mikoneh smiled. "Please." He uncurled his fingers and studied the plain gold ring glowing with heat in his hand. A circle had been branded into his palm. If the brand hurt, he couldn't feel it. Everything was numb.

"Please," he said again. "No more fury. I just...want to heal."

He slumped forward and fell against the cold ground. The flames around him died.

Chapter 61

A Feral Instinct

"Though the idea that they know of something beyond life does comfort me, it does not remove my guilt for the lives I have taken. That is something even the loyal earth spirits cannot quiet for me."

- *A Treatise on the Magic of the Hidden Realm* by Sariolin the Solitary

Maya, now!

She pinched the ring on Latta's finger and jerked it off. Latta screamed, then fell still.

"Stop!" Akonn's shout gave Maya a mere breath's warning before Feresse rammed into her, knocking her from the bed.

"How dare you?" cried the queen, clawing at Maya's face.

Wrestling back Feresse's hands, Maya glimpsed Akonn looming over them, unable to swing his blade for fear of striking Maya. She tried to send him a reassuring smile, but Feresse cuffed her cheek. Scowling, Maya snatched Feresse's hair and wrenched hard. The queen screamed and scratched Maya's chin, drawing blood.

Water fell against the grappling women, then caught Feresse around the middle, forcing her to roll off Maya. Sitting up, Maya dragged hair from her face to find her rescuer. It was Penn, gripping an empty pitcher in one hand. His other hand clutched ropes made of water which held the disgraced queen in place. Penn's eyes had turned a vibrant blue. At his feet, the second healer lay unconscious.

Feresse struggled against the viscount's elemental attack, spitting out curses. The dragon scale necklace the twins had given her slipped from under her collar, flashing in the torchlight.

A feral instinct bubbled up from somewhere deep down and seized Maya. She lifted her hand and closed her fist over the air. The dragon scales responded, tightening. Feresse gurgled. Her hands scrabbled at her throat, trying to loosen the necklace. The water still held her fast.

Rising, Maya shoved back her hair, and staggered toward Feresse. "Justice demands penance," she said. "The dragon scales seek your blood."

Like a silent voice crying from the necklace, Maya understood Feresse's past actions in a flash. Feresse and Hilker had been unfaithful to their spouses. The queen had begun the affair, finding Hilker a more suitable man to rule at her side than her temperamental and narrow-minded husband. They were both passionate by nature and discontented with their lot. They found they both sympathized with Mages, and feared and resented Rokahnians—especially the Dragon King. Both hungered for more power than even a human throne could offer.

Feresse hated Latta—threatened by the princess's song, and her popularity among the people of Simynshin. It was Feresse who obtained the gold rings from a shady dealer in Lintha at the start of summer. At first, Hilker hadn't wanted to hurt his grandniece, but Feresse had chipped at his resolve, whispering all the ways Latta's magic could be useful, until Hilker's ambition had swallowed his affection.

So, too, Feresse had stirred up Hilker's old bitterness surrounding his quarter fae blood. Unbeknownst to her lover, she'd stoked the flames of prejudice against the fae at court, reminding Hilker of the pain of his youth.

All of that, because the queen was bored of her old, stubborn husband, King Prettem, and because she feared the rise of dragons.

Sprawled before Maya, Feresse whimpered. Her knuckles were white from trying to wrench off the necklace.

"Tell me, Feresse," Maya said in a low voice. "Do you deserve death?"

The last hints of blood fled from Feresse's face. She shook her head.

"I'm not convinced," said Maya, setting her hands on her hips. "Crim is *dead* because of you and Hilker. So are several others. Latta almost joined that number. You worked with Dark Mages, betraying your people, betraying your marriage vows—all because of greed and fear. What *does* that deserve, I wonder? What *is* justice?"

"P-please," Feresse squeaked. "Mer—mercy."

Maya's eyes narrowed. "Do you even know what that means?"

"*Please.*" Cut off from air, Feresse's eyes lost their focus. She slumped backward against the ropes of water.

Maya flicked her hand open, and the dragon scales loosened their grasp. Akonn marched forward and bent over Feresse, seeking a pulse.

"Still alive." He sounded disappointed.

"For now," said Maya. "Let Simynshin judge her sins." She

strode close, stooped to unlatch the necklace, then straightened up. "These are Jensirin's scales. I won't dirty his hands. He's suffered enough."

"It might've been cathartic for him," said Penn, standing near the bed. He set the pitcher on the stand, then eased Feresse to the floor using his watery ropes. The ropes then slackened and broke form, puddling around the queen.

Maya sighed. "Maybe so. But I won't make that call." She tucked the necklace into her dress pocket. "Is Latta all right?"

"Yes." Penn glanced at the sleeping princess. "It seems you and Mikoneh were successful."

"Yes, indeed," Ter said, reminding Maya with a jolt that he was present. "You pulled it off most excellently."

"Thank the Nijaal for that." Her body was beginning to ache, and the scratch on her chin felt wet. She wiped away a trickle of blood. "I'll feel like celebrating after I know Mikoneh's safe—that reckless, stubborn, headstrong man."

Ter and Penn chuckled. Akonn was too busy trussing up Feresse's wrists with a fine braided rope to react.

A commotion came from the doors, then Prince Atlanse burst in, followed by King Prettem. A slew of men in armor followed, along with several noble spectators.

"My daughter?" Atlanse asked.

Ter lifted a placating hand. "She will make a full recovery. Entirely thanks to the Rokahn family, I might add."

Atlanse threw a look toward his father, then marched across the room to peer down at Latta. "Celes be praised."

Prettem stood near the open door, looking as though he'd aged ten years. His gaze fell on Feresse, and his eyes hardened. "She was locked up."

"She had help escaping," Penn said, nudging the foot of the second unconscious woman.

Fishing out a handkerchief, Maya dabbed at her bleeding chin. "I think," she said, "we ought to find out what happened outside. Can we send someone, or should I go myself?"

Ter beamed at her. "I will go and return as swiftly as I can." He vanished on the spot.

How he managed that technique without a Void anchor, she couldn't guess. Disappointment tugged at Maya's chest, but she ignored it. Traipsing beyond the castle borders in pursuit of a Mage sympathizer was foolish beyond her acceptable levels of rashness. She would wait, as much as she hated to.

Please let Mikoneh be all right. Please.

She glanced at Penn. "Since when have you been a Water Elementalist?"

He grinned, wiping a stray droplet from his cheek. "Since Owenekiras's war camp. I asked Ter to test me, and once I knew which element I could control, I found a mentor who helped me awaken my element, but I didn't want to say anything until I got better."

"So, that's what you were doing, sneaking off in the dead of night, worrying us *sick*!" Maya laughed. "Oh, Penn. I'm so happy for you."

He studied the droplet on his knuckle, smiling. "I've got a long way to go, but I'm glad I can be useful now." He looked up. "I've been practicing here, too. Crim found me a proper Water Master, and I sneaked off to train as often as I did to research Simynshin." Pink brushed his cheeks. "I'm glad you're not angry."

"Not a bit! That's wonderful." She hugged him. "Wait until Mikoneh finds out. Water, of all things. But then, you've always been good at putting out his fires."

Penn only laughed, but the sound was music to Maya's ears. It was just like Penn to work harder than anyone else, just to help out, and not make a show of it. She smiled fondly at him. Whatever their futures, however their paths might diverge, she would always care about him.

Even if her love for him wasn't quite the kind she'd expected.

INTERLUDE V

ALWAYS NEAR

"Can your heart hear mine across the chasms of life?"

\- From the Corpse Poet's 57th Sonnet

The soft green of the forest stretched before him, padding his bare toes. He moved along the edges of a great lake, and the lapping of the water soothed his soul.

"Where are you?" he called into the stillness.

"Here." Her voice came from behind him.

He turned and spotted the lady standing close, cloaked in white.

"You look exhausted," she whispered.

"I lost him."

"Minno?"

"Yes."

She nodded. "It will be well. He knows what he's about."

"Still, I hate that he's alone."

"When next you see him, tell him so." She reached up and

brushed Mikoneh's cheek. "He will resist, but it will soothe him a little."

"Why is he so stubborn?"

The lady laughed. "Why are *you*?"

He grinned at that. "I miss you. So much."

"So do I." She stroked his cheek again. "But soon, perhaps, we shall see each other once more."

"Why do I never remember when I wake?"

"The time isn't right yet." She turned away, but her voice trembled. "Hopefully, soon..."

He caught her hand. "I don't want to leave you."

"You never have. We are always near."

Chapter 62

Until the Spring Thaw

"It is because of my unceasing guilt that I escaped from my former life and sought solitude and healing among the Spirits Elemental."

- *A Treatise on the Magic of the Hidden Realm* by Sariolin the Solitary

Sunlight columned the bedside in slanting pillars, sparkling with dust motes, churning with warmth. Mikoneh stared at the beam near the canopy above his head for a long moment before comprehension settled in. He was alive. Breathing. The air smelled of faint snow and woodsmoke.

His palm burned where the ring had branded his skin.

Turning his head with a faint scratch of hair against his pillow, he wasn't surprised to find Maya sleeping on top of the coverlets beside him. Her dark hair was spread around her, loose and glossy. Her breaths were even and deep. A faint scratch ran down her chin.

Shifting his head, Mikoneh found the window. The blue

curtains were open wide, letting in the ample glow of midmorning. Penn had fallen asleep on the window seat, a heavy tome resting against his chest. His mouth hung open.

Mikoneh tried to sit up, but every muscle protested. Setting his teeth, he tried again and managed to win.

Feet padded across the rug, coming close. Mikoneh lifted his head and found Akonn leaning over him.

"Easy there," the Captain of the Sword murmured. "You've taxed your body a great deal."

"I'm alive, aren't I? That's good enough."

Akonn shrugged. "Princess Mayanaleh is the authority. Ask her."

Mikoneh grimaced. He had no intention of asking Maya's opinion. It was easy enough to predict. "How long have I slept?"

"Two days."

Not as bad as Mikoneh had feared. He nodded, trying to order the events that had led to his collapse.

His heart twinged. Crim.

Drawing a breath, he trawled for matters that might be less painful to discuss. "Princess Latta. Is she…?"

"Alive," Akonn said. "Your timing was perfect. I was with Maya when she removed the ring. Ter was guiding her in the process of using your twin bond to communicate. Queen Feresse tried to stop them but failed. Feresse is now a prisoner in the dungeons, awaiting her trial."

Mikoneh stirred. "She had a necklace of dragon scales."

"Maya got it back. That was an interesting highlight, actually."

Something to hear about later. "And Hilker?"

"There wasn't enough remaining of him to scrape off the forest floor, judging from what Lord Owenekiras and Lord Jensirin described. You were most thorough."

Mikoneh grunted. He'd certainly wanted to be. "Anyone hurt? There were Mages."

"Lesser Mages only. Lord Owenekiras dispatched them easily enough. And we've combed every inch of the castle and Elenth proper for any remnant. Nothing so far." Akonn settled himself against the mattress. "We also collected Lord Crim's body from the storeroom. His burial will be tomorrow."

Inhaling, Mikoneh nodded. His lungs remained tight, but he spoke anyway. "How did his wife handle the news?"

"She was inconsolable, I understand. No one has seen her since Lord Crim was taken back to his estate."

Mikoneh traced the pattern on his coverlet, unwilling to look up, or to imagine Namirsha's grief. He couldn't—not yet. His mind played over the events leading to Hilker's end. Recalling the Mage circle and Minno's sacrifice, Mikoneh tensed. "Where's Owenekiras?"

"In the adjacent room. You wish to see him?"

"Yes, please."

Akonn moved off, and the sound of the door opening whispered in Mikoneh's ears. Akonn left it open a crack. Voices drifted into the bedroom, one lower and deeper than the other, then the door swung wide. Owenekiras Rokahn entered, his armor and cloak absent. Instead, he wore a black tunic over trousers, with matching boots. His sword gleamed in a sheath at his hip.

Mikoneh leaned forward until he caught his father's eye. "Minno was sent to the Mage Queen."

Owenekiras halted. His eyes narrowed. "You're certain?"

"Yes. Hilker meant to send me. Minno shoved me from the spell array and was taken instead. He told me to tell you he's sorry for what he did, then he vanished."

Silence fell, then Owenekiras nodded. "Then he's beyond our aid for now."

"You can't mean that."

The Dragon King moved closer to the bed, positioning himself in a strand of golden sunlight. The blue highlights in his dark hair shone. "Minno is my spymaster. He's the most capable of all my scouts. If anyone can survive the Mage Queen, it's certainly him." Owenekiras's gaze drifted to Maya sleeping nearby, then flicked back to Mikoneh. "You met Minno in an underground Mage sanctuary, I think, yes?"

"Yeah."

"He allows himself to be caught and tortured now and then, in an effort to gain vital information. At that time, he had been tracking Sathe's movements, trying to determine what the man wanted. Minno didn't know you were the target, but he could guess that Sathe was hunting someone. He allowed himself to be caught in order to rescue whoever it was."

"And then he betrayed us," Mikoneh said, unable to dowse his anger. "I still don't understand why that's acceptable to you."

"It was a moment of weakness for him." Owenekiras sighed. "And I believe he made amends when he switched places with you in Hilker's Mage circle."

Mikoneh chewed on that. "Fine. I suppose we're even. So... we just leave him be?"

"Minno is tenacious. He will survive."

"He can't afford to get any odder. If the Mage Queen drives him to insanity—"

"She won't be the first to have tried," Owenekiras said. "In many ways, Minno *is* insane. But I trust him with my life, and I trust him to find the Mage Queen's location. This may be a game changer in this war. If we can discover her exact whereabouts before the Mages overtake Cimin, we stand a good chance of putting an end to her machinations. That would leave only my sister and Rokahn itself as a viable threat."

"What about Lintha?" asked Mikoneh.

"On its own, it's little trouble. Lintha has always been loud rather than strong. Without allies, it will soon slink back into its old habit of waiting and sulking. All Lintha is good at is trade."

"Isn't Lintha allied with Rokahn?"

"They have a tentative truce, but my sister is nearly as paranoid as were my parents. She's reluctant to hold true to any alliance without absolute proof of loyalty to her—and Lintha only cares about itself."

Mikoneh folded his arms. "So, what's next for us? I assume Cimin."

"Your instinct does you credit. Yes, Cimin is our next priority. And it may prove a greater challenge than Simynshin. Assuming King Prettem doesn't go back on his word, you and your sister have made the difference here. Apart from the fae, who have long been loyal, we have our first true alliance in this kingdom."

"The fae do side with you then?" Mikoneh hadn't been certain on that point. "All of them?"

"Enough of them," Owenekiras said. "The Nijaal are high fae. What they do, the rest do as a general rule. Even the dark fae will answer the call should we demand it—except those already controlled by the Mages. Lady Katanni and her armies are striving even now to break the bindings on many of the fae races long enslaved. It is a meticulous and prolonged campaign."

"Sounds like it." Katanni's image flashed across Mikoneh's mind, and something in his chest loosened. "With Cimin being so close to the High North, will we see much of the Nijaal once we're there?"

"It is possible." Owenekiras drifted toward the window. "But no one can journey to Cimin until the spring thaw. The weather is too severe. That's just as well. You need time to recover your strength, and I will be working with King Prettem and Prince Atlanse to secure new agreements in our alliance. That's a rather tedious and time-consuming venture."

"It won't take me the whole winter to recover," Mikoneh said. "I could go ahead—"

"I would prefer you to remain here and study." Owenekiras glanced over his shoulder. "Jensirin is a worthy teacher, and you have much to discover of your dragon blood. Ter tells me you and Mayanaleh successfully tapped into your twin bond. That will serve you well in the future." A faint smile brushed his lips. "Your mother would be delighted with your progress."

Mikoneh tensed. Something in that statement—perhaps Owenekiras's faint tone of grief, or Mikoneh's blank where his mother ought to be—sent a ripping pain through his heart.

"I don't remember her at all."

Owenekiras nodded. "That isn't surprising. Her death was...unsettling. I have wondered often how much you witnessed that day. She hid both of you, and you—being the brave soul you have always been—held your sister near to protect her. But you may have seen something of the attack. I suspect you blotted out the memory, and as a consequence, you recall nothing of Rathana."

Mikoneh's pulse quickened. Breaths came short and sharp. "I—"

"Put it from your mind for now," Owenekiras said gently. "The time may come when the memory is not so painful, and thus, not so frightening. Be at peace, my son. Rathana wouldn't blame you for forgetting. She would understand."

Swallowing, Mikoneh nodded. He dropped his gaze to his hands and found them tightened into fists. His knuckles were white. Loosening his grip, he drew breaths, willing his heart to slow.

Let it go. Deal with it later. There's enough to focus on right now.

"I've given you more than enough to wrestle with for the time being," Owenekiras said. "I will take my leave." He dipped his head, then strode toward the door.

"Wait." Mikoneh spoke before he understood what he was going to say. But something inside him didn't want this man to leave. Though they knew little of each other, Owenekiras was his father, his connection to a past he didn't remember, and to the people who'd raised him. Crim was gone—severing a connection to Seranni. He didn't want to lose Owenekiras, to lose any more connections. Somehow, the idea terrified him, as irrational as it was.

Owenekiras was watching him. Waiting.

"I...I'd like to have dinner with you. Soon. If—if that's not inconvenient. Just us—you, and Maya, and me. Here, maybe."

A light sparked in the Dragon King's eyes. His lips twitched up. "Crucial matters prevent my being available today or tomorrow, but I will clear my schedule later, if that is acceptable."

"Oh, that's— If you're too busy, don't—"

"I will be here for dinner two days hence, at the eighteenth turn," Owenekiras said firmly, then stepped out, and shut the door softly behind him.

Maya shot upright and threw her arms around Mikoneh. "That's my big, brave brother!"

"Get off." He shoved her back, laughing.

She beamed at him. "Really, Mikoneh. I'm proud of you. And I'm so relieved you're awake. You had me worried!"

"That's not exactly hard. You're a fusspot."

She poked him in the ribs. "Be that as it may, you give your twin license to worry." She flopped against his pillows. "So, then, we have until spring to learn all we can about our dragon heritage and get better at our elements." Pain wiped her smile away. "We've both lost our Elementalist teachers, though."

Mikoneh's breath hitched. "I'm sure we'll get new teachers soon. We need to be ready for Cimin."

"Hard to believe we'll be traveling the world." Maya sighed. "I always thought we'd live out our whole lives in Relvin Province, except maybe a visit once or twice to Nauttia. It's a good thing I never wagered on that."

He grunted. "We're a long way from home."

"I'm not sure it ever was our home," she said. "I mean, Fa and Mama were, of course, but Relvin—and even Oceana—they were just places with people. I wonder if we'll ever know what it's like to really call anywhere home."

Mikoneh turned toward the window and stared out into the glittering white world. "I don't know, Maya. I hope so."

CHAPTER 63

THIS WRETCHED KINGDOM

"Perhaps when my life comes to a close, I will at last be able to shed my past and feel that I have paid penance. Certainly, living with these ethereal beings has softened the hurt. Is that allowed for one such as I?"

- *A Treatise on the Magic of the Hidden Realm* by Sariolin the Solitary

The next morning, a fresh quilt of white sparkled over the castle grounds. Mikoneh squinted as he plowed his way to the stables. Pushing open the door, the musty scent of hay and horsehair intermingling with the sharp odor of manure made him sneeze.

Rook nickered a greeting.

Mikoneh moved to the black stallion's side and stroked Rook's neck. "Hi there, my friend. Ready for a ride?"

"Only if I can come with you."

He whirled toward the stable door. Princess Latta stood in the block of light, bundled in a fur-lined cloak of silver, her cheeks and nose red with cold, her dark hair coiffed atop her head. Her blue eyes shone with a challenge.

Mikoneh shrugged. "If you like. This isn't a joy ride, though. I'm visiting Lady Namirsha."

Latta blinked, then nodded. "Then I should definitely come with you. I need to apologize to her."

"If you like," he said again, then began to saddle Rook. "Can you sing now, Princess?"

"Yes. My music is restored in full."

"That's good."

Latta moved over to Firechaser and started saddling up the horse. They worked in silence, both lost in their own thoughts. At last, Latta looked up from checking her straps.

"I want to thank you for all you and your sister have done —for me and for Simynshin."

He shrugged. "We couldn't just look away. That's not what friends do."

"Have you recovered, Mikoneh?"

"Enough for this."

"You sneaked out, did you?"

"And you didn't?"

She shrugged. "What if we run into Mages?"

"Then they'd better move out of my way quickly. I'm in no mood to spar." He moved over to help her swing up into her saddle. "But," he went on, "I doubt we'll see much of them over the next few months. According to Jensirin, my father scared the life out of several—quite literally—and the rest aren't eager to return."

Latta chuckled. "Owenekiras *can* be rather fierce."

"I've noted it." Mikoneh mounted his stallion and caught up the reins. "Ready?"

"Yes."

AT THE CASTLE GATES, a dozen guards were mounted on horseback and waiting, with Akonn at their head. Clouds hung low and dark, heavy with the promise of more snow.

"To Lady Namirsha's, I presume?" the captain said with a grim smile.

Mikoneh rolled his eyes. "This isn't necessary."

"With all due respect," Akonn said, "it is. You're a prince now, Your Highness. Better get used to inconvenience."

"He's not wrong," said Latta.

"Yeah, yeah." Mikoneh nudged Rook forward, and the guards flanked him along the road. Despite his reluctance, something eased in his gut with the faint clatter and clop of the escort surrounding him.

They made good time through the gloomy woods to the keep where Mikoneh had once dined with Crim and his wife. Against the naked trees and looming pines, the ivy-laden fortress looked stark and forlorn. The soul that Crim had infused into the stones was absent. Mikoneh's heart throbbed, but he adjusted his shoulders and rode into the bailey. Hooves clattered on the flagstones.

Looking up, he glimpsed a figure in an upper story window. The figure retreated before he could be sure, but he'd have wagered it was the lady of the keep. As he swung from the saddle and handed his reins to a stablehand, Mikoneh steeled himself against what was to come. She might refuse to see him altogether, which he honestly found the most welcome scenario in his head.

Latta accepted Mikoneh's arm, and they swept up an icy path carved between snow drifts and into the keep at a servant's beckoning invitation. Akonn and a handful of guards followed.

"Lady Namirsha has been expecting you," the servant said in monotone, clutching a lantern to stave off the gloom. Few torches were lit inside. Luckily, Mikoneh's slitted eyes attuned well.

They were taken to a drawing room where a fire smoldered in the grand hearth. Flicking a glance at it, Mikoneh willed the fire spirits to brighten the chamber, and they obeyed with a cheerful pop and crackle.

Lady Namirsha stood behind a wingback chair, one slender hand clutching the piece of furniture like it alone held her upright. She was draped in layers of black silk and a billowing lace veil, hiding most of her features. Despite that, Mikoneh could tell that in the past few days she'd lost weight. He winced.

The servant left. Several guards waited outside the door, leaving Akonn and two others to station themselves at the royals' backs.

Silence filled the space between the visitors and their hostess. Then Namirsha stirred and gestured to a settee.

"Please, have a seat."

Mikoneh guided Latta forward. They sank into the stiff cushions and waited. At last, Namirsha sighed—a long, weary sound—then glided around the wingback chair and sat at its edge, perched like a delicate bird.

A log fell in the hearth, and the fire hissed.

The wind outside rattled the glass panes in the drawing room window.

"Why have you come?" asked Namirsha in tones as bitter as ice.

"Crim was my friend as well as my mentor," Mikoneh said readily.

"Yes." Namirsha's voice dipped into a whisper. "And you killed him."

"That's not true," Latta cut in. "Hilker did that. He caused *everything.*"

Namirsha's veiled head swung toward the princess, and somehow the drawing room grew colder. "Yes, I've heard the report, Princess Latta. And I see you survived despite how close you came to death. How happy for you that the Rokahns managed that, despite failing to rescue my husband."

Mikoneh's stomach clenched. "A regret I'll carry for the rest of my life. I'm in your debt, Namirsha." His words tolled through him, a great weight he felt in his soul.

"I want *nothing* from you," she whispered.

Latta's fists clenched. "That isn't fair—"

"Silence, Princess," Namirsha spat out, rising to her feet. "I blame you still more for Crim's death. He sacrificed *all* for the sake of this wretched kingdom. He worked with your great uncle every day, yet what good did that do? Treachery and betrayal are all that await good men in Simynshin." Her concealed face turned back to Mikoneh. "If this is the cause your father serves—if this is the justice he demands—then I renounce it. I'm returning to Lintha. To *my* people. Crim was a fool to side with you."

Her words bit deep, but Mikoneh had braced for that possibility. He rose to tower over the petite Linthian woman and peered into her veil until he could see the outline of her fair features. "Crim was my friend, my lady. I came to love him like an older brother. He fought bravely to his last breath against Hilker's control. For that, I won't turn my back on the cause he chose. I'll fight on to make certain his sacrifice and loyalty mean something. If you can't do the same, so be it. But don't lash out blindly. Don't bury his dreams because the memory hurts too much.

"Grief is coming for all of us before this war ends," he continued. "It will touch everyone, old and young alike. And with its touch will come a private choice each must make: concede defeat and defile the memory of those who have fallen, or battle on and keep that memory pristine."

A noise between a sob and a growl escaped from beneath the black veil. "How dare you lecture me?"

"I've seen the monsters grief can create," he said. "I've seen the husks, too. The first loss strikes hardest, and that's when it's most important to make a stand rather than fold. But I can't force you to make the better choice."

"Get out." Namirsha stepped toward him. "Get out. I'll never forgive you. I'll never, ever forgive. I *loved* Crim—against everything I believed. I chose him and his philosophy—and look what it's cost me."

Latta stood up, and moved to Mikoneh's side. "Please, Namirsha—"

"Don't you dare offer the hand of friendship now," she snarled. "You and your ladies at court disdained and dismissed me. It's too late to pretend you didn't."

"You're right." Latta reached out a hand. "That was wrong of me. I suspected you—"

"And now you have cause. Now, Princess, I am your enemy —and that is on you."

Latta flinched back.

Mikoneh's eyes narrowed. "No, Namirsha. Whatever you do now—it's on your head alone. No one else can be blamed for our conscious choices. No one. Even if Latta ostracized you. Even if I failed Crim. Even if Hilker betrayed you—and me—and all of us. Your choice, your consequence. No one else's."

"*Get out.*" Namirsha spun away. "Once I leave Simynshin, pray we never meet again, son of Rokahn. At that time, I may try to kill you."

Mikoneh's shoulders fell, and something in his chest

cracked. He'd feared this outcome, but he'd resisted accepting it. "I hope you don't always feel this way. Crim wouldn't want—"

"Get out!" Namirsha's scream was full of heartbreak and wrath.

Mikoneh caught Latta's arm. At the same time, Akonn stepped forward to shield them. They all moved from the drawing room, down the corridor, toward the front door. Latta's cheeks glistened with silent tears, and Namirsha's bitter words burrowed into Mikoneh's memory, wrenching at the guilt and loss he bore.

I'm sorry, Crim. I tried.

He stepped out into the frosty world, where crystals of ice fell like maddened wasps, stinging and swirling. He helped Latta onto her horse, then swung into Rook's saddle. They rode within the protective circle of guards, buffeted by howling wind. Glancing at Akonn, Mikoneh found the fae captain scowling, but no one spoke.

Mikoneh bowed forward during the ride, letting his failure fold in around him. When he reached Elenth Castle, he would shake away the guilt and restore the armor he'd constructed for his soul—but for this moment, he allowed himself to wallow.

To grieve.

To regret.

HALFWAY TO THE CASTLE, the storm lessened, and the snow fell more gently.

Latta cleared her throat. "I have something to give you, Mikoneh."

He glanced at her. "I don't need—"

"It's not much," she said, her sapphire eyes bright despite

the redness rimming them. "Just my way of thanking you for all you've done. Please let me. It—it might help with what just occurred."

He nodded, unsure what to expect.

Latta opened her mouth—and sang. The words were in the Old Speech, which Mikoneh had never learned, yet he understood the meaning just the same. Latta sang an aria of hope and healing, of light and rebirth. Every note was heavenly, piercing his core as if the spirit of spirit within him answered. Warmth flooded Mikoneh's chest, chasing off the shadows of Sathe's touch, and the sorrow of Crim's death and Namirsha's wrath.

The hollow feelings would be back—he knew that—but like the unicorn's touch, the Songbird Princess gifted him with peace and healing for a time.

Grief lifted. Guilt died. Regret cowered.

Tears filled Mikoneh's vision. He bowed his head, giving Rook the reins. The song floated over the snow-crusted world, lifting toward the heavens until even the clouds rolled back to reveal the sun.

When at last Latta finished singing, the wind had settled to a hush. Their guards were silent as though they'd been stunned.

Mikoneh struggled to find his voice. "Thank you," he choked out.

"You're very welcome." Latta reached out to brush her fingers against his cloak. "It's the very least I can do for my brother."

Mikoneh's smile deepened. That was a relationship he could understand and embrace. Catching her gloved fingers before she retreated, he squeezed them. "Thank you, *sister*."

Chapter 64

What He Could Control

*"Or shall a hidden life of peace and harmony condemn me
nonetheless for being what I am—a Mage?"*

- *A Treatise on the Magic of the Hidden Realm* by Sariolin the Solitary

Namirsha didn't attend Crim's state funeral at
sunset. Afterward, word reached Owenekiras that
she'd sailed from the western port earlier that
evening, despite the dangers of the winter ocean, determined to
head for Lintha at once.

The next day, Feresse stood trial for her crimes and was
found guilty on all counts. King Prettem had her executed by
beheading that same afternoon. The Rokahn twins didn't
attend either the trial or execution, content to remain aloof
within their common room with Penn and Jensirin. This was a
matter between Simynshin and Lintha.

"One thing's certain," Penn said, moving a game piece
across the Fang and Claw board. "War between the two kingdoms is a mere matter of time. Between Namirsha's fury and

Feresse's death, Lintha won't stay silent. Their pride is on the line."

"Amazing how many wars are caused by that vice," Maya said, moving a game piece to counter Penn's. He grimaced, seeking an escape.

Mikoneh looked up from the book of dragon poetry Sir Kalet had lent him. The fire spirits in the hearth crackled and stoked the flames, hopeful that he would acknowledge them. "War was inevitable even without these recent events. The Dark Mages won't rest until they either secure every kingdom or drive a divide between the factions. Cimin's next."

"It's too bad we can't head there immediately," Penn said.

"Are you coming?" asked Maya, setting a dragon piece beside her gryphon.

Penn frowned at the board. "I thought I was."

"I'd rather you stayed here, Penn." Mikoneh stuck a ribbon in his book to mark his place. The poetry *was* excellent—easily the best he'd ever read—but he couldn't concentrate, and he was tired of pretending otherwise. He took a sip of *tiassana* tea; its healing properties immediately eased the hole where Sathe's shadows clung once more. "You should be our representative in Simynshin. Maybe help keep Prettem on task?"

"The king *does* have trouble maintaining a sense of urgency," Maya agreed. "You can keep lighting a fire under his posterior every time he veers off course."

Penn glanced between the twins. "You're not just saying this to keep me safe, are you?"

"No," Maya said at once.

"There's more to it than Prettem, though." Mikoneh set the book aside. "Listen, Penn. Oceana is a shell of itself, but the struggle there isn't going to end soon. I'm not done fighting for that land—and once we secure a treaty with Cimin, I fully intend to march back into Oceana, fend off the little squabbling nobles, and put someone trustworthy on the throne. That someone is you."

Penn blinked. "Are you—"

"Perfectly serious," said Mikoneh. "Which means we *do* need you to stay safe for now. Practice your water element, and learn all you can about digging a kingdom out of the ashes."

"That isn't a bad plan." Jensirin's voice drifted from the shadows near the window. He stepped into sight, smiling at Penn. "You've proven a resourceful man. Oceana will need that in the years to come. And you do have noble blood."

"But..." Penn swallowed, then shook his head, laughing. "I thought you hated royalty and nobility, Mikoneh. That can't have changed just because you're now—"

"It's not that," said Mikoneh. "I've just come to accept that people vary. That a peasant can be just as corrupt as a prince. And a nobleman can be as kind and generous as a healer. If nothing else, Crim taught me that much—as have you, Penn."

"Well." Penn smiled. "King of Oceana, huh? It's something to consider, I suppose. I..." He paused, then nodded to himself. "Very well, I'll remain here and—and at least explore the idea."

"Good. It's all settled." Mikoneh looked at Jensirin. "You'll be coming to Cimin, though, I expect."

"Yes." Jensirin drifted forward, his eyes set on the twins. "I will follow you into the nether realm itself if need be."

"Let's hope that's never on the agenda." Maya beamed at him.

"Agreed," said Mikoneh. "I'd like to remain on this side of life for a while yet." He glanced out the window to the snow flurries thick in the pale gray sky. Something tugged him toward the view, and he left the others to resume their strategy game.

"It's almost time for dinner," Maya said.

Penn sighed. "Good. I relish the chance of reprieve."

The Dragon Princess giggled. "Coward."

Kneeling on the window seat, Mikoneh stared down into the bailey. Servants were scarce, and the guards on watch were huddled under shelter against the growing cold. Something glinted upon the castle's outer wall. Searching, Mikoneh found a lone figure standing on the parapet. Despite the distance, he could feel eyes on him.

He tensed. A Mage?

No. Instinct assured him this was something else.

Something...familiar. Yet, he had no name for it.

Sathe's words of warning returned to him: "*You have an enemy. You, yourself. A great one. He hates you—but he doesn't want you to die.*"

Chills ate at Mikoneh's insides. The figure on the wall raised one hand, and blue flame flickered above an open palm. Then the figure vanished as though it had been a ghost. Snow swirled from the heavens, and wind rattled the glass panes.

Friendly laughter swelled behind Mikoneh, and the fire crackled, shredding the eerie silence.

Sathe had said the stranger wanted Mikoneh to suffer tremendously. That he knew more about Mikoneh than anyone.

There's nothing I can do about that now. Whatever he wants, whatever his grudge, I'll have to wait for him to make another move.

In the meantime, Mikoneh would focus on what he could control. For now, that meant dragon lessons and mastering his element, so he could eventually take on the Mage Queen and her armies.

Come springtime, he must journey to distant Cimin, where Emperor Thyfinn Kingbreaker ruled over a conquered people—and somehow the Rokahns must persuade the tyrant to become an ally, or they must overthrow another kingdom.

Think about that later.

A knock sounded on the door, marking the arrival of Owenekiras Rokahn—just in time for dinner, as he'd promised. In mere moments, Penn and Jensirin would excuse themselves, leaving the Rokahns alone.

Nerves writhing, Mikoneh turned toward his companions as Maya sprang up to answer the door. Tonight, the twins would come to know their father better.

In a few days hence it would be Wintertide. Mikoneh would exchange gifts with his companions, toast the failures and accomplishments of the past year, and bask in the warmth of friendships, old and new alike.

For now, in the soft silence of winter's music, he would grieve what he'd lost, cherish what he had, and make each turning of the sandglass count.

Continued in
BOOK THREE:
THE BURDEN OF A BROKEN CROWN

Dear Reader

Thank you so much for continuing the journey of the *Dragons of Rokahn*! Please consider leaving a review online for *A Silent Song in Winter*. Reviews truly do help the right readers find the right books.

This series is a true labor of love for me. These characters and this world have been part of my life for over twenty years, and bringing everyone and everything in Sirinhigha to life at long last is absolutely magical!

This story is, at its core, one of healing. The twins, in particular, continue to help me lance old wounds and heal from newer injuries of the heart and soul. My earnest prayer is that they may help you in some small way with your life struggles as they navigate their grief and find their courage.

If you want to know when my newest books are coming out, access behind-the-scene tidbits, take a peek into my writing process, and be among the first to see cover reveals, along with other gems, considering joining my Dragon Hoard over on Substack!

In chapter eight, Latta mentioned a play called *The

Minstrel and the Dragon, which I've written into a short story that can be read as part of the *Reign of Dragons* anthology co-edited by Jasmine Young and Robert Zangari.

Lastly, here is an **exclusive** bonus epilogue tying directly into the ending of this book. *One Last Song* features the twins and Owenekiras at their private dinner together, which was omitted from the main ending for pacing reasons.

Stay magical, my friends!

—M. H. W.

Acknowledgments

This book proved a special challenge, as my chronic pain flared up before I could dive into rewrites and edits, then I got pneumonia for two months, and then even more health issues came along to join the party. Needless to say, I wondered if I'd ever have enough brain power and energy to complete ASSIW.

BUT I DID. Which I couldn't have done alone.

Enormous thanks to R. K. Goff, Heidi Wadsworth, and Robert Zangari—my amazing alpha team—who all went above and beyond to make sense of the *mess* that was the early draft.

Colossal thanks to my beta team: Beba Andric, J M Archer, Laura A. Barton, Jaxon Charlton, Cathryn DeVries, Amena Jamali, and Mandi Oyster. Handling a plot like this requires a lot of outside insight, and the feedback I was given was tremendous for helping me identify where weaknesses lay hidden.

Epic thanks to Sarah B., my patient and long-suffering editor who always takes my edits and elevates them with a little tweak here and a new addition there. Her final touches really bring out the full potential of characters and plot points!

Huge shoutout to my Kickstarter backer, AJ McDunn, who opted into the Name A Future Character add-on tier, allowing them to name Swordmaster **Donivan Kriv**! Such a perfect name, too. I hope you enjoyed his character, AJ!

Loving thanks to my family for cheering me on! Your tireless support means the world to this anxious little author.

Particular thanks, as always, to my parents, Duane and Deborah, and my sisters, Heidi and Tawnee, who read *everything*, write special notes, and listen to me chat endlessly about writing stuff they (probably) don't always care to know.

Special thanks to my readers! You're one of the main reasons I keep writing. I'm so grateful for every purchase, every review, every subscriber to my email list, and every follower on social media. Your united message comes across loud and clear: *Don't you quit*! And I don't mean to, Mr. Frodo—

Er, sorry. Got carried away there. Anyway, I WON'T QUIT!

Also, heartfelt thanks to J. R. R. Tolkien, for inspiring me ceaselessly across so many years with the most soulful and impactful fictitious story I've ever consumed. You showed me the hidden passages in my soul and gave me the map to navigate them. To the Professor!

I would be remiss if I didn't pay special tribute to Cheryl Benner, my dear friend, to whom this book is dedicated. She was a super fan who devotedly read each of my books multiple times in anticipation of the next one. When I told her about my *Dragons of Rokahn* project, she was ecstatic, but unfortunately she was called to her heavenly home just before *When Darkness Hunts the Dawn* was published in 2024. I deeply regret that ill timing, but I know she's still rooting for me from above. Thank you, Cheryl, for your steadfast belief in me, for your bright and mischievous smile, and for your vibrant soul!

Last, and most of all, I thank my Savior for his compassion, love, and healing. He is the source of my strength and courage. He is my banner and shield. He is my all.

—M. H. W.

Glossary

People

Akonn – Captain of the Sword.

Atlanse Chenta – Crown Prince of Simynshin.

Athonen d'Ereth – A Scholar of the Spire.

Brentin – A stablehand at Elenth Castle.

Crim – A wealthy nobleman and merchant lord in Simynshin.

Dalter – Deceased father of Lord Fontinn.

Donivan Kriv - Royal Swordmaster at Elenth Castle.

Drayve – Earl of Relvin Province in Oceana.

Duck – Minno's mallard companion.

Eddan – A hired hand working for Lord Crim.

Elayorah – Usurper queen of Rokahn, younger sister of Owenekiras and Milann.

Feresse Chenta – The new queen of Simynshin.

Fontinn – A Simynshinian lord.

Gredd – Head of the Guild of Words in Simynshin.

Hilker – A Master Wind Elementalist.

Jensirin – A dragon lord. Formerly the Revenant.

Jossen – Princess Latta's protector.

Jonatten – The twins' surrogate father. Deceased.

Kalet – Leader of the Valor Knights. Also called the Corpse Poet.

Karrad – The Mage ambassador in Simynshin.

Katanni – A Nijaal. Also called the Lady of the Wood.

Kevva – An Oceanean woman who betrayed the twins.

Larkynven – Owenekiras's dragon mount.

Latta Chenta – The Songbird Princess, daughter of Atlanse.

Mage Queen – A legendary figure from the Age of Dragons.

Maya – Mikoneh's twin sister. Dragon Princess of Rokahn and a healer.

Milannetirin - Twin brother of Owenekiras Rokahn. Called Milann.

Mikoneh – Maya's twin brother. Dragon Prince of Rokahn and skilled strategist.

Minno – A mysterious boy clad in gray. He has a mallard companion named Duck.

Namirsha – Wife of Crim and daughter of the merchant guild leader of Lintha.

Nilo – King of Oceana. Deposed.

Owenekiras Rokahn – The Dragon King. Also a banished prince of Rokahn. The twins' biological father.

Penn Lendir – Viscount of Relvin Province in Oceana. The twins' friend.

Prettem Chenta – King of Simynshin.

Rathana – The twins' deceased biological mother.

Sariolin – A solitary historical figure who forsook humanity to live life apart and study the Spirits Elemental.

Sathe – A Mage General serving under the Mage Queen. Deceased.

Seranni – The twins' surrogate mother. Deceased.

Suld – A Mage General serving under the Mage Queen. Sathe's brother. Deceased.

Tayvin – The royal tailor at Elenth Castle.

Teev – A lord of Simynshin.

Ter N'Avea – The Ever Present. An Ephe'ahn.

Thyfinn Kingbreaker – Emperor of Cimin.

Tikar – An ambassador from the Isles of Kwilaj.

Tryss – Queen Feresse's handmaiden.

Vomm – The royal dance instructor at Elenth Castle.

Zevier – A student of Donivan Kriv.

PLACES

Andyan Mountains – The mountain range separating the Fae Lands of the north and the human kingdoms of the south.

Blighted Lands – A barren scape in the west of Cimin.

Cimin – An empire in the northeast of the main continent.

Crestfel – Capital of Cimin.

Elemeer Plains – A place lost to history.

Elenth – Capital of Simynshin.

Holore – Capital of Lintha.

Hyanython, Citadel of – A ruinous fortress in the heart of the Simynshin Forest.

Kagon – An Ephe'ahn village at the foot of the Andyan Mountains near Cimin.

Kenooshin – A Ephe'ahn village in the Simynshin Forest.

Kwilaj – A cluster of islands to the east of Cimin.

Lintha – A kingdom in the southeast of the main continent.

Mithrinn – The universe.

Molten Gold, Isles of – A cluster of islands to the south of the main continent. Pirates make their home there.

Moon Veil – A fairy ring on the main continent.

Nauttia – Capital of Oceana.

Oceana – A kingdom in the east sandwiched between Cimin and Lintha.

Pae'Tal – An island in the high northwest.

Principal Plain – The living realm where mortals dwell.

Relvin – A province in Oceana ruled by Earl Drayve Lendir.

Rokahn – An island kingdom in the southwest. Ruled by the Rokahns.

Serielias – The realm of Lady Katanni in the Fae Lands.

Simynshin – A large kingdom spanning most of the western half of the main continent.

Sirinhigha – The name of the main continent and the world.

Spire, The – A natural mountain fortress in Cimin where a clan of scholars dwell.

TeshRelle – A blackened land in the northeast above the Andyan Mountains.

Vorsah – Capital of Rokahn.

Terms

Age of Dragons – An era 20,000 years ago that broke the Complété, which the fabric of space and time. A faulty substitute was erected in its place. Dark Mages rose to conquer all and were defeated at a high price.

Complété – The fabric that once held the universe together. It was shattered in the Age of Dragons.

Dragon Healers – A rare type of magic user (human or fae in origin) who could heal dragons of various types of ailments. Their gifts varied. No known dragon healers exist on Sirinhigha.

Elementalist – A person who can consciously control an element (or several) and can see the Spirits Elemental.

Hollow – A type of tainted magic. Half of the fabric holding the universe in balance.

Jarsui - A rare leaf used to patch dragon wing wounds to allow for flight. Does not work on magically inflicted injuries.

Korta – A fruit strong in nutrients for young dragons. It is poisonous for humans to eat.

Renemm – An highly addictive drug manufactured in Cimin.

Sword, The League of the – Elite swordsmen serving under the Dragon King's banner.

Tiassana – A kind of leaf that keeps dragon bonds healthy. It can also be used to soothe broken bond wounds.

Void – A type of light magic. Half of the fabric holding the universe in balance.

World Between – Where magic is traditionally said to come from, the World Between may be the origin of the Spirits Elemental. Not to be mistaken for the Realm Above (heaven) or the Realm Below (hell or the nether realm).

RACES

Celes – Guardians dwelling between Heaven and Hell. Simynshinians worship them.

Dark Mages – Once called Mages (or Light Mages) before they succumbed to corrupt magic. Mages were once all human, but their magic has been tapped by fae races upon rare occasions as well.

Ephe'ahn – A type of woodelf.

Fae – A broad term for the magical races of Sirinhigha. These include the many kinds of elves, as well as dragons, fairies, gryphons, Pegasi, Nijaal, and many more.

First Kin – The first five beings born on Sirinhigha, tasked with protecting order, mortality, nature, magic, and balance.

Humans – A broad term for the different races of humankind regardless of origin. The non-fae. These include the Cortharans (most Simynshinians, Linthians, Oceaneans, and Ciminians are of this race), the Jemarri nomads, and the Kwilaj Islers. Rokahnians have traditionally been included in this category, but emerging evidence suggests that the Rokahnian people may in fact be dragons in disguise. This is still a debated point among scholars.

Nijaal – The oldest race of fae. Also called elder elves or high fae.

Spirits Elemental – Guardian spirits over the living realm (also called the Principal Plain). The five main types are: Fire, Wind, Water, Earth, and Spirit. Sub-types include Lightning, Ice, and Metal.

Undrik – Nightmarish toad-like monsters capable of controlling dreams under certain conditions. Favored pets of Dark Mages. They can absorb magic and store it as energy.

ABOUT THE AUTHOR

Writer of fantasy, magic weaver, dragon rider! Having spent the past two decades devotedly writing fantasy, it's safe to say M. H. Woodscourt is now more fae than human.

All of her fantasy worlds connect with each other in the Mithrinn Universe, forged with great love and no small measure of blood, sweat, and tears. When she's not writing, she's napping or reading a book with a mug of hot cocoa close at hand, while her quirky cat Wynter nibbles her nose.

Learn more at www.mhwoodscourt.com

Also by M. H. Woodscourt

The Ember Lily
High Fantasy/Young Adult

The Crane Maiden

Dragons of Rokahn
Epic Fantasy/Adult

When Darkness Hunts the Dawn

Mark of Valliath
High Fantasy/Young Adult

The Storyteller True

The Shattered Arch

The Marked Prince

The Blood Fountain

Record of the Sentinel Seer
Science-Fantasy/Adult

Prince of the Fallen

Rule of the Night

Song of the Lost

Paths of the Broken

Heart of the Sentinel

WINTERVALE DUOLOGY

High Fantasy/Young Adult

The Crow King

The Winter King

PARADISE TRILOGY

Portal Fantasy/Humor/Young Adult

A Liar in Paradise

Key of Paradise

Beyond Paradise